The Audacity

Noah Coleman

ISBN-13: 979-8-9987289-0-7

Library of Congress Registration Number: TXU002485172

Printed/Electronic Copied in the United States of America

TO
MY MOTHER AND MY FATHER

In Loving Memory of My Dearest Friend and Most Wonderful
Companion, Frodo.

THE AUDACITY

PART I

DORMANCY

One

July 15, 2019

Jude Monroe would die in 18 minutes. Of course, he had no way of knowing this. Ironically, his thoughts were nowhere in the vicinity of a reflection on mortality. They were not on the mission at hand, nor even the integrity of the rocket named *Audacity*. Rather, his thoughts dwelled upon the students of Perryville High School, the school where he taught history, and the thumbs up he promised to send them when a tiny red light would pop on at the front of the compartment to signal a live camera at T-14. He hoped this image would bring a new level of credibility for his "chase your dreams" classroom mantra. Sitting in his padded chair, strapped to a rocket, his thoughts were on his students and nothing else.

At T-13, exactly 30 seconds after the red light from the cockpit camera turned off, Jude could not help but think, for the first time, that he was completely useless. He sat back and watched as the four others inside the rocket methodically completed each of their pre-launch tasks. As he observed the command pilots, Link and Sarah, complete their final superstitious motion through the reflection glass at the front of the cabin, his mind started to drift off. He thought of his sister and how, despite the fact that his presence on this mission was originally her idea, she probably hadn't taken a breath since she arrived at the observation bleachers hours ago.

"Monroe, are you with us, Monroe?" asked Sarah, startling Jude. "You've been staring at me through the mirror for about 60 seconds now. Can we keep the crush outside of the billion dollar missile?"

"You wish, baby," Jude, with a smirk, quickly responded, "but that shit is going to space with us."

Looking to her partner, Link, Sarah said, "See, I told you he'd become one of us. Say, Monroe, aren't teachers supposed to not use expletives? Especially when they're being recorded and listened to by a couple hundred scientists and whoever else?"

"Look, *shit* happens. Besides, what are they going to do? I'm an astronaut now."

"He makes a good point," replied Caroline Smithpeters, the Mission Specialist and only veteran astronaut on board, "astronaut celebrity status awaits you all upon return."

"Exactly!" said Jude, still looking at Sarah in the reflection glass. She made no effort to conceal her smile. "As we leave the Earth, I am simply Mr. Monroe, but when we return, I shall be Mr. Moonroe! *Am I right people?*"

After a brief pause of silence containing the ringing of the emphasized word 'people,' the crew let out a mixture of true laughs and pain-filled groans. "Good God, that's painful. You've been holding that in a while, haven't you?" asked Sarah, cheeks red.

"No way, on the spot. You guys selected me for my potential to top lines like 'one small step' and whatnot." Jude responded, barely able to turn his head but doing his best to look around the cabin.

"T-3 minutes," stated a voice from Mission Control, "and can we please skip the puns, otherwise we might not let you come back down in a week."

"Come on guys, we're adults..." said Abe, the payload specialist, with as sarcastic of a tone as he could manage.

An anxious calm fell over the cabin as the crew continued to monitor their respective screens, and the gravity of the final few minutes began to sink in. Humor could no longer remove the crew's attention from the inevitable. By this point in the process of pre-launch, there was not much to do in the cabin except listen for the countdown cues. No puns, no small talk, nor the beepings of machines around the crew could detract from the reality of the situation. The adrenaline each member felt staring straight up into a perfect baby blue sky became overpowering. Each crew member knew that, in a matter of minutes, that blue would fade to the darkest black.

Jude closed his eyes and tried to cement the reality he had known for the last 30 years of his life. However hard he tried to maintain normalcy, he was fully aware that in ten minutes, everything he thought he knew would be forever changed.

"T-2 minutes, close and lock your visors," the familiar voice from mission control stated.

Jude watched his new friends shift and close their visors. Sarah, with a hand on her helmet, looked back through the reflection glass, gave Jude a wink, and proceeded to lock her visor, which, like everyone else's, was completely transparent. Jude felt warm as he locked his own visor and continued to watch the others in the rocket. He had become so very close with the people around him. His eyes shifted from Sarah to Abe who watched their tiny interaction before sealing up their helmets. With eyebrows raised and a friendly smugness on his face, Abe was the last one to close his visor.

* * *

Abe was the first person to meet Jude at the welcome party for the crew three months earlier. Looking like he had just bitten into an onion, he approached Jude. "Do NOT eat the ants on a log," Abe said, holding out a hand to be shaken. He was much taller than Jude and he had cool blue eyes. However, he was far from imposing. "They taste like they've been left out since *Apollo 13*. I mean hell, I know budget cuts, but get us some damn hors d'oeuvres!"

"Are you always complaining?" asked Sarah, who came around the buffet table to join the conversation. "Hi, I'm Sarah Lazerous. I'm one of the two command pilots... but the only one that matters." She reached out her hand, and Jude could not help but be intimidated by her poise and ability to dominate eye contact. "Abe," said Sarah, still maintaining eye contact with Jude, "since day one, you complained about the fabric of the lining inside your jumpsuit and now free food? What's next?"

"Well," stuttered Abe, "probably having to be taken to space by some second-rate Navy pilot."

Sarah's head slowly turned toward Abe. Her blonde hair fell slightly over one of her eyes, but her glare was undeterred. They stared at each other for what felt like an hour and then began to laugh loud enough to drown out any of the neighboring conversations. The pair turned back to Jude with genuine smiles. "This guy and I have been through too many simulations during this whole training process," said Sarah, pointing her thumb at Abe. "He's not worth a damn for anything, besides some good jokes, but you gotta love him." She slapped Jude on the back. "Welcome to the team, champ. See you bright and early tomorrow. I'm headed back to the kitchen to see if I can make some real food."

The two men watched Sarah walk away. "She's a lot to handle, but damn, she makes things interesting," said Abe with a smile."She's single too bud, so do with that what you will." He walked away, only to briefly turn around for a quick second with eyebrows raised, smugness on his face, and left Jude to take in his first encounter with two people; the likes of which he had never met. He knew, despite the fact that he never thought of anything to say during the entire encounter, that he would grow to love both of those very brazen, yet very welcoming people.

* * *

Abe, sitting directly behind Jude, smugly raised his eyebrows in the reflection glass. Jude had to laugh, but he had no way of knowing that this would be the last moment he would see one of Abe's iconic expressions.

"T-1 minute."

"You good, kid?" said Caroline to Jude through the microphone built into her helmet. "Haven't heard you make any puns in a few minutes and it's kind of... eerie. Just breathe, it's going to be a smooth ride."

"Uh, yeah," said Jude, "just taking it in... trying to keep it in... y'know."

Because of the angle he was sitting, Jude could not see Caroline's face through the reflection glass, but he knew she was smiling. Three months of training and through high points and low, Jude could always count on Caroline to be there supporting him with a smile. "The smartest people in the world are sending you out of it, and they are going to bring you back safely... Don't sweat it."

"Yeah," laughed Sarah, "no reason to be nervous, the autopilot does all the work... Link here won't be touching anything, and we're all the safer for it."

"Just another pretty face," Caroline laughed, "easy job when everything is planned out for you."

Link, captain of *The Audacity*, had no comeback but laughter as he finalized his pre-launch procedure. Jude appreciated the humor and the words of encouragement from Caroline. He had missed the feeling of maternal support ever since the death of his mother. It was like having her back in his life. Leading up to the launch, it helped him with his anxiety more than he ever realized.

* * *

Three months of intense training led up to the moment of the launch. Each step of the way, Caroline Smithpeters was there. During each simulation, each exhausting exercise in the ice-cold pool, each moment of nausea, she was there.

"Y'know kid, we all know you're a teacher and not a scientist, or a pilot, or filled with experience," Caroline said after the first day of training. She had found Jude standing outside staring up at the night sky. "You were selected for a reason, though. The other four of us made it to where we are right now because somewhere down the road there was a teacher who made us want to keep chasing our dreams.

My first time into space, it was impossible to not reflect on my journey there. I thought of my mom, who was on the ground watching, I thought of my sister who pushed me every day, and I thought of Mrs. Abbots, my ninth-grade science teacher. She would stay for hours after school with me just to discuss planets. Fact is, when you start to feel that Imposter Syndrome, realize this: we have your back. You are an astronaut now. You are on my team, and I've got you every step of the way."

She patted him on his shoulder, gave him a smile, and said, "Now come on, let's go eat some dinner, but don't eat anything you like. The simulator tomorrow is a real bitch, and it'll ruin your appetite for whatever this meal is forever... Trust me, I know..."

* * *

"You sure you're okay, kid? Kid?" Jude heard again through his headset.

"Yeah. Yeah, I am solid... My stomach is a little *rumbly*... I'm really kind of hoping it's just the rocket..." said Jude, trying to hide his nerves with his usual humor.

"You are such a weird guy, you know that?

"Listen Ace," said Link, "there's a lot of talk about how good the filtration is in those suits... they'll get the vomit out, sure, but they don't get the smell out... I learned that the hard way."

"Link here did one too many corkscrews in an F-14 a few years back apparently. It's a great story," said Sarah as she laughed with everyone in the cockpit, including Link.

"Don't worry," said Link, "the feds told me I couldn't intentionally do any corkscrews in this thing, so you should be good... but really, don't hurl, I'm not kidding about the smell..."

"He really isn't," said Caroline, still laughing.

Link was smiling as he looked in the reflection glass and back at Jude. "Y'know," he said, "that actually reminds me of this story about when I was stationed in Norway and I had just had a huge plate of Fårikål..."

* * *

Link always had good stories. Nights after long days of training would be matched with stories of good food from sausages in Germany, to curry in Southeast Asia, to authentic empanadas in Argentina. The stories would be wildly unbelievable and somehow always ended with the same line: "...and then the next morning I had to sneak out and I had this feeling... like I was forgetting something."

The day before takeoff, Link woke Jude up. "Come on, Ace, let's take a bike ride." He was not someone anyone could say no to, especially for any adventure, large or small. The two emerged from their onsite living quarters as the final minutes of night began to tick away. They straddled their bicycles and rode in silence. The breeze of a cool morning crashed their faces as they rode next to each other. Link's dark hair flowing in the breeze made Jude feel almost self conscious about his choice to wear a bike helmet.

As the sun began to break the horizon, the two slowed down to watch. Pulling up next to Jude, Link finally broke the silence. "Listen, Ace, I know you've kept this cool composure about liftoff tomorrow. I admire that. We all do, but, seriously, are you alright?"

"Uh, yeah, not too bad, I guess," said Jude, looking away. "I've been trying hard not to think about it."

"There's a lot of people working to make sure that we get there and back safely."

"People a lot smarter than me, that's for sure."

"And me. I trust them, though. I trust them with my life." Link took in a deep breath and closed his eyes. As he reopened them, he stared at the sky and smiled. "Nothing more perfect than a sunrise, is there? All the potential for a new adventure... all the life that can be lived... All the bike rides with new friends. Come on, let's keep going." Link took off, and Jude took a moment before following. He looked back at the sunrise as he let Link's words settle in.

The two, in their matching navy jumpsuits, rode for a few more minutes while a group of reporters arrived early and took pictures of the two on their bikes. This would make for a few feel-good images for the Internet later. Because of quarantine procedures, they had to stay further away.

"Listen bud, when I was in Cairo, I had to do a solo mission. I flew over a small village 30 miles south, and my right wing was hit by an RPG, one of our old ones, and I had to bail. I had to hide in a local village. My parachute was bright white... anyone could see that I made it out of the plane. Enemies searched all over for me, but they couldn't find me. I was able to send coordinates to my team in Cairo. I was only able to move around at night. Food was hard to come by on the first night... rough situation. However, my team was incredible, and fortunately smarter than those bad guys also looking. My team found me first, and then the next morning I had to sneak out with them and I had this feeling... like I was forgetting something."

"Was it your plane?"

"Obviously, it was Einstein, but also the lady's name who I hid with on night two... Egyptian girls, Ace, I know where we're going when we come back to Earth."

"I'm just a teacher, man, I have responsibilities. I can't go gallivanting around the globe and live some superhero life like you have. There's the life of Link and the life of Jude... You've got this James Bond life, and I've got this... this... well, I'm a teacher. I inspire kids to live the life you lead. That's good enough."

"My brother," said Link, pulling his bike over again, putting one foot on the ground, and looking straight at Jude, "listen to me. Tomorrow night, you are going to be in space. Off this planet. Reality as you know it will be changed. But, dude, seriously, are you actually going to wait for zero gravity to realize that you can *do* anything and *be* anything you want to be? Why not listen to your own damn lectures and inspire yourself? Don't wait for zero gravity to fly. Just step out the door and fly. Do anything. Be anything, Ace."

Standing next to Link, he truly heard each word. Link had hit a chord with Jude that had always been there. The feeling to do more, to be more. "You're right," said Jude.

"Damn right I'm right... I know you like the classroom, but two words Ace: *book sales*. You write about this adventure when we get back and you'll be loaded. We'll take the funds and fly across the planet for some Arabian nights, eh?"

Jude just looked at him, a smile growing on his face...

"*Ehhhhh????*" emphasized Link, laughing and nudging his elbow into Jude's side.

Jude laughed and looked down at the ground. He kicked a rock that was close to his foot. "I don't think anyone has said no to you before, Link."

"Nope! But hey, speaking of women, let's get you back to the dorms to see your new best friend."

"Who?" said Jude, starting to get embarrassed, "Sarah? No..."

Link settled his bike and pointed at Jude. He shoved his index finger into Jude's chest. "Ace, remember what I said: do anything, be anything, it's in you. It always has been... Don't wait for zero gravity to realize that."

* * *

"... and then I snuck out that morning and I couldn't help but think I was forgetting something..."

The story fell on deaf ears as the bright red numbers blinking to takeoff seemed to speed up.

"T- 20 seconds."

"Godspeed, everyone," stated Caroline, whose hands instinctively became fists.

"This is as good as it gets," Abe yelled, trying to speak over the cacophony of sounds around him.

"Not yet, in 10 minutes, you'll see 'as good as it gets,'" Caroline yelled in response.

The vibrations were unreal to Jude. Everything began to flash before his eyes, his sister, his students, the simultaneous loss of both parents three years ago, the decision to try to be more, and then finally, Sarah. All of the nerves one could possibly feel sent his eyes to the reflection glass.

"10...9...8...7..."

The clock counted down, ticking closer to the death of the crew. The numbers faded away as he looked at the reflection and through Sarah's visor. Despite the enormity of the situation, he chose to look in her direction, locked his focus, and became calmed by her brown eyes.

* * *

The night after the welcome party, this mysterious woman was on Jude's mind. Actually, it was her laugh. It continued to ring through his ears. He had never heard anything like it before. He replayed the scene, the eye contact, the firm grip, the soft hands, and how idiotic he felt for not saying a single word.

He stared at the ceiling of his dorm as all of this was on his mind when a pair of knocks hit his door. "Monroe," said Sarah Lazerous, "get your ass up and come with me. I have something you need to see."

Jude sat up, trying to be composed, and slowly got to his feet. He tried to think of something witty to say, but she was out of the room before he could get a syllable out. "Great," Jude thought to himself... "0 for 2."

He finally caught up with her before she exited through a door that said "To Roof." The two climbed the stairs until they arrived at the top of the complex. Without any light exposure, there were twice as many stars as Jude, forever the city boy, had ever seen. His eyes were wide, and he couldn't hide any bit of his reaction to the sky above.

"Beautiful, isn't it?" Sarah said as she walked up next to him and joined him in looking to the sky. "I mean Earth, yeah, amazing, beautiful, and the Alps might be the prettiest mountain range in the entire galaxy, but come on, the real beauty... it's out there." She paused and then said more quietly, as if to herself, "it's out there."

Jude continued to look to the night sky. There was something about where he was in that moment that made it seem all the more peaceful. Yet, when he looked back at Sarah, whose eyes were fixated on the stars, he could not help but also think how the Earth had just as many mysteries as any other celestial sphere. This woman, this interesting human, with more complexities than Jude could ever dream of unraveling, and the way she looked at the stars as if she were attempting to decipher the secrets of each one, he was transfixed.

The two stood and looked to the night sky in silence. Not awkward silence, not uncomfortable dawdling; it was a calmness which Jude hadn't felt since he could remember.

Sarah finally broke the quiet. "Look, it took a lot of courage for you to do what you're doing, and I really appreciate you for that."

"Aren't you the one who flew a solo mission into Baghdad?"

"I'd probably do that 100 more times rather than deal with 30 brats like you do every day."

"Ah, they're not too bad..." Jude said, looking at Sarah from the corner of his eye.

There was another peaceful moment. Sarah had yet to take her eyes off of the stars. Jude turned his head back to the sky to join her gaze.

Sarah took in the cool night air through a deep breath and began to laugh. "I saw your interview on CNN a couple mornings ago."

"No, please, no!" Jude started to laugh in humiliation. "That was in the top five of the most embarrassing moments of my life."

Mimicking Jude, Sarah put one hand on her hip, pointed one index finger to the sky, and said, "Uhh, yes, I hope I don't get kidnapped by aliens, *I have no training for that!*"

"Stop!" Jude yelled, laughing, "what was I supposed to say?"

"True, true... they literally asked the worst questions..."

"Thank you, I'm glad someone understands me... my students are going to give me so much shit over that..."

"Oh no, profanity! Not the teacher profanity. Do you know when my childhood was ruined?" asked Sarah, watching Jude wipe away tears in his eyes from the laughter, "when I realized that teachers cuss, and drink, and have weird adult lives away from school buildings... honestly, it's a terribly creepy thought..."

"Terribly creepy," repeated Jude, looking back at Sarah, "terribly creepy... except me, of course, I enjoy my twin-sized cot under my desk. I never leave the school; all of my meals are cafeteria cuisine... It's a humble life I lead, but it's the path I've chosen."

"Hey, living at a school, hard to get kidnapped by aliens on federal grounds."

"My thoughts exactly..."

Laughing, Sarah looked at Jude. She smiled as she took a long look into his eyes. Her smile faded as she maintained her characteristically intense eye contact. He was already beginning to adore how she did that. "Y'know," said Sarah, "speaking of which, there was one thing in that interview that I particularly loved... you said... let me get this quote right... I loved it... 'I guess I just agreed to do this thing because... aside from pressure from my sister... because after my parents' car wreck, I got so scared of death that I forgot about wanting to live my life... So, I guess this is me, deciding that I want to live my life.'"

Sarah finally looked away from Jude when she finished the quote, and he was almost certain she was holding back tears. "I guess this is me, deciding that I want to live my life," she repeated quietly... She took in another deep breath.

She looked at him again. "Jude, I fell in love with that sentence."

He didn't know what to say. Somehow, he felt completely understood in every way by this woman whom he had just met 24 hours ago. The way she looked at him and the way she repeated his cheesy one-liners, it was as if they had known each other for years.

He looked at her as she strengthened her gaze into him. "You've really done your research on me over the last week," said Jude, immediately kicking himself for not coming up with something more witty.

Sarah moved in closer. She lightly put her hand on his shoulder. "Well, it's because I think you're cute."

"Really?"

"No, dumbass, it's because I'm about to be strapped to a rocket and launched off this rock with you."

The two laughed, their entire bodies shaking from the humor. Tears of joy came back into Jude's eyes. Sarah looked back up to the night sky. "You know, my mom had two of us kids. I was the oldest, and she died when I was 13... I never shook this feeling of loneliness. Not until I realized something when I looked up at the sky and I saw all these planets and stars... It's hard to feel alone when there's so much out there, y'know? People... They like to think of the Earth as some small inhabited space dangling in an unimaginably large abyss... but it's just the opposite. Just the opposite. I always felt comforted by the sky... I never had words for those feelings until you said that in your interview..."

Sarah turned and looked at Jude, her cheeks were red, and she had a growing smirk. She took his hand and made a short laugh. "I understand you, Jude Monroe. I really do, and we're going to become very close over the next few weeks... Just you watch..." She smiled as she leaned closely into him and kissed him on the cheek. Pulling away slowly, she smiled and resumed looking deeply into his eyes. After a moment, she quickly turned and walked away.

Jude stood there alone for a few moments. He couldn't help but laugh. He touched his cheek where her lips had just rested. Feeling truly elated, he noticed that he had been staring too long at the door Captain Sarah Lazerous had just exited through. As he looked back to the night sky, he wondered how he could have ever felt as alone as he had before beginning this new journey. How could anyone feel alone in a universe with so much beyond any imagination, or even in a world with someone like that unfathomable woman who had just made him feel weightless?

* * *

"3...2...1... " The countdown was spoken, but it was not heard by Jude, nor any of the other voyagers in the cockpit. The immediate pressure took the wind out of him. He closed his eyes and tried to catch his bearings. The pressure only intensified. He tried to scream, but when he opened his mouth, nothing came out.

To Jude's surprise at this moment, it was not his life that flashed before his eyes, but the last three weeks. He thought of the bets the crew would take each night on how long it would take for Abe to complain about the health food served for their dinners. He thought about how many stories he heard ending with *"...and then the next morning I had to sneak out and I had this feeling... like I was forgetting something."* He thought about the heart-to-heart conversations over cards after long days of training. He thought about how often Caroline would come up to him, put her hand on his shoulder, and tell him how glad she was for his presence on the team. He thought about three weeks of sitting in lawn chairs on the roof with Sarah and trying to work up enough courage to be witty. He thought about how he finally took Link's 'be anything, do anything' speech to heart on the night before takeoff. He thought about how he used that speech the last night on the roof with Sarah as he took her hand, pulled her in, and kissed her. "About time," she said, and the words were still ringing in his ears even above the roar of the rocket.

He thought of these beautiful friendships he had cultivated over three months. These four humans had changed his life. These four humans somehow became more important than the mission itself. These humans became more impactful than a ride to space could ever be. Mortality was the furthest thing from his mind.

Ignorant to his imminent death, he managed to reopen his eyes. He peered into the reflection glass and looked at Sarah. He thought about how beautiful she looked while in control of the magnificent machine propelling them into the sky. It was this contemplation that was the final thought Jude Monroe had, four minutes into flight, when *The Audacity* exploded and everything went black.

Two

March 17, 2019

There was only one light on in the room, and Jude was completely surrounded. As he stood there, he could feel 28 pairs of eyes staring at him. Slowly, in the circle formed by this large group, Jude turned to look every single person staring at him in the eyes. With his dress shirt sleeves rolled up and his gray tie with a light coffee stain, he raised his hand, pointed to the ceiling, "and that is why we chase our dreams," he said, "because the world is better when we do. We have one life. All the people we study, they all faced the choices to live their lives or to die, never chasing their dreams. We study them because they made the choice to live."

John, sitting on his desk with his feet in his seat, asked, "Mr. Monroe, we study bad people too. Is the world really better for them chasing their dreams?"

"John," said Jude with a smile on his face, "I can always rely on you to ask the hard questions." Everyone in the room laughed, only to become immediately quiet as they waited for him to answer. "You're right. You may damage my *kindness changes the world* speech that I was trying to finish this school day with... Thanks for that... I do refuse, though, to believe that there is a person in this room whose dream we'd be better without... In history, sure, there are dreams we might have been better off without. But, do you know what we should give more credence to than anything else? The people who stood up when those bad dreamers' dreams became too big. The Harriet Tubmans, the Rosa Parks, the Ida Tarbells, the Lazowskis, and the Schindlers. History is filled with evil being met with good. It's the good people triumphing over evil that we should discuss. It is a must that we study the evil in the world, sure, but also, we should learn how the past has been fought and challenged by those brave enough to meet evil with good. Because we learn from the past to do what, class?"

In a full group, like clockwork, because this was Mr. Monroe's favorite way to end class, *"to be better."*

When the bell rang, John, one of Jude's favorite students, walked up to him with a couple of friends. "I really enjoyed the lecture today."

"Oh, yeah," said Becca, "I like this strong women route that class has taken over the last week. Deborah Sampson dressing up like a man and joining Washington's army? That's some inspirational stuff."

"How did I get so lucky to have my nerdiest hour at the end of the day?" asked Jude with a smile. "Now, get out of here. No congregating today, I have to leave early."

"Ooooh," the group said with cheesy grins.

"Big plans tonight, big guy?" said John, with a grin.

"It's Mr. Big Guy, and yes, as a matter of fact, I am meeting my sister for dinner."

This was met with a comedic silence. "*That* is way less cool than what we all thought," said another student, smirking at John.

"Yeah, well, sorry to disappoint," said Jude, looking playfully sympathetic. "I meet her every year on this date, and I am not going to be late. I was late last year, and I still haven't heard the end of it. Now get out of here. I'll see you all tomorrow."

They all said their goodbyes as they headed for the door. "Have a great day!" Jude yelled and listened to the replies of reciprocated kindness. This was a daily routine: end 8th hour American History with Jude's favorite class, a handful stay well after the bell, and he eventually herds them out and sends them on their way. Jude sat down with a smile, a deep sigh, and exhaustion from a long day of seven lectures. Loosening his tie, he leaned back into his desk chair and thought about what he taught today: "be brave, and chase your dreams." This theme was almost always present in Jude's classroom. Sometimes, a thought would enter Jude's head: was he living up to his own mantra?

He truly enjoyed the moments after school with his students. He never minded that they distracted him from completing tasks that he would have to stay even later to tend to. Getting to know these individuals outside of lectures is what brought the most meaning to his career. After all, those who stayed after class were often the ones who needed to be heard the most. This little band of friends, members of the "Nerd Club," they called themselves, responded well to Jude, and he responded well to them.

Jude saw a lot of his younger self in this after-school group. They always made him think of the friends he used to have and the ones that stayed in his life. Some had become more distant than others as of late. No matter, he thought, teaching offered him the daily smiles and assurances that he was doing what he was supposed to be doing with his life. Most days, this was enough. However, every so often, a morning would come when he would feel differently. These days tasted bitter to Jude. He knew something was missing. Over the last few years, the bitter days became more frequent. He would feel lost, without any direction. Though these students offered some purpose, he felt like he was making a difference, still, something was missing. There was a piece out of place –a phantom limb.

After this long day, Jude sat in silence. For a brief moment, he let the reality sink in of what today really was: the anniversary of his parents' death. Every year, on this day, Jude and his sister, Hazel, met to cook dinner together. Hazel always bought the groceries. Ever since Jude showed up with only spinach when Hazel requested lettuce, he was relieved of all grocery shopping duties. His argument that "all green leaves taste the same" did not offer any redemption.

* * *

"I know how you feel about red wine," Hazel said, entering Jude's house later that evening, "but if I'm going to sit through more chick flicks tonight, I get to choose the alcohol."

"Whatever you say, your highness," said Jude, feeling happier than usual to see his sister.

Hazel was older than Jude. The two years she had on him were used only for developing an intense protectiveness over her brother. Roughly a year ago, when Jude had his engagement broken off by his fiancée, Hazel showed up to his house with ice cream, wine, a collection of action movies, and a suitcase. "I'm moving in for the foreseeable future. Don't like it? Tough." She moved right by Jude and did not give him a moment to react. She then set everything down on the kitchen table, turned around, grabbed Jude by the shoulders, and said, "look, this is really hard right now. I'm sorry for that. But, just like all the other terrible things that have happened in our lives, you're not alone." They spent the rest of the night watching *Die Hard* movies and eating like they were 10 years younger.

Their parents were never going to name her Hazel. From the moment they found out they were having a baby girl, they planned to name her Ophelia. Their mother used to cup her face and say to her, "you were always referred to as baby Ophelia, but when you were born and you looked at your father and me with those big, beautiful hazel eyes, we had no doubt what your name should actually be... You are our Hazel."

Wielding a bottle of red wine, her sleeve pulled up to reveal the tattoo that said, "Their Hazel," and a copy of *When Harry Met Sally*, Hazel looked to her brother and said, "I *do not* know why we moved from action movies to rom-coms, but at least dinner is going to be good, I brought home rib-eyes."

Every year on March 17, the two would cook, eat, and enjoy a movie together. After enough years, they stopped needing to invite each other to be there; they knew they would be together. Three years prior, their parents died in a tragic accident. Jude was in Chicago, and Hazel was just outside the city in their hometown of Perryville. Jude was at a concert when he got the text from his sister. In slow motion, the people and lights danced around him. He read the words, "you need to come home. Something terrible has happened." Somehow, he knew. Deep inside, he knew that he was alone. He turned to Grace, who had just become his fiancée, grabbed her by the hand, and they left.

Since that day, Hazel and Jude had worked in tandem. Hazel spent the next few years pushing Jude to become what he was before the deaths of his heroes. However, Jude seemed to be more reserved and less outgoing. That concert was the last concert he ever went to. Although it broke her heart that Grace decided to leave Jude, Hazel understood why. Jude was not who he once was. Hazel knew it was still in him, she knew. True, the separation from his fiancée had obviously made the challenge at hand more difficult, but Hazel didn't care. She never cared. She loved her brother and would do anything for him.

Three years since the death of their parents, Hazel found herself frustrated. She found so many of her efforts to be in vain. Years spent trying to lift the spirits of her brother, she found nothing resembling anything close to a result. She tried buying concert tickets, hockey tickets, weekend trips, movie nights, cookie baking at Christmas time... nothing. She always felt fortunate to have Grace around. It was always 24/7 positivity projected toward Jude. And yet, the results never came. Jude was a shell of his former self. When Grace decided to leave, Hazel didn't blame her. She wasn't mad at her. Grace couldn't stand by and throw her soul into the black hole that had become her relationship. She very clearly loved Jude, but Hazel understood that it was simply best for Grace to leave.

Another year went by that was filled with Hazel trying to find new avenues, new people, new adventures for Jude to find a spark. From speed dating to German-speaking night classes, Hazel searched for something, anything. Eventually, no idea was too small. Her brother had gone through the motions for three years, and she looked to the stars, praying for a miracle. She never dreamed that the stars would be the answer.

* * *

Space, the last frontier, always seemed tangible only to government-based entities, like NASA. Since its inception, NASA has been the face of space travel. The space race started by Kennedy in the 1960s, culminating with the broadcasted walking on the moon, cemented the name of NASA as the household-named hero of the galactically unattainable. While the t-shirts with the NASA logo never went out of style, decades passed with a slowing of public interest and multiple scandals. The loss of *The Challenger*, and later *The Columbia*, on public airways was something the public never forgot. Still, though, NASA and other governmental agencies seemed the only people going to space. That is, until billionaires started asking what they always ask when boredom strikes, "why not us?"

When citizens began their own space race, government agencies, like NASA, started to quickly realize that new faces on the space exploration scene would certainly step on their toes. NASA always relied on perception and public interest to keep the funding coming its way. But when space travel started moving its way into the private sector, NASA had to react and fast. What would people think when they realized their tax dollars did not need to fund an agency when a CEO can fund it all on their own?

Hundreds of hours were spent with board meetings, advertising experts, social media gurus, politicians, and focus groups. NASA knew they had to get out in front of the private space race. When the dust settled, it had to be NASA who everyone continued to look to as the real expeditionists.

Finally, late one evening, as the most recent focus group was leaving, Tom Metzlebaum, the man leading the effort to save the face of NASA, was thanking everyone for coming in. The last person to walk through the door was a woman named Alice Jones.

"Thanks for coming in, you guys really did help," said Meltzlebaum, forcing a smile.

"Thanks for letting me be a part of it," said Alice, somehow still filled with energy after hours of focus group activities, "I had a lot of fun and I can't wait to tell my kids about it. Alice Jones, by the way," Alice said, extending a hand to shake.

"Tom Metzlebaum... How old are your children? Maybe I can find a model shuttle as a thank-you gift for having such a helpful mother?"

"Oh," said Alice, laughing, "I don't have children, my kids... It's what I call my students. I teach sixth-grade science."

"Ah, well," stuttered Metzlebaum, "make sure you tell them NASA wants them to come work for us... It always starts with the teachers."

"Oh, I know. I wouldn't be doing what I do if it weren't for my sixth-grade science teacher," said Alice, smiling, and beginning to walk away.

"Yeah, if only ole Mrs. Taxon could see me now at NASA," laughed Metzlebaum, "she might give me a better grade on that model volcano I failed in sixth grade."

Alice paused and looked over her shoulder. "I don't think so," she smiled, "I bet ole Mrs. Taxon would probably say the failures are what led you to such a wonderful amount of success." Alice walked away, and Tom Metzlebaum stood in place speechless.

When Alice turned the corner and out of sight, everything, absolutely everything, became crystal clear... Metzlebaum knew how to save the face of NASA... It wasn't a new idea they needed, but an old one... even a failed one. He rushed back into the room and started scribbling on a legal pad what would become the official rebranding event of the organization.

At 8:00 am the following morning, Metzlebaum's colleagues arrived to find him disheveled. Surrounded by numerous balled up pages from his legal pad, some spilled coffee, his tie loose, he stood up and welcomed everyone. Behind him on a whiteboard were the results of his all-night planning. In big letters at the top of the board was one circled phrase: "Operation Audacity."

Metzlebaum's team sat quietly as he painstakingly went through his idea. He started with the conversation with the teacher from the previous night, and how he was inspired to rethink the possibilities to retry NASA's attempt some decades earlier to send a teacher into space. Mission STS-51-L, the twelfth mission for the space shuttle *Challenger*, for a brief period of time, made the world fall in love with the idea of space travel. Not only that, but the world fell in love with Christa McAuliffe, a teacher who became the face of the mission. She was the human interest story NASA needed to regain the eyes and interest of the public. She was followed closely by the media, and the more they found out about her, the more they wrote about her, the more people fell in love. The tragic ending to this mission still haunts NASA. Still, it is impossible for anyone to deny the attention they gathered leading up to the launch. If they could recapture that amount of attention again, if they could bring sympathy to the name of NASA again, and if they could make the organization the people's organization again, they might be able to stay relevant and funded through the space race of the private sector.

Convincing the higher-ups took time. Rebooting the space shuttle program was an almost impossible task. The cost to do so would be immense, let alone the even higher price should anything on the mission go wrong. The board of directors knew that the fix to their problem would require vast amounts of media, sure, but to redo a failed mission... that would involve every bit of the media consistently alluding to one of NASA's darkest hours. However, if it all went well, the positivity could cement the organization for at least the rest of the 21st century. Metzlebaum's plan was voted on by the board by a count of six to two. It was the image of a teacher in space, the human-interest potential, and the nostalgia of a shuttle lifting off that landed a win for Metzlebaum and his team.

The crew, with the exception of the lucky teacher, was set after only a month of the go-ahead for the plan. After two years, the plan of sending a teacher to space went public. Advertising for this new mission could be seen anywhere from *Entertainment Weekly* to the sides of Coca-Cola bottles. All someone had to do was send in a video, a resume, some letters of recommendation, and pray.

So, when Hazel Monroe got home after a long evening of failing, yet again, to reengage her brother with the world, she went to her fridge to get something to drink and grabbed a Coke. As she sat down on her couch, and before she opened the bottle, she saw the ad: "In Need of a Teacher Who is in Need of an Adventure." She looked at the words. They were as loud as if someone were standing in her room yelling them. She set the soda down and immediately went to her computer. She had the application completed on Jude's behalf in one hour. She collected letters of recommendation from the administrators at Jude's school. Two weeks later, without any word to Jude, she had a video. With the help of the kind people at Jude's school, positive messages from Jude's students and colleagues were recorded. The video ended with a one-shot message from Hazel.

"My brother..." started Hazel, "I love him. Wholeheartedly, I love him. No one could need this more than he does. Have you ever known someone who was so filled with potential, but life squashed it before it ever had a chance to be fulfilled? That's Jude. Jude. The world is at his feet, and he could be anything he wanted to be, but after the death of our parents... Well, it's as if I lost him in their car wreck, too. He loves life and this world and the people in it. He is an amazing teacher and brother and friend. He is the perfect candidate to send to space. He is the perfect person to be the face of your mission. He is not just a teacher who needs adventure... he is a *person* who needs adventure. You could save him from the void he has been trapped in for so long. He is so loved, as you've seen, and with good reason. Everyone sees it but him. Give him a shot. You'll love him like everyone else. He is the teacher you need. Jude Monroe and NASA need each other. Trust me."

She sent in the video and the information, and though she hoped, she never actually believed anything could come of it. That is, until two months later, when she received a phone call from the secretary of a Mr. Tom Metzlebaum.

"Hi, uh, is Jude Monroe available?" asked a young woman's voice on the phone.

"Hi there! Uh, this is his sister," replied Hazel, confused. "Can I take a message?"

"Well, the Teacher Selection Committee for the Audacity Mission reviewed information submitted on behalf of Mr. Monroe, and he has been selected to be on the final list of the 100 candidates, and I am calling to set up an interview with him."

Hazel dropped the phone. Though she could hear the voice on the other line, she remained frozen. She could not believe that any part of what she had just heard was real. There were tears rolling down her face before she even realized it. She picked the phone back up.

"Uh, hey, yeah, sorry... Name the day and he'll be there. I'm sure," said Hazel, filled with an excitement she had not felt since far too long ago.

* * *

"So hey," Hazel said, looking at her brother when the movie ended, "I saw this thing and I thought you'd be perfect for it and I signed you up... I didn't think anything would actually come of it... But well, it's gotten a little farther than I had planned."

"If this is some speed dating nonsense again, count me out," said Jude, picking up candy wrappers and stray pieces of popcorn.

"No! Of course not. It's nothing like that... again... It's just something I saw an advertisement for and... well... I signed you up... and now they want an interview with you."

"What is it?" asked Jude, knowing that Hazel would tell him anyway. He just knew by now that it was better to humor her.

"I signed you up for something. And now it is actually getting some traction, and I think you're going to love this new idea," said Hazel, becoming filled with more joy.

"Okay, fine, tell me what it is?" said Jude, exiting the room but remaining in earshot.

"Well, you know... You know how you are always telling people to live like there's no tomorrow, or to buy that plane ticket, or chase your dreams?"

"I know the speech," Jude said from the other room, clearly uninvested in the conversation.

"Well, the thing is, I signed you up about two months ago. I had to write a resume and collect some letters of recommendation from your bosses and get some good video interviews from your students. It was a process, let me tell you..."

"You did what? What the hell are you talking about?" Jude said, rising in volume and frustration while cutting his sister off. Over the last three years, Hazel had signed Jude up for cooking classes, yoga classes, book clubs, and whatever else she might think would be able to rekindle his interests. Jude, who knew what she was doing and loved her more for it, did not want to go through with any of it. The thought of going out the front door and being spontaneous again was not something that he concerned himself with anymore. Sometimes, sure, he woke up in the morning, looked himself in the mirror, and realized life was passing him by. His daily commutes on his bike to school to teach his students were his only carefree moments of his day-to-day living.

"Okay, it was intrusive, but listen, it's super cool. They liked your resume and they liked what your students and bosses had to say," said Hazel, her eyes gleaming with excitement.

Jude looked at her. He could not help but enjoy the enthusiasm Hazel was feeling. "Okay," he said, "who loves me and what do they want from me?"

"I knew you'd be interested. Okay, so, it's NASA--"

"Damn it, Hazel, I thought you were serious," said Jude, turning to walk away from the conversation.

"I *am* serious. NASA is who the ad was for. They're looking for a teacher to go to space. I sent in a ton of stuff about you to them, and you made their list of the top 100 candidates."

"You've had too much wine. Let me take you home," said Jude, reaching for his keys.

"I am being real with you, Jude. Listen to me. I saw the ad and hopped on it. It's a legit opportunity to do something literally no one else gets to do. They selected you. NASA. Who the hell chases their dreams like the people who work there? They follow the mantra you tell everyone to live by; don't you want to actually start living by your words and stop watching other people do it? I sent in the stuff, they called this morning to set up an interview, and you're going to go."

"Okay," said Jude, with condescension, "I'll play along. Even if this was a thing, I'm not going to go to space. Why would I want to go to space?"

"Because the *Apollo 11* poster that's been in your room since you were five, for starters. Because I have looked all over this damn planet to find something to make you happy, and I have found jack-shit. Maybe it's time to start searching somewhere else."

"None of that matters anymore. I'm fine, Hazel, I'm fine. I'm alive." Jude regretted humoring any bit of this conversation.

"Yeah, but you haven't lived in years," said Hazel, unapologetically.

"Hey--"

"Damn it, Jude, listen to me," yelled Hazel, becoming, somehow, more adamant. "NASA is looking to redo the idea they had in the

80s when they planned to send a teacher to space on the *Challenger*. They're looking for a teacher, and I sent your story in."

"I mean, good for them, seriously, but *story*? I have no story. I am no one," said Jude, his back turned to Hazel as he pretended to wash dishes.

"Hey," said Hazel, walking up and punching Jude in the shoulder, "I'll kick anyone's ass who talks about my brother like that, especially if it's you. I told them how much you love teaching, and I brought up mom and dad. I brought up how you gave up on chasing the days and chasing life, and how you struggle to stay present. I just said how this is the very thing you need in your life to bring back the meaning we all know that you feel you lost."

There was a pause. Years ago, after hearing something like this, Jude would have fought back, but not now. Deep inside, he knew she was right.

"Is that what you really think about me?" said Jude, his hands completely still in the soapy water.

"Yes. It's what all the people in your life think. It's what Grace thought. It's why she left. She couldn't stand to watch it anymore."

"You stayed," said Jude, still not looking at his sister.

"Yeah," Hazel said, trying not to smile, "we're stuck together, dude."

"It's just... y'know, since mom and dad, I just haven't..."

"I know," said Hazel, leaning up against her brother, making eye contact in the reflection of the window above the sink, "I know, but you have to live. You have to make it count. Doing the opposite is not the lesson mom and dad would want you to take from their deaths."

There was a pause. Jude turned to look Hazel in her eyes. With a smile, he thanked her. He didn't know what he would do without her, but he knew he would be lost. "Okay, fine, sure, I can go to an interview," he said, "what do I need to do now?"

"Recruitment interview is next week. Wear your blue tie, and I'll iron your shirt, so that it's done right. Just lay into the sob stuff, I think it really worked to begin with."

"How much sob stuff did you talk about?" said Jude, starting to laugh.

"Enough for them to love you, apparently. But, it's getting late and I've had too much wine to drive, so I'm going to need you to take me home. Besides, it'll give me more time to tell you about the process in the car," said Hazel, her excited disposition having returned. "I really do think you have a good chance. They only selected 100 people to interview. Just keep spewing that 'chase your dreams' BS you spew at everyone but yourself."

"Hey, it's a good speech," said Jude, with a shrug.

"It's a damn good speech," said Hazel, grabbing Jude's keys. "It wouldn't be so good if somewhere, deep inside, you didn't believe it yourself, and it's time to start realizing that." Tossing the keys to her brother so that he could take her home, Hazel walked to the front door and opened it. "Now, come on, future astronaut, there's a big universe out there, and it's right this way."

Three

November 5, 2393

Darkness. That's all there was. Not even a minute ago, Jude was looking at the reflection glass inside *The Audacity*. But now, only darkness underscored the one question burning in Jude's mind: what happened?

He finally began to catch his breath, and time slowed down. He tried to assess the situation. Was he asleep? Did he just wake up from a terrible nightmare? The last thing he remembered was Sarah's visor... and that terrible, terrible noise before nothing remained but darkness. But was this darkness a dream, or did he just wake up in his corridor on NASA grounds? No. This was different. Jude's eyes were open, but he could not see. He tried to get up, but as he made his first move, he heard something move close to him, and he realized something that made him immediately go cold: he was not alone in the darkness.

"Who the hell are you?" A voice whispered inches from his face. The voice was electric and gave no sign of humanity.

Jude didn't respond. He continued to look around, attempting to see anything. But as he tried to reach out, he became aware of something even more terrifying: his hands were tied behind his back. In panic, he fell over onto his side, and as he did so, he realized his vision was blocked by a cloth covering his head. Tied up, blinded, confused, Jude tried to scream, but nothing came out. This certainly wasn't a fantasy, but what the hell was it? Where was the shuttle? Where was the crew? Where was Sarah? This may not have been a dream, but it was definitely a nightmare.

As Jude began to struggle again, the voice came again, the tone was harsher, yet still a whisper. "Who the *hell* are you, and what are you doing here?"

Jude tried to talk, but his throat was dry. He opened his mouth to scream, but still, nothing came out. He couldn't stand. His feet were locked to something immovable. He was completely defenseless. Whoever else was in this room... They had complete control. Jude knew he could fight to move, but the battle was lost before he even woke up.

"Listen to me. I'm only going to say this one more time," the voice growled again, not raising above a whisper. Jude heard what sounded like a high-tech drill. Finally, after what felt like a lifetime, his head cover was removed. The light of the room blinded him, but when his eyes began to focus, he saw, inches from his face, a black gun with a green light shining down the side. He had never before seen anything like this weapon. The light bouncing off the overly white walls mixed with the intense fear made Jude close his eyes. The figure pushed the gun against his forehead, and Jude managed to make some words come out.

"I don't know where I am!" He groaned, his voice raspy and strained. "I'm... I'm just a... please don't hurt me. I don't even know why I'm in this room. What happened? Where am I?" Jude began to open his eyes again. The gun had not moved, and the person holding it was rigid and unflinching.

"Stop the act. I don't have time for this. I need to know where the vest is," said the voice in strained patience.

"I... I swear... I have no idea what you are talking about...Vest? Five seconds ago, I was sleeping. No. I was on the shuttle. Please, tell me what is going on?" asked Jude, tears forming in his eyes.

"What's going on? I'll tell you what's going on. Outside that door are two dead guards. The gun pointed at your face right now is the cause. I came into this room to find something very valuable, and all I found was you unconscious in this corner. Last chance, you have five seconds to explain yourself. I don't have time to listen to your stuttering. There's been an increase in Shadow activity, and if my loot isn't here, I need to get the hell out."

"Shadow activity? Please. I swear. Please, don't hurt me. I have a sister. She needs me." Jude said this as the tears broke through and streamed down his face. Shock was starting to set in. He was slowly accepting that all of this was real. Even though he had no idea how, he realized that everything, the bright room, this person in front of him, was real. Jude was starting to shake, his mouth drier than before. He didn't even realize he was cold.

"Sister? You have a sister?" asked the voice, surprised. The person standing in front of Jude began to slowly lower the gun, and their stoic posture slightly relaxed. "My parents broke the single child law too... They eventually caught us, and we lost her... Where's yours? Was she with you?"

Jude's eyes finally focused. The person standing in front of him was dressed head to toe in a tight red, gold, and black suit. He barely noticed the blood on the black gloves, the way the suit accented the outline of the body, nor the several weapons attached to the black boots or belt of the person. Rather, he continued to stare into the fully black glass mask which prevented any visual. Jude looked into the visor, and he was only met with his own reflection. He was still wearing the slim white and gray jumpsuit which he wore under his space gear. The collar of his padded t-shirt underneath seemed only slightly whiter than his pale complexion. Despite the fact that the gun was no longer pointed at Jude, he still knew danger stood two feet in front of him.

"My sister was taken, too. She was taken to the camps almost 17 years ago," said the figure after a long pause, looking at the door behind. "When was yours taken?"

It was at this moment that Jude, for the first time, began to wonder where Hazel might be. Was that loud noise and the following darkness the shuttle exploding? Did he go unconscious and end up somewhere he shouldn't have? This person in front of Jude was not from his reality, but he was certain he was both awake and alive. No matter where he might be, Hazel would know something was wrong, and she most certainly would be a mess. Tears began again to come to Jude's eyes. "I... I didn't lose my sister... Look, I don't know what is going on," said Jude, frantically, still staring at the dark visor.

Again, the gun was pointed at Jude. "That's impossible," yelled the voice with the same aggression that Jude had woken up to. "Every house was raided in the country to take extra kids. This is your only chance to answer honestly. Are you *Volgen?*"

"Am I what? What the hell is a Volgen? I'm a teacher. I was selected for a mission with NASA, and here I am. That's what I am. A nobody. A teacher. Please, please, stop pointing that at me."

Continuing to point the gun at Jude, the figure said, "Stop, just stop. NASA hasn't existed for over 100 years. Teachers stopped being used after the discovery of The Imminent Collision, and anyone who has been around for the last 18 years knows about the Volgens. You're either very stupid or the best liar I've ever seen. You better hope you're just stupid." Again, slowly, the figure pressed the gun to Jude's forehead. Silence filled the room.

Jude didn't know what he should say. Clearly, this person was doing the math. Everything Jude said seemed to be the wrong thing to say, and he knew that every second of silence made him seem more suspicious. His wrists were raw from the bindings, and he hadn't felt his feet since he had woken up. He just stared back hoping that whoever this was would see whatever they were looking for. The tension was causing sweat to form on Jude's head and back. The gun was still pointed at him. He could hear the rubber in the glove holding the gun tighten.

After studying Jude for a full minute, the figure put the gun back in its holster. The person took out a knife and immediately sliced a deep one-inch cut onto Jude's forearm. Still tied down, Jude could do nothing but let out a yelp. The figure put a hand over Jude's mouth to muffle the scream. He couldn't breathe. Quickly, whoever this masked person was took a vial out of a pocket, scooped up a little amount of Jude's blood, and put it into a small electronic box.

The figure was silent. Even though he could not see through the visor, Jude knew that he was being studied. He could feel a piercing stare looking deep inside of him. Quickly, the figure pressed the knife to Jude's throat. "Tell me your name. Now."

"Jude, Jude Monroe, and I swear, I'm no one."

The figure paused. No sign of life came from behind the visor. Seconds later, in one movement, the figure took the gun out again and fired two shots. Jude jumped, only to realize that his hands and feet were now free. "Stand up," the figure said. "Stand up and turn around."

Jude stood up, terrified. All the action movies he watched with Hazel, this was always how it ended for the hostages at the end of the films. Their hands were freed for "humane" appearances. Jude began to turn around to plead one last time for his life.

"I didn't tell you to turn around yet," he heard the voice say, as there was a click and a quick burst of air. Jude, still scared, was all too aware that the figure had taken off the intimidating mask. He knew that Darth Vader-like sound from watching *Star Wars* with Hazel hundreds of times.

"Okay, raise your hands and slowly turn around," Jude heard a voice say. This voice, however, no longer had its deep, electric sound. It was softer, almost welcoming.

Jude slowly turned around. The figure before him was a young blonde woman. She still held the gun to Jude's chest as if begging him to make a wrong move. She looked steadily at him and then spoke. "I'm Elise. You can put your shocked look away now."

She was right. Jude was shocked. He didn't know what to expect behind the mask. The gun, the lights, the suit she wore; he thought anything could be behind that mask. He never expected her, though he didn't know why. No matter what he thought before or even thought now, he was surprised to find that he was even more scared than he was when she had the mask on.

"Why did you show me your face?" Jude asked. They were the only words he could think to say.

"Do you know what this is?" asked Elise, pointing to the box on her belt.

"No. I don't. It looks like something from the movies," said Jude, completely aware of how moronic he sounded.

"I should think you wouldn't. Considering who you are. This screen tests the blood, and I can see whether or not you are human. Judging by your relief at seeing the green light, I can see that you understand that the green is good. Congrats, you're not an idiot... despite the look you've had on your face for five minutes. However, what's strange is that underneath your A positive blood type, it says that you are over three hundred years old. Either this machine is wrong, or you're very misplaced in time."

"Three hu--- What? No. I'm twenty-s—. What the hell are you talking about?" asked Jude, completely confused.

"You really have no idea about anything that is going on, do you?" asked Elise. Behind her eyes, Jude was certain he saw concern.

"Please," begged Jude, exhausted, "please. Where am I?"

When Jude finished his sentence, an ear-splitting alarm began to ring. Elise's face went from subtle concern to complete fear.

"Shi–. Okay, tell me. How are you here? Did you come by a portal? Do you have a Houdini Vest? How are you here and so out of your time?" asked Elise, the pace of her speech becoming quicker.

"What does any of that mean? Portal, Houdini what? What are these alarms?" Jude's hands were cupped over his ears. The sound of the sirens made it impossible for him to think.

Elise moved to the door and quickly looked outside. Flashing red lights from the hallway filled the completely white room when she cracked open the door.

"Okay. Listen to me," she said, moving back to Jude. "Say this whole damn routine is real and you really just ended up here from 300-something years ago, and I'm the first face you saw, you need to know this: the year is 2393 and the entire world is at war. Those sirens. Those sirens are in every building in this city. They alert us when the Shadows are loose. Which means we need to get out of here right now."

"I--" began Jude, but he was immediately interrupted. The sirens, ever present, were unyielding.

"Listen to me now," yelled Elise, grabbing his collar and running through the door. "I believe this whole thing you've got going for you, okay? I've heard stories of people through time being grabbed by the portals... these are like doorways from one time to another. Maybe that's what happened to you. I don't know. I can see in your eyes that you're completely lost. No one can fake it that well. You're looking at me the same way my father looked when they took my sister away from us." She paused as they approached a corner in the hallway just outside the room Jude had woken up in. "That look is why I am going to help you out of here, and we can sort all of this out later. Okay? I be-

lieve you, Jude. Now, you have to believe me. If only for ten minutes." She looked into Jude's eyes as he stared back in total disbelief.

He looked deep into Elise's eyes which were inches from his face. At this moment, for whatever reason, he trusted her. He gave a slow nod. She looked at him for a moment longer, and she gave a smirk. Quickly, she grabbed his hand, pulled him around the corner and into the new hallway, and took an immediate right through a small room and into yet another similarly looking hallway.

Quickly, they ran down corridor after corridor. Each hallway was empty. "People hide when these sirens and lights go off. They are safe if they stay out of sight," said Elise, pausing to let Jude catch his breath. "Shadows don't spend time looking. They only attack what they find in their path. Some people think they only track residual energy from time travel."

"Time travel?" asked Jude, still lost on what Elise had said earlier, "grabbed through time, portals..." This was becoming far too science fiction.

"You really have no idea what is going on, do you?" asked Elise, gritting her teeth and looking at Jude. "Listen, if your story is true, that you were on some NASA mission and you were a teacher, then you are not from my time or now or whatever. The building you are in is called The TTI. Time Travel Institute. This building is a tower dedicated to one purpose: time travel. It was built shortly after the discovery of The Imminent Collision. The government explored all avenues of escaping the comet... even time travel. The first portal was found in this very building, Jude. All of these things, you from a different time waking up in a building meant for time travel, it all adds up to one thing: you were somehow taken from your time and put here. I don't know how you got tied up and blindfolded, we can sort that out later, and I know this probably all sounds crazy, but trust me... if you'd have lived through the last ten years during this time, you wouldn't be surprised by anything." She grabbed him, and they began to run again.

"Okay, fine. Fine. Say I'm 350 years in the future, you're telling me there's something called a Shadow loose and chasing time travel energy?"

"Yes. That is what I am saying. Which is why the Shadows always come to this building," said Elise, growing impatient. She was clearly only running at Jude's pace, and he could feel her frustration.

"Why can't we just hide like everyone else?"

"Because... aren't you listening? If you are from 350 years ago... You have time travel energy on you. They'll be looking for someone just like you." Elise paused a moment, looked around the corner, and began to run down a new hallway. Clearly, she was looking for something.

"What the hell would they want me for? Even if I had this energy 'on' me. Did I wake up in some demented Neverland where I'm Peter Pan and I pissed off my vengeful, murderous Shadow?"

"...I know you did not just make some dumbass joke with sirens surrounding you in a time you have no knowledge of."
"Yeah, my jokes are often mistimed," said Jude, regretting literally everything in that moment.

"Listen, I'll go into it later. But the Shadow people are from far away, and they are only known for one thing: seeking and killing anyone with the residue of time travel on them. They kill everything in their path as they try to find the residue. They'll kill me just for being right next to a time traveler."

"And... and at this moment, I have that... this residue?" asked Jude, somehow, somehow beginning to believe Elise.

"Yes. They are relentless and ruthless. They---"

As Elise was turning another corner, she stopped, and her eyes immediately looked to the very end of the hallway. She went silent. He slowly looked to the end of the hallway with her.

This one was different from all of the others. Each hallway they ran down, and there were many, was incredibly well-lit. This hallway was bright like the others for about fifty yards. But at the end of it, where there should be a door, or a new hallway, or something, there was complete darkness. No light could be seen. What looked like a man stepped out of the darkness, and under the last visible light of the hallway, Jude could see no face or anything at all. The figure took one more step into the light and stopped. The figure was completely black. It was a nine-foot silhouette resembling a man, but only in shape. If Jude didn't believe Elise before about Shadows, he did now. The only thing he could make out when looking at this human-looking Shadow was its bright red eyes. Slowly, the darkness from which the Shadow had stepped out had somehow moved to where it was standing, and it disappeared again. The darkness moved down the hallway at a crawl, and Elise and Jude stood motionless, almost hypnotized in fear. The darkness began to move more quickly down the hall, and as it did, the figure exploded from it at a full sprint toward the two.

Elise was the first to run, grabbing Jude. They turned down another corridor. Jude, looking back over his shoulder, saw that the

Shadow was not far behind. The black wall of darkness followed the figure at a lightning pace.

Deep inside, Jude could feel the Shadow calling out to him. In his mind, the Shadow had already taken him. He was startled awake by the sound of a blast. Elise had drawn her gun again and was firing upon the Shadow. Each shot seemed not to faze the seemingly evil creature. The dark figure continued to advance. Elise took Jude to a door that led to the nearest stairwell. Outside the door, "Floor 15" was posted. Elise kicked out the door and seemed to be in shock. The entire stairwell was black. She immediately froze. Jude was still looking over his shoulder at the charging Shadow as it was running to catch up. Elise put her arm out to stop him from running into the completely dark stairwell. Frozen again, they stared into the darkness. A wall of black charged after them from behind, and now the stairwell was filled with the same abyss. They could hear growling and stomping from within the solid black stairwell. They were running out of options for escape. Before they had time to start running again, a shadowed hand reached out quickly and came within inches of Jude's face. It barely missed. The darkness began to move into the hallway from the stairwell. Within the dark mass, Jude saw a dozen red eyes staring at him.

Without needing to be grabbed this time, Jude turned and ran. As he ran, Elise quickly caught up and passed him to lead him down a different hall. They entered some sort of conference room full of windows, tables, and chairs. Elise, gun still drawn, pointed and shot out two windows that led outside. The two ran to the window and looked down.

"We have to jump," said Elise, looking at Jude.

"Your escape plan involves death?" asked Jude, completely out of breath and looking fifteen floors down.

"Death by jumping is a much better choice than death by Shadow. I promise you that. But, there'll be no dying today."

Elise looked to the ground below as she finished talking. The door exploded open. The two looked back, and there was only darkness. No light from the hallway could be seen. Finally, within the solid black wall on the other side of the doorway, the now familiar red eyes could be seen. The Shadows paused in the threshold of the room as if they were watching to see what fate the two humans would choose. Slowly, the walls began to disappear as the blackness covered them.

"Do you trust me?" asked Elise, trying to speak over the sound of the wind coming through the open windows. She grabbed Jude by the shoulders and looked at him. He wasn't looking back. He was speechless, still looking at the darkness creeping into the room. "Do you trust me, Jude?" she yelled again. Finally, he looked at her, but words didn't come. "I'm going to have to take that as a yes," Elise yelled, and without hesitation, she threw him out the window, 15 stories above the ground.

At first, Jude didn't know he was falling. He felt like he was flying, and he couldn't help but think that it was peaceful. For just a second, it washed away all thoughts of Houdini vests, Volgens, Shadows, time travel, and anything that led him to a world where any of that could possibly exist. Peace, however, lasted a matter of seconds before he realized how quickly the ground was approaching. Gravity ushered him to certain death. The walls, the city he was in, everything was a blur. He was moving too quickly to make anything out. The only thing he could see was the ground below and how quickly it was approaching before unconsciousness took him and the world, once again, faded to black.

Four

March 24, 2019

The sounds of the lights in the room were starting to drive Jude crazy. He had sat in this room, alone, for what seemed like an eternity. The entire time he sat there, he could not believe that he had flown all the way from Chicago for this–what was sure to be a gigantic waste of time. At least, he thought, it was on NASA's dime. He was brought to this waiting room almost an hour ago; enough time for whatever nerves he had to leave. He noticed that as he was sitting in the chair, he was playing with the tie that Hazel had picked out... and tied for him before she put it in his suitcase. Okay, so maybe some nerves still remained. After all, no one truly enjoys an interview, even if it is for something they didn't sign up for, let alone actually wanted. Although, deep down, something Jude was completely oblivious to, he really did want it. For so long, he yearned for something incredible to come into his life. Since his parents–since Grace, he needed something like this.

After realizing he had moved his tie out of place for the 13th time since he entered the room, he readjusted and stood up to walk over to the *Apollo 11* portrait on the wall. Jude thought of the poster he had in his room as a child. How many times did he fall asleep looking at it? The bravery of humans... It was really the reason he became a history teacher. He loved that history was filled with people becoming greater than they ever dreamed that they could. He loved that the future would bring more people to follow in their path. Hazel, Grace, his parents, his friends, they would all tell him that he could be whatever he wanted. There was a time he believed them, but that had since passed. Teaching truly was a dream realized, but deep down, he wanted more.

"Pretty incredible, huh?" A man's voice said behind Jude. Before the silence was broken, Jude was fully unaware that he wasn't alone anymore. He was so deep in thought at the portrait, he didn't even hear the door open behind him.

"Oh, yeah... I had a poster that looked just like it when I was a kid," Jude said, trying not to sound as caught off guard as he felt.

"So did I... well, still do," laughed Tom Metzlebaum, still standing in the doorway. "The wife let me keep it when we bought a new house and moved out of the apartment. Hard to let go of the past, isn't it?"

Jude chuckled in agreement. "That's why I teach history. I hold onto the past for a living."

"History was always my favorite subject in school... Don't tell my science professors that. They might take my PhD away," joked Metzlebaum, as he moved toward Jude. "Tom Metzlebaum, it's really nice to meet you, Mr. Monroe."

"Nice to meet you. I still can't believe I'm even here... I mean, I'm grateful, but, I mean I'm... I'm thankful," stuttered Jude, looking down at his tie again, trying to summon the courage Hazel repeatedly told him on the phone that was inside of him before he left his hotel room this morning.

Metzlebaum had not stopped looking at him since he opened the door, waited half a minute while watching Jude study the *Apollo 11* poster, or since he walked over and shook hands with him.

"You know, my father was actually there," said Metzlebaum, pointing at the poster. "My grandfather took him to the launch. Said it changed his life... It's why he came to work here after college... hell, it's why I, his only child, came to work here." Metzlebaum continued to look at Jude, who was looking down at his tie. "I think about him every time I look at that poster at home... or here. Some people, they wake up one morning knowing they're going to experience something that is going to change their life, like my dad did when he woke up to go watch that... It's not always that easy, y'know? Sometimes, sometimes, it takes waking up and manifesting our life-changing events."

Jude looked up at Metzlebaum, who was now looking at the poster. "Two groups of people that day," said Metzlebaum, smiling at the mounted picture. "Those who showed up to have their life changed and those who carved their path day by day to change their life. But you know what both did? They showed up. Sometimes life can change just by showing up."

Metzlebaum's words were left hanging in the air. Jude wondered which man in the room the words were meant for more. The two men looked at the portrait for a few more seconds.

Jude turned to Metzlebaum and laughed. "You sound like you heard the speech my sister gave me before I left this morning... really, every day since we lost our parents. But I want you to know. I'm here. I'm ready. I really do think I can do this," Jude said the words, and they were noticeably forced.

"Y'know, I'm really sorry to have heard about that loss," said Metzlebaum, putting his hand on Jude's shoulder. "I know how heavily that can sit on your shoulders. Lost my dad about a year ago. I couldn't look at this portrait for six months. Your sister loves you, that's for sure. I watched the video she made... We got about 2,000 submissions from entries who didn't even know they were entered, which was clearly the case with your submission. But it was not just what your sister said, it was how she said it. Your sister's video got you to the top 250 people, which was where I came in to start watching, and I remember I watched it early on and your story... Well, let's just say I can connect. Sometimes, life makes you look at that portrait that you've been averting your eyes from for months. Mr. Monroe, it's time to look at the portrait."

Jude was speechless and yet captivated. This man in front of him had summarized years of pain in a way that he never could put into words himself. "Mr. Metzlebaum, I..."

"Don't mention it," Metzlebaum said, waving his hands in the air. "Humans, we gotta stick together. Listen, you feel like coming inside to interview with us, it'll just take a minute." He smiled, turned, and walked to the door. He paused in the doorway, looked back, and put his hands in his pockets. "Make the decision, Mr. Monroe, to look at the portrait because you already made the decision to show up."

Five

November 6, 2393

Jude had yet to wake up from his fall. Elise was standing staring at him. How she would explain to him her ability to catch him was beyond her. Honestly, if this guy's story really was true, how she would explain using her flying pod to catch him during his freefall from 15 stories above the ground after being chased by Shadows... he's going to think he lost his mind. For the last thirty minutes, from meeting, to running, to falling, the two people were as unbelievable to each other as they could be. She had to be just as unreal to him as he was to her. This thought, as she watched his unconscious body in the back of her pod, was all that kept her from leaving him where she had parked her pod after the Shadow sirens had faded away.

Of course, there was the other thing keeping him in her pod. Looking down at Jude, one thing was for certain: this stranger from potentially long ago had something to offer. What she went to the 15th floor of the TTI to retrieve was not there. She was able to access the whereabouts of where her desired treasure was in the room next to where she found Jude. In order to get into where she was about to go, though, she would need assistance. She needed Jude's assistance. There was more to this guy than what met the eye, that was certain.

Enough to break into a Volgen prison camp? Elise had no other choice than to find out.

Jude awoke to the sound of rain beating down upon the metal of the exterior of Elise's pod. He felt calm, a terrible headache, but calm nonetheless. He had no memory of getting to the bed he was lying in, nor how he got the black blanket which was now covering him. Elise was standing in front of him with her arms crossed.

"Sorry about that," said Elise, not giving Jude time to speak, let alone internalize the newest environment that he had found himself in. "I didn't have time to find out if you had the guts to jump or not."

He rolled over, sat up, and put his feet on the floor. The wall was lined with tally marks. From floor to ceiling, black tally marks covered a gray metal interior. When Jude stood up from the bed, he felt a throbbing pain in his leg and fell down immediately. Elise caught him and helped him back into the bed. He looked down and noticed some makeshift stitching binding a large gash on his lower left leg.

Gesturing to his bandages, Elise broke the silence again, "sorry about that, too... It's been a while since I've had to do any stitches. You sliced your leg jumping out that window." Her voice, Jude noticed, sounded actually compassionate.

"If I remember correctly," said Jude, not looking up and still staring at his leg, "I was thrown from that window."

"Semantics," replied Elise, staring at the wound, a tinge of pain behind her eyes. She paused and, with as much kindness as she could muster, asked, "you okay?"

"I'm not sure," said Jude, finally looking at Elise. She was out of her form-fitting jumpsuit and had the appearance more of someone recognizable from Jude's time. She seemed more vulnerable. However, Jude knew from seeing her in action that she was not someone who could be underestimated. "It's nice to wake up and not be handcuffed or blinded. I have to admit that."

Elise laughed for a moment. "Yeah... We'll find the bastards that did that to you. Not exactly a solid welcome wagon to the future, was it?"

Jude looked to Elise, then he looked to the ceiling. "Listen, not to sound rude, there's a lot to unpack, I'll give you that, but I'm not crazy. Time travel is fantasy. I live in reality. So, where am I?"

Elise looked at him, trying to figure out how to help this man connect the dots and come to terms with reality. Still, she wasn't 100% sure that this wasn't an act. However, she stood up, walked to the edge of the bed where Jude sat, and opened up a curtain on the wall. The sunlight, which broke through the rain clouds, shined through the window and briefly blinded Jude. Quickly, however, his eyes adjusted. Elise held out her hand and helped Jude to his feet. He moved slowly to the window. Buildings crowded the sky. High in the air, between the skyscrapers, were flying cars that looked like floating piles of pieced-together garbage. To Jude, the most noticeable thing was how brown everything seemed. Rust had waged war and won with apparent ease upon all the buildings in sight. Jude and Elise were parked at the top of one of the skyscrapers. Jude's eyes left the brown buildings and became fixated on something he saw in the distance. He stumbled to the door of the pod.

"How do you get out?" he asked. He started pressing random buttons.

"Why? Where are you going? Stop pressing all of those. You might hit the self-destruct."

"Just outside. I'd like some air... wait, self-destruct?"

Elise laughed, "I'm just messing with you, that button doesn't exist. You are going to be so fun to mess with, old man."

Elise pressed a lever near the door, and the entire chamber was filled with cool air. Jude stumbled out. He cautiously stepped onto the roof of the building they were parked on. His eyes were fixed on the beautiful water around the buildings. Through wisps of smoke, he could see the water that he had grown up looking at. Growing up in the suburbs of Chicago, Saturdays meant going into the city, picnicking at Lake Shore Park, and walking around the banks of Lake Michigan.

"What is it?" asked Elise, seeing the look on Jude's face as he stared at the water.

"That's Lake Michigan, isn't it? I'd know that water anywhere. I used to sit near it on weekends with my parents and my sister as a kid. Then later, when my high school girlfriend cheated on me, when my engagement fell through, and almost every night for a year after my parents... after... well. Well, let's just say, I know that water, but there is no way that this is Chicago."

"Still Chicago," Elise said, gesturing to all of the rusted buildings, "but Jude, it's just not your Chicago anymore. Your Chicago is centuries behind us right now."

Jude's eyes never left the water, though they began to fill with tears. Emotions took him. Reality set in that he had, in fact, somehow ended up in the future. He could hear the junkers flying by stories below; he could smell burnt rubber, but his eyes never left the one place that brought him so much calm in his life. Suddenly, Jude began to laugh. He began to laugh like Elise had just told the funniest joke he had ever heard.

How funny, he thought, that when he needed the lake for calm more than ever, he stepped outside, and it was within sight. Jude, looking at this new world, was somehow ready to welcome conversations of Shadow monsters, of Volgens, of portals, and of Houdini Vests. He was hit with a cold wind, and he was thankful that not everything was different from this very old city.

He looked down and saw humanity, 300 years later. Jude continued to laugh, somehow harder. "Stubborn-ass Chicagoans," he turned and said to Elise, only to quickly turn back to the water. The sun broke through the clouds and bounced off the waves. The beauty of the moment overtook him. Humans, the indefatigable, the defiant. They battled against time and continued to build and continued to exist. Pride was the only word he could find to describe it. Five minutes passed of internalizing the world around him, and he didn't notice the complete silence that had overtaken the conversation.

"Speak to me, partner, what's going on? You haven't gone comatose on me again, have ya? You don't wanna fall out here," joked Elise, looking at Jude and not the city.

He looked at Elise, back to the city, back to Elise, back to Lake Michigan, and he began to smile to himself as he thought about what he should say. Finally, he said, "I mean, all I can say... all I can say is thank *God* the future lived up to the flying cars cliche. I would have been so damn pissed."

The two laughed out loud and simply looked at each other, and for a moment, anything that divided them melted away. Just two humans in the year 2393 laughing at a bad joke.

Jude, still looking at Elise, said, "Okay, I believe you." Elise nodded back at him; her blonde hair flowed in the wind. She didn't say a word. She only smiled at him and took his hand. Despite the cold winter air, the events of the last 24 hours, and the fact that somewhere Shadow monsters were on the run, peace was the only thing that the two felt.

Six

March 24, 2019

"Mr. Monroe, thanks for flying all the way to Lyndon B. Johnson Space Center in Clearwater, Texas, to join us today. Sorry we kept you waiting so long out there," said Metzlebaum, when he got seated at the head of the table. There were 15 people sitting at the same large table, and they were all staring at Jude, who was sitting directly opposite of Metzlebaum. There were five cameras also pointed straight at him, and he could only feel that this was more of an interrogation than an interview. "Also, sorry about all of the bells and whistles in here, you know how government processes are." Every head turned simultaneously to Metzlebaum when he began talking again. "We could be filming history here, y'know? Speaking of which, Mr. Monroe, you teach history... tell us a little bit about that." Like one organism, the entire group simultaneously turned their heads and were, yet again, staring at Jude.

"History, yeah, well, I've always loved it," said Jude, knowing he somehow pulled a strike when the question was teed up for him.

"...and why is that, Mr. Monroe," pushed Metzlebaum.

Jude paused and really thought about the question. "...Well, I guess, it all started when I was younger. Dad, my father, would sit with us after dinner and when the dishes were clear, he'd just tell us the best stories. He told us stories of war heroes and inventors... If we listened to music, he could tell us stories about the musicians. I remember thinking how I would always want to be able to tell stories like him. I spent my life trying to be as good of a storyteller as him. Which is why I became a teacher. I remember, on the night he renewed his vows with mom, he took me outside, gave me a cigar, and told me some incredible story about the building the ceremony was in. I just looked at him, and all I could think was damn, I wish I could be that smooth."

The room laughed, and Metzlebaum, who had smiled from the moment Jude started talking, was eyeing around the room to gauge reactions.

"You really shouldn't get me talking, because I can't stop when you get me going, just ask my students," laughed Jude, and everyone smiled and nodded. "I never really liked cigars, but I liked sharing cigar moments with dad. Does that make sense? That night, though, I asked him, what's the secret? How do you make every story seem like it's the most important story in the world? I remember it so clearly. He looked at me, put his hand on my shoulder, and said, 'because each story, to someone, *is* the most important story.' That's never left me."

Jude paused. He thought of his dad and his mom. He remembered that his father continued saying, "you and your sister, to your mom and me, are the most important story to us. One day, when people tell our story, they'd better tell it like there was nothing more serious... or more fun." That was the last cigar Jude ever smoked with his dad. It was the last time the world seemed to make any sense.

"I think I love history because it's filled with everyone's most treasured memories," continued Jude after he realized that he had paused a moment too long. "Good versus evil. Happy versus sad. It's all important to someone. That's the point, I suppose."

The room stayed silent, and for the first time, no one was looking at Jude, except Metzlebaum. The other 14 people lowered their heads and thought about their most important stories. Moms, dads, pets, wives, husbands, exes, clearly, each person was lost in thought for a moment. For Metzlebaum, however, his thoughts didn't dwell on the past, but on the future. Here in front of him, this man who, though filled with grief, was also filled with the exact amount of passion he had hoped to find in a candidate. There was something about this Jude Monroe. In one question, he had connected to every person in the room. Deep inside, humans are collections of important stories –histories that are often forgotten. Every so often, though, reminders come along and moments are relived. Each person in the room was lost in thought for a moment until the interview resumed.

The interview lasted a full hour, though it only took thirty seconds for each person on the selection committee to make their decision about Jude. He shook each hand before exiting the conference room. Metzlebaum walked him out.

"Well, thank you, sir, for allowing me to have a chance," said Jude, walking through a door opened for him by Metzlebaum.

"Son," Metzlebaum replied, "thank you. That was one hell of an interview."

"Th– thank you, seriously, Mr. Metzlebaum. It just... once we started talking, it just felt right, you know?"

"You decided to show up today. You made your sister proud. Hell, I haven't known you more than just the last few hours, and you made me proud," laughed Metztlbaum, adding, "call me Tom. It was really grand to meet you today."

"The pleasure was mine, thanks, Mr–Tom," said Jude, shaking hands with this man who had been so crucial to making Jude feel comfortable before and during the interview. "I wish you guys the best of luck with the interviews."

"Yeah, we have about 25 more of those left. But, you're going to be hard to beat. Keep your phone on," smiled Tom.

"You can't be serious," said Jude, smiling but in disbelief.

Tom turned to walk away and let the door close behind him. Though before the door fully closed, he yelled over his shoulder, "sometimes life makes you look at the portrait whether you feel ready or not."

Jude stood there. In the reflection of the glass door that had just closed, he could see himself. Somehow, he seemed taller than this morning when he had put his tie around his neck in the hotel mirror. He almost looked like a different person. He looked at himself for a few moments in the reflection until he noticed a picture over his shoulder.

He turned around and walked up to a portrait of *Apollo 11*, and in that moment, he wanted nothing else. The voice that had been in the back of his head for years was now louder than ever. It was calling to him. He felt a fire within himself that had been dormant for so long, and he realized something: it was time to finally answer that call.

* * *

Hazel picked Jude up at O'Hare airport the following morning. She followed the usual tradition, which Jude and Hazel always did when they picked each other up at the airport for the last couple years. She stood on a chair and yelled his name loud enough for complete humiliation.

"JUDE MONROE! JUDE! OVER HERE, JUDE!" she yelled, and Jude only smiled and picked up his pace to make the humiliation stop a little sooner. Still, despite the public display of embarrassment, the two always loved being welcomed home with so much love. They gave each other a big hug, and Hazel picked up Jude's suitcase to carry it to the car.

"Seriously," said Jude, "I can get my own suitcase."

"Oh, shut the hell up and tell me about the trip. You didn't answer any of my questions on the phone last night, and I've been *dying* to hear," asserted Hazel as she led the way.

"Well, I was really nervous, you know, but I think it went alright."

Hazel stopped in her tracks, put the suitcase down, and pointed at Jude, her index finger in his chest. "You listen to me. I want better details. I want the questions. I want the answers. I want the reactions. I even want the amount of breaths everyone took. I want the deets, and I want them now... Or at least when we get in the car, because you know how I feel about being in public too long."

Jude told her all about it on the way home. He told her about the trip and the flights and finally the interview. He told her about Metzlebaum's words and what he said when he was leaving. Hazel slammed on the brakes.

"Keep your phone on?" She yelled, "MY BROTHER IS GOING TO SPACE."

"That's just some BS they say to everyone, I'm sure," said Jude, to which Hazel immediately punched him in the arm before letting off the brakes and moving forward in the car. There was silence between the two for a few minutes, the duration of which Hazel never stopped smiling. Jude didn't realize she was crying until she allowed a small sniffle.

"You know, I'm really proud of you. Mom and dad would be, too. So damn proud."

Jude looked at her and put his hand on her hand. "They'd be proud of us."

The two drove home in quiet joy. Words aren't always needed to express love, joy, or pride. Though, something was strange when they turned the corner and could see Jude's house. There was a red car with rental plates in his driveway, and a man sitting on the top step of Jude's porch. Tom Metzlebaum waved at the pair when they pulled into the driveway.

"It might be a little unconventional for senior staff to come all this way, but I had to," said Metzlebaum, extending his hand to greet the Monroes. "After you left, we decided to cancel the other 25 interviews." Hazel let out a squeal, unable to contain any emotion.

"So, what do you say, Mr. Monroe, want to talk about becoming an astronaut over some of this Chicago deep-dish pizza I've always heard so much about?"

Seven

"Here, you must be starving," said Elise, handing Jude a bowl of what looked like eggs and bacon but in no way smelled like eggs and bacon after an hour of Elise cooking. Jude gratefully said thank you and ate the meal without tasting it. "I was right, you were hungry. I'm not the best cook, but sometimes food is food."

Jude looked at her and laughed. "True. True. I've had worse meals...." The sun was setting behind them. It reflected on the water in spurts of yellow and orange. The engine kept the inside of the pod warm as a cold night was beginning. The two sat quietly and watched as the sun disappeared. Fires were becoming visible throughout the city. Smoke could still be seen in the early hours of the night. No lights were turned on in the city, only fires.

"Not as pretty," said Elise, looking through the windows and out at the small visible camps, "the city without the natural backdrops. I'm sure the hype about beautiful cities didn't fully come true here in the future."

"You'd be surprised. If you had watched any movies during my time, this is more than any of us expected this far in the future. I'm surprised anything is still standing." Jude continued to look out the window and to the city as he worked through the almost inedible meal. "So, all those fires..?"

"Uh, yeah, you'll have to learn the differences between big pockets of smoke and smaller ones. Look over there, those intermingled sets of smaller smoke clouds, they're crowds of people. See, it's too dangerous to live alone inside of buildings anymore. It's too easy to be trapped with Shadows constantly hunting and feeding. Over there, though, the big throws of smoke are from the prisons. The biggest one is where they are holding the largest imprisonment of Volgens."

"Why are there so many fires and no lights?" asked Jude, still wrestling with differences of reality and from what he was promised in futuristic science fiction films.

"All streetlights were outlawed when the Shadows began descending upon major cities."

Jude looked at Elise, and there was pain behind her eyes. Because of a small amount of mutual trust, he felt as though she was beginning to let a bit of her guard down. Likewise, Jude was beginning to allow himself to believe in the reality he had woken up in. Finally, he looked to Elise, trying to comprehend both the Shadows and the Volgens. It was taking a lot to allow himself to believe any of it. "Okay, I'm willing to listen. Houdini Vests, Portals... but first, I have to know: what exactly are Volgens?"

Elise looked back at Jude and then looked away. He could see in her eyes that she was reliving the entire story before telling him. "Where do I begin?" Elise paused again. "Tell me, Jude, what did you guys know about aliens during your time?"

"Nothing really, only stories. Only in movies. I mean, there were always conspiracy theories and Area 51 things, but everything always seemed very fictional."

"Jude, let me tell you, they were there. They were everywhere. They were far from fiction."

"No offense, but there were no aliens. I mean, there were some funky-looking people. Mick Jagger and whatnot, but no aliens."

"Movies, Mick Jagger, I swear we don't speak the same language," said Elise, still solemn, her lightheartedness failing.

"What, no Stones fans 350 years in the future?"

Elise stared at him, attempting to decipher the joke. She looked away and moved on with her story. "Listen, aliens have been around for centuries. The Volgens are appearance-shifting aliens that have roamed the Earth since your time and before. They were first nick-named guardian angels when people started realizing what all they did for humanity. How many centuries were humans scared of aliens? When we discovered their existence, already on Earth, and what they had done for us while disguised as humans... Well, we celebrated... Everyone celebrated except the major governments. Then, shortly after they came out of hiding, we found out about The Imminent Collision, and we found out why the Volgens came out from hiding."

Elise paused, peering hard into Jude to make sure he followed. Jude put his fork down on his plate and looked to the ceiling. "Okay," he said, "pause on the Volgens. What is The Imminent Collision and what does it have to do with them?"

"Okay. Good questions... So, The Imminent Collision was supposed to be an event where Earth was struck by a comet in 2376. The North American Government discovered it over a century ago and decided to keep it secret from regular citizens. This wasn't too hard for them. They banned education, and they worked really hard to hide any information from the past. Apparently, all of the major governments knew about the comet, the Asian Government, the European government, but it was the best-kept secret on the planet. Here's what we know: somehow Volgens figured out how to harness the energy someone creates by escaping death, and they were waiting for the comet to bring a potential mass death for a mass escape."

"What the hell does that mean? Energy from escaping death?"

"So, it's like, kinetic energy versus potential energy. It takes energy to die... so when someone does die, their potential energy becomes kinetic as their life exits their body, right? So, if you escape death at the exact moment it happens, the kinetic energy that was going towards removing life, can actually be harnessed for something else... My dad was a scientist and explained it to me like 1,000 times... I'm still not sure I understand it..."

"So, if people escape death, they can actually capture the energy? I'm not sure that's science as much as... "

"Witchcraft? Sure as hell sounds like it and that's what I told my dad. He said it was almost like some combination of science and religion that these aliens had somehow figured out."

Jude was silent for nearly a minute as he tried to piece all of this together. As unrealistic as all of it sounded, in order for him to accept the reality that it was time travel that led to him sitting on this bench eating a terribly cooked breakfast for dinner, he had to go out on a limb and accept what Elise was saying.

"Okay," he started again, "okay, so these creatures figured out how to harness the energy from escaped death... sure... so why did they come out of hiding?"

"Well, that's where The Imminent Collision comes back into play. See, word started to get out about the comet. People began to lose their minds. The end of the world was coming, and there was seemingly no escape. Wars began to break loose. Bombs were dropped around the world. It looked like no human would actually make it to see the comet. Until, finally, these guardian angels came out of hiding and offered an escape plan just a few months before impact. Apparently, during pandemics of the world, each world war, even hyperactive climate changes, the Volgens were the ones who, disguised as humans, would steer the world back on course for survival and offered to do it again. They even offered to sit down with the top scientists in the world and explain how they could use their energy to escape the comet."

"So, these aliens were simply helping the Earth out of the kindness of what, their hearts? I don't get it."

"See, that's what they wanted us to think... Apparently, all along, they were waiting for the comet... but when they saw the amount of destruction that began when the secret of The Imminent Collision came out, they saw that the chances of humans making it to when it was going to happen were unlikely. What we didn't know is that they needed us as much as we needed them. So, they worked with these scientists named Leo and Goliath, we think, even before the news broke of the comet."

"Leo and Goliath?" asked Jude, taking a final bite of eggs.

"They were these two crazy scientists. They are the reason the TTI exists in Chicago. The North American Government was trying to beat all of the other governments to discover an escape route from the comet... They accepted all ideas; even unrealistic ones. So, when these two scientists, Leo and Goliath, were brought in and they suggested time travel, miraculously, they weren't laughed out of the room. What no one knew, the government official that had brought them in to speak to The North American Leadership was actually a Volgen who had infiltrated the government from the inside. Leo, Goliath, and the Volgens had actually known of each other before the public knew of the aliens surrounding them."

"Okay... I'm following, but I really don't understand how any of this connects."

"Let me put this simply: There was a big comet coming to Earth that would kill everything. Humans, aliens, everything. The Volgens needed to escape just as badly as the humans. They had two human scientists they trusted, and they had advanced technology or religion or whatever you want to call it that allowed them to harness crazy, unheard-of energy. They needed the labs, the humans had them. Human technology plus Volgen technology equaled an escape. They were going to use the energy to escape."

"Through time travel?" asked Jude, trying as hard as he could to follow.

"Through time travel. The Volgens were smart, but Leo and Goliath were just as smart. Together, they figured out how to use their energy to travel through time."

"Well, that could explain, somewhat, how I'm here?"

"Yeah, maybe, but we'll get to that. The Volgens had secrets they kept from everyone, though. They were stuck here. Why? Why did they need to wait for the comet? What was their plan? They needed to get a way to harness the energy all at once. What better way to harness vast amounts of energy than escape the catastrophic extinction of everything on a planet? Which leads me to the Houdini Vests."

Elise went to the room that Jude had woken up in and came back out with what looked like a bright yellow life jacket one might wear to go white water rafting. It was covered in tubes and had what looked like an oxygen tank connected to its back. She handed it to Jude, and it was heavier than he expected.

"Everyone on Earth was given one of these. They were going to save us all. They were what the Volgens and Leo and Goliath had come up with. The vests were supposed to be triggered at the moment of death and simultaneously capture the energy and teleport the humans to another place and time. So, if every human were wearing one when the comet hit... well, anyone wearing it would immediately have their vests triggered and sent to another time. A, hopefully, safer time."

Jude continued to look at the vest. He looked up at Elise and asked the obvious question: "Well, here you are, they must have worked? Why do you hate the Volgens? They had to have saved you, right?"

Elise sighed and stood up. She walked to the window. "That's where it gets interesting, Jude Monroe. You see, the day of the comet came. My dad put his arms around me and my sister and even though the sun was shining, we could clearly see the comet coming straight toward Earth. It was massive, and then the strangest thing happened:

74 | NOAH COLEMAN

it disappeared just before hitting the atmosphere. No one knew how...
We just saw it disappear... A few days went by, and we started hearing
terrible stories of suicides... People tried using their vests to time
travel, and that's when we realized, the vests never worked... they
were just for comfort to keep us civil until the mass death. That vest
in your hands, like the rest, is fake. That was until Volgens seemingly
started disappearing... Even Leo and Goliath were gone, and people
realized something: there were vests that worked, and Leo and Goliath and Volgens had them. They were going to travel to the future to
an uninhabited Earth. They couldn't go back to their home for whatever reason, so they were going to steal ours. They were going to use
the comet to kill us and send them to the future. The Government
began arresting every Volgen they could find. Strangely, though, they
never found a Volgen with a working vest. So we're told."

"That's terrible. What about Leo and Goliath? What happened to
them?"

"That's the thing... they were never found. They must have used
their working vests and escaped. Every Government was pissed. Riots
were happening all over the globe. Food supplies were only stocked to
make it to The Imminent Collision... the Volgens ruined everything."

"I just don't understand. Why would they do that?"

"Because they're evil. That's why." Elise punched the wall of her
pod, leaving a dent. "Guardian angels, my ass. They're demons. That
wasn't even the worst part, Jude."

"What could be worse than that?"

"The Governments around the world kicked open every door
there was. They kidnapped children. Any house that had multiple

kids, they took all but one. That's how they got my sister. They promised to trade any child to any parents who brought forward any Volgens. They starved the children in the camps. I don't know if they really wanted to find any Volgens. I think food supplies were low, and they needed an excuse to eliminate a large part of the population. The worst part, Jude, they had remnants of the designs of the vests that they found in Leo and Goliath's lab at the TTI. They experimented on any Volgen they could arrest or any child who would never be saved. It was the worst savagery you could imagine. I cry thinking about my sister every single night, Jude. Those bastards."

"Elise, I... I'm so sorry."

"They only captured Volgens that were turned in... but, the thing about those aliens is that they can change their appearances... so, parents rarely got their kids back... They're still arresting Volgens... That's why you can see those Volgen camps way over there in the distance."

Jude looked back out the window for the first time since Elise began telling this horrific story. The entire world was somehow completely different yet again. His heart broke as he looked and saw the smoke.

"They still do the tests in those camps. Trying to figure out the science. Even the Volgens they arrest, and they've arrested millions, can't get any of the science to work for whatever reason. But, my father and I, as we watched my sister get taken away, we realized the governments, the Volgens, they're all just as evil as each other. Wars ended, rebellions were squashed by the governments. Everything became very totalitarian. That's when the Shadows began appearing. They were found all over the world where time travel buildings were and around camps testing time travel. Every day, they seem to get worse. I don't know much about them... but they are somehow more vicious and evil than the Volgens. All we know is that somehow, they're attracted to time travel. Which only makes sense why they came at you so viciously. They come out almost always at night, which is why buildings have built-in alarms for them, which is why humans sleep outside these days."

"How do you have so much information about all of this? You say this like it's common knowledge, but I have to think if the government is as powerful as it is, they can't be spreading these things..."

"Right you are again, Monroe, but you know how stories spread. Nothing can be a secret forever. Just look at The Imminent Collision. There are resistance groups all around the globe. My dad leads the biggest one in North America: The Chicago Resistance."

Jude paused, Leo and Goliath came back into his thoughts. "So, no vests work anymore? I mean, did the scientists take them with them or destroy them or..?"

"Well, The North American Government released a statement that the Houdini Vests don't actually work and there was never a truly working one."

"Do you believe that?"

"I do and I don't," said Elise, becoming somehow more solemn. "I don't think any of the stolen children have time-traveled, but I do believe there are vests that work, and I do believe the energy has been harnessed. There are silos all over the world that are not nuclear, but they are much bigger... Listen, Jude, my sister was taken to those camps. She died in those camps. The Volgens, I hate them. They're vultures that tried to feast on the worst moment of humanity.... but the institutions around the world... They've done much worse. They've ripped families apart. My father has led the Chicago resistance for years. He joined when they took my older sister. I think they have vests that work. I really do. That's what I was looking for at the TTI when I found you. Imagine my surprise when I kicked open the door and I saw your scrawny-ass tied up in a corner."

"You were looking for a vest, so you could do what?"

"I was going to try to save my family."

Jude looked at her when she said this and couldn't help but think of what lengths he would go to were he in her shoes. He would do anything to bring his parents back, and if his sister were ever taken... Well, he would do anything by any means necessary. He looked at Elise and saw her strength and her courage, and he admired her now more than ever before.

"You see, my father was arrested for hacking into The North American Government's technological grid. It was a last-ditch effort for our group. We had all but lost. They kicked the door down while I was hiding in a panel in the ceiling. He managed to get all the information downloaded to a secondary drive before they barged in. He tossed the drive against the wall and got down on his knees. They immediately arrested him. I followed them with my pod, but they were too fast. I tracked his ID chip to the building you were in. I was going to find him, steal a vest, and go get my sister. But I found no vest, and he had been moved by the time I found you."

"Okay, okay, so the institution is corrupt, the Volgens are evil, and the resistance is fleeting... Where is everyone? What can we do?" asked Jude, wondering where this small burst of courage had come from.

"After the comet disappeared, most of the Volgens realized how evil their actions were and tried to make peace with humans... We wouldn't listen. Any Volgen that surrendered or was captured was put in extermination camps all around the globe. The North American Government uses them as well as captured children to test the Houdini Vests or any other scientific research. From what I have gathered from reading my father's intel, they haven't yet successfully accomplished time travel... All we know is that they have vests, but time travel hasn't happened yet. Billions of deaths, and for what?" Elise paused, then looked at Jude with tears rolling down her cheeks. "My sister died for nothing. The comet didn't land, the science is flawed, and she is gone for nothing."

Elise looked away from Jude and back at the billowing smoke that filled the sky and made everything seem foggy against the moonlight. "Maybe the comet should have collided, so we could hit some sort of reset button."

"Then I wouldn't have gotten to meet you... or eat any of this... uh... food?" joked Jude, making a Hail Mary effort to lighten the mood.

"You really pick the worst moments to be funny," said Elise, humoring him with a soft laugh.

"Where is your dad now?" asked Jude, after a moment's pause.

"He's at the Chicago extermination camp. They send traitors to the same camps as the Volgens... It's a sick joke. Oddly, though, my dad's intel says that in the most secured part of the camp, there's The North American Government's collection of Houdini Vests and time travel files. It's in their records building. I actually have all the information we really need for the camp, thanks to dad."

Elise looked at Jude. "Listen," she said, "do you want to get home?"

"More than anything…. It was nice getting to meet you, don't get me wrong… but I need to get home… Damn, I don't know how I'll explain surviving the explosion…"

"I think I can get you a vest… My dad's stolen intel can lead us into the file building in the camp. Maybe, maybe the three of us can work together and figure out how to find a real vest and make it work. Besides, you have already time-traveled once, and it happened at the exact moment you were supposed to have been killed, right?"

"Do you think the energy from our deaths sent me here?" asked Jude, concerned, thinking of the others from his shuttle.

"Maybe," replied Elise, "I mean, it's the only way it could be possible. You got lucky once, maybe we can get lucky again. We need to get you a working vest to find out."

"You would do that for me? I have to imagine breaking into where they keep the vests would be a death sentence," said Jude, nonetheless excited at the possibility of being homeward bound.

"I'll help you if you help me," said Elise, looking into Jude's eyes.

"Whoa, whoa, I can't be of any help… I wouldn't know how to begin to help in any situation with that camp."

"Listen, I have a plan to save my dad, but I need a second person… I have a plan that can work. There's a clear path for us, just look at the intel... Come on. It's the only way you'll make it home and see your sister again..." Elise took Jude's hand and leaned closer to him. "I lost my sibling... Your sister is somewhere in the past broken because you apparently died. Yet, here you are... I can get you home and reunite you two... Help me and I can help you."

Jude thought about this proposition. He thought about how secure he was in the belief that he was nobody... just a teacher, he would tell everyone. However, as he looked over a dark Chicago skyline 370 years in the future, where Volgens roamed, where Shadows led him out of a 15th-story window to a fall he survived, to a new friend who made him feel full of confidence as they spoke outside of her flying pod, he thought anything was possible. If anything was possible, then it was possible for Jude Monroe to be someone. For the first time in a long time, he felt like he was worth something.

"Okay," Jude said, standing up and offering his hand to Elise, "where do we begin?"

Eight

March 25, 2019

"I gotta say," laughed Metzlebaum, putting his fork down on his plate, "I never thought one slice would fill me up, but here we are."

"Congratulations on your first real slice of pizza," said Hazel, after putting a second slice of Chicago's finest on her plate. "Here, I'll dish you up another slice, too."

Jude laughed and looked at his sister. She had yet to stop smiling since they came home from the airport to find Metzlebaum on their front porch. "Maybe you can let me take a few slices of this on the rocket," he said, still working on his first piece.

"Tell you what," said Metzlebaum, eyeing his new slice of pizza and working up the willpower to continue eating, "you figure out a way to make pizza rehydratable and we'll talk."

"Deal," chuckled Jude. "I can't even begin to believe any of this. This conversation, what's to come, it's a dream."

"You're the right guy for the job. I told you, we knew right away."

"Of course he is," Hazel confirmed, looking at her brother, her eyes shining with pride. "My brother..." She put her hand on his shoulder. "My brother, who is doing incredible things. Look at you. All this potential we always knew you had, and voila: going to space."

The three at the table let a tranquil silence take over as they enjoyed the moment. Finally, Hazel turned to Metzlebaum and resumed the conversation. "My brother may be going to space, but don't think for a second that NASA is the only one trying to keep him safe. You guys make sure you do your job or I'll build my own rocket, I'll go find him, and then I'll come find you guys in Florida or Texas or wherever and kick some ass."

"Oh, trust me. I believe it," humored Metzlebaum. "Jude is in the best hands he could be in. Jude, you're going to space, and you're going to inspire so many people. That's why we wanted a teacher. You guys inspire people every day. Now, we're going to strap you to a rocket and make the world your classroom."

"The history teacher makes history," laughed Hazel. "Are you going to be humble and skip your chapter in future textbooks?"

"Oh hell no," said Jude. "We'll probably spend a full semester looking at my selfies from zero gravity."

"Look at this guy... a week ago, he claimed to be nobody over a sink of dirty dishes, and now we've got some hotshot... Where did my brother go?"

"Oh, he's here, baby, and going nowhere... well, except to space, no big deal."

"Metzlebaum, I hope the size of his growing ego won't pull the Earth out of orbit."

Metzlebaum laughed as he watched the two banter. Every bit of the conversation they had shared since entering the car to go eat made the decision to choose Jude even more cemented. Everything made more sense as the night progressed. Hazel loved her brother, truly she did. Jude was a man who very clearly needed every ounce of this opportunity. His back was straighter than it was a day ago, and his smile was as genuine as it could be. Jude Monroe was the right guy for the job. Metzlebaum had never been more sure of anything.

"Look," said Jude, "Forgive me for feeling alive. I don't know... When I left the interview, I realized how much I needed something like this and now... well, I haven't felt like this in years."

"Look at this guy, filled with life," smiled Hazel. "Thank you, Tom. Look at him. My brother is coming back to us!" She reached over and firmly grabbed his shoulder and shook him as she felt overwhelmed with pride and love.

Tom looked at the two Monroes at the table and laughed. There was nothing to be said. The atmosphere was filled with so much joy and pride and life. The three laughed together, and Metzlebaum raised his glass, "To living."

"To living," they all said and clanged their glasses.

"So, when are you guys taking my brother away from me?" This was the only question Hazel needed to build the courage to ask Metzelbaum. Despite all of the excitement and even beyond any fear of her brother taking such a potentially dangerous trip, the saddest thought she had was the time she would have to spend away from him. He was her best friend, after all. Sometimes, she felt like she needed him more than he needed her. The loss of their parents was equally hard on both of them. What family she had left was the most important thing in her life; having to spend time apart would surely be the hardest part of what was to come.

"Well, that's just it. We have a lot of training to get through and tests to run on you, Jude... We're going to have to leave relatively soon... We have a plane ticket for you to come to our facility in Texas the day after tomorrow."

"The day after tomorrow," erupted Hazel, before she could stop herself.

"Oh... wow," said Jude, looking at his sister. "That *is* sudden... What about my classes and students?"

"I know it's sudden, and you're going to have to take immediate leave. There is so much to do and, well, we're already behind schedule. You'll have interviews first and then some wild training, and then you'll be going to space in just a couple of months."

There was a long pause at the table. "Well," Jude looked to his sister. "How long have you been telling me that life isn't going to just happen and that I have to meet it in the middle... Looks like it's time to do just that... You going to be okay?"

"Yeah... Yeah. I'll be good. Let's make the most out of tomorrow. We can go for a walk at Lake Michigan and enjoy the day before your flight. Anything else you'd like to do?"

"Honestly," said Jude, looking at his sister and smiling, "let's just have a regular movie night."

"Deal. But no romcoms," laughed Hazel.

"Fine... Fine... *Die Hard* it is."

Hazel looked at her brother. Pride continued to fill her heart.

After a day of spending time together, Hazel dropped Jude off at the airport. They hugged, and she watched him walk away. Look at him, she thought, off to do incredible things.

Each night, Jude would call his sister, and she would fill him in on what he was missing in Illinois, and he would tell her about his adventures on the NASA compounds in Texas. He would tell her about the exercises, the days he would make it without throwing up, and his new friends. She tried not to pry when he would spend a little more time talking about one of his crewmates named Sarah. The most obvious thing, however, was how he sounded on the phone. When they would hang up, she would sit back and smile. Finally, her brother, so filled with life, had come back.

Jude and the rest of the crew had been flown to Florida for the launch. Hazel went alone to watch the takeoff, and she arrived several hours early. She was the first one on the bleachers, roughly seven miles away. Even from that distance, she could still see the rocket standing in place, awaiting takeoff. She took pictures from where she sat. Alone, she drank her coffee and tried her best to see if she could view any movement on the ground so far away.

Pride was the only word she could find to explain what she was feeling. As hundreds began to gather around her, she found so much joy in seeing the excitement of others as they came to watch her brother go to space.

On her phone, she watched the news. She watched as her brother walked across the camera, walking closely to a taller man and a younger blonde-headed woman. She watched as her brother walked to the elevator that would take him up to enter the rocket. The most obvious change that she noticed was that he was walking more confidently than he had in years. With tears in her eyes, she put her hand to her mouth and thought, "that's my brother."

If only mom and dad could see us now was all that Hazel could think as she watched on her phone at T-14 when her brother gave a thumbs up to the camera from inside the cockpit. Hazel had watched countless videos of previous launches to prepare her for what to expect on the day of *The Audacity* launch. Even though she knew the schedule of the takeoff procedure by heart, each sound from miles away still made her jump. She watched the clock tick down 3-2-1. As her brother began his ascension, she laughed when she realized she had not breathed since the clock reached T-10 seconds. The thrusters erupted as Jude was carried straight toward the baby blue sky.

When the catastrophe occurred four minutes later, the sound of her brother's certain death took a few seconds to reach her ears. The sound rattled the bleachers beneath her, though she never heard it. She didn't hear the screams or any commotion around her. The world stood still. Reality wasn't setting in. Even as the smoke began to dissipate in the sky, she looked up as if to see her brother still continuing on his journey.

She sat on the bleachers miles away as the flaming pieces of *The Audacity* floated to the ground. In slow motion, some in the surrounding crowd fled to seek shelter, some crashed to their knees in immediate sobbing, and some filmed on their phones. The cacophony of madness framed the ever-still Hazel as she sat motionless, staring at the sky.

An hour went by, and Hazel was completely unaware that she was the only person still sitting on the bleachers. She was alone. She had gone to Florida to watch the launch alone, she would return to Illinois alone, and, without her brother, she would have to figure out a way to live alone.

She walked back to her rental car, a mile from the bleachers, and sat completely still in the driver's seat. She was parked near a small bay, and the sun set behind her as she stared at waves crashing on a shore just ahead of the car. Hazel was completely numb, and she never felt any of her many tears.

In nearly three years, she had lost everyone. Today, a day more painful than she could ever fathom, her brother, her best friend, was gone.

She continued to stare at the water as the last rays of sunlight finally disappeared. On her dashboard was a small Polaroid picture taken by her mother of her and Jude on Halloween night in 2005. She smiled at the kids in the photo who beamed at the camera without a care in the world. Though pain filled her, and the sorrow was unbearable, the pride that she had arrived earlier with was still the emotion she felt most. Jude had decided to live. She watched him return to form. She had heard his voice on the phone each night. He had been renewed with life. He died, filled with courage and chasing something more. The potential she always said was in him had become as clear to Jude as it always was with her.

My brother, she thought as she looked out her car windshield and to the darkness ahead, *my brother* who died doing amazing things.

Nine

November 7, 2393

"Are you sure you can handle this?" asked Elise, her hand resting on Jude's shoulder. The two were standing at the open door of Elise's pod as they looked down upon the compound they intended to enter. They had spent the entire day going over the plans, studying schematics, and building layouts. To Elise's surprise, Jude actually had some solid suggestions. Fortunately for them, Jude, being the only person who had seen the likes of *Ocean's 11, Baby Driver,* or *Inception* in centuries, had much to contribute. Jude's old school perspectives, Elise's obvious skills at breaking into forbidden areas, and the intel from her father helped them create what they thought would be, at best, an alright plan.

All day, Elise would check in on Jude to make sure he was prepared for the night's events. Each time, he would look at her and say, "hey, come on, it's me." Each time, of course, she would bring up his passing out right after first meeting each other. Nonetheless, confidence in the plan or no confidence in the plan, they had confidence in each other, and somehow, for them, that was enough.

"Are you sure you can handle this?" asked Elise, checking once more on Jude.

"Hey, come on, it's me. What could happen?" he responded, smiling at Elise.

"Who's this brave guy that replaced the crying one from two days ago?" asked Elise, laughing.

"In my defense, I had just been blown up. That affects people, you know."

The two laughed and looked back at the camp below them. The reality of the situation saturated the lightheartedness. Looking down, Jude saw where they planned to land and the path they would have to take from the inner-Volgen cells to the records of Leo and Goliath. The plan relied on time to be on their side. Clearly, there was an unfathomable amount of variables, but the risk for both Elise and for Jude was far outweighed by what they were trying to acquire.

"Okay, cloaking setting ignited, this ship is invisible," said Elise, pressing a few buttons on her armband. Jude watched as the floor below his feet vanished, and it looked like he was floating. "It'll be here when the three of us make it back."

Elise handed Jude a new armband. "Take this... Like I told you earlier, this armband is your life. You can activate the zero gravity in your suit with it, but only a few feet from the ground. It is amazing to help with a fall. It would have been great if you had had one when you fell out of the window a few days ago."

"You push... excuse me for only having clothes from my time."

"Yeah, well, welcome to the year 2393. Remember, red means stop, green means go. Gravity is your friend... unless you forget to hit the red button. Then, gravity is most certainly not your friend."

"I can't believe I'm about to jump out of this thing without a parachute. What the hell am I thinking?" said Jude, contemplating out loud.

"Listen. Do you wanna be like that Danny Ocean guy or what?" asked Elise, trying to build Jude's confidence.

"Danny Oc--- nevermind. Okay... Let's do it before I change my mind," said Jude.

"Not yet. Remember, wait for the alarms."

Elise and Jude had spent most of their time figuring out the beginning of the plan. It was both the most crucial and most dangerous part. According to Elise, Shadow monsters would attack at 11:30 PM every night. Because it was the epicenter of time-travel testing and Houdini Vests in North America, this extermination camp in Chicago was where the largest amount of time residue existed. The night attacks happened like clockwork. Apparently, The North American Government never minded. According to Elise, the government liked to use these nightly occurrences as practice on how to fight them, though they had yet to figure out how. Some of these parts didn't quite make complete sense to Jude, however, he understood a good distraction when he heard one.

It was this distraction that would help them get into the camp and make their way to where they kept the top security files, like the records of Leo and Goliath. They mapped out that their return would follow through the area where resistance prisoners were kept in solitary confinement. Two stops. In and out. They would get the vest, rescue Elise's father, and then they would go their separate ways.

Jude heard a click behind him. Elise had sealed her helmet back on her head. "I never get tired of things like this," she said, her voice back to the unrecognizable tone that she had when Jude met her days before... Jude had put on a suit that matched Elise's. As he stood there next to her, he could see himself in the reflection of her helmet. He knew it was himself. It obviously had to be. But, it certainly did not look like the Jude Monroe he saw in the mirror only days ago. Two days had passed since *The Audacity* explosion, and he was still battling his disbelief in the possibility of whatever reality had become.

"This jump is going to be terrifying," Jude said, looking at his feet.

"Nothing is more terrifying than the Shadows. Volgens, humans, no one can win against them. Our war is pointless. If they wanted more than time residue, we'd be screwed."

"Who are the Shadows? Where did they come from?"

"No one really knows, as far as I know. The intel dad stole, there's not much there. All I know is that I've seen them kill before. When they touch someone... it's like they burn them from the inside out... I've never seen Volgens run from anything like they run from them... They had clearly seen them before coming to Earth."

There was silence as Jude internalized Elise's words. There was no need for further explanation. She looked to Jude, who was still staring below and obviously reflecting on everything.

Finally, the silence was broken by chuckling coming from Jude while he looked down at the suit he was wearing as he stood in the doorway of the pod. Elise looked at him, and he had the largest grin on his face she had seen yet. "I feel bad ass, I won't lie," he said. "Do I look as bad ass as I feel?" The only answer Jude received back was from Elise joining in the laughter from behind her mask.

The two stepped toward the edge of the now invisible ship. The laughter died away as they reflected on the odds of survival and what was coming. Jude was more scared of the jump than anything. Elise, however, was more terrified of what would come after they made it through the first few steps of her plan and what they would inevitably come face-to-face with.

The alarms finally began to sound below, and the two knew it was time; the Shadows were now moving inside the camp. Below them, Volgens, Shadows, guards, and other unknown threats waited for them. They were about to willingly charge into a camp with Shadows roaming and looking for the type of residue that was already on Jude. It didn't matter. All that mattered was Jude getting home and Elise getting to her father. They would stop at nothing. Family was on the line.

To Elise's surprise, Jude jumped first. "Damn," Elise thought to herself just before taking a step to jump out after him. "There really is more to this Jude Monroe than meets the eye."

Ten

November 7, 2393

Even though Jude had jumped out of the pod first, Elise still landed before him. She waited for him to gain the courage to drop the seven remaining feet to the ground. While she only had to hit her red button once, Jude hit his button roughly six times before landing on his stomach at her feet. The two began to laugh in the ominous shadow cast by the barricades of the camp. Ungraceful as the landings may have been, they still managed to land right where Elise had planned for them. They were a little over a mile from where Elise's father's intel had said was a collection of Houdini Vests and files from Leo and Goliath. There were five cell blocks that lined the pathway to reach the building. They had to wait for their distractions to come closer to where they were.

When Jude stood up, he was greeted by the eyes of dozens of Volgens. They were still in human form. Imprisonment had been torturous on their bodies. They looked mutated with peeling skin, pus draining from their nostrils, and many missing limbs. Most lacked hair and were covered head to foot in burns. Each had a ragged piece of cloth draped upon them. The jaws of some hung without connection to their skulls. The horror of their appearance made Jude sick, but he could not look away. It wasn't the horrid features, nor the smell, nor the sounds of wailing from within the mass heaps of these creatures that affected Jude the most. It was their eyes, dark and sullen. Excruciation in its purest form. They remained blinkless upon Jude.

In all his life, even the death of his parents, he had never felt so much pain as to see these caged beings gathered behind impenetrable bars. Elise fought to regain Jude's attention, but he stood transfixed. From above, in the pod, he had seen block after block that made up this camp for miles. Sure, Elise had told him of the creatures that stood confined to these barricades. However, nothing prepared him for what stared at him when he landed.

Only standing here, in the presence of tortured masses, did Jude see that the true evil was not the imprisoned, but whoever the imprisoner might be. Jude didn't even realize he was crying. After 30 seconds of trying to regain Jude's attention, Elise grabbed his arm and started to pull him to a wall to hide behind.

"Listen to me," said Elise, "I get it. It's sad. Yeah, but we've got bigger issues. There are Shadows running wild down here. We don't have time to be sad. Hesitation gets you killed, you hear me?" Elise grabbed Jude by the shoulders as he continued to look over at the caged Volgens. "Look, I get it, you've got this good guy thing going for you, but hesitation will get you killed."

Jude was speechless. He knew she was right. He turned his head and looked at her, but he did not see her. In his mind were the eyes of the Volgens. Everything about where they were was wrong. Sure, they infiltrated the world. That's what Elise said... but he had to think, does anyone deserve a fate like what he just witnessed? He was at a loss for answers. His thoughts were interrupted by a high-pitched screech. This scream was like nothing Jude had ever heard, and it paralyzed both him and Elise. He didn't have to ask what it was, because in his heart he already knew: Shadows.

Within moments, all of the guards who were at nearby gate doors down the path began to sprint in the direction of the scream. They ran past the passageway in which the two were hiding.

Jude took a step forward to take advantage of the opportunity, but Elise grabbed him and hugged him against the wall. They were silent as the entire passageway went black. Jude recognized this evil darkness from the black stairwell at the TTI only days before. They heard the poundings of large footsteps which quickly became louder. Sounds like boulders crashing into the ground came closer and closer. As streaks of red flashed by the opening of Jude and Elise's passageway, the screeching was at its loudest. Elise braced Jude harder against the wall, trying to smother him from the view of the raging creatures as they passed by. The Volgens in the cages next to them were screaming in horror. They had lost too many loved ones to these monsters, and here they were: trapped in cages as the Shadows crashed by.

Light began to return to the passageway. The two were frozen in place. The pure malice that flashed by had stunned them.

"Why didn't they stop? Don't I have the residue they're looking for?" asked Jude, confused.

"Shadows are locked in when they're attacking," said Elise. Behind her mask, she was pale from fear. She was thankful that Jude couldn't see. "We just got lucky they were drawn somewhere else... we need to get moving though."

"Right," said Jude, his heart racing. "Turn left, then one mile straight, right?"

"Right," said Elise, still gathering her bearings. "Right, then straight..." She looked at Jude and began to count, "three- two- o–" Before she could finish counting, Jude was already running.

"What was that?" yelled Elise, catching up to Jude with ease.

"What?" yelled Jude back at her. "You got to one!"

"Damn it, you always go on 'go!' You are such a moron."

"You're just mad that a dude that's like 400 years old is faster than you."

"Oh, just shut the hell up and run."

The two, winded, continued down the path. Jude kept his eyes locked. He did his best to block out the hands that reached through the bars at him from the Volgens. He kept his head straight. He regretted his callousness, but he knew that if he looked, he would not make it to their destination.

An eighth of a mile from the arsenal, the two heard the screeches of the Shadows as they once again filled the air. Their legs stopped moving, and they were frozen in terror. When they turned around to look behind them, they saw the very thing they feared to see: everything was black. The darkness was 50 feet from them and quickly closing in on the two. Looking closely, Jude could see that red specks filled the blackness. Hundreds of red eyes were charging at them. Elise and Jude turned and began to run again, though much faster than before.

The intense pounding upon the ground from the Shadows grew stronger as they closed in on the pair. The Shadows were locked in and charging. Closer they came as the two ran, digging their toes into the ground as they sprinted for the doors of the building ahead. The screams of the Volgens were louder than ever. They had seen this sort of event far too many times. Their screams nearly drowned out the cadence of the footsteps of the Shadows.

100 feet from the door of the records building, the walls of the pathway had become fully dark. The Shadows were on their heels. Jude and Elise could hear intense growling and scraping intermingled with the barbaric pounding of the charge. The air grew thin as more and more of what surrounded Jude and Elise became black.

20 feet from the door, and they could see that it was already open, though the two didn't consider themselves lucky yet. They gave everything they had to continue running. Their legs burned, and they could hardly breathe. They focused on the light penetrating from the doorway. As they got closer, they could make out the bodies of dead guards who must have been stationed outside.

10 feet from the door, the image of the bodies became more gruesome. Jude could see that their eyes were still open. They were clearly burned. Burned from the inside, Jude thought, remembering Elise's words about the Shadows. He closed his eyes during the last five feet. Everything was dark except for a small sliver of light breaking through the abyss. He made it through the entrance of the records building just ahead of Elise. He dove and rolled inside with his eyes still closed.

The door of the entrance was slammed by Elise when she entered, and it was immediately met by the Shadows crashing into the exterior wall. The building shook, and dust from the ceiling crashed down upon the two. The screech of the Shadows filled the room that the two were now standing in. The rage from the monsters continued as they pounded upon the outside of the building. True fear shook them as Elise opened a visor on her helmet, they looked at each other, and stared into each other's eyes as they caught their breath.

"Are you okay?" asked Jude, panting.

"Am I okay? You're the one who is new to the action," said Elise, between deep breaths, her hands on her hips.

"Yeah, but I made it through the door first... We leaders have to look out for the weaker ones," said Jude, trying to laugh between wheezes.

Elise, still regaining her breath, walked up to Jude and punched him in the arm.

"Hey! What was that for?" said Jude, a smirk growing on his face.

"You were saying about being weak?" replied Elise. "Now, come on. My dad's intel on the schematics has the records we want two doors down that hallway over there. Apparently, the Houdini Vests are 15 levels below our feet. Let's go to the records first to see which cell my dad is in."

The two ran to a door on the other side of the room and went through it. Inside were two new guards and two women in white coats.

"What the hell? You both are lost," yelled the taller of the guards. Both guards drew blasters similar to the gun Elise had with her when Jude woke up a few days earlier. They began to shoot at Elise and Jude.

Elise pushed Jude back through the doorway that they had just entered. She rolled onto the ground and withdrew her own blaster. She
dodged the first few blasts from the guards and landed a shot in the
knee of the shorter of the two. Using her momentum, she sprang onto
the taller guard and straddled his face, tackling him to the ground in
one quick motion. He tried to stand up, but she planted her heel into
his jaw and knocked him unconscious.

The other guard was on the ground, howling in pain. She ran over
to him, grabbed him by the lapels, and yelled, "Where can I find the
resistance prisoners?" The guard continued to scream in pain. She
tried again, this time slower, "where can I find the resistance prisoners?" She put the blaster between his eyes. He did not look at her. "Tell
me. Now," she yelled.

One of the women in the white coats finally spoke up. "Wait! We
keep all the files in this room... The resistance prisoner files are down
that row." The scientist pointed to the left of Elise and didn't say another word. Remnants of prayer could be seen behind her eyes.

Elise looked at the two workers and then back at the guard. He had
passed out from the pain. She looked at Jude. His eyes were wide, and
he was speechless.

"Yeah, I know," said Elise, "I have that effect on men. Now get your
ass up and let's find these records."

Pointing her blaster at the two workers, she asked, "Where are the
Leo and Goliath records and Houdini vests? We know you have them
here."

"Row 67, at the end. But they're sealed, only someone with time
residue can get access..." said the other scientist in the room, surprised

that she had the courage to speak. The other woman who spoke first took over and said, "It was a trick created by Leo and Goliath so that no one could get in. I'm sorry, but only someone who has that residue can unlock the verification panel to get access. Those files are the only non-copied files in the camp. No one has read or seen them since we missed the collision."

Looking back at Jude, Elise said, "Lucky for us, we have a way in. Get yourself to row 67 and find us whatever files you can on Leo and Goliath. I'm sure there's stuff that my dad's intel doesn't have. I'll meet you back here in five minutes."

Jude ran down the hallway lined with files. Watching the numbers increase on the wall, he thought of libraries from his own time. 60, 61, 62, he counted in his head. He got to the end of the room and stood before two large metal doors. On the right door was a sign that said 'Row 67.' There was a single screen built into the wall next to the doors.

To his surprise, Jude didn't hesitate as he placed his hand on the screen. A white line went up and down the monitor under his palm and then outlined his hand. The screen went black, and there was a moment of silence. The doors began to rattle and creak. Then, they separated, and a stale air exploded through the door.

Jude stood in the opening. He looked around, hoping Elise would arrive, but he was alone. He hadn't taken the time to acknowledge his surroundings. Books and folders took up hundreds of rows behind him. With heaps of brown and rust, Jude thought that the massive room resembled the Chicago he had woken up in.

A blue light crashed through the doorway and contrasted with the entire aesthetic of the records building, leading to where he stood.

He looked around until he built up the courage to step into the room alone. There was an obvious change in the architecture within this room. Clearly, there was a significant amount of reinforcement built within the walls, which made the room feel narrow. The dusty air felt thin. Jude slowly crept forward. His situation reminded him of watching Indiana Jones movies with his dad and all of the traps Indy would inevitably have to evade.

Step by step, Jude looked around the room, but there was very little to see. The walls were a deep navy, which added to the darkness. In a space the size of a small gymnasium, the only visible light came from something ominous that loomed in the center. A perfect cube of a glass box, roughly 20 feet high, sat 50 feet from where Jude was advancing. With each slow movement, Jude was surprised to find what exactly the light was coming from: a small yellow desk lamp plugged into a small black box in the very center of the glass case. The lamp sat upon an old wooden desk straddled by two wooden chairs. One chair was pushed in under the desk; the other was lying on its side. There was a tattered briefcase sitting closed on the desk next to the lamp with a single blue folder lying on top of it. There was a lone blaster, similar to that of Elise's, lying on the ground next to the chair, which had clearly toppled over.

In moments, Jude stood feet from the translucent box. No poison darts were shot from the walls, nor any large rolling boulders like the one from Indiana Jones. Jude easily walked straight to the box. The ease of the approach made Jude feel all the more unsettled. Strangely, with an area rug on the ground under the desk along with the furniture, and the old lamp, Jude couldn't help but feel the inside of the box had an oddly warm feeling that contrasted with the rest of the world he had woken up in. The glass case was like a museum; the past was here on display only to see and not to touch.

There were no doors into the box. There was only one small white box that rested chest level to Jude on the other side of the cube. He walked around and tried to analyze it, but there was not much to make out of it. A simple white box that looked like a large bird house sat placidly suspended against the much larger clear block.

By the time he even realized he was doing it, it was too late: Jude's hand was already moving toward the small opening, and it disappeared inside. Quickly, his wrist was grabbed by a hidden restraint, and he felt something sharp slice the palm of his hand. Before he could scream, he was released by the box, and he fell backward upon the ground.

Blood poured from his hand, and he began to feel lightheaded. He heard footsteps running around the glass museum toward him. He was relieved to see Elise, helmet off, coming to help.

"I was wondering what the hell was taking you so long. What happened to your hand?" she said, out of breath but concerned.

Jude didn't respond; he was trying to regain his bearings as he winced through the pain. Elise looked from his hand and slowly followed the drops of blood to the small white opening on the case. She looked back to Jude.

"Did you put your hand in that thing? What the hell were you thinking?"

Jude opened his mouth to respond, but no words came out. Elise, waiting for him to speak, watched as his eyes went wide. She turned around just in time to see what he was looking at.

Slowly, the white box sank into the larger case and disappeared. Seconds later, the walls of the glass room disappeared, and there was nothing separating the two from what was locked inside. Elise helped Jude to his feet, and the two stood immobile as they looked at the unguarded objects before them.

"That cut looks really bad," said Elise, looking at Jude's hand. "But, either stupid or brave, it did something helpful."

"This stuff has to be some of the most protected items in this place," said Jude, as more of a question than a statement. Almost simultaneously, the two crept forward. They stood on the rug at the desk.

"Leo and Goliath did not play around," replied Elise, moving slightly less cautiously than Jude.

"Shouldn't this be the part where one of us asks who left the light on?" Jude asked semi-jokingly, trying to understand what the lamp was plugged into.

"I was wondering the same thing," said Elise, confused. "Surely, that means someone has been here recently?"

"What is this little black case? It is not attached to anything. It's like a battery."

"That's exactly what that is, but I've never seen anything like it before.... Here we are in a room clearly meant to house some things from Leo and Goliath... If that battery has anything to do with the energy they learned to harness, well then, this lamp could be powered for ages."

"Are you trying to tell me that Leo and Goliath left this lamp on?"

"It's all hypothetical," said Elise, trying to string together thoughts. "When I entered this room, I became just as out of my element as you are. But, clearly, this room... it's full of mysteries."

The two paused for a moment. Chills went down Jude's spine as he thought about Leo and Goliath leaving on this light that was sitting before him. Two people whose decisions and creations had led him to where he was standing, they had seemingly plagued his life since the explosion of *The Audacity,* and the more he learned about them, the more confused he became.

"What's in the leather box?" asked Elise, breaking the silence. She eyed the blue folder and picked it up as she asked the question.

Jude, startled away from his thoughts, turned to the briefcase. To his surprise, it wasn't locked. He slowly lifted it open. Inside was, to Jude, what looked like a life jacket someone might wear while boating on Lake Michigan. It was white and black with a miniature touch screen on the left breast. There were multiple straps that hung loosely from the sides. In bright red on the back was one word: "Goliath." On the large collar of the vest was a single metal bar with three small words: "Imminent Death Detector."

"Oh my God," said Elise, dropping the folder while her eyes became wide. "This must be an original Houdini Vest."

"Are you serious? This? This looks like something I'd wear on a boat." Jude held the random item in his hands, unsure whether he fully comprehended the magnitude of it.

"If this one doesn't get you home, nothing will," said Elise, a large grin across her face.

"I can't believe we did it," said Jude, looking at Elise, whose joy was overwhelmingly contagious. "Look at us... We make a good team."

"A lost old man and an angry woman. Who'd have thought that was a recipe for success?"

Standing on a rug at the desk of Leo and Goliath, Jude somehow felt calm for the very first time since waking up. He laughed again as he thought about Elise, an unlikely friend from the future. "Some recipe," Jude repeated as a response.

The two maintained eye contact for a brief moment until a strange, ominous feeling crept over them. Sending chills down both of their spines.

"Jude?"

"Yeah?" he responded, his tone matching the sudden change in the atmosphere.

"Do you feel that?"

"I do... But what am I feeling?"

"...like we're not alone," said Elise, still looking at Jude, who returned her gaze in complete agreement. At the same time, the two slowly began to raise their eyes to where the ceiling should have been. Rather than the expected tiles, replacing the top of the room was a sea of black with thousands of red eyes swimming amongst it.

"Run!" yelled the two simultaneously, though neither heard the other. Elise grabbed the vest as they were already moving to the door, which was left open. Elise caught up to Jude with ease. The Shadows above them screeched, and the two had not heard anything as loud as this in their lives. They were both almost knocked to the ground as the screams of the Shadows filled the entire space. With the crashing force and sound of an avalanche, the Shadows fell onto the ground in menacing form to chase after Jude and Elise.

The two ran for the door, and the crashing and screaming became nearly too much to handle. They didn't even realize the sudden temperature drop in the room. Above the door were red numbers. These numbers were quickly decreasing. As the two got closer to the door, they were able to make out what was written on a sign beneath the screen of red numbers. It read:

Safety Protocol One:
Room will secure itself
at -300F if vest
removed from case

"Damn it," yelled Elise, quickening her pace as she finished reading the sign.

"Could they have put that in a more inconvenient place?" yelled Jude, as he tried to keep up with Elise.

The doors began to close in front of them as the digits flashed to -40F. The room was freezing from the ceiling. Fortunately, for Jude and Elise, the floor was the last thing to be touched by the cold. The Shadows still on the ceiling were affected first, but the smaller ones kept on the tracks of Jude and Elise. Frozen Shadows began to fall from above and crashed, sounding like broken glass, onto the ground.

For the first time, Jude was able to make out, only briefly, what the creatures truly looked like: demented manlike creatures but with four legs, long claws at the end of long hands, a tail covered in long black blades, and deathly red eyes. Frozen, there was no darkness cast from the creatures. They were smaller than Jude had expected, dead, yet still threatening. Jude couldn't decipher if the coldness he felt was from the creatures that were crashing to the ground around him and Elise or from the temperature in the room.

Nonetheless, Jude and Elise continued to run. The only creatures not frozen and falling were closely following from behind.

The doors were closing slowly, yet were still slightly open when the two were feet from the opening. Jude made it out first when he heard Elise scream from behind. She had fallen. Her legs were lost in darkness as the remaining Shadows reached her. She had pulled out her blaster while the two were running, and when she was tackled, it flew forward. It sat at Jude's feet.

"Jude, the blaster! Help!" yelled Elise. Immense pain could be heard in her voice.

Jude didn't hesitate. He reached down, grabbed the gun, and pointed it in the direction of the darkness surrounding Elise. No light could be seen in the room now. The lamp was already a distant memory. He had never fired a gun before. Truthfully, he never thought he would. But here he was, in the future, a friend in danger, he pulled the trigger, and it was like he had been doing it his entire life.

Screeches came from the abyss surrounding Elise. Jude continued to fire even as Elise crawled for the doors, which were now almost closed. She reached out with the vest, and he grabbed hold of it and began to pull her in. The doors were closing, and another Shadow grabbed her foot. Jude looked into Elise's eyes, which seemed red with fire.

Somehow, he pulled her through the doors, which were now frosted, and the Shadow holding Elise was becoming clearly visible as it too froze. Her leg was caught in the now icy claws of the monster as the doors finally closed and slowly severed the limb from the Shadow. Elise's entire boot was frozen. Through gashes in the leather of her pants, Jude could see that there were severe burns all down her legs, and she was fighting as hard as she could not to scream.

She slowly sat up, wiped tears from her eyes, and tried to catch her breath. Suddenly, a thought entered her head, and she punched the floor as a new anger took her.

"Damn it," said Elise as she punched the ground again. "There was a folder on the desk, and I forgot to grab it. Damn it."

"The fol-" tried Jude, but he was cut off.

"I grabbed the vest, but I forgot the folder."

"Yeah, El-"

"What the hell were we doing to get so distracted? Gawking at Leo and Goliath's desk."

"Seriousl-"

"What the hell–"

"Elise!" yelled Jude, finally getting her attention. "You mean this folder?" He pulled the large blue folder from behind the zipper of his jacket. "I mean, come on, I'm not totally useless."

Elise stood up and looked Jude up and down. She gave no expression. "Yeah… not totally." She walked up to him and grabbed the folder from his hands. She completely changed when she opened it. All signs of pain from the burns had vanished.

"Jude. Jude! These are all the notes from Leo and Goliath. This is huge. We're going to get you home… These can help so many people. Think about it… What if we were able to use Leo and Gollaith's energy harnessing to give power and electricity to everyone on Earth… We could make life better for everyone. My dad will know what to do with these. I found which cell he is in. It's close."

Jude looked at Elise's eyes, still red, and then down to her legs. "Are you sure you can keep going? That Shadow got you really good."

"Listen to me, Jude. Nothing will stop me from getting to my father. Nothing."

Nothing else needed to be said. Jude saw behind Elise's bloodshot eyes that she was fully committed to her cause, and nothing could possibly stand in her way. Jude took the vest from Elise and handed her back her blaster. The two slowly walked back to the entrance, which they had rushed through only thirty minutes before. The two women in white coats who had pointed Jude and Elise in the direction of row 67 were lying on the ground, dead. Their eyes seemed burned, and their white jackets were covered in blood and scorch marks. They laid next to where Elise had knocked the two guards unconscious. The two women had their hands interlaced as they tragically died with a final act of love.

Jude and Elise stood only feet away from these corpses as they looked at where the door of the entrance used to be. It was now rubble, and the door was torn into pieces. Cracks from this new opening raced to the ceiling.

Strangely, outside, everything was calm again. Guards were back at their posts as if nothing had happened. They seemed to be fine guarding the entrance to the record building, whether there was a door or not. Clearly, this type of occurrence was not new.

The two moved slowly from one place to another. Elise pointed the way, and Jude helped her limp to wherever they had to hide from sight next. They crept past new hordes of imprisoned Volgens. These creatures, and their cages that lined the way to blocks that held the resistance soldiers, were silent. The Volgens simply stared at the two. Their eyes screamed for help, but their mouths remained shut.

Following the path Elise discovered in the records, they worked their way, slowly, to block 73. Inside was where her father was apparently being kept in isolation. Elise entered the dark hallway first. Light from nearby fires illuminated the passageway through barred windows.

"He is in isolation in cell 22," said Elise as they crept through. It was completely silent in block 73. The long hall was lined with large cage doors. It looked like something out of the Middle Ages. Small numbers marked the cells from above the doors. There was virtually no movement from within the cages. Nights when the attacks were as severe as this night, the prisoners knew to hide in silence. Finally, after an hour of traversing the camp from the records building, they stood in front of cell 22.

Cell 22 was different from the surrounding cells. There were no bars, and there was no caged door. There was a single 10-foot metal door with 10 locks from ceiling to the floor. Strangely, it was completely unlocked. They opened up the doors, and their hearts dropped. Inside, a lonely guard was sitting on a single cot in the room.

"Who the hell are you?" yelled the guard as he stood up and swung a fist at the only person he saw, Elise, who was too weak to even react. Jude, reacting without realizing it, put the vest forward to block the fist and then threw an elbow into the jaw of the guard. All three people in the cell were stunned, most of all Jude. The guard pulled out his blaster and pointed it at Jude. Elise landed a quick kick into the side of the knee of the guard, who immediately fell to the ground. Before he could move, Elise was back on her feet with her blaster pointed at his head.

"Where is prisoner 22?" asked Elise, through gritted teeth.

"The last guy? That bastard?" asked the guard, in fear.

Elise aimed the blaster at his head. "Where is he?"

"They flew him out this morning to St. Louis. He's set to be exterminated in a few days. I'm just here to take a nap on one of the only free beds in the camp." The guard began to laugh to break the tension.

Elise was unamused. "St. Louis? You're lying." She pressed the gun against the guard's temple.

"I swear, I swear!" yelled the guard, cowering and coming to terms with the gravity of the situation. "It's too late, though, the St. Louis prison is impenetrable."

Elise's anger, pain, and exhaustion finally caught up to her when the guard said this. She put pressure on the trigger. "Shut the hell up," she said to the guard. "It's never too late."

As Elise began to pull the trigger, Jude grabbed her wrist. Elise's reflexes caused her to point the gun straight at Jude.

He stared down the barrel of the blaster and at Elise. "If you do this, you're no better than them. We can find your father and rescue him. But, you can't do this. *You're better than this, Elise.*"

She looked at Jude in surprise. "You have the vest, you can go home."

"I'll help you," said Jude. "But, I won't help you like this."

Elise stared hard into Jude's eyes. "Why? Why would you help? You have no stake in this."

"You saved me from the lab when you had no need to. This world I woke up in is terrible. It has to be worse on your own. I'll help you, Elise... I'll help you rescue your father, and then I'll go home. But if you kill this man in cold blood, you're on your own. I'll take the vest, I'll take the notes, and we're finished."

She continued to stare straight through Jude. It was obvious no one had spoken to her like he just had in a long time. Elise, calculating, calming down, lowered her blaster. In one quick motion, however, she raised it and slammed it into the head of the guard, who fell over unconscious.

"What?" asked Elise, "I'll be humane, but not stupid."

The two stood awkwardly for a brief moment in the silence of the cell. "Jude..." hesitated Elise. "Y'know..."

"Don't mention it," said Jude, putting his hand on Elise's shoulder. "So, to St. Louis then?" He did his best to sound positive.

"I guess so," said Elise, "but I really have to warn you, it's a shit-hole."

Slightly laughing, the pair braced themselves against each other as they began their trek back to Elise's pod. Covered in blood, burns, and whatever else, the two remained undeterred.

"An old man and an angry woman, huh?" said Jude, thinking about Elise's words from earlier, as they made their way out of block 73.

"An old man and an angry woman," repeated Elise. "St. Louis doesn't know what's coming."

Eleven

November 8, 2393

E lise and Jude arrived back at the pod after a long secret journey to where they first entered the camp. To Jude's surprise, being lifted up to the pod was even more terrifying than jumping out. Hitting a button on his armband, he was immediately launched upwards toward the invisible pod. His eyes were closed for the entire duration of his climb. Elise, who had made it to the pod first, was laughing at Jude when he finally opened his eyes.

"You're one smooth guy... Anyone ever tell you that?"

"Constantly," said Jude, relieved to be safely back on the ship.

Elise crashed on the bed. Taking off her pants and stripping down to her underwear, she revealed the extent of her wounds.

"Don't stare, creep. We're still human even centuries later. Nothing new." Elise laughed, paused, then said, "All this pain and to not even be in the same camp as my father."

She reached onto a nearby shelf and grabbed a purple bottle. She rubbed some sort of gel up and down the burns on her legs. "My father... We're going to St. Louis. We're going to save him... it'll be worth it."

Elise switched to putting gel on her other leg. The two people aboard the pod were lost in a brief moment of thought. Finally, Jude broke the silence. "Tell me about your father."

Elise looked to Jude and took a moment to think about the question. "You know, he's the best. He went through his wife being murdered and his child being taken... He stayed strong. He felt like he had to for me, I think. He worked as a scientist in the military until they took my sister. I was so young when she was taken. We were both broken. He kept it together, though. He was pretty high in the ranks when the wars broke out amongst the continental countries... But when the Volgens came and when The Imminent Collision passed... Well, he sat back and watched. He kept me safe, but he didn't want to support either side. That's why he founded the resistance in Chicago... From the rubble, he thought, the humans who didn't support the institution would rebuild the world... here we are... Still trying to rebuild... While he's glad the Volgens lost their part in the story of humanity, the resistance still fights, and the institution still imprisons those of us who want change. My father, he just sees this world for how it should be... free of the institution... free of Volgens... free from the Shadows... just people... free to be people."

"He sounds incredible," said Jude, with a genuine smile. "Really. It makes sense why you seem so strong."

Elise became lost in thought again. This was fine with Jude. She had answered his question, and he could see that she was content to be lost in her memory while she treated her wounds. Jude found a lot of comfort in the fact that Elise was so willing to discuss her past. Not just her past, but the difficult parts, too. In just a short amount of time, the two had seemed to become close friends. It must be hard to meet people in this world, Jude thought. Nonetheless, Jude took Elise's momentary meditation to do some reflecting of his own.

He leaned back against the wall of the pod and thought of his own father. He thought of playing catch in the front yard. He thought about kayaking on Lake Michigan with him. He thought about the final things they said to each other. He became so lost in thought that he didn't even realize that Elise had stood up, walked past him, and sat in her pilot's chair.

"Jude…" He finally heard. "Elise to Jude. Are you there, Jude?" She laughed when he finally startled back to consciousness. "Lost ya there, man."

Laughing, Jude said, "yeah, sorry… I do that."

"I noticed… so, listen, are you sure you want to go to St. Louis? It could be… What was it that you called last night's mission? A death sentence?"

"I'm sure," said Jude, confidently. "Family is the most important thing."

"Family is the most important…" repeated Elise.

Before turning on the engines of the pod, Elise turned back one more time and said, "You're a good guy, Jude Monroe, ya know that?"

"Just wait til you get to know me," joked Jude.

"Oh, I'm looking forward to it," smiled Elise, back at him.

"Still though, I'm apparently still getting to know me. Did you see me elbow that guard in the face? I'm such a legend."

"A legend whose ass needed to be saved like five times back there... Super hot."

"What can I say? Everyone loves an underdog."

The two laughed, and their cackles rang throughout the pod. When it quieted down, Elise said, "I'm glad you're here, Jude."

"I am too," he replied. Truly, somehow, he knew that he meant it, and he realized that he would do anything to help Elise save her father. After the events of the last few days, Jude felt like he could do anything.

"Alright," said Elise. "I'll set the pod's course for St. Louis. You can probably already smell it from here."

Smiling to himself, Jude looked at the wound on his hand, still not fully believing how he got it. He stood up and moved to a window that was on the side of the pod. Sitting down, he turned his head and looked out to see the morning sun break through the skyline of the brown and rusted Chicago. The beams reflected off of Lake Michigan. As the water seemed to turn red and orange from the rising sun, he removed a picture that he had in the pocket of his undershirt. This picture he had taken with him everywhere, even aboard *The Audacity*. He looked at it and replayed old memories of when things were simpler. When his parents were still alive...

Twelve

March 16, 2016

Jude sat back and watched his parents dance to their favorite song, "Handle With Care" written by the Traveling Wilburys. They danced a slow sidestep, and Jude had never seen his parents filled with so much love as they held each other. Though the tempo was upbeat, they continued to dance slower and slower as if they were washing everything away from the world except each other. Love, at its finest, was on display for all those who came to celebrate the Monroes' 34th wedding anniversary.

* * *

"Why are we throwing such a large party to celebrate the 34th anniversary?" Jude asked two weeks earlier as he sat in his parents' kitchen, sampling a small spoon of his mother's marinara sauce that slowly boiled on the stovetop. "Shouldn't we have done this for the 30th or wait for the 35th? 34th seems out of place."

"I agree, and it's so sudden..." said Hazel, entering the room and joining in the taste testing. "You want to send out invites only two weeks in advance for some crazy-big 34th anniversary party? You guys are crazy."

"Crazy in love," responded their father, Peter Monroe, a man with hair graying too early for his age. He proceeded to wrap his arms around his wife's waist as she was mixing batter for a cake that she should have put in the oven an hour ago.

"We're unconventional," joined Olive, their mother, to the defense of Peter, "and we like to celebrate that way." She turned her head back, kissed her husband on the cheek, and snuggled into the crook of his neck while never missing a spin of the whisk in the cake batter.

"You both are disgusting, but I love it," said Hazel, smiling.

"Love is in the air. Look at Jude. He and Grace are just like we were when we were their age... Give it time, they'll be just as repulsive as your parents while celebrating their 34th," said Olive, in a sing-songy way that only she could, and not making eye contact with either of her children. "Speaking of which, where is your fiancée anyway?"

"Oh, she's on her way; she just *had* to get a new pair of jeans for the concert the day after your anniversary. With the preparations, she didn't want to wait too long, and apparently none of the pairs she already owns are good enough for 'date night,'" said Jude, sarcastically, as the other three laughed at him.

"Okay," said Hazel, turning the attention back to her parents, "what do we want for this soi·rée? Food, music, dancing, et cetera?"

"I'll let your mom pick everything," replied Peter, still holding his wife and smiling, "I just want our first dance of the evening to be to 'Handle With Care.'"

"Oh no, that song is too lame for the opening number," replied Hazel.

"I've never understood why that is your 'song.' It's cheesy," said Jude, rolling his eyes with Hazel.

"You watch it, young one," said Peter, beginning to laugh. "I'm pretty sure that was the song that you were conceived to."

"Gross! Stop!" responded Jude and Hazel in unison, while dropping the dinner samplings they were about to eat. "Too damn far, dude," continued Hazel. "What the hell?"

"Peter, stop. You're being raunchy," replied Olive, turning from her husband and putting the batter in a metal pan. "Besides," she paused for dramatic effect, "you're thinking of Hazel."

"I. Am. Done." Hazel groaned and immediately left the room with her hands over her ears.

The three remaining in the kitchen continued laughing as she left the room. When Olive turned around, her husband embraced her again, and he said, "34th, 35th, 36th, and every day in between I'd celebrate my life with you." Olive kissed him and smiled back at him. Jude sat at the kitchen island in the middle of the room and watched his parents. It was not unnatural for Jude to see his parents overly affectionate with each other, but there was something even more kindled between them than usual at this moment. Nonetheless, Jude smiled as he reflected on how fortunate he was to be surrounded by so much love.

* * *

"Our parents had sex to this song. It's disgusting. And no one watching them slow dance to this shit has any idea," said Hazel, pulling up a seat next to her brother. The pair had spent the last two weeks attempting to find mismatched chairs for the occasion, per the request of their 'unconventional' parents. The velvet seat, which Hazel sank too far down in, only made her all the more uncomfortable. However, as she watched her parents, she recognized the facade that she was putting on as she dreamed of finding a love like they had. Like her brother had. She wondered when her turn might come.

"I think it's sweet," said Grace, holding Jude's hand.

"That's just our parents," said Jude, watching Peter and Olive, whose smiles had not disappeared all night. "They are exactly who I want to be."

The slow dance ended with a small twirl and Olive dipping Peter. Their guests laughed and clapped their hands in a standing ovation for them. Still, the two looked longingly into each other's eyes, and the world was still clearly vacant to them. Silently, Peter whispered something in Olive's ear, and they both slowly turned to look at their two children, who were also standing and clapping. Cheek to cheek, the parents smiled at their kids. This moment, full of joy, was all the Monroe family could ask for.

The night was filled with conversations, food, and dancing. "Do you think we'll celebrate our 34th anniversary?" asked Grace, as she slow danced with Jude later in the evening.

Jude pulled Grace closer to him so he could whisper in her ear, "Love, I think we'll celebrate many more than that."

As he leaned his head back from hers, she grabbed him by his lapels and kissed him quickly yet tenderly. "I love you. So much," she said, looking into his eyes.

"Who could blame you?" laughed Jude and immediately dodged a playful punch from Grace. "I love you, so dearly," he finally said and then spun his fiancée as the music faded out. As he looked at her, he felt truly lucky. The dark brown curls in her hair bounced against her cheeks. Her dimples were even more prominent with the wide smile she flashed at him. He looked to his parents and then back to Grace. 34 years would be a cake walk. The only fear he had in this moment was the fear of the years going by too quickly.

The night ended with the Monroes in a line, hugging their guests as they filed out of the hall. Hugs and smiles capped off what was the perfect evening. Olive and Peter stood in front of Grace, Jude, and Hazel, and gave them hugs and kisses. They thanked them for all their effort and for making sure the evening was perfect. Finally, the parents stood only feet away from the three for a brief moment, and they seemed to take a mental picture of them. One more round of hugs later, and the couple who had been married for 34 years walked out the door. Grace, Jude, and Hazel were the last three out the door from the party.

* * *

Five days later, they sat in the same order that they had received the final round of love from their parents: Hazel on Jude's right, Grace on his left, holding his hand, as they sat in front of the two closed caskets.

Jude wore the same black tie that he had worn a few days prior to the anniversary party, less than 24 hours before his parents' death. It was Hazel's idea to have the mismatched seats from the party lined in front of the coffins in the cemetery. This time, she didn't even notice the give in the velvet seat as she sank in it once again. The three sat under the canopy and waited for people to arrive. There was no line, no eulogies, and little sentimentality. Olive and Peter, agreed Jude and

Hazel, would not want too much of a show for this occasion. They had the toasts, the celebrations, the gatherings, only a few days before. Nothing more was needed.

Rain came as fellow mourners began to arrive. They sat in the assortment of chairs in silence. Grace volunteered to say a few words during the funeral, which lasted only five minutes. The three sat in silence long after the guests had left and stared at the two brown boxes before them.

They quickly became numb to the word "tragedy." It was on the news when reporters covered the car wreck that took the lives of their parents. It was in the texts and cards sent to them. His parents truly were together, in everything, even to the end, thought Jude. The path ahead was dark to him. How could he move forward without at least one of his parents? How could he endure without the people who had been there every step of his life? He had to be strong for Hazel; he knew that. She was broken, and while he knew he couldn't fix her, he could be her source of strength and support.

The three remained as the two caskets were lowered into the ground. Jude felt something deeper than pain. He was lost, he was drowning, he was terrified, and he knew he would be for a long time. He would be broken well after the funeral, after years of attempted coping. There was an emptiness that seemingly could not be overcome.

When they got back to their parents' house later that night, Jude opened an envelope that contained photos from the party only days ago. The top picture was of the four members of the Monroe family with their arms around each other. They were not looking at the camera. Olive, Jude, and Hazel were looking at Peter. Their heads were thrown back as they laughed heartily at something raunchy he had said. Peter's eyes, though, were fixed on his wife. A perfect moment.

This was exactly how Jude wanted to remember his family. He folded the picture, and he put it in his pocket. He always had it on him as a reminder that love endures, love transcends death, love is constant. This reminder was the only spark of light he felt in the years following the loss of his two heroes.

* * *

Jude looked out the window and at the sun reflecting upon Lake Michigan as Elise began to pull away, and then his gaze returned to the picture he held in his hands. Though the tragedy may have occurred centuries ago, the love of his parents was still alive in the future, his future, the Earth's future. They were there with him, he thought. He folded the picture and stuffed it back in his breast pocket. With a single tear in his eye, he looked at Elise in the pod's cockpit. He would help her save her father. He knew what it felt like to lose the most loved people in one's life. He couldn't save his parents, but maybe, he thought, he could save one of hers.

Thirteen

February 4, 2369

Neither Leo nor Goliath had seen this woman before. Yet, here she was strolling into their laboratory as if she were invited in. The two scientists looked up from the 142nd trial of the experiment they had been working on for months as this stranger pulled up a chair and sat only feet away. She called herself The Sphinx. The two scientists had only heard the name before and had never seen the face.

* * *

Leo and Goliath had spent their careers attempting to break through the field of teleportation. They believed it could become fact, not fiction. Years flew by, and the two scientists yielded no fruit. They would have been laughed out of the science community had their research not stumbled upon new ways to utilize energy. For this, they were highly regarded. Yet the pair was still held at arm's length for their radical ideas and dreams.

Their discoveries in the field of energy were enough to make for the early retirement of any scientist, but for Leo and Goliath, they knew their job would not be done until either death or the discovery of the one thing that always eluded them: transferring matter from one place to another.

The pair continued their work slowly until one day a mysterious package was sitting in their lab when they entered on the morning of October 14, 2368. The package had a note that said:

Only the pair of you could use
this for what is to come.
Good luck.
The Sphinx

As the two scientists opened the package, they quickly realized that it contained the answers to all of their questions from the moment the two dared to dream of teleportation. 141 trials later, they could feel that they were close, though they felt so far from mastering what The Sphinx had laid out for them. For months, the two had put an old rocking chair in front of the machine built from the blueprints of The Sphinx, and always the rocking chair remained when the test was complete. The pair, though frustrated, kept making adjustments, looking over the blueprints, and trying again.

So now, after strolling into the room after Leo and Goliath had finished so many trials, The Sphinx introduced herself. She said nothing more as the two proceeded with trial number 142. Ten minutes later, the trial was another failure. The stranger sat and looked over the machine and proceeded to study Leo and Goliath. She then stood up after some time, removed her hat, and walked over to the rocking chair. She sat down in it and then said only seven words: "Try again, but point it at me."

Still unsure who this person, The Sphinx, was or whether or not to make adjustments, Goliath walked over to the machine, pointed it at the woman in front of them, and pushed a green button. The machine buzzed, and a large wind filled the room followed by a loud crack. Leo and Goliath stood still and could not believe what had just happened. The machine had worked. The Sphinx had disappeared, and so had the chair.

Nearly five minutes later, the stranger walked back into the laboratory. "This science does not work on the inanimate, but the living. Sure, you can transfer materials, but something living must be touching them at the moment of impact from the cannon. I am The Sphinx. I am not of Earth. I am Volgen. In a month's time, the world will find out about a comet that will hit your planet in the coming future. I tell you this as a friend and to earn your trust. I will come back when the news breaks. Teleportation is not enough. We must move beyond what you think possible."

In June of 2369, word was released of The Imminent Collision. A comet would destroy Earth and everything on it in 2376. Leo and Goliath were in their lab watching the news break. When the president of The North American Government closed his speech, the door opened in Leo and Goliath's laboratory, and The Sphinx, as promised, walked in with a new set of blueprints.

She explained to them that with the science of teleportation came the penultimate step to traveling through time. The three worked through the night disassembling the teleportation cannon and re-assembling it with new parts brought by The Sphinx. The last items needed were a handful of teal rocks that The Sphinx put into a compartment at the base of the newly built cannon. As the sun began to rise outside, the three sat and looked at their new construction.

Goliath pushed the green button again, and instead of teleporting, instead of a person disappearing, instead of the hope of anything vanishing, something all the more peculiar took its place. Before the three, suspended in the air, was a floating circle. The three could see into it and not through it.

A different time lived through this "portal," explained The Sphinx. She continued to explain how the rocks were crystallized from something called Mortality Escaped Energy. Or, energy gathered from someone escaping death. The portal collapsed in five minutes, and the machine caught fire.

After this event, The Sphinx explained to the pair of scientists the Volgen science and how to create what would soon be called a "Houdini Vest."

The three spent the next six years working in the lab until finally they had created a working vest that could be mass-produced. In December of 2375, Goliath wrote in their journal:

The Sphinx had not just shown us how to create a portal to move from one place to another, but from one time to another. The vests we created are set to trigger a portal at the exact occurrence of a lethal moment of someone's life. However, if they are wearing a vest when something lethal were to happen, they would survive. The vest would use the energy from that person's escaped death and use it to allow them to travel through space or time.

The vests will be triggered by any cataclysmic event. When the vests are triggered, the person wearing it is literally suspended in time. The death that the wearer is supposed to suffer from is completely evaded. The kinetic energy from that person's imminent death in that moment is then redirected into transferring that person to not just another place, but another time.

The vests can either be triggered by a button on the gloves or the chest. By pushing the button, the vest will release an electric shock that would have the capacity to immediately kill the person wearing it. However, the person would not die; they would escape death, and again that energy is harnessed. Either through accident or intention, the vests will rescue the wearer and utilize the kinetic energy.

This breakthrough changes our entire plan of action. Should we travel to a time after The Imminent Collision or travel to a time on Earth before and live out our days? During one of our experiments, Leo traveled to the past and reappeared an entire day later, still wearing the vest. Leo had spent an entire week in the past. In Leo's hand was a feather from an ostrich which has been extinct for 100 years.

Our findings are this: A Houdini Vest can help any person wearing it to escape death. The vests are designed to use the energy to open a portal that only someone wearing the vest can enter. In the case of a fatal attack, cataclysmic event like The Imminent Collision, or anything else likewise, the vest will automatically transport the person wearing it to another time. The person can also use it to voluntarily travel through time. They should be wary... According to The Sphinx, the vests are only good for three trips until one needs a new one. Bottom line, however, we believe we can save everyone on Earth. This is the breakthrough we were looking for, not just for our careers, but for the fate of humanity. Rather than teleporting the comet where it could do damage somewhere else, we will let it destroy itself, and the humans will survive.

* * *

Jude read all of this aloud from the files of Leo and Goliath to Elise as the two were in flight from Chicago to St. Louis. When Jude finished reading the journal entry from Goliath, the pod was silent for a brief period of time.

"So, it's like you said, the vests take the energy that should be used for the death of someone, and transfers them somewhere else," said Jude

"Right... Volgen technology... of course, they would find the most vile way to complete time travel."

"I'd hate to find out how they figured it out..."

"I'm sure those monsters had no problem testing it out on themselves. Still, Leo and Goliath seemed to not have any idea of the selfish intentions from The Sphinx. To use the technology for the Volgens and not the humans... Does it give any explanation about where they went or why none of the vests worked on the day the comet disappeared?"

"Let's see," said Jude as he flipped through schematics of the vests, a few years of journal entries, until he got to the last few pages. He read from an entry dated January 1st, 2376.

"Here towards the end, it says, *'Today, Thomspon told us to only build 200 vests that worked. No more were needed. They intend to let the world perish in a few months. We must find a way to do more...'* What the hell does that mean?"

"Thompson was in charge of the Department of Homeland Security. Those bastards. They were going to just let the comet come and kill the Volgens and every other human. That is worse than evil."

"Let's see, you said nothing worked, and Leo and Goliath all escaped, right?"

"That's right. Do they give any explanation? What about The Sphinx, anything about her?"

Flipping through pages, Jude finally found what he was looking for. "The last pages are scribbled on...

Here at the end of things, Goliath and I shall leave. We have done what we set out to do. Though we lost The Sphinx, we saved humanity. What we leave in our wake, we know not. We left dormant portals all over Earth. The vests are the only way to enter in and out of the portals left suspended in the sky. They have the energy to last for many millennia. Though they are high and out of reach, they can be accessed if one simply knows the place and is wearing a vest. The Volgens know the places... Goliath and I know the places if we ever choose to return, though that can most likely never happen. These portals will stay dormant without the presence of vests. Should anyone want to step through the doorways of these portals, they must be wearing one of the Houdini Vests which humans and Volgens created together... If you are reading these words, you are in danger. I don't know if what we did was right or not. The world continues to spin. Whoever reads this next, the Houdini Vest is dangerous. Very dangerous. The North American Government will kill us if they make it to us and kill anyone who has the last remaining vest that sat next to these files.... please, use it to flee from them. Remember to take precautions. The vest will only open a portal at the exact moment of death. We lived well.

Good luck.

L&G

The two in the pod paused as the last lines from the files reverberated throughout the flying capsule. Deep in thought, the two finally spoke up and asked the same question at the same time.

"Why didn't they say how they saved the planet?"

"There is no way they made the comet disappear," said Elise, slamming a fist into her steering console.

"They had to have something to do with it... right? Maybe, another portal?"

"Like they sent the comet somewhere else?" asked Elise.

"Yeah, like maybe that's what killed the dinosaurs," said Jude, half joking, half serious.

"No idea what you're talking about... movies?"

"Right, deleted past and whatnot, well, anyway, I feel like there is so much that they are saying and yet not saying."

Elise remained quiet in thought.

"I guess all that matters is that the world was saved," said Jude, flipping back through the files.

"The resistance can use all of this for good, like Leo and Goliath did. We can use this vest to get you home and then to win."

"Should anyone use it? Should we just destroy it rather than let the institution get it?" asked Jude, still looking through the files, hoping that something would pop up to make everything make more sense.

"Are you crazy? We have to take the institution down. This science is more advanced than anything they can create. We're going to save my father, get you home, and then kill those bastards that left the entire world for dead. They won't get away with this. These files are going to spark the rebellion to its truest potential."

"Maybe you're right," said Jude, nodding, "I just... I get it. It obviously worked and all. The world was saved, the scientists did disappear, it's obviously more fact than fiction... It's just, I can't wrap my head around it. Y'know?"

"True... I feel like this left us with a lot more questions than answers."

"Too many unanswered questions."

"...but all of this has to have something to do with what happened to you. I had heard of portals before. Everyone had. I mean, you must have traveled through one when your rocket exploded, and it must have brought you here. It happened at the exact moment you should have died, and you traveled to the future... but how could that portal get there?"

"I don't know and I don't get it... I wasn't wearing a vest, y'know. I just don't get it... Only Leo and Goliath would know. "

"Maybe they can help us," said Elise, growing excited.

"I was thinking the same thing. We can find them, and then you, me, and your father can work with them to save the world one more time."

"We need more information. We need to find more answers. All of this, though, this *is* game-changing. Like Leo and Goliath said, 'this is the breakthrough we needed.'"

"This could make all the difference," said Jude as he walked up to the cockpit and put his hand on Elise's shoulder. "We can do this."

"You keep signing up for things that are keeping you from going home. You have the vest. You could leave anytime. Why keep fighting for a world you don't belong to?" asked Elise, looking up at Jude.

"Because it's the right thing to do. My dad always said that we should live in a way that would make the world better than the way that we found it. This future... This horrible future... Maybe I can help leave it better than I found it before I go home."

Elise looked at Jude as the light from her windows shined upon him, and he glowed. His confidence radiated. She looked into his eyes. "Let's burn those bitches down," she finally said, "but first, get some sleep. We have a big mission ahead of us in St. Louis, and we're going to need our rest."

Jude walked to the back of the pod and laid down. He tried to break down all of what he had learned of this new world he had woken up in. The Volgens had helped the humans, and it was the humans who ultimately were the most evil. He thought about the vests and the terrifying science behind them. He thought about Leo and Goliath. Were their efforts in vain? What did they truly save? Did he find the future through what they called a dormant portal in their files? He closed his eyes, certain that he could dream of no nightmare more terrifying than the reality he had traveled to.

Fourteen

November 8, 2393

Jude was surprised to find that the St. Louis Gateway Arch still remained hundreds of years later. It wasn't uncommon for the Monroe family to take trips to St. Louis, and each time, as they crossed the Mississippi River and into the city, Peter Monroe would always say, "I just don't get how it works. How does that thing stay up?" The rest of the family would laugh in the car as they crossed over the water below.

Jude thought of his dad as Elise lowered her pod and parked on top of the monument that his family used to ponder many years prior. He couldn't help but laugh at the fact that despite his father's bewilderment, the structure still stood. Without missing a beat, Elise opened the side doors of the pod and stepped out onto the structure.

"You need to hit the purple button on your wristband. That will help you stay secure on the slick surface out here."

Jude nodded to Elise, speechless as he poked at the screen on his arm. "Thanks. I can't believe where we are," Jude finally said as he crept to the threshold of the pod and not a step further. He looked down and could feel the Arch, which was fully corroded on the outside, sway beneath him. He could feel himself struggling to make the decision to step down.

Elise was patient as Jude took in the new scenery. He had come through in each situation they found themselves in, and she knew she didn't need to push. When Jude finally decided to look up from the Arch below, he was even more taken aback. Here, 630 feet high, he was surprised to find the contrast of the new St. Louis from the new Chicago. Chicago, at the very least, seemed to have some life in it. St. Louis, on the other hand, was decimated. Rubble surrounded the entirety of this city. He could remember skyscrapers that cast their shadows across the river and into Illinois, but no such buildings remained. He looked to his right in hopes of seeing his home state, but flooding had taken over the Illinoisan banks and spread for miles. No land remained in sight, even from the top of the Arch.

Jude looked back to where the city used to stand, somehow still surprised by the desolation. Clearly, something more than age had been the cause of the scene he was looking at. Only one building stood amongst the hundreds of miles of scattered debris. Nothing, not a single sign of life, existed with the exception of The Arch and a distant structure. The golden tower in the distance seemed to reach miles higher than the top of the Arch.

Jude barely gave two glances at the tower. The land below is what he was still trying to fathom.

"The war left this place in ruins. After the Volgens came forward and after The Imminent Collision passed, the continental armies immediately went to war. More bombs were dropped. The wars that broke out were worse than when everyone found out about The Imminent Collision. After time, though, the Shadows began to appear and joined the fight," said Elise, trying to decipher Jude's thoughts.

"Did the humans work together or..?" asked Jude, not looking at Elise.

She looked to the sky and paused. "Well, not exactly. They stopped fighting each other, sure, but that doesn't mean it got better. You see, after the Volgens came out and we all started looking to the skies wondering who would come next... The Shadows began appearing and answered the question for us."

"Is that what happened here?" asked Jude, the images of the Shadows in the records building were still clear in his mind. He began to imagine the St. Louis he knew from the past filled with those evil creatures. "I mean, this is terrible."

Elise walked to the edge of the Arch and looked below. "I wish I could say the Shadows did this. I really do." She turned to look back at Jude. Her blonde hair, alive in the wind, contrasted the dead world behind her. "When the Shadows began overrunning the cities, The North American Government, like the other governments around the world, tried to stop those monsters by dropping nuclear bombs in the center of each one."

Jude, still standing at the threshold of the pod, let the information set in. "You mean... You mean they just killed innocent people? Their own people?"

"That's what they do. The greater good," said Elise, sarcastically. "Evil, right? They killed everyone. They sent soldiers into the fray to keep it sealed and then dropped it... It was horrible. We watched it from streamed footage from local resistance fighters. There was fighting all over the city, and then all footage just went black."

"There's nothing left. Nothing."

"Only this damn Arch."

"The institution really didn't care about anyone, did they? They just wanted to stay in power."

"Exactly," said Elise, walking back to Jude. "They are the root of evil. Yeah, the Shadows were here to kill, but the institution... they're the real murderers."

"History always repeats itself... It takes different forms, but it always repeats itself," said Jude, more to himself as he thought about his last lessons before leaving for NASA headquarters.

"Funny how it managed to repeat itself after they made it illegal to study the past."

The two looked at each other until Elise turned and walked backwards and leaned against the side of the pod. Jude finally stepped down onto the Arch. He kept moving until he reached its edge. He looked down to what seemed like miles below. Since he had woken up, he had slowly learned how much was lost over the last few centuries. He was heartbroken. The imprisoned Volgens and the innocent people murdered... The world was filled with pain. He finally fully understood what Elise meant when she said that the comet could have been a reset button. Leo and Goliath may have somehow saved the Earth, but what did they save it for? It couldn't have been for the cemetery beneath Jude's feet. A single tear rolled down his cheek and fell to the Earth below.

Elise walked up to him and didn't say a word.

Jude looked to the sky and then to the horizon. "We have to make this right. I refuse to believe that this is it."

"Now you see the world as I see it... As we all see it. The resistance is the first step. We need all the help we can get."

"Why not the Volgens? You can't tell me they wouldn't rebel against their captors, too."

Elise looked back at Jude, fire in her eyes, "No. Absolutely not. They abandoned us. They tricked us. They were parasites waiting for us to die... They deserve death just as much as the institution."

"But, didn't you see their eyes? Didn't you see the pain? All the help, right? They could help!"

"You just don't get it. You weren't here. You didn't see the war. They could have prevented everything. Guardian Angels– Demons. That's what they were. They lurked. At least the institution had the gall to screw us over where we could see them. The institution, the Volgens, the Shadows, none of them deserve life. The revolution wants a reset. To do what the comet should have done. That's what they deserve."

"How does that make the resistance any better than the institution dropping bombs on the innocent? It doesn't."

"You just don't get it, you don't. You don't know what all they took. They all deserve to die. They all ruined everything. Everything."

"But, is that how you really want to build back humanity?"

"Look, it may not be perfect, but humanity isn't perfect. You know what, let's get that vest and then we'll get you home to where things are fair and full of sunshine. Maybe the future is too much for you."

There was silence. The two, only feet apart, had not yet been so distant. There was awkwardness filling the void where the debate had been. Finally, Elise looked over at Jude. The cold wind blew through his hair while the dust from below rose and danced around his head.

"Look," Elise said, "I'm sorry. You've done more than anyone could have asked of you." She paused and watched the sun reflect off his eyes; they were filled with tears as he continued to survey what was left of St. Louis. "You never asked for any of this. You were just a guy trying to inspire a lot of kids, and you wound up here... I get it. Imagine being one of those kids, though. Here. Growing up looking at this... You're broken before you start."

Jude turned to Elise. The sun was close to setting. A new calm filled the air. "Elise, I understand. I get it. Look, I'll help. I want to help... But, we need to fight for better, not for the same evil just under a different flag. I won't help only to help history repeat itself."

Elise looked away and then at the pink sky above. "Okay... Yeah... Okay... It's so hard, y'know, to live that black and white..." She paused and then smiled and looked at him. "Not everyone can be as pure as the extremely old and wise Jude Monroe."

"Hey, I've learned some things in the last 400 years. I've been around."

The two laughed until silence crept back in. "We good?" said Elise, offering her hand to Jude.

He nodded and accepted the handshake. "Of course. Let's go get your dad. I assume, since nothing else is around, that he is locked up in that tall-ass gold obscenity?"

"You got it," said Elise. She nudged her elbow into Jude's arm. "But good news, thanks to my dad's intel, I already have a way in."

"I can't imagine it's as easy as it sounds."

"It can't be worse than what we just did in Chicago. On the 95th story, there is an exterior shaft that, if we move quickly, we can infiltrate. 50 feet into the building is an internal vent that we can drop through. Luckily, according to the intel, they keep resistance fighters on the 100th floor. We just have to make it up five stories, and we'll be there."

"Sure, it's as easy as getting to the 95th story... How the hell are we supposed to get to the 95th story of that monstrosity? I sure as hell am not climbing," replied Jude, losing his smile and staring straight ahead to the gold building.

"Easy... I already have it covered. My sister and I used to ride hover cars all the time when we were kids. She was wicked smart... Smart enough to modify ours to be able to fly 400 feet in the air and to scale buildings. We'll just ride it down that side of the Arch, cross over to the prison, ride the wall up, and then break in. Couldn't be more simple."

"Yeah, when you put it that way... It's just an easy trip across a desolate St. Louis to a future prison where we'll casually ride your side-by-side hover car up 95 stories to where we'll break into said building by way of a shaft. Really simple."

"Exactly. Simple. Besides, it's only a future prison to *you*," said Elise, giggling as she made her way back to her pod. She went into the cockpit, hit a button, and air exploded from underneath her pod. From the bottom compartment came a two-seated hover car. The machine was red and yellow and floated a foot above the ground. Elise hopped in first and revved the engine. "Listen to this thing purr!" she yelled over the engine that made very little sound at all.

"That is a death trap if I've ever seen one," Jude responded in a normal tone, frozen as he looked at the hover car and played Elise's plan in his head. "Shouldn't we wear helmets?"

"Oh, yeah, good idea! Get in, and I'll hand you one."

Jude hopped in and sat next to Elise. "Wher–" was all he could get out by the time Elise threw her foot down, and the two were speeding down the side of the Arch. They made their way across barren lands. There was no sign of life anywhere. Jude swore he could see blurs of red eyes mixed in the rubble, but he convinced himself that his mind was simply playing tricks.

After a few minutes of flying, Jude felt dizzy and out of breath. He was terrified as they sped through the remains of St. Louis. Elise rushed toward the gold building. Even as they got closer, she was not slowing down. Seemingly impossible, the building became bigger and bigger.

"Elise?" yelled Jude. Again, "Elise! Elise, what are you doing?"

"Pipe down, ya coward!" Elise was smiling widely and thoroughly enjoying the ride.

"Elise!" yelled Jude, one more time, 20 feet from the base of the building.

"Ah, fine!" yelled back Elise as she pulled up on her steering handles. The car began to ascend the wall. They climbed the wall faster than they flew on the ground. Jude closed his eyes and gripped the side of the vehicle. 95 stories up, Elise slammed on her brakes.

" I hope this is it," she yelled, "I lost count." She was laughing loudly and wiping away tears as Jude had yet to open his eyes. "God, that was fun."

"That was terrible," yelled Jude, refusing to look at where he was. "All the stuff we've done so far, that was the worst."

"Look, you're doing some cool things. That kind of stuff works on girls. Chicks dig cool wall-scaling stories. I would know, I've been called a girl once or twice."

The joke made Jude open his eyes, and when he did, he found that Elise was looking at him. There was a short pause, and the two began to laugh with one another.

"You really do trust me, don't you?" asked Elise.

"Apparently. I'm hanging out of a hover car that's 95 stories high, aren't I?"

"*Yeah, you are.* Such a legend, the old and wise Jude Monroe. Such a legend." She looked at Jude and began to laugh again. "How lucky am I to find a guy like you in a shithole like this?"

Jude looked back at her. He didn't need to say anything. The two shared a perfect moment in perfect silence. Elise turned and, using her blaster, blasted the gate of the vent open. The cage fell to the ground 95 stories below.

Elise moved into the building first. Jude did not hesitate before jumping from the pod and following her.

Jude kept repeating Elise's words. "I'm a legend.… I'm a legend."

Elise, hearing Jude's whispering from behind, paused and looked back. "I'm going to stop giving you compliments if you start letting them go to your head."

"Oh, just keep moving," said Jude, slightly winded. "You don't want to hinder the legend."

Elise smiled, rolled her eyes, and continued moving. Fifty feet in, just as Elise had read in her dad's intel, they found the entrance they were looking for. Elise worked the opening of the vent until it popped free. She hopped in first and landed on her feet. Jude immediately dropped in behind her, though slightly less graceful.

"See? How about that?" said Elise, putting her hand out to help Jude up. "Too Easy."

"Yeah, too easy," said Jude, with a smile. "You know, I think I'm getting pretty good at this."

Elise pulled out her blaster and walked slowly to a door at the end of the room that was slightly cracked open. She put her finger to her mouth for quiet as she slowly opened it a little wider. She held up two fingers to Jude to let him know how many guards she could see. As she began to open the door wider to move into the hallway to take on the guards, Jude thought about stopping her. He might have, had he not seen how she handled the two guards in Chicago. Elise continued to slowly open the door when it let out a loud creak that may as well have been the loudest noise Jude had ever heard.

"Hey!" yelled a voice from outside.

"Get down!" yelled Elise, as she rolled backwards and into the middle of the room. Jude fell to the ground and crawled under a nearby table.

The two guards entered the room. Elise let out a few shots from her blaster. One guard took both blasts straight into the chest and flew against the now open door. The second guard grabbed Elise by her gun-wielding hand. He punched her square in the jaw. She didn't flinch. She grabbed the guard by the neck with her free hand and threw him to the ground. She pointed her blaster at him and put her finger on the trigger.

Before she could get a shot off, a few blasts came from outside the room and made holes in the wall above Jude's hiding spot while debris fell onto the table above him. Elise pointed her blaster at the doorway and let off a few shots of her own. She ran and slid to where Jude was hiding. The two made eye contact for a brief moment, and he would have sworn that she was smiling. Jude thought to himself, there was no way she could actually be enjoying this, could she?

She flipped the table and continued to blast toward the door. The guards and Elise exchanged blast after blast until it was completely quiet in the hallway outside the room. Elise poked her head up and saw that the coast was clear.

"What did I say about welcome wagons in the future?" said Elise, looking down at Jude, who was looking back at her in disbelief. "I think now is when we get going. Wouldn't you agree?"

Jude couldn't believe what he had just witnessed, and when he stood up from behind the table and saw the guards lying in the room, his legs became weak from the shock that was taking him.

"Jude, buddy, c'mon, don't lose it now. We're almost there." Elise put her hand on his shoulder and then walked back to the door to see if it was safe outside. She turned around and smiled at him before looking back into the hallway. He wasn't used to her smiling, but it was truly reassuring. All this time that they had spent together, she really hadn't smiled much at all. It was enough to put some stability back into his knees, and he stepped around the table to move toward her at the doorway.

As he moved, he saw something out of the corner of his eye. The second guard that Elise had taken down began to sit up. Seeing this, Jude yelled, and Elise, the smile still on her face, turned around quickly. Though, it was too late. The guard let loose three blasts from his gun, and they all hit home in the middle of her chest. She fell to the ground in slow motion as Jude rushed to her limp body. The guard stood up and pointed his blaster at Jude.

Seven more guards rushed through the doorway, stepping over Elise's motionless body, and immediately began to attack Jude. They were relentless, but Jude never felt the blows. As they beat him, his eyes were fixed upon the corpse of his dear friend, who was lying lifeless on the ground only five feet from him.

He began to lose consciousness, and the last thing he saw was the girl who just wanted to save her father, and then it all went black.

Fifteen

November 9, 2393

Jude finally awoke, and he was alone. Rays from a new sunset were already exploding through a barred window in the wall only feet from his head. He rolled over onto his side and tried to stand, but he quickly fell back to the ground. He felt every bruise from his arrest the previous night. Lying on his stomach, he did a slow push-up and grunted through the pain until he managed to get his feet underneath him.

"Some welcome wagon." The words from Elise before tragedy struck were still ringing in his ears. He took a step toward the window and fell against the wall for support. Though his head was foggy, he knew he was imprisoned. He knew that the cage door and the windows of his cell were a part of the prison he had broken into the night before. He wished that Elise were there. She'd know what to do. The small box he was in was cramped like the cockpit of *The Audacity*. If only he could escape this fate like he had the explosion a few days before.

Jude used the wall to brace himself as he took another two steps to the window of the cell. The final sun rays still illuminated the remains of St. Louis. The golden clouds in the sky only made the desolation below seem all the more of a wasteland.

The sun was a deep orange as Jude looked to the horizon in the west. Despite his current state, bruised and locked away in a tower centuries away from anyone who knew him, he couldn't help but think how beautiful the sky looked. He had stepped out of his door a few months prior, looking for adventure. Well, here he was, he thought, and what a nightmare he had found. He closed his eyes and breathed in freezing air from outside. He pictured his parents and his sister. What would they say right now, he thought.

He thought about Leo and Goliath and how he wished for a floating portal in the middle of his cage like they had in their lab. Or if only he had brought the vest from Elise's pod, maybe he could escape with that... No, it would have fallen into the wrong hands. He wondered where he would go even if he did have a vest to travel in time. Would he go to the days before the launch and enjoy time with Sarah, that wonderfully mysterious woman? Would he go and spend those last few weeks with his sister that he missed out on leading up to the launch?

No, he knew the exact place he would go. The most perfect night. His parents' 34th wedding anniversary. He wouldn't do anything but stand in the back of the room and watch all of the people he loved most dearly laugh and dance the night away. Jude began to smile as the memories came back to him. The cell disappeared, and he could see the dance floor, his sister in the middle of it, making sure that it stayed lively, and people around talking about how full of life she was. He could see his parents off to the side, in their own world, fully entranced by one another.

He could see Grace... Grace. He opened his eyes, and the cell seemed all the more narrow. If he could only see Grace again. He closed his eyes once more, and there she was, in her blue dress at the anniversary party. The white Christmas lights hung from the ceiling, twinkling in her eyes. He fell in love with her over and over again with each dance that night.

Jude looked out the window and wondered how he could have become so lost. What was it that led him here, he wondered. He was imprisoned long before he found himself in this cage. The night of the anniversary, Grace and Jude had stayed up the entire evening, talking about kids, marriage, and love. His future was supposed to be filled with love and laughter, with his parents and Hazel holding the kids he would have with Grace. His future wasn't supposed to be imprisonment. It wasn't supposed to be Volgens, or Shadows, or death. It was supposed to be life.

The sun disappeared into the horizon as a few stars broke through the intermittent clouds. Jude put his head down as all of these thoughts sank in. No. He thought. Enough. He looked outside the bars as far as he could see. "Enough being a prisoner," he whispered. "My future is not death. It's life." He closed his eyes and repeated. "I choose life. I choose life."

He turned around, eyes still closed. "I choose life," he repeated.

"That's great and all," a voice said from outside the cell. Jude immediately paused and opened his eyes. "That's a great choice, y'know, but I'm not so sure that decision is in your hands anymore."

Jude looked into the eyes of the man standing before him. He had dark sunken eyes and was easily a foot taller than Jude. Behind him were two men, much wider than the man with sunken eyes. They held blasters in their hands and were motionless.

"I am glad to see you're finally awake," said sunken-eyes, as he walked slowly to the door of Jude's cage. He wore a solid black suit with a red tie. Jude could only be surprised that, of all the things to remain from his time, suits somehow made the cut. "I was beginning to wonder if our guards were going to have two corpses to bury rather than just the one from last night."

Jude's blood boiled with rage as he heard these words spoken so coldly, so unremorsefully. He bit his tongue. He knew he was still alive for a reason. Someone from the institution, he thought. Elise might still get her revenge if he could make it out of the cage. Jude just focused on the red tie and didn't say a word.

"Ah, you like my tie? Are you still surprised that we still wear them so far in the future?" He took a few steps closer to Jude, until they were only three feet apart. "People still enjoy the classics. Even in the future." Jude's jaw tightened even more. "Yes, Mr. Monroe. We know. We know where you are from. We know your name. We know everything. There is nothing to hide, because we already know it."

Jude opened his mouth wider to say something, but quickly closed it and tried to take a step backwards. The pain from the bruises on his legs shot lightning bolts through his body, and he fell backward to the ground. He slowly sat back up through the pain to find the man in the red tie squatting and staring straight into his eyes.

"I want you to know, and I am being genuine when I say this, I am glad to hear you choosing life. So, few want to do so these days. It's going to make what comes next much easier for you. Much easier. We're on opposite sides of the cage. You don't want to talk, you don't want to trust me, then don't. I get it. But, listen, kid. You choose not to talk upstairs, well, things are going to become a lot harder. *That,* you can trust me on."

Still squatting, the man's sunken eyes never broke contact with Jude's. He tilted his head to the side, and Jude remained motionless as he continued to sit on the ground. Finally, the man stood up and gestured to the door of the cage. The two larger guards stepped forward, opened the door, and entered the cell. Jude was terrified. The words from the man outside the cage were beginning to sink in. *They need me alive, for some reason.* This was all Jude would let himself think. It was the only thought that gave him any calm.

The guards each grabbed a separate arm and lifted Jude to his feet. Pain filled his entire body, and he fought back a scream. Barely able to feel his legs, he was escorted by the guards through the cage door, through another door only feet away, and into the hallway outside. Sunken-eyes led the way down the narrow passageway and to an elevator with golden doors that matched the outside of the building.

The four men rode to the top floor of the building in silence. Not even the elevator made a noise as they sped to their destination. The doors opened quickly, and the smell of mahogany filled the elevator. The man with the sunken eyes gestured for Jude to step out first.

Jude looked from his captor to the room that stood before him. After a discreetly taken deep breath, Jude took one slow step, followed by another one. Each one he took seemed more painful. Though it was already dark outside, Jude could still see that the room's walls were all windows that allowed for a 360 panorama of the surrounding St. Louis area. The room was tiled with black and gold bricks. Directly in front of Jude were two rows of gold-lined wooden chairs that were all positioned in front of a large wooden desk. Behind the desk was a tall leather chair with its back turned toward Jude. On both sides of the desk were two figures that looked like closet-sized boxes, which were covered in baby blue sheets.

Jude continued to take slow steps into the room. The elevator doors closed slowly behind him. Standing behind the desk was a tall man dressed head to foot in black. Only his cufflinks, which were gold, and the top of his collar, which was white, had any color to mention. His hair was a sleek ebony. He was clean cut and tailored and looked easily 15 years younger than he actually was. He didn't turn around immediately when Jude entered the room, but Jude could feel the man watching his every move.

Slowly and steadily, the man in front of Jude turned away from the window and made eye contact from across the room. The wrinkles from his eyes flowed into the wrinkles on his temples that shot back to his ears. Nothing was said for nearly 30 seconds. Jude could have sworn that he saw a tiny smirk creep onto the face of the man in front of him.

"Hello, Jude," this ominous man said, his voice nearly melodious. "My name is Reginald Becket. I understand you've come a long way to be here, and I'd like to thank you for joining us this evening."

Reginald Becket's eyes were cold, dark, and unyielding in their intensity. Jude's knees were shaking, but he did his best to stand. He didn't know if it was nerves or pain that were causing him to tremble. He didn't say a word.

Reginald waited for Jude to speak. The smirk on his face quickly disappeared. "When people say thank you, it is polite to say you're welcome. Is it not, Jude?"

Still, Jude remained silent, more focused on staying standing than speaking. Reginald remained unmoved as he waited a few moments more. When silence remained, Reginald pulled a device from his pocket and pushed a red button at the top of it. Jude felt electricity jolt through his entire body, and he fell to the ground in anguish.

When the pain slightly subsided, Jude put his hands to the back of his neck where the jolts originated and felt a piece of metal poking from the top of his spine.

"We don't need handcuffs here," said Reginald without even the slightest change in his melodious voice. "We find pain keeps everyone in line."

Jude was on his hands and knees, panting shallow breaths through the pain. He tried to raise his head to see Reginald. Sweat poured into his eyes and burned when he looked up. His vision became blurry. He had to fight to stay conscious through the pain.

"Let's try again, shall we?" said Reginald, who walked to his desk and leaned back against the front of it. "I'd like to thank you, Jude, for coming all this way to my office. I hope it wasn't too much trouble."

Jude, slowly wiping the sweat from his eyes, leaned back onto his knees, still breathing shallow breaths. "You're... You're welcome... Mr. Becket."

"Much better." Reginald put the remote back into his pocket. "Isn't it easier when we all just get along?"

Jude breathed in the first deep breath he could manage since stepping off the elevator. He slightly nodded and agreed with Reginald.

He did his best to maintain as tall of a posture from his knees as he could.

"Now Jude, do you know why you're here?"

Jude thought about the question for a moment. Sunken-eyes had told him they knew everything, and Jude had no reason anymore not to believe it. He decided to listen to the advice. "I came to help someone escape. I was helping someone else… I've never even met the prisoner before."

"Helping break someone out you've never met before, Jude? Perhaps you've noticed that such generosity is not common these days."

Jude put his head down, thinking of Elise. Thinking of all the brokenness she told him about. He didn't look up. He only shook his head.

"Times are different now, Jude Monroe."

Jude felt horrible chills every time Reginald called him by name. "How do you all already know who I am? What the hell is this?" he asked, surprised by his volume.

Reginald immediately took the remote out of his pocket and triggered the electricity through Jude's body once again. Jude rolled on the ground in complete agony. He could hear Reginald speak over the volume of the jolts. "You really must watch your manners in this room, Jude."

Jude curled into a ball as he attempted to bear through the pain searing through his body. When Reginald ended the electric shocks, Jude tasted blood in his mouth. It took a minute before Jude was able to sit up. He rolled over onto his stomach, pushed himself up, and sat on his knees. He didn't realize that a drop of blood was sliding from his mouth and down his chin.

Jude caught his breath just enough to say, "O-okay. I am sorry-sir, but how do you know my name?"

Reginald flashed his grimacing smirk once more. "Didn't they tell you downstairs that we know everything up here? We know all about Jude Monroe who misses his dear big sister back home. The poor teacher who lost his fiancée after the tragic deaths of his parents. Truly, you are a sad story."

"How–" Jude began to yell, but Reginald held up the remote as a threat. Jude ground his teeth to remain calm. "How could you possibly know all of that? I don't understand... Did you test my blood while I was unconscious? There's no way blood samples can tell you any of that."

"Blood samples?" Reginald let out a small laugh. "Blood samples can't tell you anything but what type of blood you are."

"There are—"

"Portable blood testing devices that can tell whether you are human or Volgen? You really should learn what's real and what's science fiction."

"But— How—" stuttered Jude, more confused than he had ever been since he woke up a few days ago.

"How do I know all of this information? Well, the answer to that is quite simple. It's not fancy machinery. It's much simpler than that. I believe you have met my daughter."

Before Jude could process Reginald's words, the leather chair behind the large wooden desk turned around. There, sitting before Jude, was Elise. She stared straight into his eyes from across the room like Reginald had only moments ago. She wore a smirk identical to that of her father's.

Jude was speechless. His head started to spin, and he fell over, catching himself with his palms on the ground. He looked up again, hoping this was still a dream, that all of this was another daydream from inside his cell floors below. She didn't say a word. She only looked at him, continuing her cold sneer.

"I hear you grow attached quite quickly," said Reginald, not giving Jude much time to work his situation out. "Especially with the Volgens in those death camps."

"I– I don't understand. Why are you doing this? Wh–"

"Why are we doing this to you?" asked Elise, finishing Jude's thought for him. "Don't you get it? You were always supposed to end up right where you're sitting right now."

Reginald looked at his daughter with pride and continued the thought. "Everything that has happened has been to my design. The Rocket explosion was right near a connecting portal left dormant by Leo and Goliath... Not so dormant after we sent someone to set the wheels in motion years before you were even selected for that mission. You and everyone on board exploded right on schedule."

Elise chimed in, "We even got Leo's Houdini Vest on you without you knowing it."

"Do you really think you would just wake up in front of someone so willing to help you escape Shadows? Jude, you need to understand this: your fate was in our hands for much longer than you realize. We brought you here. You never made a decision to be here. We made every single one for you."

Jude's mind blew right past the manipulation. He was focused on only one thing. "You killed. You murdered. All the talk about being better, about saving Earth for the better... That was all a lie to get me here? For what?

"Oh, we're going to save the Earth," said Elise, rising from the leather chair. "The resistance is going to win. Getting you here was all we needed to get the ball rolling."

"I— just don't get it. What does any of this have to do with me? Why did you need the Houdini Vest if you're already able to go back in time? Why would you go back in time and choose my life to ruin? What did I do?

Elise began to speak, but Reginald turned his head and stopped her with a glance. Silence filled the room as Reginald stopped leaning on the desk and walked across the room. He grabbed a chair and sat right in front of Jude.

"Listen, thanks to you returning the Leo vest and helping steal the Goliath vest along with The Sphinx vest we already had, we have three working vests. Now, there are 200 others that are faulty, and we have a missing comet. Only two people in the history of time know the solution to both of those problems. If we fix the vests, find the comet, well– Well, then, we can rid the world of all of its evils and start over."

Jude was starting to regain his strength. "No, your plan is what is evil."

"It's a solution, kid, and you're the key."

"Me?" asked Jude, looking past Reginald and to Elise. She looked squarely at him without a glimmer of remorse in her eyes.

Reginald pointed at him. "You. You are the key to unlocking Leo and Goliath's science. You see, we needed you for two reasons. Number one, we needed your blood to recover Leo and Goliath's secured research in Chicago... And number two, we needed you to be our hostage for future negotiations." Elise let out a slight laugh after her father finished his explanation.

"Negotiations? What good could I possibly be as a bargaining chip?" asked Jude, still refusing to look at Reginald.

Reginald was visibly filled with anticipation as Jude tried to work everything out. "That, Jude, is the exact question that I hoped you would ask. Why are you the center of all of our plans? Why are you the perfect hostage? Why are you the key to the comet and the vests and the research? I told you, only two people in the world know the answers to all of my problems."

"Leo and Goliath, yeah, I get that, but what do they have to do with me?" asked Jude, finally looking into Reginald's cold eyes.

"Everything, Jude. They have everything to do with you. I think you know them quite well." When Reginald said this, he raised his remote, pressed another button, and the baby blue sheets were lifted from the boxes that were on opposite sides of the large wooden desk. Under the sheets were two cages with a person in each. Jude looked from cage to cage.

The only words he could utter were: "Mom... Dad?"

Sixteen

November 9, 2393

It had been three years since Jude had seen his parents. However, for Olive Monroe, it had been fifteen since she had seen her children. It felt longer. Olive and Peter had fears that, because of their decisions, their children would face the consequences. Olive Monroe never dreamed it would look like this.

As she sat, chained underneath the baby blue sheets in her cage, she felt every ounce of pain that her son felt when he was shocked by Reginald. She wanted to rip the chains apart, to scream, to break free and save her son. But she knew, as Reginald had warned before Jude exited the elevator, any sound from the parents would make Jude face more anguish.

While Reginald and Elise spoke with Jude, Olive had closed her eyes and thought of every scenario possible to save her son. She had to be careful. The government was going to let a comet wipe out the world, and they dropped bombs on their citizens, but Reginald... No government had someone in its ranks as evil as him. She remained in deep thought, knowing that her husband, 10 feet away, was doing the exact same thing. She stayed still, knowing her time would come. Reginald was a problem long before she or her husband were captured. He would pay for the pain he'd caused in due time. The fact that he brought her kids into the equation, well, that would make things all the more swift. Besides, she thought, there was a secret that only she knew, and it was going to make all of the difference.

Still, there was nothing that could have prepared her for when the curtains would rise and she would see her son for the first time in so many years. She fought back tears as she saw her second-born, covered in blood and dirt. The pain that she heard was confirmed as she saw him sitting on the ground, eyes bloodshot, bruises on his neck and face, holes in the sleeves of his futuresque jacket that revealed deep wounds. She didn't know how he was still conscious.

Jude looked from parent to parent in disbelief until finally locking eyes with his mother. He fell backward from his knees. The shock mixed with the pain became almost unbearable. He wanted to run to them, but his legs had no more strength. The parents had to watch everything unfold and were, themselves, as helpless as Jude. They knew what Reginald wanted. They were the only ones who could fix the 200 vests and who knew where the comet had disappeared to. They knew what Reginald wanted, and they refused. They had anticipated all of the moves from Reginald. They knew how successful he had become in his endeavor to recover their files and the lost vests, of which he thought there only to be three.

Reginald never took his eyes off Jude. He kept his eyes locked so that he could watch each emotion cross the face of his newest prisoner. He watched as Jude's eyes widened and as he fell backward. The smirk on Reginald Beckett's face only grew wider. "What do you think, Olive?" said Reginald, still looking at Jude. "Still think my plan won't work?"

"Go fuck yourself," said Olive, her eyes burning into the back of Reginald's head.

"Watch yourself," ordered Elise, who was still standing only feet away and pointing her blaster right at Olive.

With the same gentle movements and composure Reginald had shown during his encounter with Jude, he stood up and raised his hands for civility. "Now, Olive, we talked about manners." In his right hand, he held the remote up and sent electricity through Jude's body once again. The Monroe parents had to watch from their cages as their son writhed on the ground. This time, Jude couldn't hold back the screams.

"Perhaps the Monroes still forget who has the power," said Reginald to his daughter as he walked slowly up to his desk while the last few jolts made their way through Jude's body. "Perhaps, we should continue to show them." Reginald held up the remote once again.

"No!" yelled Olive, pleading. "Enough. Enough." Reginald turned around and looked back to Jude, who was lying on the ground. Jude didn't have the strength to sit up. He simply remained on the ground, his eyes staring at his mother across the room.

"You see, Jude, I have nothing personal against you. You're just, how did I put it, the bargaining chip. Do I want to cause you pain? No, not really. But I have an agenda, and it will be completed without any more pause."

Reginald turned to his daughter and nodded. She set the blaster down on the desk and immediately walked around the table, grabbed Jude by the collar, and dragged him to one of the many glass panels that lined the room. With one hand, she lifted Jude to his feet, and she opened the panel with her other. A cold wind exploded into the room that made Elise shiver, and Jude became more awake. The other three in the room didn't budge. The Monroe parents knew Reginald wasn't bluffing. Reginald was calm as he seemingly held all of the cards.

"No more pause, Monroes. You know what I want. Tell me where the comet is and how to fix the vests, and my daughter won't throw your son to his death."

Jude wanted to scream, he wanted to say something, but with the pain and the blood that was pouring into his mouth, he was unable. The wind was loud as it filled the room, and yet it felt silent.

"Okay—" said Peter, speaking for the first time. He had been silent for days, processing everything. When he knew Jude was in the year 2393, his heart broke as he felt every bit of guilt possible. As he watched his son be tortured in front of his eyes, he couldn't bear even to speak. But, when his son was being held out a window by his collar nearly 100 stories high, he knew he'd give anything, even the end of the world, to save him.

Olive cut him off before he could say any more. "Okay, we'll help. But Jude has to be kept safe."

"I am a man of my word, am I not?" responded Reginald, not moving. The temperature in the room was dropping quickly. Jude still dangled out the window, and Reginald waited for the information he had worked so hard to retrieve. "One more time. Where is the comet? How do I fix the vests?"

"I can fix the vests. You need them to access the portal we sent the comet through." When Peter said this, Olive looked directly at her husband with sympathy. The two held eye contact for only a few seconds, but even so, they held a long conversation. Reginald walked over to the cage that held Peter.

"You'll activate the portal, you'll fix the vests. You'll bring back my comet," said Reginald. Each short sentence seemed to take forever as the cold became oppressive. Elise's strength while holding Jude was beginning to waver.

"All of it. I promise," said Peter, stuttering. "I am Goliath. I can do it."

Reginald took his time as he looked Peter up and down. He then looked over at Olive, back to Jude, and finally back to Peter. "Deal. You'll have a week to fix a vest that we will test out on your wife over there. In the meantime, we'll keep your son downstairs. If we don't retrieve the comet by the end of the week, I'll throw him out the window myself."

With that, he nodded to his daughter, who threw Jude back from the window and into the room. He picked himself up onto all fours. Elise walked away from the window, leaving it open to allow for a little extra pain. She knew Leo and Goliath would remain in those cages for the night. Reginald pushed a button on his remote, and ten guards entered the room.

"We'll leave some guards for you and we'll bring you a vest to work on. Of course, if you try anything funny with any vest, you know what will happen to Jude," said Reginald, beginning to leave.

"Reginald," said Olive, her voice shaking not from the cold, but from the pain she felt for her son. "Reginald, what if we said we could do it in two days. We could fix the vests in two days."

Reginald turned around, the smirk grew on his face once again. "Two days, eh?"

"Maybe less. Just let me hug my son. Please, I haven't seen him in 15 years." Jude's head popped up. It was the quickest motion he had made since entering the room nearly half an hour prior. For him, it had been three unbearable years, but for them, fifteen...

Reginald paused, then looked to Elise, who was shaking her head.

"Please," pleaded Olive. "We know how this works. We're never going to see him again. Just let me hug him goodbye. Please."

Reginald looked at Olive, who was staring straight into his eyes.

"No. Dad, no. They don't deserve it," said Elise, moving her gaze directly at Olive.

Reginald looked at his daughter and then at Olive. Everyone in the room could see on his face that he was calculating something. "Two days?"

"Two days," said Olive, tears rolling down her cheeks.

"Two days or I will kill your son."

"You won't have to. I promise."

Reginald looked to Peter to see that he understood the deal being made without his input.

"We can do it. Please, let my wife have this," said Peter, looking at Olive.

"Fine. You have sixty seconds," said Reginald, who stood still but motioned to his guard to unlock her cage. Elise couldn't believe it, but she stayed still, only feet away from Jude.

Olive rushed to her son and wrapped herself around him. He was almost too weak to even lift his arm. She kissed his cheek, which was bloody and sweaty. It didn't matter. She was holding her son.

What strength Jude had left in his legs finally vanished. For a brief moment, he finally had his parents back. Despite what was to come, his heroes were alive, and he was being held by his mom. He fell into her as his strength gave out, and she didn't budge. She only pulled him closer.

The wind from the window picked up and was louder and colder than ever. Olive whispered something in Jude's ear. "Only nod if the answer is yes. Do you still have the undershirt on that you wore during the explosion?"

Jude almost didn't hear her; the wind was so loud, and she said it so quietly. He didn't move.

"Jude. Nod if you still have the shirt on."

"Enough. That's it. Two days begins now," said Reginald, motioning to his guards to split up Olive and Jude. Before separating from their hug, however, Jude gave the slightest nod which Olive felt on her collarbone. Elise took a step closer to make sure they separated immediately. Olive maintained eye contact with her child, and for the first time in 15 years, she smiled at him.

"I love you," she said as the guards began moving in to grab Jude. "We are so proud of you."

"So proud," yelled Peter from his cage twenty feet away.

Elise put her hand on Olive's shoulder to lead her back to the cage. Olive never took her eyes away from her son. As Elise began to push her backwards, Olive grabbed a thermal detonator from Elise's waistband and pushed her away, causing separation only for a moment. A moment is all she needed as she grabbed Jude by the breast of his jacket, armed the detonator, put it in his pocket, and threw him out the window he had been dangling from only moments before.

Jude quickly plummeted from the top story of the prison. The cold wind crashing against his face was deafening, and he could only slightly hear the ticking of the detonator in his pocket. It ticked away, each beeping noise getting closer together. His hands were frozen, he was in pain, and the ground was getting closer and closer as he tried to reach into his pocket and remove the grenade. The beeping intensified, and he fought to get to it. He never did.

The detonator exploded sixty floors into his descent. He felt the air get knocked out of him, and everything went black. All of a sudden, Jude felt like he was flying sideways and upwards. Everything was warm, but he couldn't see anything. He knew he was still alive, he knew the detonator did not kill him, but as he felt his body moving in hyper speed, he couldn't comprehend what was happening. Still, upwards in total darkness, he flew. The only thing he had time to think was the one question his mother asked: "'Do you still have the undershirt on that you wore during the explosion?'"

Jude felt himself falling again, this time at a much greater speed, like a bullet from a gun. Finally, light became visible beneath him, and he crashed down toward it. He looked to where the light was coming, and it seemed miles away as he barrelled toward it. The closer he came to the source of the light, the more he realized it was shaped like an oval. Most surprising, on the other end, the lights that were breaking through were definitely city lights. He crashed through the oval doorway and was immediately surrounded by skyscrapers whose lights were only a blur. There was a warm breeze in the air that completely contrasted from the cold winter air he had felt only a minute ago.

He continued to fall as he heard what sounded like the roar of an engine seemingly falling right next to him. He felt a hand grab his arm and pull him into what seemed like one of Elise's hover cars. He was thrown into the seat next to the driver, and they sped away, weaving between the tall city buildings.

Jude's vision was blurred, and he couldn't see anything. He turned to look at the person who had interrupted his fall, but he couldn't make it out. Slowly, he blinked his vision back, but he couldn't believe what he was seeing. There, looking back at him and into his eyes with her unmistakably mysterious smile: Sarah.

"Hello, dear," she said, one hand holding the steering column and the other cupping Jude's face. "Did you miss me?"

PART II

AWAKENING

Seventeen

July 16, 2019

H azel Monroe sat in 7A, a window seat, having boarded her early morning Chicago-bound plane only a few minutes prior. Even though the folks at NASA offered to book her a hotel room for 'as long as she needed,' she knew the best thing to do was to get back home as soon as she could. Putting off going home would only make it more difficult, she thought.

She appreciated Tom Metzlebaum for reaching out personally to offer condolences and to secure her a flight on the plane she was sitting in. She also appreciated his assurances that he was only a phone call away– should she need anything. Still, his words, just like those in the texts and emails from friends and colleagues, had yet to register.

As she looked out of the window of a 737 jet, she was lost in thought and didn't even realize when someone sat down in 7C, the seat right next to her. She was too busy thinking about Jude and what his last few days must have been like.

"Hi there," the person sitting next to her said quickly, and Hazel offered a gentle smile as she turned back to the window to resume her thoughts. She wasn't prepared to allow herself to think of Jude's final moments. Be strong, she repeatedly said to herself.

She focused on the last few phone calls she had shared with Jude. Did she spend too much time talking about herself or Chicago? Did she pry too hard when he would subtly bring up Captain Lazerous? Did she tell him she loved him enough? She stared at the outside of the Orlando International Airport as if she would find the answers to her questions written on its outer walls.

"The airport is huge, isn't it? I've never flown here before," said 7C, trying to create some small talk.

"Yeah. It is," said Hazel, trying to be polite but completely uninterested in a conversation. 7C nodded his head and looked back up the aisle as Hazel went back to her thoughts. Did she–

"So, where are you from?" 7C, again.

Hazel turned her head back to the stranger once more. Yet again, she offered him a kind smile. "Chicago. I'm headed home."

"That's cool. That is cool," said 7C, pausing as if he were waiting for her to ask him the same question in return. When she didn't and turned back to the window instead, he spoke up once again. "... family in Chicago as well?"

Hazel looked at the man sitting next to her. He wasn't reading the context clues she was clearly sending. He wore jeans, a white t-shirt, and a Miami Marlins hat that was made to look worn, but was clearly new. She didn't feel like having a conversation, and she definitely wasn't prepared for the stranger's last question.

"Yeah, they're there..." Hazel paused. "... well, they used to be." Tears flooded her eyes when the answer came out, and she started to unbuckle her seatbelt when the captain of the plane gave orders for the flight attendants to prepare the cabin for departure. She looked out the window and wiped her eyes on the cuff of her sweatshirt that she only wore when she traveled on planes.

The stranger allowed her to have the moment to herself. He had clearly asked the wrong question. Hazel calmed herself down by going back to the questions she had been thinking to herself before the small talk from 7C.

Jude had asked about Chicago, he wanted to know how the city was and how his sister was. Jude was clearly rolling his eyes by the last time he responded to the words 'I love you and I am proud of you.' Thinking back, she wouldn't have done anything differently with their last few conversations. Would she have done anything differently with signing him up for the entire thing to begin with? Hazel knew she would be asking that question for a very long time.

7C began to fidget in his seat. "These seats are always so uncomfortable, and I swear they make us wait a long time on purpose to get going. Some weird power thing." He looked to Hazel, who didn't say anything in return, still holding back some tears, though none were falling. "Sorry, I hate to complain. I sound like this old friend of mine." The man turned and looked up the aisle again, and Hazel was allowed to return to the window and to her thoughts.

The plane began to pull away from the terminal, and the sudden jolt made Hazel grab her armrest. The plane began revving its engines, and Hazel immediately started having flashbacks to yesterday's launch. She began to feel claustrophobic. She was breathing heavily. The plane moved and bounced for what seemed like an eternity before finally turning onto the runway. The engines were still revving as the captain prepared for takeoff. Hazel looked to the front of the plane, thinking about how her brother must have felt as he waited for his own takeoff only yesterday. A bead of sweat rolled down her temple.

"Nervous flier?" asked 7C, this time clearly trying to distract Hazel from the takeoff. She welcomed his words for the first time since they met a few minutes prior. She nodded. "Nothing wrong with that. It's a weird science. I'll be honest, my last flight... it was rough." He raised his eyebrows and tilted his head to Hazel. "Like, really rough, but you know what, here I am. Because flying is never as bad as it seems. Being nervous is alright. I'm a pilot, and I still get nervous sometimes."

Hazel paused her near hyperventilation and turned toward 7C. "Pilot?" She was still breathing heavily.

"Yep. Been flying a long time. I think it's not so much the flying as the relinquishing of power that most people are scared of."

"Oh, it's definitely the flying," said Hazel, who actually laughed when she finished her sentence.

The stranger laughed with her as the plane began to move, and Hazel's laugh turned into a long, deep breath. "Now, listen, okay, he's just about to put the throttle down, and the wheels are going to leave the runway just a few seconds after. Totally normal."

7C began narrating the takeoff, and to Hazel's surprise, she found it slightly comforting. Having a pilot explain the procedure was almost therapeutic and certainly a welcome distraction from her thoughts of her brother's launch.

"... so now the wheels are going to come in and the flaps will be lifted to avoid any extra drag." Immediately following the stranger saying this, Hazel could hear the wheels retract.

"... and if I'm not mistaken, we're going to bank to the right in a few seconds. Be prepared, it's going to be a hard one." A few seconds later, the plane indeed banked hard to the right to set a course for the northwest. Hazel turned to the stranger. She couldn't believe it, but her fears were assuaged. He narrated everything that the plane would do on its way to its cruising altitude.

After a while, Hazel didn't even realize that she hadn't thought about the plane or even yesterday's launch for quite some time. She just listened to this stranger next to her narrate the flight and then tell some stories of his own. She was apprehensive at first while this person was talking, but then she figured that maybe some stranger's kindness was what she needed at that moment. She sat back and listened, and her pain subsided just for a bit. Besides, she thought 7C's stories were very interesting.

"...and in the morning, I couldn't help but think that I had forgotten something."

When the man finished his story, he and Hazel let out a loud laugh that turned the heads of the people sitting in the row in front of them. Hazel lifted her complimentary bottle of water as if to say cheers to the man sitting next to her.

"Thanks for the stories. They're helping more than I could ever say," said Hazel, as 7C raised his complimentary bottle to tap hers.

"Glad I can help. Very glad. Oh, man, I'm so rude, I never asked your name." He checked his wristwatch that, like the hat, looked faded but was brand new.

"Hazel. Hazel Monroe. It's nice to meet you."

"Hazel, huh. Like your eyes... which are stunning by the way."

Hazel laughed for a second. She'd cried through the night and morning, but with the stories and a little bit of charm, she was slightly warming up to the stranger's distraction. "Well, I don't know about that. But, it is a pleasure to meet a pilot such as yourself. And you are... captain..?" she asked, holding out a hand to shake.

"Link. Just Link. But trust me, the pleasure is all mine."

Eighteen

July 15, 2019

Sarah Lazerous parked her hover car in the exact location she was given by Leo. She made it there with only a minute to spare. Like Jude, she had a terribly long journey to make it to where she was now sitting: 400 feet above the ground in downtown St. Louis, Missouri, just above the old city courthouse. She hit a small green button on her steering column to make the hover car invisible and began to wait.

Sarah could see nearby buildings illuminated in the colors red, white, and blue. United States flags, such as the ones on top of nearby buildings or the one in front of the old courthouse, were at half-mast. Though it had been six months for Sarah since the explosion of *The Audacity*, it had only been a few hours for the world below. A few hours, a few months, it didn't matter; she still couldn't shake the sound that the rocket made when it exploded. The thought, while she looked at the symbols of unity and condolences around her, sent shivers down her spine.

Six months felt a lot longer to Sarah. The trials she faced, the objectives she had to accomplish for Leo and Goliath, and watching them get caught by Reginald's St. Louis Resistance... it all took a toll on her. Still, six months later, she couldn't help but be excited that, if Leo's plan worked, if the Houdini Vest built into Jude's undershirt was calculated correctly, she would be with her old friend once again. As she prepared to see him for the first time in what felt like forever, she couldn't deny the butterflies in her stomach.

She checked her wristwatch as the numbers changed from 11:29 to 11:30, and she immediately looked to the sky. There, breaking through the light pollution, Sarah saw it, directly above, a perfect oval. She had seen an oval like this only a few times: ten years before the launch, immediately following the explosion, and about six hours ago. She prepared herself. Leo had told her that Jude's fall would not be graceful.

He broke through the oval, flailing his arms and legs like he was trying to catch something. He plummeted toward the courthouse below. Sarah accelerated the hover car to meet him. She changed directions quickly as Jude fell, and she matched his falling speed. She reached out and grabbed his arm, pulling him into the car with only 150 feet to spare from the top of the courthouse dome.

"Hello, dear," Sarah said to Jude as she accelerated the pod forward and weaved through nearby skyscrapers. "Did you miss me?"

Jude blinked his eyes repeatedly at Sarah. He simply could not believe what he was seeing. In the last sixty seconds, Jude was thrown out of a window by his mother, evaded yet another explosion, clearly flew through another portal, and found himself sitting next to Sarah. Sarah, over whom he had grieved the last few days.

Sarah smiled at him and gave him a few moments to collect himself. She navigated the hover car to the Mississippi River and traversed it to the North, traveling at a speed much faster than Jude and Elise had traveled from the Arch to the prison in her hover car.

"What the hell is going on?" Jude asked, finally able to speak. He hadn't taken his eyes off of Sarah. "You—you're—"

"I'm alive, Jude. And so are you. Not easy to stay alive in 2393, nice work."

Jude blinked again at Sarah, still unconvinced that he wasn't hallucinating. He had wondered a few times over the last few days that if it were possible for him to survive the explosion, maybe someone else did, too. He chalked it up to wishful thinking, but here Sarah was, some lights from the outskirts of St. Louis reflected in her eyes as she turned her head and looked at him.

He continued to look at her, and he had to laugh. Everything started to click, and to his surprise, despite everything he just lived through in the last few hours, despite the pain that remained from his beating by the guards and the electricity from Reginald, he felt joy. He grabbed Sarah and tightly hugged her. Sarah chuckled when he pulled her in, causing the hover car to slightly shift position.

"I'm so glad you're okay. I don't get it. I don't know what the hell is going on, but damn it, I am just so glad to see you."

Sarah allowed the hover car to pilot itself north as she hugged him back. "I'm so glad to see you, too. It's been so long, and I have to be honest when I say that I did worry about you."

Jude pulled away from the hug and still looked into Sarah's eyes, bright blue, even though he'd have sworn they were brown when he last saw her. That was a lifetime ago. "I know," he said, "this past week has seemed like a year."

Sarah knew that Jude had only been a few days separated from the explosion. Leo had planned it that way. She paused as she looked back at him. She had wondered, when she thought about the reunion with Jude, if she would tell him the difference in time they had spent apart. She knew he would be processing more than he could handle. Still, she thought that he should know. "Jude, it's been six months for me," she finally said.

Jude became exasperated as he looked at her and digested her words. "Six months?"

Sarah nodded, watching his reaction.

"Sarah," he started, completely in disbelief. "Where were you?"

"I was a little less than six months before you showed up in 2393."

"Seriously? What were you doing?"

Sarah took a second to think of the answer to Jude's question. She had thought through this conversation numerous times, but now, being here with him, her mind blanked.

"I had a lot to do. Jude, you need to know something, and this is going to be a lot to take in, but you need to know that all of this, every bit of it, was in motion well before *The Audacity* explosion."

Jude nodded as he took in Sarah's words. She waited for him to react, but he didn't. "I kind of figured. Someone said something along the same lines about an hour ago." Sarah continued a course north on the Mississippi. The pair floated 400 feet above the river.

"This plan... You knew who I was then? Or were you in the same boat as me when you woke up in the future?"

Sarah looked back at Jude; the smile she had only moments ago had vanished. "Jude, I knew who you were. I knew Leo and— I knew your parents."

"I— Why didn't you say anything? I mean... those moments we shared... Sarah, those meant something to–"

"–they meant something to me, too," said Sarah, cutting Jude off. "Jude, I came here a long time ago to accomplish a mission set by Leo and Goliath. You were only a name. But, I saw you on the CNN interview... and—" Sarah trailed off.

"Sarah, you don't have t–"

"'I guess this is me, deciding that I want to live my life,'" quoted Sarah, still looking at Jude. "It wasn't until I heard you say that... It wasn't until then that I truly believed in the mission."

Jude thought about what Sarah was saying and about his own quote. "You know, I really thought they selected me bec–"

"Jude, no matter what, you were the right choice. Whatever led to you being selected for that launch, that was you. As far as I'm aware, both sides of this battle were playing with the cards that were already dealt. You being selected for *The Audacity* was a card already dealt when we decided to play."

"Wait a second," said Jude, starting to really pick up on the bigger picture. "Both sides. Was there someone else on the rocket involved besides us?"

"Link. Link's playing ball for the other guys."

"Where is he?" asked Jude, who was unfazed when Sarah expected more of a betrayed reaction from him.

"Well, that's a good question. We–"

"How do you not know? I mean—"

"Jude. This has been a chess match that has lasted a very long time. We're trying. I was chasing him down over the last few months. He came back here. We're going to find him."

"I want in. I want to find him. I'm tired of these people screwing with my family."

"I was hoping you'd say that. But, Jude, about your family... I believe he came back here for your sister."

"No," said Jude, finally showing some more emotion. "Hazel's all alone. We have to get to her. How much of a head start does Link have on us?"

"That's where we're headed now. We're headed to Chicago, where she has a ticket to fly in tomorrow. We only technically just blew up a few hours ago. It's still July 15th. Well, 16th soon. We will get to her, Jude."

There was a pause. Sarah saw Jude clenching his fists, and there was obvious pain on his face. They were miles away from any city at this point, and the moon crashed through the front window of the hover car. Sarah could see the dried blood that formed three crooked lines on the side of his face. Silence filled the small space separating the two, and she could see Jude calculating. She could only imagine the amount of questions he must be contemplating.

Jude finally unclenched his fists and slightly relaxed as he leaned back in his seat. He let out a painful sigh. His ribs felt cracked. He rolled his head against the headrest on his seat and looked at Sarah as she drove the hover car, not saying a word and allowing him time to work through his thoughts. He finally spoke.

"Okay, I believe you. We will get to her. We have to get to her." Looking around, he noticed for the first time that the pod had its invisibility setting engaged. Jude paused and took in a deep breath as he acclimated himself to the reality that he was still becoming used to. "I want to know everything."

"Tell me where to begin," said Sarah, who looked back to Jude. Her smile had returned, but it was laced with sympathy.

"I don't understand how I am even here," said Jude, looking down, "I'm not wearing a vest. Wha–"

"Your parents are pretty smart. It's not the vests that get people from one place to another. It's the technology that matters. They can build a Houdini Vest out of anything. Even a t-shirt like the one you have on right now."

Jude looked at the shirt he had worn over the last few days. "They really are geniuses," he said as he continued to look down. "So you knew them, then. My parents."

"Leo and Goliath is how I knew them. They knew my mom."

"How?"

"My mom was the person who helped your parents design something called a Houdini Vest. My mom's pseudonym was The Sphinx." Jude's jaw dropped, and Sarah immediately saw that he had heard the name before. "I guess your knowledge of the future is a lot more advanced than I thought it might be."

"If that's your mom, then you're a v—"

"I'm Volgen, Jude. Yeah, I'm an alien." Sarah laughed as she said this as more of a joke to break the tension than anything else. She paused and let it sink in as Jude looked out the windshield and back to Sarah. Clearly, with his reactions so far in the conversation, he had seen plenty in the time since they were last together.

There had been a lot for Jude to grasp in the last few days. He couldn't deny the future, the portals, the vests, the Shadows, but aliens, he still struggled with. Yet, he couldn't deny that when he pulled away from the kiss with Sarah the night before the launch, he gazed into her dark brown eyes. As she gazed upon him now with her cool blue eyes, he accepted her words as truth.

"What the hell is this world that I've been living in?" asked Jude, who, to Sarah's surprise, was slightly laughing. He smiled at Sarah, who expected him to feel like he had been fooled, but instead looked at her with the same smile that he had before he locked his visor on *The Audacity*. "An alien, huh?"

"I'm still hot," laughed Sarah, shrugging her shoulders.

"Not denying that one bit," laughed Jude, as the atmosphere in the car became light for the first time since they were reunited. "But, if it's true what I hear, y'know, that you can change your appearances, well the–"

"Oh, you are not suggesting my attractiveness is fabricated, are you?"

The two continued to laugh as Jude looked Sarah up and down as she sat next to him. "Like I said, no denial. No denial." Jude still gazed at Sarah, who was blushing. "Volgens, from a different planet, they can change their appearances—"

"All of this is true," said Sarah, as she looked to Jude and changed the color of her eyes from blue and back to the brown she had when she first met him. Jude reacted, more impressed than shocked. "What else were you told about us?"

"Oh, you know, just that your people waited in the wings for the comet to strike and that you guys, with the help of my parents, were going to let the world burn so that you could have it when the humans were incinerated."

The mood immediately shifted. Jude's attempt to relay Elise's words in a light-hearted way severely missed the mark. Sarah's eyes immediately shifted back to blue when Jude finished speaking.

"We tried to help. My mother tried to help. I lost her because we tried to help." Jude eyed Sarah; it was now her turn to clench her fists. She punched the steering column. "I came here to do what my mother would have wanted."

"Now *I'm* listening. Tell me what really happened," said Jude, who put his hand on Sarah's fist, and she relaxed her grip.

"I was only a kid, y'know, when the news of the collision was broken to the world. But, my people, the Volgens, we knew about it for a long time. Generations. And yeah, it's why we chose to come to Earth, but not for the reasons she told you. For millions of years, my people harnessed the kinetic energy those vests use to power things for their day-to-day living. We never used portals. They were around our world, but we were responsible. Still, something came through. Our planet, Volgeria, was overrun with darkness, and the Shadows destroyed everything. We fled to Earth, the closest inhabitable planet for us. When we got here, we knew the comet was centuries away. We also knew we could help. We did our part. Centuries later, when the comet was only 100 years away, we told the humans in charge, and they tried to hide the comet from its people. The governments terminated education and any space agency that existed. Still, the Volgens worked to help and waited for the day when we could help the people of Earth survive the collision. That's why mom went to your parents. When they were only given the materials to save a few humans, they went from putting the technology into the hands of people who would use it for evil to putting the technology toward stopping the comet."

Jude processed everything as he looked out the window to the ground below. It was just then that he realized how fast they were traveling. He looked to the sky where a comet was currently hurling in his direction. "How did they stop the comet?"

"They opened a portal and sent it somewhere else," said Sarah, a tear formed in her left eye.

"Sarah, where did they send it?"

"Jude, they sacrificed my planet so that yours would survive. The way portals work, they build a connection from one place to another.

They had to destroy the comet, so they landed it in Volgeria. Volgens weren't here to take your planet. We sacrificed ours so you could keep yours."

Sarah looked to Jude and watched him work through what she had just said to him. She expected him to ask more questions, or to comment, or to even tell a poorly timed joke. Instead, he took her hand again and just looked into her eyes, which were now brown again.

"I'm so very sorry." He continued to hold her hand, but didn't say anything else.

Tears rolled down Sarah's cheeks. "I never saw my mom again after the comet disappeared. Someone had to open the portal. It took her with it."

Silence filled the car yet again. Jude didn't know what to say, so he didn't say anything. He knew that the pain of losing loved ones doesn't just subside. It's there, and it stays. Sarah turned the hover car slightly to the right to head northeast.

"You get it, though. You lost your parents," Sarah said without looking at Jude, focusing on the steering column.

"Yeah bu–" Jude started, but was cut off.

"She's not gone as long as we keep doing what she truly wanted. The resistance wants to go back in time, find the comet, and put it into the Earth rather than Volgeria."

"Wouldn't that save your mother if they saved the comet from going into your home planet?"

"It doesn't work like that. Events can be altered, but lives can't. Once peoples' lives end, it's over. The event might be over or changed or whatever, but the people never returned. The Houdini Vests work when the energy is harnessed from an escaped death. When a person actually dies, that's it. Their timeline is done. Nothing can change that. Volgens tried that very thing, and that is what created the portal that Shadows came through. My people had the energy harnessing down to a science, but they unlocked something terrible when they tried to use it for something more. According to your parents, the Shadows came to Earth through the very portal that took the comet away in the first place. That's how the Shadows got here. When someone messes with the timeline of a human and brings them back from the dead, the Shadows also come through a portal that disrupts that timeline."

"I don't understand," said Jude, rubbing the back of his head, "if Shadows come through portals that disrupt someone's timeline, then shouldn't they come when every vest is activated?"

"From what we know, Shadows only come through portals when people who are dead are brought back to life. Technically, if someone escapes death, they never died to begin with. So, it's like their timeline was always set for them to survive anyway. That's why the people on Earth can live on, and my mother can't."

"So, if the resistance finds the comet..."

"Then my mother died for nothing." Sarah's jaw tightened as she said this. Jude could tell that, though all of this information was painful for her, she needed someone to hear her. Now, it was Jude's turn to let Sarah have a moment to collect herself. She knew what he was doing, and she turned to him, wiped her tears away, and let out the slightest giggle. "Talk about baggage, amiright?"

Jude busted up laughing. "Yeah, good thing this plane doesn't charge extra for too much carry-on luggage."

"You're such a dork, anyone tell you that?"

"Pretty much daily. And, not for nothing, but I believe I have sole privileges over 'amiright.'"

"Whatever you say." Laughter returned as the two flew through the night, traversing through the upper part of central Illinois. "I know you have more questions about Volgens."

"I mean, yeah, they... *you* seem like good people, only trying to escape, so you guys became stowaways, you did your part, but were still left to die like the rest of the humans. Honestly, though, I guess I'm still stuck on the changing appearances thing."

Sarah laughed. "Yeah, it's weird."

"I guess my question is, what do you look like? Like Volgens, what do they look like?"

"Oh, it's very sexy," said Sarah, making no attempt to seem serious.

"I'm picturing like an Octopus... You guys look like octopuses, don't you?"

"Yeah, but like sexy octopuses."

"No. Shut up. You're lying. I wasn't right." Jude paused as Sarah let him think about it too long. "Was I?"

"No, you nerd, we look similar, just different. I can't explain it."

Jude paused and then smiled at Sarah. "Is it intrusive to ask if I can see?"

"I'm not a zoo animal," laughed Sarah, loving the fact of having something to lord over Jude's head. He laughed back. "It's not that different. But, yes, we can change our looks."

"That does seem ethically questionable..."

"Yeah, says the guy who made out with an octopus."

Jude paused and then broke out in chuckling yet again. "Yeah, okay, I'll believe it when I see it." He was finally thankful to get the answers he so desperately needed. It all seemed fantastical to him, but so did everything from the last few days. He thought about how these answers affected what he knew of the future. Then he thought about the only true interaction he had with Volgens. He paused as the images of the camps came back into his mind.

"What is it?" asked Sarah, feeling the new vibe.

"I saw the camps," said Jude, putting his head down. "It was the worst thing I'd ever seen."

It was now Sarah's turn to take Jude's hand. "I know," she said, "I never understood why so many allowed themselves to be captured... and when they continued hunting for them... Jude, the world you woke up in is sick, and there's so much that needs to be saved, but it's like Leo– your mom told me: the comet is the greatest threat to all things living on the Earth. We can't save those who are eviscerated.

So, we solve one problem at a time. The resistance is moving to kill everyone and we have to stop them."

"Okay, so we get to Chicago. We save Hazel. We save my parents. We save the planet. Am I leaving anything out?"

"Nope. That pretty much covers it,` said Sarah, still holding Jude's hand.

"All in a day's work. Step one, Hazel."

"We already have someone looking after Hazel. I know you're worried. But, she'll be alright until we get to her tomorrow."

"Just how many of us is it against how many of them?"

"Well, we have you, and me, and your parents, plus one, against... Well, against an entire resistance."

Jude looked to the sky as if he were doing some quick addition. "Seems even."

"I think it's pretty lopsided with the Monroes on our side," said Sarah, more serious than anything.

"Just a couple kids of genius scientists going to battle."

"We can do anything. It's in our blood." Sarah smiled to herself as she said this. Jude went to say something else, but stopped himself. "What is it? Go ahead, ask."

"Well... it's just—" Jude stuttered, trying to get his thoughts out. "I feel like my parents are total strangers. Sarah, it's difficult to know what to believe anymore or who to trust."

"I know you have questions about them, but they should probably answer those... but let me ask you this. Your parents, they were great your whole life, right? They loved you? You loved them?"

"They were amazing. They were the best."

"Then that's all that matters," said Sarah, looking back to Jude with a smile on her face. "They're good people. There's not an answer to any of your questions that changes that. Finding out my mom was The Sphinx... I thought it changed everything, but I was wrong. It only made me want to be a better person. That's why I decided to join the fight and help Leo and Goliath."

"Just tell me this. Why is it just them... us against the resistance?"

Sarah nodded. She clearly believed that this was the right question for Jude to be asking. "You know, when we lost mom and the comet vanished, and they started headhunting, they wanted your parents more than anyone. Even the Volgens. Your parents ruined a lot of people's plans. They did what they wanted to accomplish, and then they left and went somewhere in the 1980s or something. But when Reginald and the resistance put their plan into action and sent Link to your time, that's when your parents were told, and that's when—"

"–that's when they had their accident."

"Exactly. They went back to save the world from the comet once and for all. Which is where I got involved and came here to your time. I think they knew they would be captured. They knew Link was sent here to capture you and your sister, too. We knew Link would some- how find himself on *The Audacity* with you. That's why I was there and I'm here now."

"Elise called you guys guardian angels," said Jude, more to himself than to Sarah.

Sarah looked down at Jude's hand, which was still lying in hers, and looked into his eyes as Chicago became faintly visible in the dis- tance. "We prefer to just be called friends."

"I can live with that," said Jude, smiling back at Sarah.

* * *

Using the moonlight for assistance, Sarah parked the hover car in Hazel's backyard. Jude hopped out and lifted a stone by the back door to get the spare key. He wasn't surprised to see the TV left on. Hazel, living alone, always thought leaving the TV on would make people believe that someone was home. He wondered about where she was. He knew she was somewhere, dealing with the events of the day. There was no way she was sleeping. He couldn't imagine what she was going through. What she watched, only hours ago, no one should have to live through anything like that.

And then he thought of something that he realized he should have thought of sooner: when she gets home tomorrow, how will he ex- plain any of it? Jude stood in the middle of Hazel's living room as this thought dawned on him. Sarah walked into the room to join him.

Reading his expression, there was only one thing he could be thinking. "Thinking about how you're going to explain any of this to your sister?"

"I literally died a few hours ago. Her only brother. I'm worried she'll have a heart attack when she opens the door. What am I supposed to do? Sit in the chair and say, 'hey sis! Good to see you!' when she walks in?"

"I don't see any other options," said Sarah, walking up to Jude, sympathy on her face.

"We always pick each other up at the airport. Bu–"

"Bad idea, anyway, with Link out there. He's bad news, Jude. He's a big part of the reason why the resistance was given St. Louis."

"Did he know who you were during the training?"

"No. It helped that I was here for nearly a decade before launch."

Jude hesitated; he had hundreds more questions, but he'd had enough answers for the night. He had so much to process as it was. There was only one thing left that needed to be answered. "You're sure... You're sure Hazel is safe until she gets here?"

"I've got my best man on it," said Sarah, hoping to see relief on Jude's face. It didn't come.

Jude sat down on his sister's couch and rubbed his face in his hands. Sarah sat next to him and put her hand on his thigh.

"Look, why don't you get some sleep. You must be exhausted. It's going to be okay, and there's nothing more to do right now." Sarah looked deep into Jude's eyes. They were bloodshot. She offered him her hand and kissed his cheek.

Jude put his fingers to where Sarah had just kissed. He sighed and looked at her. "You're not too bad for a weird creature from a distant galaxy."

"I know. Neither are you."

Their eyes lingered for a moment before Sarah grabbed a throw blanket from off the back of the couch and threw it onto their laps in one quick movement. Jude's head bobbed, and he rested it on Sarah's shoulder. He was asleep before he knew it.

* * *

Jude woke up at noon the following morning, still under the throw blanket on the couch. Sarah walked into the room with a plate of bacon and eggs.

"Good morning!" she said with a smile on her face. She put the plate on the side table next to Jude. "I let you sleep in. I can only imagine when you last had a decent sleep. I know it wasn't this past week or the week of the launch. How do you feel?"

"Hungover," said Jude, looking around the room for a clock. "You cooked?"

"I'm a nervous cook. Today has the potential to be really long." Sarah rocked back and forth on her heels.

"...wow, thanks. It smells incredible. I don't remember the last time I had real food. What time is it?"

"Noon... Eat up, your sister should be home shortly."

Jude felt too nervous to want to eat, but still, the last sit-down meal was the food he choked down, cooked by Elise. He knew he had to eat. He had no clue what he was going to say to Hazel when she walked through the front door. How could she possibly understand? He finished his eggs when Sarah walked back into the room. "Alright, she's here. You ready?"

Jude, somehow still surprised, stood up quickly and looked out Hazel's front window and saw a taxi. The driver quickly got out and grabbed Hazel's things from the cab trunk. Finally, she slowly stepped out of the car and onto the curb. She held a wad of tissues in her hand. Her flying sweatshirt was tied around her waist. The driver handed her the bags, she handed him a tip, and the cab was soon gone. She stood motionless as she stared at the front of her house. She was clearly working up the courage to approach the door.

Hazel took two steps, her hand was on the handle of her rolling suitcase. She stopped yet again as tears poured down her face. She fell to her knees. The suitcase fell by her side as she brought her hands to her face. Jude took a step to go outside, and Sarah put her hand on his shoulder. He looked back at her, and his face was also drenched with tears. She let go of him, but as he turned to go to the door, Hazel was already making her way up the stairs.

She entered the house as Jude stood only feet away. She closed the door, wiping her face, and set her bags down. She was completely unaware that she wasn't alone. Sarah stood a few feet behind Jude as Hazel lifted her head and saw her brother.

Jude wanted to say something. Anything. The words just didn't come. Hazel gasped. "What?" was the only thing she could conjure.

Jude still looked for words, but none were found. Tears crashed down his face as he stepped forward and took his sister in his arms and hugged her. The emotional anguish he had suffered over the last few days came flooding, and he wept in her arms. Hazel couldn't believe it. She had walked into the room and saw the impossible. She had prayed from the moment of the explosion for a miracle, and her wish had come true. As her arms wrapped around Jude, he felt real. She was certain she wasn't dreaming, but she didn't understand. For the moment, though, it didn't matter. Her brother was there, and the pair cried together for minutes.

Sarah, content with the interaction, kept watch out the window. Still, she looked at the siblings, holding each other and was glad for Hazel. Sarah wished a miracle like this could have happened for her and her mother. At least these two Monroes could share it. Hazel finally pulled away from Jude. She looked at him, and her knees became weak. This couldn't be reality, she thought.

"I just– I just don't get it. You– the rocket– I was there... in Florida yesterday. Wha–"

"I know." Jude took his sister's hands and walked her to the couch. "Hazel, there's so much I have to tell you, and it's going to sound crazy."

"Did you somehow get off the rocket? Why didn't you call? Wh–"

"Hazel, I was on the rocket. That—"

"Jude. Then you died yesterday. Died. The rocket exploded. That was you." Tears filled Hazel's eyes again, and Jude hugged her tightly. "I don't understand."

"Yes, that happened. I know. I was there, but I lived and I'm here now."

"That's impossible. I've lost it. This isn't happening." Hazel stood up and paced around the room. She pointed at Jude. "You can't be here right now. I sat on bleachers yesterday and I watch–"

"Everything you saw was real, and everything you're seeing is still real," said Jude, standing up and meeting Hazel at eye level. "Hazel, listen to me. You're not crazy. I am here, and I can explain. But what I will tell you will be what sounds crazy."

Hazel continued to pace and, after a few laps back and forth on the living room carpet, she sat back down on the couch. "Okay. Clearly, you're here, so something magical must have happened. If I've lost it, I've lost it; so basically, there's nothing you can say now that can truly be too crazy. If you're here... then..."

Jude looked to Sarah, who shrugged her shoulders, unsure of what to say, but offered a supportive smile. "Hazel. You're right. Something crazy happened. But I'm here now."

"Tell me. I'll listen... Of course, I'll listen. It's you," said Hazel, trying to smile but absolutely unsure of what to feel.

Jude took her hands and looked at Sarah and then into his sister's eyes. "Hazel, mom and dad are alive."

Hazel stood up. "Nope. Nevermind. This is definitely all in my head."

Sarah finally stepped forward. "Hazel, he's telling the truth." It was only then that Hazel realized there was a third person in the room.

"You–" Hazel began, pointing at Sarah, but she was interrupted by the loud stomping of someone running up the steps of her porch. The person didn't knock. They simply came on through the front door. Sarah pulled a blaster out that was hidden in the back waistband of her pants and pointed it at the intruder. She didn't fire when she saw the person's face.

"Sarah, it's time to go," a familiar voice said, nearly out of breath. "Link is only two minutes out."

Hazel looked at the figure standing in the doorway and became lightheaded. If there had been any doubts about what Jude was saying, there weren't anymore. Because if *she* were here, then something extraordinary truly must have happened. The woman standing in front of Hazel didn't look at her. She didn't even look at Sarah, the person to whom she was speaking. No. Grace, with both fear and love in her eyes, only looked at her former fiancé as the screen door slammed behind her, and tears began to roll down her cheeks.

Nineteen

May 8, 2014

It was one of those days as Grace entered the grocery store and headed straight for the frozen food section. The trials from work on this day could only be cured by a pint of Häagen-Dazs chocolate ice cream. She had come to the store straight from work, and she still wore her Barnes and Noble apron as the sliding doors with the words "Exit Only" cranked open, and she rushed in. She didn't even hear the greeter say 'hello' as she entered the building. She had had enough dealings with people today.

She had recently been promoted to assistant manager as she prepared to graduate early with her Bachelor's degree only 10 days away. The homework, the promotion, and the second job at a nearby Starbucks had her completely exhausted. Today, after dealing with a shipment that never showed, one too many customers complaining about prices, and being short-staffed for the fourth day in a row, Grace had met her limit. It was Thursday, the stress was behind her, and a three-day weekend was finally here. The ice cream was going to be the perfect segue from terrible week to relaxing weekend.

She turned down the second aisle in the store, and there was only one person in the row with her, which would have been fine had he not been at the exact door she was headed for. She slowly approached as he pulled out the last pint of the exact ice cream that she wanted. She stopped in her tracks as she looked from the empty shelf in the freezer and at the man's hand that was holding the one thing that got her through the long day. She wasn't surprised. That's exactly how this day had gone from the moment she woke up ten minutes after her alarm was supposed to go off.

The man immediately noticed Grace lurking some feet away. She couldn't find it in her to even pretend like she was in the aisle for anything else. He followed her eyes and read the situation immediately. He didn't know this woman, but she had clearly had a rough day. Her work apron was still on, her hair was disheveled, and the bottom right leg of her jeans was slightly tucked into her sock.

"You know," Jude Monroe said, looking at the pint of chocolate ice cream in his hand. "I think today is more of a cookie dough ice cream kind of night." He offered her a smile, replaced the ice cream, and moved towards the end of the aisle.

Grace tried to say thank you, but the words didn't come out. Before Jude turned, he looked back and smiled once again at her. As the two made eye contact, she felt all of the stress of the day immediately disappear. He didn't say another word as he exited the aisle, but he didn't have to. It wasn't his light eyes or his dark hair, nor was it his immaculate taste in ice cream, it was the way he looked at her before he exchanged the frozen treats. A glance so filled with kindness and positivity, she was smitten instantly.

She opened up the freezer, grabbed the last pint of Häagen-Dazs chocolate ice cream and went on with her evening. Because this was a very busy grocery store in downtown Chicago, she figured that she probably wouldn't see him again. Still, on her drive home, neither the ice cream nor the stress she'd been feeling were on her mind. Rather, she thought of all the clever things she should have said to this stranger during any part of the interaction as opposed to being silent the entire time. That's how it goes, she thought as she pulled into her parking spot feet away from her apartment door. Still, though, here at the end of this Thursday, today miraculously felt like a win.

* * *

A week later, Hazel was looking for a new cookbook. Grilling season was well on its way, and she wanted to hone her skills during the coming summer. Jude picked her up on his way home from school and drove to a Barnes and Noble closer to his house than hers. She thought the selection at that particular store was better than the one closer to her place, apparently making the inconvenience worth it.

The pair walked in and searched for the cooking section. Looking down the aisles, it took Hazel two extra rows to realize that Jude wasn't walking next to her anymore. She turned around and noticed her brother, frozen, staring down the Fantasy section. He didn't even budge as she walked up to him, followed his eyes, and saw what had stolen his attention.

Jude stared down the aisle and saw the girl he had been thinking about for the last week. His friends were divided as they debated whether or not he was 'smooth' during their interaction. Either way, he hadn't told Hazel about it. She'd have roasted him over every word. Though, here the girl was. Grace's brown curls bounced against the dimples in her cheeks as she rearranged an eye-level shelf. Each novel she held, even though they were each the same, she looked upon them as if they were the most prized book ever written. As she smiled at the covers, Jude could feel his stomach fluttering.

"It's been too long, and you're being creepy," said Hazel, laughing when Jude jumped at the sound of her voice.

"I– What are you talking about?" said Jude, stuttering and looking everywhere but down the Fantasy section.

"Damn, she's cute though. Ask her out." Hazel nudged Jude with her elbow.

"Oh yeah, that'd go well. What am I supposed to do? Just walk up? How is that any less creepy?"

"Than standing and staring? Gee, I don't know." Hazel began to laugh as Jude started to walk in a direction he hoped the cooking section would be. "Oh, Jude, don't be a coward. She's a human. We're all human. Just go talk to her."

"Oh, okay. I'll go up and be like, 'so hey,' all smooth and then continue with 'very fitting that I'm here in the Fantasy section with the girl of my dreams.'"

Hazel walked straight up to Jude and punched him square in his chest. "You are seriously the biggest freak that I know."

"Tell me about it," laughed Jude.

"You could go pull *The Lord of the Rings* off the shelf and brag about how many times you've read that. Chicks dig *The Lord of the Rings*."

Jude stopped in the middle of the Political Thriller section right next to a sign that said "Get Thrilled About Politics!" He looked at Hazel and glared into her eyes. "I'm only a little certain that you're giving me shit about 'chicks' digging *The Lord of the Rings*. But, I'm fully certain that I'm offended on behalf of Tolkien and all of us nerds."

Hazel laughed out loud at Jude. "Well, I don't think Gandalf would be cool about you being a wussy."

"What the hell do you know about Gandalf?" asked Jude, moving from Political Thrillers to Historical Fiction.

"What did beardy say, 'all we have to decide is what to do with the time that is given us.'"

"Don't you dare quote the sacred texts at me," scolded Jude facetiously, spotting the cooking section and not stopping his forward movement.

"If Frodo can take the one ring into Mordor, I think Jude Monroe can talk to an assistant manager at a Barnes and Noble."

The two stopped at the entrance of their desired aisle, and Jude looked back at Hazel, who was only a step behind. "I saw that girl a few days ag–"

"Whoa whoa whoa. There's been a girl on your mind the last week, and I am just now find– do the guys know? I swear if they knew and I didn–"

"It's really nothin–"

"Oh hell no, Jude. I'm the first to find out everything. It's the golden rule," said Hazel, putting her index finger into Jude's chest.

"Isn't the golden ru–"

"The golden rule." Hazel jabbed her finger into Jude's chest, which was sore from her punch earlier, to emphasize each syllable.

"Deal. Fine. Future girls, I'll tell you about. What I was going to say is, I saw that girl a few days ago. She is so far out of my league."

Hazel rolled her eyes. She hated when Jude deprecated himself. After spending years since their childhood of being his personal 'hype man,' she hated being reminded of how much progress she still had to make. Before she had a chance to say anything, the girl the two had been speaking about walked to the section just over from Cooking. Hazel looked at her while she put a few books on a low shelf in the travel section. She then looked at Jude, and a grin slowly crept onto her face.

Jude read her thoughts from a mile away. "Nope. We're leaving." That's all he had time to say before Hazel quickly moved away and approached Jude's crush.

"Excuse me, miss?" asked Hazel, with a whimsical tone that only big sisters can conjure while they humiliate their younger siblings.

"Hi there!" said Grace, a big smile on her face. Jude stayed out of sight, hidden by a stack of books on a table between the sections. "How can I help you?"

"Well, that's just it," said Hazel, looking over her shoulder, and though she couldn't see Jude, she knew that he was right behind. "My brother has recently told me that you're out of his league, and I either need directions to the Motivation section, or for him to step up and cut me off before I break out some childhood photos that he knows I have in my purse."

Grace smiled awkwardly at Hazel as she tried to decide how to react. Her decision, though, never came as Jude, horrified, walked around the stack of Stephen King novels he was hiding behind, and she felt her heart skip a beat.

Her reaction only lasted a second, but it was all Hazel needed to see to tell her that this girl was just as smitten as her brother. She looked from one to the other as she broke the lingering awkward silence with a loud cackle. "Oh wow, this must have been some meeting a few days ago." She continued to laugh as Grace and Jude looked at each other. They didn't say a word. Hazel turned to Jude. "This is the part where you speak." Jude opened his mouth, but nothing came out. "Tell her you like *The Lord of the Rings*." She turned to Grace. "Dude is obsessed."

A smile filled Grace's face, and her dimples became deep trenches. "*The Lord of the Rings* might be my all-time favorite set of books."

Hazel, once again, let out a loud laugh, clapped her hands together, and started to walk out of the aisle. She put her hand on Jude's shoulder as she made her way out. "You really should have to pay me for moments like these."

Jude and Grace were left alone, and although both had spent the last week kicking themselves for not being clever when they last saw each other, they still struggled on the second go. Grace looked down at the Shakespeare button on her apron while Jude continued to look directly at her. He was entranced.

Grace finally ended the silent spell. "I've... I've thought about you a little bit, Mr. Cookie Dough ice cream." This was a sentence that, when she got to her car after work later, she would sink into her seat and wonder what the hell she was thinking.

Jude stuttered, "Same here, but, y'know, about you... How was the Haagen-Dazs?"

"Therapeutic. Thanks for being a gentleman. By 6:00 pm that day, you were still the only nice person I had talked to."

Jude didn't know it, but he was blushing. "Oh, you know... To be honest, Cookie Dough was the right play that night."

"Oh, is that right?" Grace said with a grin, finally making some consistent eye contact.

"Oh, yeah, you get a little bit of everything. All the sweets. Sugar here... Sugar there. Honestly, the perfect dessert." Hazel was still within earshot and dramatically rolling her eyes.

"I'll remember that next time," Grace said, unaware that she was still holding a small stack of books in the crook of her left arm.

Silence fell between the two again for a few seconds. To a person looking from the outside, the encounter might have seemed awkward. But for Jude and Grace, there was something there that made the two feel completely comfortable. Later on, while Jude and Grace would separately analyze the encounter with their friends, it would seem completely cringy, but, truth be told, the two were sharing a perfect moment. There was a feeling of something bigger that was clearly present, and they were standing right at the starting line. Jude held out his hand. "I'm Jude."

"Grace," she replied, smiling deep into Jude with her dark brown eyes. The two held the handshake for longer than either anticipated.

Hazel came around the corner, three grilling books in her hands. "This is the part where you both acknowledge your mutual love for ice cream and agree to just go get some together sometime."

Jude turned back to his sister, humiliated. She matched his glance with her head cocked to the side and a large grin. Grace broke out in laughter. She took out a Post-it note from the pocket of her apron and wrote on it. "Here's my number. I'd love to get ice cream."

Jude took the Post-it and smiled at Grace. Hazel put her hand on his shoulder to help him get his feet moving to leave. "I'll call you soon," he said, and the Monroe kids moved toward the checkout counter.

"My God. I am just as good as Samwise the brave. You're welcome for the number," said Hazel, putting her arm around Jude.

"Oh please. That was all me."

"I'm sorry, but you clearly didn't listen to yourself if you really believe that." She did her best impression of her brother. "It's really the best dessert... What the hell is that?" Hazel put the stack of books on the counter and looked at Jude. "Seriously though. Way to go. I'm proud of you. Even Gandalf would be proud."

Jude looked back at his sister, and his eyes were shining. "No one is as good as Samwise, y'know." Hazel leaned into him as she laughed in response, bumping her brother with her shoulder.

Grace stood back 12 rows and watched as Jude and Hazel checked out. The two of them hilariously interacted. She smiled to herself as she looked at Jude. She had been so tired from work and school that she hadn't actually been excited about something in a long time. Not since she moved from Pennsylvania to Illinois for school only a few years ago. But, as she looked at Jude, with his head thrown backwards as he laughed at his sister on the way out of Barnes and Noble, her heart beat quickly. No doubt, she truly was excited.

* * *

"Can you believe that we had our first ice cream date 18 months ago tonight?" said Grace as she sat on the back of Jude's car, her feet on his bumper, and taking a bite from her pint of ice cream.

Jude was sitting next to her as he took a bite from his own pint. He looked at her as they sat in the parking lot of the grocery store where they first met. The light from the neon sign on top of the building glowed in her eyes. While he had been smiling during this date, the same date they took on the 22nd of each month, he smiled even wider. He put his arm around her and hugged her tightly. "I love you more every single day. 18 wonderful months."

Grace leaned into Jude and rested her head on his shoulder as she began to laugh. As she laughed, she snorted, which always made her laugh harder. Jude loved her laugh and always wished that it never ended. "Do you remember," she asked, trying to catch her breath."When we got ice cream cones celebrating our two months and you leaned in for a kiss when I wasn't looking–"

"And I ruined my favorite date T-shirt?" remembered Jude, finishing Grace's story. She loved that story. Each month, she always looked forward to ice cream night. It was their time to just get away and forget about the daily stresses. Jude didn't worry about his students or emails or parents, and she wasn't worried about her Master's Degree classes or Barnes and Noble.

Jude closed his eyes tightly as he fought the oncoming brain freeze. Grace put her arms around him. "I'll save you!" she yelled, not caring that a pair of people walking out of the store were staring. Jude laughed and was completely distracted from the pain. This inside joke from their fifth ice cream date was still going strong, and he loved every bit of it.

Jude got his bearings and smiled on. "You know, I think I'm more partial to our three-month ice cream date story."

"Where I told you that I loved you first?"

"And you had a chocolate mustache from your milkshake." The two laughed and looked into each other's eyes.

"I love these dates, Jude," Grace said as she took one last bite of ice cream.

Jude finished his one bite later. "I can't tell you how much I am looking forward to a future of monthly ice cream dates."

Grace kissed Jude on the cheek. "A life of Jude Monroe and ice cream? Count me in." She grabbed the empty containers and went to the trash can a few feet away. When she turned around, she saw Jude, not sitting on the back of the car anymore, but on one knee, a ring in his hand and the widest smile she had ever seen on his face.

* * *

Jude spun Grace around as the last song of the night ended. He pulled her in and as the two kissed on the dance floor, the entire world vanished. They had spent the entire evening of Jude's parents' 34th wedding anniversary watching the love of Olive and Peter, dancing with Hazel, flashing the engagement ring around, and talking about a beautiful future together. Still, for the two, nothing beat this moment as they held each other closely.

"What was it you said a few months ago? 'I love you more every single day?" Grace smiled as she looked into Jude's eyes.

"More like every single second," said Jude, no smile, completely serious.

They held each other, and Grace rested her head on Jude's chest. They continued to sway even though there wasn't any more music.

"Alright, alright!" said the DJ, looking at the pair refusing to leave the dance floor. "I think we can find one more song for the happy couple."

As the DJ played Adele's rendition of "Make You Feel My Love," Grace and Jude nodded at him as a warm thank you. Halfway through the song, Hazel, Olive, and Peter all ran up and hugged the two, and the five of them danced together until the song faded out.

As the sun rose the following morning, Jude and Grace sat with their backs against the headboard in Grace's apartment. They watched as the sun broke the horizon with their hands interlaced. They hadn't slept that night. Grace rested her head on Jude's chest, and the light began to fill the room.

"I wish we could freeze time," she said, closing her eyes to capture the mental picture. "I wish we could stay this happy forever."

Jude sat up and looked back at Grace. She looked at him as the rising sun formed a glow around his head. He'd never been more beautiful to her. "We don't need to freeze time," Jude finally said after a moment of just looking at his fiancée. "We're going to be this happy and more happy forever, regardless. Time doesn't change these things."

Grace put both of her hands on Jude's cheeks and gently kissed him. "Promise?" she asked, not taking her lips from his.

Jude kept his lips on hers. "Let's make sure of it. For each other."

"Deal," said Grace as she pulled him backwards and the two fell back into the bed.

As the sun rose and its warm beams exploded through the window, Jude and Grace shared what would be one of the last few carefree moments they would know for many years.

* * *

Two years and a few months after the deaths of Olive and Peter, Grace sat alone on a park bench as tears crashed down her cheeks. The reason why she was crying came just an hour ago.

When Jude came home from work, or on weekends when he would wake up, he often wouldn't say a word. He simply sat in a lawn chair in the backyard, completely alone. This had become routine for him. Sure, Grace and Jude would spend time together, but it was never what it was before the deaths of Olive and Peter. She had moved into the house shortly after the accident, but it didn't change anything. Often, Grace would pull another lawn chair next to Jude's and sit with him. After a while, however, she would just let him have his space.

It's not that she didn't understand, because she very much did. Olive and Peter were Jude's heroes. She loved them, too. She looked at them like they were her own parents. Two years later, two years of trying to keep Jude from drowning, she still hadn't had time to mourn for herself. She loved Jude with the entirety of her heart, but he was an empty shell.

When she got home on this particular Saturday afternoon, she had worked late through lunch at the library, finishing an essay. She came home and didn't even go inside. She just walked around the house to where she knew Jude would be. He stared blankly at the trees behind the house.

"Hey there, love," she said as she walked on the sidewalk that connected the front yard to the back. "I have an idea." Jude didn't respond. "You know what today is? It's the 22nd, and I think we should go on our traditional ice cream date. We haven't gone in so long, and it's Saturday, so we have nothing else to do."

Jude simply shook his head and looked back to the trees. Grace pulled up a chair and sat next to him. "Come on, Jude. There's a big world out there. We have an entire Saturday to go out and explore it."

Jude looked at Grace and tears were in his eyes. He simply shook his head again and went inside the house without saying a word. Grace sat alone outside, and she began to weep. She wasn't mad at Jude, she wasn't mad at her relationship, and she wasn't mad at herself for fighting for either for so long. Her heart was broken, though. She missed Olive and Peter, and she missed the way things were. She felt so much grief over how much pain Jude, the love of her life, felt constantly. Each day, however, it seemed like she was fighting to mend two broken hearts. Even with the help from Hazel, who had been amazingly supportive and strong, Grace felt like she was sinking.

She looked to the cloudy sky as wind violently shook the trees above. She was out of answers. She closed her eyes and imagined the mental image that she kept in her memories from the morning after the anniversary party and cried into her hands. For twenty minutes, she let everything out that had been pent up for so long.

Enough, she finally thought to herself as she stood up, dusted her pants off, and went for a walk. Finding herself in a nearby park, she sat on a bench within sight of where she and Jude had shared their first kiss. More tears began to roll down her cheek as she heard footsteps to her left.

"Hi," said a stranger, allowing the 'i' in the word to linger for a sympathetic effect. "I'm sorry, but are you okay?"

"Oh, yeah. I'm fine," lied Grace, as she turned her head away to try to hide her eyes. It was a hopeless effort.

The stranger sat down on the bench and looked at Grace. She wore a hoodie under a denim jacket, and she gave a look of condolence as she tucked her blonde hair behind her right ear. "I've cried on this bench once or twice myself."

Grace could only laugh when the stranger said that, and she allowed herself to make eye contact. Her eyes were bloodshot, and there had clearly been no attempt to halt the rivers of mascara that ran down her cheeks.

"Oh, honey," said the stranger, tilting her head and taking out a tissue, handing it to Grace. "Where is he? I'll beat his ass. Just point the way."

Grace laughed again. "How'd you know it was boy trouble?"

"Isn't it always?" said the stranger, with a snicker, as she leaned back on the bench. She turned her head and looked back at Grace. "It gets better. You know that."

Grace wiped the tears from her eyes. "I just don't know what to do... He lost everything, and I just wish I could fix it."

"Oh, the classic lost cause. We've all been there."

"Jude's not that... He's just. I know he's in there." Grace paused as tears came back. "I just know it."

The stranger sat next to Grace and let her collect herself. "There's a food stand over there. Why don't you let me buy you lunch and talk about it? It's alright, I do this stuff for a living."

Grace looked at the blonde woman and smiled. "Oh–"

"Come on. Sometimes we need the kindness of strangers. Gives us hope in the world and whatnot."

Grace nodded and stepped off the park bench. The two ladies walked to the food stand, and Grace let out everything. Once she got started, everything came out. Years of sadness, of having to be strong for her and Jude, of wishing she had time to grieve for herself. It was completely therapeutic to finally say everything that had been on her mind. As the two ate their street food, Grace's new acquaintance nodded and affirmed every feeling that was expressed.

"... and that's how I ended up here," Grace finally said fifteen minutes later. "I didn't know where to go, so I came here... I can't believe I just rambled like that. That is so embarrassing."

"Not at all. I told you, I do this all the time."

"I don't even know your name. You must think I'm crazy."

"First of all, I don't think you're crazy. I think you're courageous. Second of all, my name is Sarah. I'm glad you opened up. I could tell you needed it. Us girls need to stick together."

"I'm Grace. Thanks for being such a wonderful stranger."

"I think we're past being strangers," Sarah said, lightheartedly, as the cloudy sky became darker and rain started to set in. The two ran for a nearby pavilion to seek shelter. Grace was shivering from the cold rain.

"Here, take my jacket; my hoodie is good enough for me."

"Oh, that's—"

Before Grace could politely decline, Sarah had taken off her jean jacket and handed it to Grace. "Here," she said, and Grace accepted. She was already cold before the rain, and she couldn't deny that the extra layer, even from this perfect stranger, would help.

"Listen, Grace. You really don't think leaving Jude is your best option?"

Grace thought about the promise they made on the morning of Jude's parents' death. "I love him. More than anything. He's broken. He's not a bad guy. My Jude is still in there. Somewhere. I wouldn't be wearing this engagement ring if I didn't believe it."

Sarah studied Grace the entire time she spoke. "You'd do anything for him, then?"

"I'd do absolutely anything. Anything."

Sarah looked down and then at Grace one more time. She could tell Grace was fully devoted to whatever it would take. Sarah sympathized with the girl standing in front of her. Where she was from, Sarah knew it was always the good people that got hurt more than the bad. That's why she was here. That's why she came here a little less than ten years ago on Leo and Goliath's mission.

Grace walked to the edge of the pavilion with her back to Sarah. The jean jacket was a perfect fit. It was supposed to be. Grace had no idea of the consequences she would face for putting it on. She stopped and watched as the rain cascaded down from the clouds. The peace that came from the sound of the raindrops hitting the roof made her feel tranquil as she turned back around toward Sarah. She didn't even have time to react as Sarah pointed her blaster at Grace's head and pulled the trigger.

* * *

Grace woke up centuries later, having taken a trip through a portal created by the people who were supposed to be her in-laws. As she sat up in the bed she had slept in, she couldn't believe what she was seeing.

"No, you're not dead, and this isn't the afterlife," said Olive, who was sitting a few feet away.

"Oh my God. Olive," yelled Grace, filled with joy and tears. "You're—"

"Alive. So is Peter, he's... out." Grace moved to stand up, but Olive got up quicker and joined her on the bed. The pair shared a hug, and when they pulled away, Olive was crying as well. "I know that all of this is a lot to take in... But, I want you to know, Peter and I, we love you dearly, and I'm so glad to see you."

As the two cried and took each other in, Olive began to tell Grace everything. She explained where they were, why they were there, how they were there and, most importantly, what she needed from her.

As promised to Jude, to Sarah, and now to Olive, Grace would do absolutely anything for the man that she loved. Olive told her of the plan that would save the Earth and save her family. Grace, not surprisingly to Olive, nodded and was very receptive to the world she had woken up to in 2389 and everything that came with it. When Olive finished detailing the plan and what was needed from her, she paused and waited for Grace to answer. When she and Peter had made their plans to take down Reginald and the resistance, they knew they would be expecting a lot from Grace. As she and her husband had waited for Sarah to send Grace to them, they had spent many sleepless nights. Now, Olive held her breath as she waited for Grace's response.

Grace stood up and walked to the edge of the room when Olive finally finished talking. She looked out the window and saw the new world outside. "When do we start?" Grace finally said as she turned back to Olive, who simply stood up and walked over to hug her. As

Grace put her arms around Olive, she felt the perfectly warm maternal hug she had missed so dearly over the last few years.

"I can't tell you how glad I am to see you," said Grace, looking at Olive with the widest smile she had felt on her face since she could remember.

"Trust me, dear, the feeling is mutual."

"I won't let you down, Olive," said Grace as she rolled up the sleeve on the denim jacket and revealed a small piece of metal lined in the fabric that Olive used to coordinate the destination at the end of the next portal.

"You could never let me down," said Olive, smiling and giving Grace one more hug. "I'll see you soon, dear."

"I can't wait," said Grace, as she grabbed a package from Olive, closed her eyes, and watched Olive push a button on the denim jacket, which made her fly backward through another portal.

* * *

The plan Grace had to follow was the hardest thing she ever had to do. Leaving Jude, saying goodbye to Hazel, and not being able to tell either of them the real reasons why she had to leave was unbearable. Olive had explained that it had to be this way, and Grace believed her. Still, as she left, it was the hardest thing she had ever done. Leaving Jude was the first part. He had to end up on *The Audacity*, and her leaving was part of that happening. She had delivered Olive's package to Sarah. She had left Jude. Now, she had only one task while she waited for the rocket explosion. She had to protect Hazel.

Hazel was alone and vulnerable while Jude left for NASA. Grace had to stay vigilant. While Olive and Peter knew Link had his sights on Jude, they didn't want to take chances with their oldest child.

Still, though, nothing was harder than sitting back and being removed from Jude's life. Breaking his heart broke hers all the same. She knew it was what was needed in the long run, but even still, as he went on all the adventures Hazel conjured for him, including things like speed dating, Grace was nearly in pieces and counted down the days until she could see him again, until she could tell him that she loved him again.

July 15th seemed to be an absolutely horrendous long way away until the day finally arrived, and she sat only a few rows behind Hazel on the bleachers. Hazel had her phone open as she switched between different apps for various news organizations covering the pre-launch proceedings. Grace wore a baseball cap and large sunglasses, and Hazel even looked directly at her once or twice. She was never recognized by her former fiancé's sister.

The countdown clock reached 10 seconds, and Grace was glad that each person around her was focused on the screens broadcasting the launch or the actual rocket itself. If anyone had looked at her, they would have seen waterfalls of tears pouring out from behind her sunglasses. She knew the fate of the rocket and the crew on it. She knew that some would survive, and she knew that some wouldn't. She knew that no one else watching knew what she knew. It felt incredibly wrong, yet she had to stay. Watching over Hazel was her task, and every difficult thing that came with the mission would be worth it when Jude would be saved.

When the rocket exploded, it didn't matter that she knew what would happen. Her breath was taken away as the man she was fighting for disappeared in the sky, and hundreds around her started to run. Grace jumped under the bleachers as the area evacuated. Only Hazel remained in the seats. Grace waited for the entire hour that Hazel sat there staring at the sky. It was excruciating for her not to go and comfort Hazel. No one came. She was completely alone in the world.

Later, Grace sat in the hotel lobby through the night and watched the sunrise the next morning. She knew Hazel had an early flight. Link also knew this. Which was why Grace wasn't surprised when he came into the hotel lobby and sat at 3:00 AM and also waited. Grace sat back. She knew what he looked like from the news coverage of the launch. Link had no idea what she looked like. That was the benefit of only being an ex when Jude was selected for the rocket.

As Hazel came out of the elevator and caught a taxi ride, Link got in a cab and followed closely behind. Grace took another cab behind him and followed him to the airport. The three rode to Chicago on the same plane as Grace sat three rows behind Link and Hazel.

When the plane landed, it was a race to Hazel's house. Grace bumped into Link as they got their baggage from the overhead compartment. She slipped a tracker into Link's pocket. Hazel got her checked baggage and left with ease. Grace, however, had to deal with Link. As Link put a 50-foot tail on Hazel on the way out of the airport, Grace went straight up to a security guard, citing some inappropriate things she allegedly heard on the plane from the passenger following Hazel. The security stopped him as Grace raced to get to Hazel's house, where she was supposed to rendezvous with Sarah and Jude.

A block away, despite the dangers Link posed as he was already en route, Grace couldn't help but smile as she approached Hazel's house. She hadn't spoken to her former fiancé in so long, and despite the suffering, it would surely all be worth it. Jude was worth it. She looked down at the screen of her tracker and winced with the realization that Link, who was already away from the airport, was moving faster than she was.

She threw her Volkswagen into Hazel's driveway, left it running, ran up the steps, and flung open the front door. Hazel was crying, Sarah had her blaster pulled, but all she saw was Jude, standing a foot away from Sarah with his jaw on the floor.

"Sarah, it's time to go. Link is only two minutes out," she said, as she looked at Jude and no one else.

Awkwardness, tension, and silence were all palpable in Hazel's living room as everyone remained frozen instead of moving. Sarah walked over to Hazel.

"Hazel, I know this is a lot, but there's some bad people on their way, and we need to get out of here now." She turned to Grace. "Enough gas in your car?" When Grace nodded, Sarah put her hands on Hazel's shoulders.

"Listen, we–"

Jude cut her off as he finally snapped back to reality after seeing Grace and moved closer to Hazel. "Sis, we gotta go. We can tell you everything in the car."

Hazel fell backward into the reclining chair only feet away. Jude and Sarah looked at each other, knowing the consequences of dawdling too long. Grace looked down at the tracker.

"Guys, Link is literally about to turn onto this street."

Jude crouched down in front of Hazel. "We've got to go. Either I'm carrying you out that door, or you're coming under your own will. What's it going to be?"

Hazel paused and looked back at Grace and the tracker in her hand. "Okay… Fine. Yes. Let's go."

Jude grabbed Hazel's hand and sprinted for the front door. Sarah followed the pair closely behind with her blaster still pulled. Grace stayed motionless in Hazel's doorway as the three moved past her. Jude didn't even look at her as they sprinted toward the front yard and to the car. Her heart sank to her stomach.

Jude and Hazel got in the back of Grace's Jetta. Grace didn't have a choice but to be in the passenger seat. When she got to the car last, Sarah was already behind the steering wheel. As Sarah threw the car in reverse and peeled out of the driveway, the back glass was immediately shattered by a blaster shot from Link, who was directly behind them. Hazel screamed in the back of the car as all four immediately ducked. Two thuds were immediately heard as Link planted two more shots in the car's back bumper.

"Would somebody please tell me what the hell is going on?" yelled Hazel, too terrified to cry anymore.

"Well, that's a long story, but here's the shor–"

Sarah cut Jude off to yell at Grace. "Take the wheel and keep it straight!" She then leaned around her seat, pointed her blaster, and returned fire at Link through the back window. After two blasts, she resumed driving.

Sarah whipped the car around a corner, and Jude began speaking again. "The short version is this: I didn't die. Sarah's an alien from the future. Mom and dad are alive, which is why she is here and, I guess, why I am here. Grace is here, too, apparently, and that's going to be left unpacked for just a bit."

This was the first time in the five minutes that they'd been in each other's presence that Jude acknowledged his former fiancée. "Hazel, look. There's a lot going o-"

"Yeah, no shit, there's a lot going on. But why? Alien? Did I get stoned on the plane ride here? What the actual fu-"

"Haze-" More pounding on the back of the car interrupted Jude yet again. "Hazel, we'll explain everything la-"

"How about now? Explain it now because someone is shooting at us and we're driving too fast and that woman hasn't stopped at a stop sign yet... And I'm scared, Jude. I'm so scared."

There was silence in the car as everyone gripped their leather seats and Sarah took a sharp 90-degree turn. "Hazel, the man shooting at us is the man you sat next to on the plane. He's a very bad man," Grace finally said.

"Link? The captain? No!" yelled Hazel, completely flabbergasted.

"Hazel, it looks like our parents are in some deep shi-"

"Where are they?" asked Hazel, cutting Jude off.

"The future and-"

"If I hear the word future one more fu–"

"How else would I be here, Hazel? You watched me die, remember? There are some things that you're just going to have to let go of reality on."

Jude had yelled at his sister, and the car was silent again as Sarah cut off multiple cars, ran a red light, and entered onto I-94 already going 30 miles an hour over the speed limit. Regardless of the recklessness, Link was still four feet from her bumper.

No matter how anyone in the car expected Hazel to react to Jude's tone, they were wrong. "Okay. The future. You didn't die, you actually went to the future, saw mom and dad, who didn't come back with you, and now you've come back and people want us dead?"

Grace turned to look at the back seat for the first time, Sarah looked in the rearview mirror, and Jude put his hands on Hazel's. "Exactly, and right now nothing else matters," said Jude, trying his best to smile.

"Not until we're safe, but we have to shake Link," Sarah yelled to the backseat as she merged onto Route 137 and passed cars on the shoulder of the road. Still, Link was close behind. He planted more shots into the back of the car. As they made it onto 137, he sent one shot through the back window and put a hole straight through the windshield. They continued on down the road as if nothing had happened.

"Okay, she's an alien, you've escaped death, now what about Grac—"

Grace began to turn around to field the oncoming question. Suddenly, Link sent a shot into the back right tire of the Jetta, causing them to jolt to the right, cut off a car in the next lane, and bulldoze straight over the sidewalk and into the chain link fence that barricaded Oakwood Cemetery. The car slammed into one of the large historic trees that sat only feet behind the fence. Grace was whipped back around and slammed into her seat by the airbag. Sarah's head hit the steering wheel. Jude and Hazel each were thrown forward but restrained by their seat belts. They didn't have time to collect their bearings. Link was already out of the car and shooting at them.

Sarah rolled out of the Volkswagen and shot back at Link. The remaining three exited out the other side of the car. With their heads ducked, they immediately ran as fast as they could to a large tombstone. Jude had forgotten the pain in his legs until they had to run. They slid on the ground behind a large stone and put their backs against the rock slab. There they sat as they heard intermittent blaster shots. Each blast made Jude, Hazel, and Grace jump.

Sarah took turns with Link as they continued to release shots at each other. Sarah used the tree as a shield from the shots from her counterpart. As long as she could keep him hidden behind his car, she thought, the longer the other three would have to escape. Jude knew the next steps of the plan, and Grace knew where to go. They'd be safe as long as Link was occupied.

The bark splintered and fell down upon Sarah as she crouched against the tree. The front of Link's rental car was in no better shape than the wrecked Jetta after numerous shots from her blaster. Still, one of the two was bound to make a mistake. They were out of sight from the three hiding behind the tombstone. Each blaster shot sounded like a bomb going off in the otherwise silent cemetery. Link sent a shot into the upper part of the tree, and a large branch fell to the ground. It sounded like the entire tree was coming down.

"She needs our help," said Jude, who grew impatient and began to stand up.

Grace put a hand on his shoulder. "No. No chance. I promised to keep you guys safe."

"I have to. It's Sarah."

The way Jude said this made Grace pause. There was clearly more here than what met the eye. What it was, she didn't have time to figure out. She looked over the tombstone and saw Sarah and Link exchanging shots from behind their cars.

"We have to go. We have a way to escape, but we have to get to it. It is literally on the other side of those trees. Right on the water."

"We are not leaving Sarah behind," said Jude, fully aware that this was the first time they had held a conversation since she walked out the door and ended their relationship.

The two stared at each other, clearly at an impasse. "Alright," Grace finally said. "Alright." She looked at Jude, took his hands, and smiled. There was so much she wanted to say. After months of waiting to hold his hands, to feel his touch, and to be close, here he finally was. She knew what she had to do. Looking deep into his eyes, she tried to sum up all of her thoughts into one sentence. "I wish you could know just how much I missed you."

Before Jude could respond, Grace stood up and began to run toward Link. It was all the distraction that was needed for Sarah as

Link's attention moved to the woman charging at him. Grace didn't have a plan. She didn't even think it through. Sarah obviously mattered enough for Jude to risk his own life by staying in the cemetery. If she mattered that much to him, then she mattered that much to her. She raced forward and screamed as Link pointed his gun at her. There was only a slight opening, but it was enough as Sarah landed a shot clear through his throat, sending him backwards and onto the pavement. But, Sarah was too late. Link had managed to get one shot off before he was hit. His blast entered squarely beneath Grace's collarbone, and her world was black before she even hit the ground.

Jude watched the entire scene from behind the tombstone. Hazel tried in vain to hold him back from running forward. He was on Grace's body in a matter of seconds. Sarah rushed to Grace as well, though she never stopped pointing the gun at Link's car. Jude carried Grace's limp body over his shoulder as they rushed out of the cemetery and to a secluded bank of Lake Michigan, where Sarah had a pod waiting for them. Sarah looked behind her one more time before they exited the cemetery, and she could still see Link's feet motionless under his car.

This pod, similar to Elise's, was the escape plan all along. The group was so close to making it unscathed. This was all Jude could think as he carried Grace to the back and gently laid her down on a small mattress. She hadn't moved since she was hit with the blaster shot. Jude buried his face into her stomach and wept as Sarah rushed in and began her attempt to treat the woman that she had met in a park years ago. As she cut open Grace's shirt to expose the wound, there were two glaring details that crossed her mind immediately. Number one: Jude still, very clearly, loved this woman. Number two: Grace, her face pale white, wasn't breathing anymore.

Twenty

November 9, 2393

There wasn't a person in the room who fully believed what happened for an entire minute after Olive threw Jude out the window with one of Elise's thermal detonators. In truth, while Reginald had predicted the moves of the Monroes many times since their chess match began years ago, even he was surprised. The Houdini Vest that Link was to make sure Jude wore on *The Audacity* was supposed to only have one more trip in it before the explosion. Either Jude was wearing an additional vest or Olive had just murdered her only son.

The chess match began nearly five years ago when Reginald, with the other leaders of the resistance, finalized their plans to rid the world of its governments, the Volgens, and the Shadows. Every person, including Reginald and his daughter, would have perished had Leo and Goliath not been successful in ridding the world of the oncoming comet. He could not deny this fact and for that he was grateful. But, after St. Louis was given to the resistance in exchange for their complete withdrawal from New York City, they started to set their eyes on something much bigger. Why settle for St. Louis, they thought, when they could have the world? The idea of a reset button seemed much sweeter when they would be the beneficiaries.

Reginald and the resistance leaders knew everything they needed to do. There were only two things that they couldn't do on their own. First, they needed to find the comet. Surely, they imagined, if someone hid it, they could find it again. Secondly, the resistance knew of only three working Houdini Vests left in existence. One was locked away in Chicago, and without the blood of either Leo or Goliath, they would never get to it. The other two, and only truly accessible, vests were locked away in a top security prison. Fortunately for the resistance, that prison was the very one in St. Louis which became their headquarters.

They didn't want St. Louis originally. However, when they were given intel that two vests were in the city, well, they were glad to take it. The prison was the only building in the city that survived the war. They didn't mind the solitude as they worked and plotted and found themselves within reach of their goal. All they had to do was get Leo and Goliath back to the 24th century. The leaders of the resistance loved the plan as they began working it out, but they had one major issue: No one in the world, besides a handful of Volgens, knew who Leo and Goliath were.

Reginald had a secret, though. No one, not even his daughter, had any idea how, but he knew their identities. Not only that, but he knew where, or rather when, they would go. No matter how many times Elise would ask over the next few years, he wouldn't tell her how he knew his information. At most, he would tell her that he had special intel.

He did have special intel; that part was true. It became illegal to possess any information from the past. He possessed the contraband with no remorse. He even knew a little bit about the time travel technology that Leo and Goliath created with The Sphinx. He knew specific details like how there are events that are fixed moments in time that can only be altered but never removed. Events like *The Audac-ity* explosion that held a teacher named Jude Monroe. The explosion couldn't be changed, but somehow, someone could make sure he was wearing a Houdini Vest before lift off.

There were major pieces of information that Reginald had that even the fact of having "special intel" simply couldn't justify. Nonethe-less, Reginald never revealed how he knew the things that he knew. Being the leader or even a father, he was never pressed too hard. After all, he didn't become the head of the resistance for nothing.

The resistance knew that they needed a set number of Houdini Vests and a comet. They needed Leo and Goliath to come back for all of their problems to become solutions. Thus, the chess match began.

It wasn't a difficult task to retrieve Leo and Goliath. Reginald knew the buttons to push. He gave Link his orders as he fitted him with The Sphinx's Houdini Vest that still had all three of its journeys remaining and sent him on his way.

* * *

On a cold morning in early 2016, Olive and Peter enjoyed their coffee as they sat on a park bench and took in the cool Chicago air. Hazel promised to buy them coffee every morning that they would get out and exercise as part of a New Year's resolution. Olive and Peter didn't mind. They loved the idea of walking with their daughter every morning. They ended up rotating the responsibility of procuring the coffee when their daily walk in the park was finished.

Today was Hazel's turn to buy coffee. Olive and Peter watched her while she walked to the food truck fifty yards away as they sat on the park bench. She looked back to her parents and smiled as she waited in line. The Monroe parents held each other's hands and smiled back as they each felt a hand suddenly appear on their shoulders.

"Your daughter is beautiful. You must be very proud," said Link, as he stood behind the bench and looked towards the food truck.

"We are very proud. Who–" Peter began, but he was cut off as the stranger walked around the bench and stood in front of the two.

"Look. I'm not here to chit-chat or to play games. Reginald sent me here. We know about Jude, and we know about Hazel. We have a task for you. Either come back, or I'll kill your children. It's really that simple." He turned around and saw that Hazel was at the window of the truck and ordering the beverages. "We know you still have the capacity to make vests. It's time to make the world a better place. I will give you a little time. Don't push it, though. I'll be watching."

As Hazel began to walk back to the bench with the coffees in her hands, Link quickly walked away. Olive and Peter both wished that they were surprised. Truth be told, they were only surprised that it had taken so long for this day to come. They had been able to raise such beautiful and wonderful children. They had enjoyed a happy marriage through the end of the 20th and beginning of the 21st century. They knew that Reginald would find himself in a position to bring them back. They always knew that their job wasn't completely finished in the 24th century.

Hazel came back and sat down on the bench and smiled while she handed out the coffees to her parents.

"So, we have been talking, Hazel, and we have an idea," said Olive as she took in a deep breath of her vanilla latte. Hazel looked at her with excitement. When her parents started a conversation like that, it always ended with a party. "Our 34th wedding anniversary is a little over two weeks away. Let's make it something really special."

* * *

It wasn't complicated, really. Olive and Peter had spoken long ago, when the children were young, about how they'd go about it. It had to look like an accident. The previous night, they both agreed, was the finest night they had ever known. They danced with their children, laughed with friends, and sat back to enjoy the last remaining hours of this new life they had built so many years ago.

They spent the morning walking with Hazel and took a few extra laps. Peter bought the coffee, and they sat an hour longer than usual on the bench with their daughter. They laughed as they talked about the entire party and as they commended Hazel on her dance floor antics. They hugged her tightly as they said goodbye before getting in their car and driving away.

They didn't need to see Jude. They had told him how proud they were and how much they loved him last night when the party ended. As he held his fiancée, he had the largest smile they had ever seen on his face. It was already the perfect goodbye.

"Handle With Care" came up on the shuffle as Olive and Peter found themselves on the Chicago Skyway Toll Bridge. They each double checked the destinations on the collars of their makeshift Houdini Vests as Peter began to pick up speed. Olive kissed her husband on the cheek as they interlaced their fingers and prepared for impact. The car hit the side of the bridge with more than enough power to break through and send the pair plummeting 125 feet to the water below. Their bodies were never found.

They knew their fate going back to the 24th century. They knew what would happen. They had their moves set. Sure, Reginald opened up by moving his rook first, but Olive and Peter were already prepared. However, while they were prepared for the battle in the future, they weren't prepared for Reginald to still go after their children in the 21st century. Kids had always been off the table when they had conflicts in the past. This was a miscalculation that would later lead exactly to the moment that Olive would throw her son out the window of the top floor of the St. Louis prison.

* * *

The room stared at Olive as she turned around to look at her husband. It was always coming to this, and the pair knew it. Of all the plans they made in retaliation to the resistance, the most important were the ones keeping their children safe. Sending Jude back to 2019, where Sarah would be waiting, was the safest place.

Move after move, they responded to each other. Both sides found out at some point that Jude would end up on *The Audacity*. Olive and Peter found out about the plans Reginald had to capture him. So, when they sent Grace back to the past, they sent her with a brand new Houdini Vest disguised as an undershirt that had all three remaining trips on it. They knew that Link would fit him with a vest that only had one trip left in it. Using Sarah and Grace, they moved to keep Jude safe. They knew that getting captured was the only move they could make to successfully rescue Jude when he would inevitably end up in the future. They had to do whatever it took as Reginald moved forward, antagonized their family, and brought the world closer to destruction.

They couldn't do anything about their journals or the original vest in Chicago. They knew Reginald would get ahold of them. They needed him to. Only Olive and Peter knew of what was hidden in the notes and what made that particular vest in Chicago more special than any other. The Shadows running wild would have smelled their scent a mile away. They had no problem letting Reginald procure the items for them. Getting captured allowed them to be in the same building as all the materials they needed to finally rid the universe of the comet, of the resistance, and of Reginald.

When the shock subsided, Elise threw her elbow square into Olive's jaw, knocking her unconscious immediately. Peter lunged to the front of the cage in which he was imprisoned. Olive hit the ground hard. As Peter worried about his wife, he still couldn't help but feel a little bit content. Jude being sent back was, for now, another win for Leo and Goliath.

Twenty One

July 16, 2019

Link looked to the blue sky above as the few present white clouds became blurry. He knew it was his throat that had been shot, but it was his head that hurt the worst. With no give in the pavement, his head had hit the ground like a dropped bowling ball. He sat up, using the inside door handle for support. He touched the wound on his neck to assess the damage for the first time. The blast mostly grazed him, and because it had charred everything left exposed, there was no bleeding. Still, there was one hell of a gash visible. As he put his fingers through his hair, he felt something wet. He saw red when he looked at his hand.

He peered into the rearview mirror and looked at himself for a brief moment. There were numerous times in his life where he'd ask himself, 'how'd I find myself here?' He found that the answer to the question was more often than not connected to Reginald or the resistance. For ten years, he'd been traversing the 21st century and rising through the ranks as a captain in the United States Air Force. There was never a pilot who could outmaneuver, outsmart, or outclass him, no matter the plane. So, when he sent a resume to the higher-ups at NASA with the help of a few impressed high-ranking officials in the Air Force, he was quickly accepted. When it came to the mission of *The Audacity*, no one was more highly recommended.

Still, it was a long journey to get where he was sitting in his car looking at himself. There were hard days throughout his life that prepared him for anything. Whether it be some of the tours of duty in the Air Force or a shootout with Sarah in a small cemetery in Chicago, he kept moving forward.

As a child growing up in an extremely impoverished neighborhood, he had to fend for himself and struggle for everything. The resistance offered him a path for survival that he wouldn't have found where he lived in St. Louis. If he had stayed, he inevitably would have died a brutal death the way his brother had. He truly believed in the resistance's mission, and he had a natural talent for flight. Using the chip on his shoulder, no one, not even the pilots for The North American Government, could compete.

As he stood next to Elise one morning in Chicago, he watched the footage of St. Louis. He wanted to fight, but Reginald made him stay centralized. He sat back and watched the screens. He prayed that there would be no footage of any neighborhood like the one he grew up in. His parents, after all, still remained there. With a straight posture and a stoic face, he watched as the footage went black when the nuclear bomb exploded. A single tear traversed his cheek as the Chicago resistance broke out in an impromptu moment of silence. As Reginald began designing plans to take New York City, Link was the first person to volunteer. He was the first pilot in and the last pilot out. St. Louis was theirs in only a few days. However, like Reginald and Elise, he knew there was more that they could have.

He found no problem with his mission in the 21st century. He actually enjoyed the Air Force. While he knew what the government he was fighting for would inevitably become, there was comfort in the structure of the military. It wasn't all that different from fighting in the resistance so many centuries in the future.

The first time he met Jude, Link couldn't deny that he actually liked him. Jude was funny, full of charisma, and also had a terribly depressing past. He had no idea of the war going on around him. It was a war that he was at the center of, and his only concerns were of his family. Honestly, Link respected that. After all, Link infiltrated the city of New York as a dedication to the death of his parents. Jude was going to space because of a sadness over his own parents. To Link, they really weren't all that different.

He had assumed correctly that someone else was on the rocket that was an enemy. He never thought it was Sarah, though. Truth be told, he assumed it was Abe. So, after the rocket exploded and he landed back in 2393, he immediately had to dodge blaster shots from his copilot. He kicked himself. Again, he thought, how did he find himself where he was? For six months, Link dodged Sarah and prepared to return for the other Monroe child. Her chase made things difficult for him, sure, but Reginald was not someone that Link or anyone, for that matter, wanted to disappoint.

Sarah chased him to Chicago, where he planned to spend one more night in the 24th century. She was close by as he stood in the pod with Elise and looked down at Jude's body as he lay in the back of the vessel.

"Seems such a shame. He's not a bad guy," said Link, displaying an uncharacteristic moment of sympathy.

"The 21st century made you weak," responded Elise, unflinchingly.

"No. Not at all. Perhaps, but come on, he's just like us. He's blame-less for the evil around him."

"He is nothing like us. Nothing." Elise turned and looked at Link. "Listen, you've done your part here. I appreciate you catching this guy after I threw him out of the TTI window. I wasn't sure it'd work."

"Oh, that? That was nothing," shrugged Link.

Elise didn't even smirk. "Now, get going. The last thing we need is for that Sarah girl to get in our way. And if she's following you, she could ruin everything."

Moments later, Link found himself on the floor just under the roof that Elise had parked her pod. It was only a few minutes before he was face-to-face with Sarah. She had a blaster pulled, and he didn't even reach for his.

"This is it, Link. The game is over," said Sarah, out of breath.

"You know, this reminds me of a story," said Link, his hands raised and a smug look on his face.

"I don't want to hear another damn story."

"Such a shame," said Link, who immediately propelled himself out of a nearby window and flew toward the ground. His Houdini Vest only had one more trip left. No matter, he thought as he took one last glance at the world he grew up in, he had no plans to return.

The journey had been long, and he had the scars to prove it. So, as he moved the rearview mirror down to study the newest one that was on his neck, he didn't mind how gruesome it looked. 'A new scar, a new story.' That's what he always said to himself when a new injury would come. He took in a deep breath and locked the pain out of his mind.

He put the car in drive and rolled what was left of the broken windows down. There were two holes in the windshield, and his headrest had been blown off. Sarah had put some serious damage in his rental car. He was a little surprised to not be hearing any sirens yet. There were a few people gawking, but mostly they went on their way. That's Chicago for you, he thought, some things never change.

He took the device that Grace had slipped into his pocket and threw it out of the open window. He knew the device was there all along. He had figured that some minion of Leo or Goliath would put something on him between the airport and the oldest-born Monroe's house. He wasn't surprised when he felt it in his pocket earlier.

Reaching into his other pocket, he took out a tracking device of his own. He shook his head and laughed at the group running away from him. They had been smart enough to put a tracker on *him*, but not smart enough to check for a tracker on Hazel. He looked down at a tiny screen in his hand and, though it made his head throb a little more, he slightly smiled. They were still only minutes away.

Twenty Two

July 16, 2019

G race remained lifeless on the mattress as the tension in the room passed its boiling point. She hadn't breathed since Sarah entered the room, and CPR just wasn't cutting it. Sarah reached under the mattress and fumbled around in a small cabinet, hoping that the item she was looking for was still there. It'd been so long since she had dealt with something like this.

When she found what she was looking for, she attached the automated external defibrillator to Grace and pushed Jude aside as delicately as she could. Everything seemed to be moving in slow motion as Jude watched Sarah methodically work to save Grace's life. From the moment she entered the room, she seemed to have control of the situation. Still, the situation was dire. Sarah sent the electricity through Grace's body and, to the immediate relief of everyone in the room, breathing returned.

Jude sat with his back against the inner wall of the pod with his eyes fixed on Grace. The rise and fall of her chest had come back as Sarah treated the wound from the blaster shot with antibiotics. Truthfully, he didn't know what to feel. Grace was here, feet away, after so long. Like so many other things from the last few days, it didn't make any sense. A flurry of thoughts crashed through his mind as he tried to find the answers.

He had felt abandoned and betrayed after Grace left, but those feelings had subsided as life seemed to re-enter her body. He just couldn't be mad anymore, but he certainly wasn't feeling any joy. Grace. Grace had been shot. She was hurt for some reason connected to whatever the mess was that the Monroe family had found themselves in. His blood boiled as he thought about it. Still, his mind just kept going back to the same question: why was she here in the first place?

As Sarah packed up the few medical supplies that she had, she went to exit to the front of the pod. Before leaving, she looked down at Jude and gave a sympathetic nod. "Come on, she's going to be out for a while. I gave her something really good in the last injection." She held out her hand to help Jude up, which he took. He looked down at Grace before leaving the room, and some color was already returning to her cheeks. He moved to put his hand on hers, but something stopped him just short. Of so many things that he had witnessed recently, he saw something almost more unexpected than anything else. Looking down, he saw, for the first time during their encounter, that the engagement ring that he had given to Grace so long ago was still on her left hand. Jude couldn't believe his eyes.

Every turn of the journey, Jude came face-to-face with more questions than answers. He couldn't fathom how he could still be surprised after the last few days. Still though, he had to admit that part of him enjoyed seeing the ring on her finger. However, all the same, there was also a frustration that he felt when he saw it. Taking a deep breath, Jude simply turned around and followed Sarah through the dividing curtain.

Hazel sat on a small chair at an old makeshift table built into the sidewall of the pod. As Jude looked at where his sister was sitting, he couldn't help but think about when Elise had served him food in her similar spot. He got lost in his thoughts as the pod was silent. Elise and Link had betrayed him. His parents weren't who he thought they were. Grace was all of a sudden back in the mix. Sarah was Volgen. His head was reeling as he looked at his sister. For him, the newness of all of these details was beginning to wear off. For Hazel, everything was fresh. She looked up to meet his gaze. She was out of tears, and her eyes were dark red.

"Okay," said Hazel, her voice was hoarse. "The long version. Now."

Jude didn't know where to begin. He looked at Sarah, whose eyes were locked on the metal floor of the pod. He pulled up a chair and sat next to his sister. She turned her gaze straight at him, and he could see, for the first time, that she fully believed that he was sitting in front of her. If she could believe that he survived, he thought, then the other unbelievable things might have a chance.

Jude took a deep breath before he began. He spent the next thirty minutes telling his sister about everything and fielding questions the entire time. He told her about Elise and her father, the aliens that were Volgen and Shadows, about their parents being scientists and allies to the Volgens, and everything else that led up to when she got home, and her brother just happened to be sitting in her living room.

It wasn't the Houdini Vests, or the aliens, or time travel that Hazel got stuck on. Somehow, she accepted almost everything by the time Jude finished speaking. Hazel's last question, which was more of a clarification than anything, was ten minutes before the end of Jude's odyssey. At the end of the story, she was silent when he stopped talking. Jude looked at his sister and waited for her to say something, but nothing came. He knew she had to process it. Hell, he was still processing, but she didn't even move for an entire minute as the pod stayed completely still.

Finally, she shifted her eyes and turned her head to the left, and that's all that was needed for Sarah and Jude to see the one thing Hazel was caught up on. With Sarah, the alien, who was also on the rocket with Link, and also from the future, some things weren't fully adding up. She looked back to Jude, and her eyes were filled with concern.

"I'll let you guys have the space," said Sarah, as she turned to exit the pod.

"No, you can–"

"Thank you, Sarah. We'll only be a minute," Hazel said, her eyes never leaving her brother.

"I know what yo–"

"Don't you dare say that. You don't know what I'm thinking." Hazel, not giving an inch, crossed her arms and leaned forward. "Jude, where the hell are we? You're my brother, and I trust you. That's why I'm believing a lot more crazy shit than any sane person would. And I am so glad, so very glad, that you're alive. God, I can't tell you how happy I am. But look around, Jude. How can you even trust anyone? That Elise girl? Even mom and dad? I sat next to Link yesterday. He was an incredible guy, and then he's shooting at us an hour later? I just don't understand how we can trust anyone right now. Even Grace, you know that I love her, but what the hell is she doing back there? Something's off here. Don't you see that? The only person I know that I can trust is you."

Jude paused as he took in her words. He couldn't deny that she had a point. The common denominator of his story was the constant occurrence of the opposite of everything he thought he knew. The only thing he had was the feeling in his gut, but where did that get him with Elise?

"... and she just so happens to be the daughter of someone who allegedly saved Earth with our parents? Doesn't tha–"

"Hazel, I trust her," said Jude, cutting her off and not even realizing he was saying this thought until his words were floating in the air.

"Why, Jude? You tell me why. I'm listening. Our worlds are upside down. All I have is you. You tell me how you can possibly trust anyone else, and I'll listen. Because it's you. Don't feed me any nonsense. Just tell me."

Jude didn't need any time to answer Hazel's question. He looked at his sister, and she could see more confidence in him than she had in a very long time. "I trust her. With everything that I have, I trust her. She was there when I fell, and she caught me. I have to believe she'd catch me again and again. Sarah... She's not like anyone we've ever known. She knew where I'd be when mom sent me back, which means mom trusts her. Both of those things might not be much, but they're enough for me."

Hazel hesitated as she looked at her brother. She could clearly see how secure he was in what he believed. She looked hard at him. There was a tense moment between the two until a glimmer of joy came in Hazel's eyes. "I don't fully know what happened since I saw you last, but I'm so proud of you."

Jude was caught off guard as he looked at his sister. To him, her statement didn't seem to have anything to do with anything that he had said. For Hazel, it had to do with everything. It was not necessarily the words, but how he said them. Jude paused as he analyzed her sentiment, and he finally figured out what she meant. "I'm a lot stronger than I was before I left."

"No. You're not. You just found the strength I kept telling you was in there before you left."

Jude lowered his head and looked at the ground. Hazel took his hands. "If you trust her, then that's good enough for me."

"I really do," said Jude, looking back up to meet his sister's glance.

"She's some woman, huh?" Hazel leaned back in her chair.

"She really is," Jude agreed as the pair looked at the door of the pod that led to where she had exited a few minutes before. "She's incredible."

Hazel leaned forward and slapped his arm. "Oh my God, you guys kissed, didn't you. I knew it."

"What the hell are you talking about?" said Jude. A flicker of a smile crossed his face, and that was all that was needed for Hazel to know everything.

"You're kissing aliens now? Dude, what–"

"I haven't confirmed or denied anyth–

"Oh, okay. Sure. Was it differ–"

Jude cut her off as he stood up and moved to the door. "Listen, I'm going to bring Sarah back in. Before I do. Any more questions? Do you feel like you're up to speed and ready to go kick some ass and save mom and dad?"

Hazel leaned back in her chair, crossed her arms again, and smiled at Jude. "First, yes, I feel up to speed with the fact that this universe is batshit crazy and we're just along for the ride. Second, I have nothing but support skills that I am more than willing to help save mom and dad with. Thirdly, you may go ahead and bring in your girlfriend."

Jude rolled his eyes as his sister let out a loud laugh. He hit the button next to the door to reveal Sarah, who was standing on the other side. She looked to Hazel immediately, knowing full well what was discussed while she was outside. Hazel stood up and walked straight over to Sarah and hugged her. At first, she was too surprised to react, but Hazel waited, and Sarah embraced her.

"Thank you for saving my brother. I can't tell you what it means."

Sarah looked at Jude while in the arms of his sister. "Well, Jude's one of a kind. This world needs more people like him."

"Don't I know it," said Hazel, letting go and beaming at her brother.

Sarah moved to the front of the pod, started the engines, turned the invisibility on, and began to leave the ground. Hazel immediately fell back into her chair. Jude, already accustomed to pod flying, was braced against the wall.

"There's one thing I don't get," said Hazel, looking around. "I get that the vests bring you back, but how is this pod here?"

Jude, wondering the same thing, looked at Sarah in the driver's chair and awaited an answer.

"Well, let me put it this way," said Sarah, leaning back and looking at Hazel. "Jude told you about my mom, The Sphinx, sending the comet through a portal?" Hazel and Jude nodded. "If a comet can go through, then a pod definitely can as well." Hazel stared at Jude as Sarah hit the throttle, and the pod began to leave the ground. She looked at him in a way that only a sister could. Jude, who could feel himself blushing, quickly turned away.

As the group moved toward the sky, for the first time in what felt like a long time, they felt relatively safe. They didn't know that Link was already in the air, waiting for them in his own pod. "She's pretty cool, y'know," said Hazel, looking from Sarah and back to her brother.

"She really is," replied Jude, more to himself than as a response to his sister.

As the Monroes became lost in their thoughts, the only sound in the pod came from the engines. Grace remained still on the bed in the back and stared at the ceiling. A few moments went by, and she closed her eyes as she heard footsteps approaching the curtain that separated the sleeping compartment from the rest of the ship.

Jude had entered to check in on her as she was believed to be sleeping. He looked to see if she was still breathing normally, and to his content, she was. After a short spell, she heard him turn around and walk back to the front of the pod. He closed the curtain on his way out. When she was alone again, she allowed the tear that she was fighting back to stream down the side of her face.

Grace felt pain, but her suffering wasn't from the blaster wound nor from a fear of what was to come next in the mission. No, her pain was caused by something much deeper than any of that. While the siblings on the other side of the curtain had discussed everything about Jude's harrowing journey, Grace had heard every single word. She tried hard to block it all from her mind. She tried to make herself go to sleep. She knew that she needed the rest, but as she shut her eyes, she found it absolutely impossible not to think of the kiss shared between Sarah and Jude.

Twenty Three

November 10, 2393

Peter didn't sleep at all throughout the night. After knocking Olive unconscious, the guards dragged her limp body across the floor and into the large elevator. Elise was the last through the sliding golden doors to oversee whatever was to come to her next. Olive had taken too many liberties, and Peter knew that Elise would make her pay for every single one of them.

After their exit, Reginald pulled a chair around his large desk and sat it in front of Peter's cage. Peter watched as he slowly sat in the seat, unbuttoned his jacket with one hand, crossed his legs, and slightly smiled through the bars. There was an odd sort of standoff as the two stared at each other and waited for someone to speak. Peter remained standing, though he took a step away from his captor. Reginald reached into his pocket, pulled out his remote, and made a nod that indicated that he wanted Peter to sit down. Peter acquiesced; he'd played the game long enough to know which battles to pick. The two continued to stare until Reginald finally began to speak.

"You'd probably rather it was me downstairs with your wife than my daughter." Reginald paused to see if his words would garner any reaction. They didn't. "Pete, we know what we want, and we will get everything. You know this. This game only ends one way." Still no re-action. "You could stop a lot of pain for you, your wife, and your kids if you just decide to tell us where the comet is *now.*"

"You need us to accomplish all of your goals. My kids are safe. They're far from us. We've always been a step ahead of you. You are going to lose. You've always been one to lose."

It was now Peter's turn to watch how the words affected his coun-terpart. Just like his opponent, Reginald was unfazed. "Interesting. In-teresting indeed. But, you sent Jude back to where one of the best resistance soldiers I have is waiting. One that knows where to find both of the Monroe children."

"We're already ahead of you," said Peter, who was now the one with the slight smile.

"Oh, yes, Sarah, is it? The Sphinx's daughter."

"And if you think she'll let you desecrate the sacrifice her mother made—"

"This is the moment where we cut the bull, Pete." Reginald tucked the remote back into his breast pocket, reached behind his back and, pulling out his own blaster, he leaned forward. "We know the story. The entire resistance knows. The Sphinx helped Leo and Goliath save the planet by creating Houdini Vests, but when the big bad world only wanted to save a select few, they used the technology to get rid of the comet. The very brave Sphinx sacrificed her life to rid the world of the comet, and the Volgens so bravely lost their planet so that us Earth-lings could live on..."

"Well, then you know exactly what happened. There is no comet for me to give you anymore."

Reginald pointed the blaster directly at Peter's head. "That's all a lie, and you and I both know it."

"I don't know what you—"

"Pete. Man to man here. Tell me what I really need to know. I know the comet is still flying somewhere. Tell me one of your secrets, and I'll tell you one of mine."

"The comet was destroyed in Vol—"

"Pete, I'm tired of this banter, and I have too much to do. How about I tell you my secret first, and then you might be more forthcoming." Reginald leaned back once more and rested the blaster on his knee. "The story goes that The Sphinx sacrificed her life, right?" Peter nodded, doing his best to hide the fact that he had no idea as to where the conversation was going. "Then you tell me why she's locked away two floors down."

Peter tried to hide his reaction, but inside his blood became ice cold. "Impossible. She—"

"Oh, she lived. You think I believe the nonsense that Shadows found their way through some kind of dormant portal here? I know the stories of the Volgens who interrupted the timelines of their own kind. I know the evil that comes through the portals when someone changes the end of someone else's life. I know that they actually found their way here through the portal *you* made when you went back and saved *her* life. The Shadows are here on Earth because of your decisions. All this destruction, you 'saved' the planet, and then did what you did? You saved her after she died. Everything now is your fault."

For the first time, one of the two men showed emotion in the conversation. It was Peter as he stood up. "No. You're wrong. You–"

Reginald stood up and looked Peter in his eyes, only a foot away. "Just think. If you had only allowed her to die and let the comet be destroyed, you wouldn't be here. Your selfishness allowed us the only direction we needed. Without you, we'd be fighting in a war. Now, we have the greatest weapon of all."

Peter was completely beside himself. The Sphinx was supposed to be gone forever. That was the deal that the three made. Of course, he and his wife knew the consequences. They knew that the Shadows would come. But, they saved the Earth from the comet, then they saved their friend, and they left. There was no reason for her to be back. She... Surely she had stayed hidden...

Reginald sat down in the chair again as Peter stood gawking into space, trying to calculate what all of this would mean for his family. Finally, Reginald spoke. "Now, how about that talk, man to man. You have a comet that I need. How do you think Sarah, your son's bodyguard, is going to react when she finds out that her mom is alive and, oh, I'll trade her for one of the Monroe kids?"

Peter sat down and rested his back against the rear of the cage. Reginald leaned forward and pointed the blaster back at him and continued speaking. "I believe the phrase I'm looking for is 'checkmate.'"

Reginald grinned as he declared himself the winner. Peter put his face in his hands. He was clearly defeated. "What do you want?"

"I have a resistance. I need two hundred Houdini Vests. I need a comet. I need all of this within a week. Otherwise, I'll use the Chicago Vest and personally go find Sarah and deliver the good news. You and I both know Jude has one more trip on the vest you somehow suited him with. I'll bring him back here myself."

Reginald put the gun away and stood up. He moved toward the exit. When he got to the center of the room, he turned back and shrugged his shoulders. "Pete. We've known each other since we were kids. You knew my daughters. I never wanted to hurt you or your family. We go back too far. But, I lost too much because you messed up, and now I have to clean it up. You know I love Liv. But, I'll kill her in a week, along with both of your children, if you don't deliver. I'm not Reggie from the south side anymore. I'll burn your world and then everything else. You have one week." With that, Reginald walked to the elevator, entered through the golden doors, and stared at Peter until they closed to take him downstairs.

Peter was alone and left to unpack everything Reginald had just revealed. Since they were kids, they had been able to read each other. Everything he said was true. Peter and Olive always felt guilty about what had happened on that fateful day that they saved Earth. Was The Sphinx's life worth sending Shadows all over the Earth? They never expected the camps or the wars. Yes, they knew Reginald's kids personally when they were young. They never wanted him to lose them.

So much happened as a result of their decisions that, every day, Peter and Olive would have to look at each other and answer the hardest question they would ever ask: did the means justify the result? They always thought the answer was yes. But now—now that their children's lives were at stake and now that his wife was God knows where... Still, Peter thought, at least Reginald hasn't found out about the secret of the Chicago Houdini Vest.

It was the last secret Peter had that left the door slightly cracked for a potential victory for the Monroes. Despite any tricks that he may have held up his sleeve, he wondered if it was too late. Peter knew what he had to do. Fact is, he related, in some way, to Reginald. He would burn the world down for his family. That was the only choice he had left. Save his kids or save this world. The choice was obvious.

As the rest of the night went by, Peter sat up and was deeply concerned about two thoughts. First, where was his wife? It should have been him who was dragged away. He knew that wherever she was, she was in pain. The second thought he had: what possible reason could The Sphinx have had for a return? He could think of no answer to that question that didn't bring his family closer to danger. Reginald was wrong. At least in Peter's mind, the game was definitely still on. The Monroes, however, clearly had their backs against the wall.

As the sun began to rise while he sat alone at the top of the St. Louis prison, Peter was lost in his thoughts and had never felt so alone.

Twenty Four

July 16, 2019

Jude sat alone in the sand at one of Chicago's northernmost beaches. Taking a last bite of some microwaved pizza rolls Sarah had in the pod 'for emergencies,' he looked out over the water and breathed in the cool air. Nighttime was new, and despite the oncoming storm he and his group were sure to face as they figured out how to save his parents, he couldn't deny that he felt a sense of peace. Despite days of running and all the revelations that had come about, he was offered the tiniest amount of relaxation from the way that the small waves crashed the shore, the clear night sky, and the soft sand beneath his feet. He figured that he'd take what he could get.

"Jude," said Hazel, standing in the doorway of the pod only fifteen feet behind him. "Grace is awake."

Jude stood up, but before he even walked two steps, Grace came into view from behind his sister. His heart began to beat in his throat. Despite everything that had happened between them, this was still Grace. It was his Grace. How many nights did he stay awake, staring at the ceiling alone in his house and crying? How many times did he have to stop himself from calling her? Sure, he had many questions.

But, here she was, and as she leaned against the doorway of the pod and looked at him, the only emotion that he could feel was love.

She slowly stepped out of the pod and into the sand. Sarah and Hazel stood back. They knew that there may be dangers outside, and they knew that Sarah was truly the only protector they had, but this was a conversation that Jude and Grace needed to have. Better to have it now before they moved forward with the mission, Sarah thought.

Jude stood still as Grace slowly walked to him. The wind from Lake Michigan blew through her hair as she stepped through the sand, and she never stopped looking at him. The moonlight cascaded down, and the world looked coolly on fire as the two stood only feet apart. Finally, after what felt like forever for both of them, the two were together and nothing, not time nor a mission, was separating them. There was so much to say and so much to unpack, but where to start? Neither knew.

"Shoul–/So–" The two began simultaneously, cutting each other off. They gave a soft chuckle, and Grace spoke again. "Should we sit?"
Jude stepped to the side to let Grace cross in front of him. She sat first in the sand, followed by Jude, and she couldn't stop herself from noticing the distance between them. She tried to stop herself from overanalyzing each detail, but she felt cold as they sat a foot apart.

"How are you feeling?" Jude asked as he crossed his legs and grabbed a handful of sand.

"Sore. So sore. My arm feels miserable." Grace put her good hand on her bad shoulder to massage it somewhat. She flinched when it did more to hurt than to help.

"Gra–" Jude cut himself off. She looked at him as he paused and collected his thoughts. She'd had enough hard conversations with him to know to wait. "This beach," he began after clearly changing the direction of his thoughts.

"We used to come here a lot. Didn't we?" Grace let herself smile slightly as she looked down the shoreline and reminisced about the long walks that they took on this beach when they first started dating.

"We did. Long walks and great conversations. I loved it."

"Long walks and great conversations," repeated Grace as she looked at Jude. "Title of our relationship memoir." The pair awkwardly laughed, and both looked down into the sand as the laughter subsided into gentle smiles.

There was a tension that was palpable between the two. It wasn't malicious, but there was certainly a wall. Both clearly had a laundry list of things to say or to ask. Neither could find the segue into the looming conversation.

"So, Sarah, she's pretty amazing, huh?" Grace still stared at the sand as she said this. She didn't know what response she wanted when she said it, but she knew that she had to say it anyway.

"Yeah, she is," said Jude, taking in a new handful of sand and letting it flow between his fingers. "We're really lucky to have her."

Grace's heart sank as he responded. She closed her eyes, and there he was with Sarah, moving in close for a kiss. She reopened her eyes to escape the nightmare. "Look Ju–"

"Grace, what are you doing here?" Jude cut her off and looked straight at her. "I've been trying to figure it out, and I just don't understand."

Grace paused. She knew the question was coming, but when it was asked, all of her prepared remarks flew out of the window. She took a deep breath and looked back at him. "Jude. I'm here for *you*."

It just didn't make any sense to Jude. There had been hard truths that he had come to terms with, and this was nearly as unfathomable as anything else. "Grace, this whole nightmare, there's no way you've been in on it, too."

"I'm here for us," Grace spoke again, but this time with more confidence. "I'm just here for you."

"But, I don't understand how or why or–"

"Just give me time to explain. I can tell you everything. I have so much to tell you."

"Grace, I waited so long for an explanation. I never got anything from you. Not a phone call, not a text, nothing. I was so alone."

"Ju–"

"--and now, in the middle of all of this... Grace, I can't think of anything you can say that could explain why you're here."

"Jude. There are so many reasons why I am sitting here. But the only one that matters is that I am here for you."

"Why now, though? Grace, you weren't there. No matter the reason, how am I supposed to just accept that you're here? There's monsters and villains in the future, but I've been fighting so many demons before any of this started... and I had to do it without you."

"I know Jude, but–"

"Things got tough and you left and no–"

Grace, knowing how Jude could be when he thought out loud, decided to put an end to the tailspin of the conversation. "You think I left because things got tough?"

"I was so lost and then yo–"

"You don't know anything, Jude."

"Tell me, then. Because you came home, and it was over. The conversation was nonexistent. I stood in the driveway as you got into the car and you sai–"

"–I know what I–"

"–and you said that you never wanted to speak to me again."

Sarah stepped close to the doorway as the voices began to rise. Hazel stayed back, not getting involved.

"Grace," continued Jude, looking back to the sand. "Grace, you broke my heart. You were the one thing that I had left."

Grace closed her eyes as the tears that she'd been holding back since she walked out of the pod cascaded down her cheeks. No, she couldn't imagine what life had been like for Jude, especially after these last few days. But, he didn't know the same things about her. He didn't know the level of pain that she had also endured. "Please, please, just think about it. Don't you get it?" she asked, looking again at her former fiancé. "You really don't understand why I left or what I mean when I say that I am just here for you?"

"No. I don't," said Jude, looking back at Grace. "I've spent all day trying to figure out why and how it connects to all of this. But I have no idea."

Grace put her good arm behind her and leaned back. She looked to the sky and took a deep breath. "Jude. There's so much that I want to tell you if you'll only give me the chance."

"Then tell m—"

"Do you remember the promise we made the morning after your parents' party?"

"Of course I do."

"We swore that we would be happy and more happy forever and that time wouldn't change any of it."

"I know what we said. That meant s—"

"It was everything to me, Jude. That's why I left. I didn't walk away to lose you, I went out to try and find you... To bring you back home."

As Grace said this, all of the emotions that he had felt as he held her that morning, years ago, on the worst day of his life, flooded back into him. Closing his eyes, he could still see how the sun crashed through the blinds and into her beautiful brown eyes. In that moment, he had never been so at peace or felt more love. Reopening his eyes brought him back to his current situation. Her words were still in his ears as he reflected on the promise they had made long ago. Jude felt that the promise had been shattered when Grace left. After she drove away, he felt that it was a lost dream. Though, as she sat next to him and he heard her voice, filled with love, it somehow still felt alive.

Jude looked out over the water. He simply wasn't angry anymore. He wasn't sad anymore. He didn't fully understand what Grace was saying, but he knew it was exactly what he wanted to hear.

"Jude, you're the love of my life." Grace reached out, in pain, not knowing where she found the courage to do so, and put her left hand on Jude's leg. He looked down and saw the ring once again that he had given to her years ago in a grocery parking lot. "I've done everything that I can to keep our promise. You're not the only one who has been on an adventure. But, the sole purpose of mine has been for us. For you. Give me a chance to tell you why things had to be the way that they were. Please."

Jude remained silent as he let the words register. To Grace, everything that she said felt left in the air. This was the moment that she had been waiting for. This was the moment she had dreamed of for far too long. She missed Jude with such a fervor, and there were days that this moment was all that she had to keep her moving. She had played this moment over and over in her mind. She imagined that Jude would look at her and understand immediately. She never expected silence. She never expected a kiss between him and Sarah either. She never expected a lot of things. Yet, as she sat there with her hand on Jude's thigh, she didn't care about anything from the past. She only wanted him to look back at her and smile the way that her Jude always would when things got tough.

Jude continued to look at her hand as the small diamond twinkled in the moonlight. He could still imagine Grace's face when she turned around on the night he proposed and saw him looking at her. He had felt so nervous that entire date. A lifetime of Grace and ice cream, he thought, as she walked away to throw out the empty pints. That thought was always more of a promise than a wish. In this moment, there were so many emotions running wild through his mind.

Grace's courage radiated as she sat motionless and awaited a response. He looked back into her eyes. They were dry, yet glossy as the moon reflected from them. They were filled with hope and wonder. Whatever Grace had to say, it was going to be honest, painful, and most importantly, filled with love.

If she was being courageous, he thought, so could he. Jude reached down, took Grace's hand, and smiled at her. "I'll listen," he said, still watching the twilight dance in her eyes. "Tell me everything."

Sarah, still hearing the entire conversation, looked to the floor of the pod when Jude finally responded. Hazel sat back and watched the entire scene play out. She didn't know Sarah, but she knew heartbreak when she saw it. Hazel, kind as always, walked over to her and put her arm around her.

Grace worked through the entire story for Jude about where she went on that rainy day, about his mother, and about everything else. She answered all of Jude's questions as she detailed every move from her journey. Slowly, the distance Grace felt from Jude began to dissipate. Sarah, while she heard the story come to an end, could only feel the exact opposite.

She began to move toward the back of the pod so that she could try to avoid hearing anything more. She only made it one step away from Hazel when she heard Jude scream from outside. Quickly, she stepped into the doorway, and her knees immediately became weak when she saw a face that had become all too familiar.

"I hate to interrupt this lovely evening," said Link, walking around the pod and pointing his blaster directly at Sarah through the doorway. "But, I think we have some unfinished business."

Twenty Five

November 10, 2393

The sun was setting by the time Olive was brought back to the top of the St. Louis prison. Peter rushed over and hugged her. Reginald's people had cleared the space and had brought up all of the supplies and faulty Houdini Vests for Peter and Olive to work on. Olive fell into his arms, exhausted and bruised. Peter led her to a chair near a stack of vests. She tried and struggled to speak.

As she gasped and choked on what she was trying to communicate, Peter rushed to get her a glass of water. Even when filtered, the water tasted terrible. Olive guzzled it down and tried to take in deep breaths. Because of the bruises down her sides, each breath felt like another kick to the ribs. Peter kneeled on the ground at his wife's feet. He kissed her hands and looked up at her. He smiled to give reassurance, but Olive looked gravely at him.

"Peter," she finally managed to speak, her voice hoarse. "Peter, Mo–"

"She's alive. I know. Reginald told me."

"What the hell was she thinking? She knew the consequences of coming back."

"I know. But Olive, if she's back the–"

"Then something much worse is coming."

"Exactly."

"We have to get to our kids before he does. If Sarah fi–"

"Olive, we have to give him the comet. We've put our kids in danger too many times."

Olive sat back in her chair as she let the words sink in. She looked at her husband sitting on the ground. Their kids were in 2019 with Reginald's top assassin. She and her husband were stuck far in the future at the top of the St. Louis prison. Reginald held all of the cards, and now they had to make concessions. She looked around the room, and she knew that Peter was right. They were out of options. She turned back to look at him after finally making up her mind. "Where's the Chicago Vest?" Olive gripped her husband's hand, and he put his other on top of hers for comfort.

* * *

Not long after Olive and Peter were first married, they began their studies of teleportation. It all came from the childhood dreams that Peter and his best friend Reggie would share about exploring the world. Borders had been locked for decades, and the two young boys would pretend as they explored the world in the comfort of their dirt-filled backyards.

Shortly after their wedding, Peter was lost in thought as he held the hands of his new wife, a woman who dreamed of seeing Australia. He thought that if he couldn't diplomatically find a way to honeymoon in her dream location, well then, he'd find another way.

Peter and Olive always laughed when they would be asked how they found their ground-breaking energy-producing technology. They'd tell people that they stumbled upon it or that energy was a field they always dreamed of. Behind their veiled excuses for their inventions, there was a much simpler explanation. They were two people in love who wanted to see the forbidden world. They were laughed out of the science community as they continued to explore ways for teleportation. It didn't matter, though. They had each other.

The only friend they had was Peter's old pal Reggie. Before the resistance and before the news of the comet and before he lost one of his daughters, Reggie would sit at their table in their kitchen and grow excited. A chance to see the world, to live out their dreams. However, Olive and Peter left, and Reggie never got to see the technology for himself. When his wife was gone, and he lost one of his kids, and the world fell apart, the resistance was born.

No one knew what Reginald had known. He knew his old friends would flee to Australia. He knew they had the talent to figure it out. However, he also knew, from what they slipped in conversations about The Sphinx, that they had the technology to travel to not just distant lands, but to distant times as well.

The divergence in the paths of Olive and Peter from Reginald brought more consequences than either side could fathom. Reginald felt abandoned by a world that seemed to forget about average people. He felt abandoned by those around him who he thought cared. He felt abandoned by his friends, the people who not only knew of his shared dreams, but had dared to live those dreams without him. They left, and he felt completely alone.

In his mind, he became consigned to the idea that if he was alone, he'd achieve everything that he wanted on his own. He may not have been a scientist like his former friends, but he knew that he had talents of his own and could find another way.

By 2389, he implemented his plan with his daughter and a fully functional base in St. Louis to house his resistance. An entire decade of rage drove him to find one solution. To him, it was the only solution. The Volgens, the Shadows, the humans, they all deserved to die. He saw the world for what it could be. When the world was his, he could explore any corner that he wanted. His friends may have bent science to see the world, but his plan seemed much simpler.

They were just children when Peter and Reginald first met, but their paths led them in opposite directions. After Peter married Olive, his path with Reginald began to diverge. There was no intention to cause pain or anything close to what Reginald had to endure. Truth be told, there were many things that both sides wished had been different.

Still, in the end, Reginald knew of the technology of time travel that the Monroes had acquired. He knew everything but one secret. He didn't know the full capacity of the technology they had discovered. He knew they could travel in time. He even knew where they hid all of their materials, including a pod that the resistance sent Link back in time with later on. What he didn't know was the special ability Olive and Peter figured out with The Sphinx. He didn't know what they had built into the Chicago vest.

* * *

Peter kissed Olive's hands and then crossed to the other side of the room and held up the Chicago Vest. He turned around and looked at his wife. There was both pride and fear in his eyes. What he was holding was the last thing the two built together with The Sphinx. They had hidden the notes on how to design it in the files retrieved by Jude and Elise.

What he was holding was the pinnacle of all of their ambitions. It was their masterpiece. They simply called it the "Honeymoon Vest" when they completed it. They worked their careers studying and building contraptions to manipulate time and space, like the Houdini Vests. About two years into testing teleportation with The Sphinx, Olive and Peter finally got to live out their dreams. They used their teleportation technology and traveled to Australia. It was the perfect honeymoon. They spent the day on a beach while taking in the sun and tumultuous waves. They sat in the sand and watched the sun set. They wanted to stay there forever, but they had too much work to do and a planet to save. The perfect day ended as they took a long moonlit walk before going back to Chicago.

Three years later, the two were lying in bed and discussing the potential of time travel. Discussing happy memories, they shared the sentiment of wishing they could go back and experience each happy memory once again. While reminiscing about the moonlit walk they shared on their honeymoon, they each had the same idea at the same time. They jumped out of bed and immediately began working on their plans to create the Honeymoon Vest.

The vest could be worn by one or two people. Whoever was wearing it could go back and relive any moment in time. Because the Houdini Vests were only a transportation device, they had to be careful not to interfere with specific timelines along their journeys. But through the Honeymoon Vest, Peter and Olive could go back, sit on the beach, and relive the same day over and over again without any potential 'Butterfly Effect.'

By using the vest to enter into a dimension that existed simultaneously with the world's timeline, they could even see themselves walking in the waves on that sunny day in Australia. No one would see them, not even the earlier versions of themselves, and they couldn't affect anything. Like walking in a museum and watching from behind the glass, they could go and see any happy moment and feel the joy over and over again.

The vests were only able to open three portals like their Houdini Vest cousins, however, the portals created by the vests could be entered numerous times. The best part of the Honeymoon Vest was that they could use it as many times within the Honeymoon Dimension as they wanted. They cleared their mind as they relaxed away from their work while going and spending time together with the new vests. On that fateful day in 2376, when it was time for them to flee, they took one last trip to Australia only before locking the vest away forever. They closed the vest in Peter's old suitcase and sent themselves back in the 20th century.

Peter and Olive knew that one day they'd have to come back. So, they left the vest in the 24th century. While they knew that only a Monroe would be able to access it, they never, in their wildest dreams, imagined that it would be one of their children that would find it. Still, they knew that it would come back into their lives at some point. Whether it would be a reward for finishing what they had started or another escape plan later on, they knew that they would end up using it again.

* * *

Exhausted and sad as they may have been, they held the vest and thought of all the possibilities. Reginald had won. He had all the power. But, the Monroes, with their kids, could flee to a time set aside and live out their days in peace. It was their last resort.

"You work on their vests, I'll work on the Honeymooners," said Olive, slowly standing up.

Peter stood up as well and took his wife by the waist. It had been such a long journey to where they were. He looked deep into her eyes, she looked back, and they felt safe for just a moment. "How do you get more beautiful every day?" Peter asked his wife this, kissed her, and they set off to work. They worked diligently so that it wouldn't be long until the Monroe family was together again.

* * *

Four days, 167 functional Houdini Vests, and four functional Honeymoon Vests later, Peter and Olive were working late into the evening. They had set aside the fact that they would have to give up the comet in a few days and instead were focused on the fact that they would be reunited with their kids soon.

That's when they heard a sound that they hadn't heard since they had saved The Sphinx's life. It could only mean one thing: Shadows, somehow, were there. The screeches shook the windows that surrounded them. They could hear the pounding of the creatures running wild floors below. The thuds sounded like bombs blowing up outside. Olive looked to Peter; he hadn't tested any of the Houdini Vests, and though they did have some time residue on themselves from years earlier, they hadn't attracted any Shadows in a long time. What was it that brought them to St. Louis?

The answer was obvious. Simultaneously, it dawned on them, and their hearts sank to their stomachs. Before they could say the answer, the obvious answer, the only answer, the golden elevator doors opened up, and there *she* was.

Olive looked to the person stepping off the elevator as more screeches could be heard. "Molly. What the hell are you doing here?" she yelled as she threw down her tools.

"I don't have time to explain. I didn't have a choice. They're coming. Listen to me," said Molly as she rushed over to the Monroes. "It's much worse than we ever thought. So much worse."

"What do you mean?"

"Look, I know that we agreed that I'd stay away with my Honeymoon Vest, but the Shadows found a way into the Honeymoon Dimension. Not even Honeymoon Portals are safe anymore. They're not safe."

Olive and Peter's jaws dropped as they stared at The Sphinx. If the Honeymoon Portals were compromised, where would they run to with their kids? The world around them was collapsing as the thuds from floors down were seemingly getting closer.

They barely had any time to absorb Molly's words. Peter went to speak when he was interrupted by a screech and the elevator doors opening. As the golden doors separated again, Elise and Reginald stormed into the room. Elise had her blaster drawn as she pointed it straight at Peter. "What the hell did you do?" she yelled while advancing on the three.

"It wasn-" began Olive, but she was cut off.

"I wasn't talking to you, Leo. *Goliath*. What did you do? We haven't seen Shadows in St. Louis in years."

"It wasn't us," said Olive, trying again to be heard.

Elise pointed the blaster at Olive. Peter got in between the two women. "I don't know what happened. I haven't even teste–"

Reginald stepped forward, adjusting his tie. "Perhaps, our third prisoner might know what our issue is." He was calm despite the fact that the pounding of the monsters below was louder than ever. His cool disposition completely contrasted the atmosphere in the building.

Molly turned toward Reginald, and sadness was in her eyes. "They're everywhere, Reggie. It's not their fault. It's mine."

Elise turned to look at The Sphinx and was completely confused. She'd never heard anyone call her father that. While she was distracted, Peter took a quick step forward to try to steal the gun from Elise. She was too quick as she landed her elbow squarely into his jaw. He hit the floor hard as she immediately pointed the gun back at him.

"Molly. You know far too well it's all three of yo–" Reginald was cut off by the sound of the pounding filling the room. The Shadows had found their way up the elevator shaft, and only the golden doors separated the humans from the monsters. With immeasurable force, they began to break through and into the room.

The Sphinx turned toward Olive and Peter. "You have to make this right." That's all that she said as Elise and Reginald were distracted by the infiltration from the creatures. She took the opportunity to lunge at Elise to make yet another attempt to steal the gun. The two women fought each other for two seconds only until one shot went off. It went straight through Reginald's right calf and sent him to the ground.

Truthfully, Molly had no intentions of actually retrieving the weapon. Warning the Monroes was all that she had come back for. She had no more plans now. As she wrestled for the gun, she simply wanted to cause a diversion long enough for Peter and Olive to each grab a Houdini Vest and make a getaway.

Elise was distracted, and Reginald was on the ground in pain. Nothing could be heard in the room but the sound of the Shadows destroying the elevator doors. Olive and Peter each had time to put on a vest and type their coordinates. Before they could trigger the vests, Elise knocked Molly to the ground. The Monroes took each other's hands and looked back as Elise stood just above their old companion with the blaster pointed directly at her head.

Olive screamed and reached out as Molly looked back into her eyes. She opened her mouth to say one last thing to her old friends, but no words were heard before Elise pulled the trigger. Just like that, The Sphinx, Molly, was no more.

The two Monroes each hesitated in shock at the murder. Even Reginald, now on his feet, lost his emotionless demeanor for the slightest of moments. Olive went to jump at Elise, but she didn't make it. Elise whipped around, pointed the gun at Olive, and pulled the trigger, releasing a shot that only shattered the glass behind where her target was standing.

Before they could even realize what had happened, Olive had already flown through a portal and landed only a mile away from her kids. Olive looked around, and she was alone. This wasn't supposed to be how it had happened. She and Peter were supposed to return to the 21st century together to save their kids and take them somewhere safe. Instead, they were separated, and her husband was trapped with two homicidal sociopaths centuries away in the future. She thought about triggering her vest and going back to Peter, but with only two trips now remaining on her device, she had to proceed without him. She had to get to her kids. She'd have to figure the rest out later. After taking a deep breath to compose herself, she took out a cell phone that she had long concealed and dialed her daughter.

The three that remained alive in the room after Olive disappeared came to their senses as Shadow screeches filled the room. They were only seconds away from breaking in. Peter knew it was time for him to join his wife as he pushed the button on his vest. The trigger malfunctioned, and he remained at the top of the prison. He turned around and saw the open window that had been shattered by Elise's blast. He began to run. With one foot in front of the other, he put everything he had into his escape.

All he had to do was jump, and the vest would do the rest of the work. He made it to the threshold, and the glass beneath his feet broke into even smaller pieces. One step away from leaving the building, his collar was immediately grabbed, and Reginald pulled him backwards.

After weeks of too little sleep or hardly anything to eat, Peter was no match for his old friend, who was always much bigger. The metal doors began to give out as the weight of the Shadows against them became too much.

Reginald took Peter's vest off of him with little resistance. He handed it to his daughter. The gold door was now fading to black from the Shadows. "Take this. Go wherever they calculated it to go.

Keep an eye on your watch. If I'm not with you in 24 hours, kill them all."

Elise immediately secured the vest, nodded to her father, and jumped out of the window. The wind crashed against her face, and she relished in the feeling of flying. The vest triggered, and she began to journey through a portal. She landed on her feet with ease in the 21st century. She was all too glad to see that she wasn't too late. Olive was still in sight as she took off after her, and the 24-hour clock began ticking.

Peter hit his head when Reginald pulled him back and threw him to the ground. He was still dazed. He couldn't take Reginald's hits like he used to when they were younger. Reginald picked him up by the breast of his shirt and held him against the wall, only feet from the window. The back half of the room was full of darkness, and while nothing had yet managed to enter the room, both men could see a flood of red eyes in the crack of the doorway.

"Time's up. I'll let the Shadows kill us both, and then Elise will slaughter everyone you love. You saw what she did to Molly. She'll do worse to your family. *Where is the comet?*"

Sweat poured down the side of his face as Peter looked at Reginald. The room was almost completely dark. He closed his eyes as he searched for some way to forgive himself. He knew that he'd have to give up the comet. He still wasn't ready, but he had to give in. "The comet. It's in the Honeymoon Dimension. You need a Honeymoon Vest to get to it."

"Pete, I swear to Go—"

"That's where we hid it. We figured out how to hide it in another dimension. We locked it away where it could never do any damage. I swear on my children's lives that's what we did. That's why no one can find it."

The screeches and poundings from the Shadows nearly drowned out Peter's words. Their long arms and claws were reaching into the room, and the two men could hear the floor being shredded within the surrounding darkness. Reginald looked into Peter's eyes. They'd known each other too long, and he could always tell when his friend was either telling the truth or lying. Peter was clearly telling the truth. "Okay," he said, still holding onto the shirt of the man who knew him so well so many years ago.

"Hurry, grab that purple vest that has four straps. I'll take you. I'll take you to the comet."

Reginald quickly grabbed the purple vest and handed it to Peter. As Peter set the coordinates, Reginald grabbed four Houdini Vests. Peter attached the Honeymoon Vest quickly while the Shadows finally broke through the door and charged after the two men. The entire room was completely black as they came within feet of their prey. Peter grabbed Reginald by the shoulders, and they fell out of the window and toward the ground below. A crowd of Shadows, unable to halt their charge, followed them out of the opening.

Peter and Reginald were safe as the Honeymoon Vest was activated, and they flew through a portal to a new dimension. At the end of the journey, the two men gracefully landed in a field of dirt. Reginald looked around in complete amazement and then back at Peter. It was impossible for him to hide any of the many things he was feeling in this new setting. He took a few steps forward and looked around the world he was standing in. It was completely new and yet all too familiar.

He looked back at his old friend, who only replied by shrugging his shoulders. Reginald continued to look around, but it just didn't make sense. He couldn't believe where he was.

Twenty Six

July 16, 2019

"The kids are coming with me," Link said, coldly, as he pointed his blaster at Sarah.

"You're going to have to shoot me first," she replied, taking a step toward Link. He turned the blaster at Hazel, and Sarah froze.

"If I wanted to shoot you, I'd have shot you, but I think a much better punishment for this wound in my neck would be for you to suffer the loss of them like you did your own mother."

"Fuck you, Link." Sarah's words reverberated in the pod as Link turned his blaster and shot her in the thigh. She hit the ground immediately.

"Let's go, Monroes. If either one of you attempts *anything*, I'll kill the other."

Sarah tried to stand, her blaster was only feet away, but the pain was too much. Hazel looked straight at her brother; both knew this battle was over before it had started. Grace would be left behind, Sarah would live, and the siblings had to go to protect the others.

They'd figure out their next move later. Link began to move out of the pod with his blaster pointed at Hazel. "Let's go," he said, as Hazel and Jude put up their hands and followed.

In her pocket, Hazel's phone began to vibrate. She checked her smartwatch while her hands were in the air, and she couldn't believe what she was seeing. She hadn't seen her mom's name pop up since the morning of the crash. She quickly put her hands together and answered the call. In her mind, she knew, if everything Jude had said was true, this was their only chance.

Link, Hazel, and Jude all quickly faded from view as they hurried to Link's nearby pod. Grace, out of fear, hesitated only for a moment before rushing to Sarah's side to help her. The blaster shot had hit the lower part of her outer leg. She was in a lot of pain, but she was going to be okay. Grace helped Sarah to the same chair Hazel had been sitting in just a few minutes prior. Sarah pointed to where the medical supplies were as Grace moved as quickly as she could.

"I guess, it's my turn to return the favor," said Grace as she came back and opened the first aid box. This short sentence, underscored with an awkward laugh and a few pain-filled grunts, was all that was said while Sarah did most of the treating of the wound.

Grace wrapped the leg in gauze as the reality of the situation became more and more oppressive with every second. These two women had failed in their task. They lost both of their subjects to Link and weren't able to keep them safe. Sarah leaned back in her chair, and Grace sat on the floor and put her own back against the side of the open doorway. A cool wind from Lake Michigan blew in. They knew that the three could be anywhere by now. They knew that Link had to have a pod like Sarah's. He most likely had parked it close by.

They were already 10 minutes out, and Link was too good to chase. The odds were becoming stacked against them.

Grace checked her tracker just in case. According to her device, Link was still where he had been shot only hours before. She chucked it against the inside wall of the pod and put her face in her hands. Sarah stared at the metal floor as the pain from the wound began to fade away, thanks to the last injection she sent into her upper thigh.

Time ticked by, and silence remained constant. The two were dissecting the situation they were in. They weren't going to let Link just win, but they needed to figure out what to do next. They didn't have a clue. Still, the two women could feel the extra layer of tension between them. It was the elephant in the room that made their failure all the more agonizing. Both Grace and Sarah were clearly in love with Jude, that wasn't a secret. They both knew it, and they both were just as scared as the other about losing him.

Grace could feel Sarah's eyes burning into her. "Look, Grace, I feel like I–"

"Sarah, you didn't owe me anything before, and you don't owe me anything now."

"But, about Ju–"

"Really. I'm serious. There's nothing that you can say," said Grace, looking outside the pod and to the water that was thirty feet away. She was right, there wasn't anything that Sarah could say. Silence crept back into the pod for a brief moment before Grace spoke again. "Listen. We can table everything for later. Right now, no matter what, we have to work together to save them."

"You're right," Sarah said, looking at the wrapping on her leg. "Right now, we're all they've got."

"We just have to think. You've chased Link over the last few months, right? What's his next move?"

"Well, I know that Link brought a pod back to the 21st century like I did. Leo and Goliath had two that could go through a portal if the driver had their vest connected to it."

"Is there any chance that he went back to the future?"

"No. Not unless he has another Houdini Vest. He's used all of the trips on the one that he had. Jude should have one more trip on his, but I don't think that Link knows about the one that he is wearing."

Grace took a deep breath as she thought about Jude and his sister. "I can't imagine how scared they must be."

"I know, but, Jude, he's really shown a lot of strength through all of this. Hazel, too."

Closing her eyes, Grace could only agree. "That's always been in him. He can do anything, you know. He's incredible."

"He really is," replied Sarah, as the awkwardness continued to swell. "Honestly, Link's no match for him."

"You're right. Or Hazel, for that matter." Grace stood up, put her back to Sarah, and looked back outside. "I didn't risk all that I had to come this close and lose everything now. We have to get moving. Is there no way for us to track them or to find them? There must be something."

Grace's words set in quickly. Sarah had no intention of failing now either. Her face lit up as something clicked. "Grace, you're absolutely right. There must be something. Jude can do anything." Sarah's mood had shifted drastically, and Grace immediately picked up on it.

"What are you thinking?"

"Jude can do anything, right? And, Jude the nerd... How many movies are there where the hero gets captured and somehow manages to let his friends know where he or she is so that they can be saved?"

Grace began to match Sarah's mood. "... and if there's one thing Jude is, he's a movie nerd."

"Exactly. Hand me that black case that's resting under the driver's seat." She pointed, and Grace immediately moved and picked it up. Opening the case, Sarah pulled out a small, sleeve-looking device that Grace recognized as something similar to what she had seen on Jude's arm earlier. She had no idea what it was. Sarah powered it on. "Jude had one of these on, and I saw him tuck it under the sleeve of his shirt when he walked away with Link, but I didn't think about it at the time."

"Can you find out where he is with your device?"

"Well, these are resistance arm bands. They don't give an exact location, but they can tell you if there is another armband close."

"Resistance?"

"It's– complicated. But look," Sarah pointed to a red dot on the screen of the device, "if you can see that, then he's close."

Grace was a fast learner. Sarah had picked up on that the first time that they met. Still, she was surprised by Grace's stoicism as she took everything in. Grace pointed at the screen, "so–"

Sarah cut her off, already knowing the question. "So, basically, they are close, but they could literally be anywhere in our vicinity."

"Let's get moving then. We have some Monroes to find."

"Link's smart. He's not foolish enough to think that we won't find him. No matter what, this is going to be risky."

Grace paused for another moment and then nodded at Sarah. Whatever friction that had been between them had been stored away, at least for the moment. "This whole thing has been risky. But, you know what, Link is just one man, and *we* are two badass women." She took a step backward and put out her hand as an offering to help Sarah to her feet. "No matter what, let's do it for Hazel and for Jude."

Sarah looked up at Grace, and she could see what Jude saw in her. "Two bad ass women, huh?" she said, smiling at her counterpart for the first time.

"He doesn't stand a chance," said Grace as Sarah took her hand and the two moved to the front of the pod. Sarah sat down in the pilot's seat and began powering everything on. Both women knew the risks. They recognized the dangers ahead, but none of them mattered. Jude was captured, and so too was his sister. There was nothing that was going to hold either Sarah or Grace back from rescuing them. Both women had put everything on the line for Jude Monroe, and they weren't about to lose him nor his sister now.

Sarah looked over at Grace as they settled into their seats to prepare for the chase of their lives. However, before any further action, they were startled as they heard thuds on the metal floor behind them. They quickly turned around to see that someone else had entered the pod.

"Where the hell are my children?" asked Olive Monroe, closing the pod door as she stood only feet away and stared straight at the two women who had promised to keep her kids safe.

Twenty Seven

July 16, 2019

Link hadn't even sat down by the time that he had the pod in the air. He knew that if he was going against the likes of Sarah, he would need every advantage he could get. Even though he had confiscated the armband from Jude and despite the fact that he was one of the best fighters within the entire resistance, he had to be honest with himself. When it came to Sarah Lazerous, he was outmatched.

Jude and Hazel sat on the floor of the pod with their hands tied behind their backs. Link was in full view from where they were sitting. Jude looked over at Hazel to say something, but he stopped short when he saw the look in her eyes. He was amazed at how strong she had been as her world was flipped upside down over the last few hours. Certainly, she had handled it better than he had. Though, right now, there was nothing to distract her from the nonsensical environment that she was sitting in. Here, clearly a prisoner in a flying metal box from the future, her world was closing in on her.

Hazel's eyes glossed over as Jude scooted a few inches closer to her. He nudged her with his knee. No response. He nudged her again, and slowly she turned her head toward him. He looked at her sympathetically, and she gave no response.

"We're going to be okay," Jude whispered, forcing a smile. "I know it's a lot to handle. Trust me, I know, but we're going to be okay."

Hazel was emotionless as she looked vaguely at him and said nothing. Clearly, shock was setting in. Jude moved his head into her view and forced eye contact. "Sis, are you in there? Can you hear me?" Jude paused one more moment. "Hazel, I need you to answer me."

Finally, she looked at him, and the fear became obvious in her eyes. "Jude." She paused, taking in a deep breath and trying to fight the urge to vomit. "What the hell is going on?"

"That's a pretty good question," said Link, chiming in. Jude hadn't noticed that Link was turned around at the front of the pod and listening. "Jude, how many days have you had to rationalize this versus how many days for her?"

Jude didn't respond. He just kept looking at his sister. "Y... You," said Hazel, turning her head toward Link. She started to attempt to stand up.

Link pointed his blaster at her. "Now, let's not get ahead of ourselves here."

"How could you just sit next to me on the plane and make casual conversation like that when you knew we'd end up here?"

"It's all part of the job, dear. All part o—"

"You're a monster. A *monster*."

Link stood up, walked over to the Monroe children, and knelt down. He looked Hazel deeply in the eyes and chose his words carefully. "I might be. You know, that's always a possibility. Although, if you think that I'm bad, just wait until you meet the person at the end of this little trip we're taking."

Hazel and Jude remained quiet as Link sat on one knee only a few feet away. Link turned and looked at Jude, his finger was wrapped around the trigger, though he wasn't pointing his blaster anywhere in particular. "What do you think, Monroe, up for *another* reunion?"

Jude stayed quiet. It took all of his strength not to say anything. He only glared at Link, who smiled back at him in a way that had become all too familiar. "I hope you know, and I'm being as honest as a man can be here, that this isn't personal. It's not you guys that we want."

"You're not the first person to say that to me, and I'm being as honest as a man can be when I say that it sure as hell feels personal," said Jude, finally failing to stay silent.

"Be that as it may, it's the truth."

"Bite my a–" Jude was cut off by a beeping in Link's pocket. He pulled out a small device, looked at it, and smiled back at them again.

"Looks like it's time for more fun," he said, looking back and forth between the two Monroes. He stood up, walked to the cockpit, and paused. He turned around and looked back at his two prisoners on the floor. Jude felt rage as he looked up at Link, but even still, he couldn't deny an authentic sympathy that seemed to radiate from him.

"It really has never been personal, Ace. This is just bigger than all of us," said Link, who looked to the ceiling of the pod in tranquil reflection. Jude watched his captor as he moved his eyes from the ceiling and back at him. The interaction almost felt nearly identical to the conversation that they had on their bikes before the launch several days ago. Link, with a subtle yet consoling smile on his face, continued speaking. "Look, I know that you wouldn't be sitting there if you didn't decide that you could be or do anything that you set your mind to... but that's why I'm here too..."

Link turned away from the pair and looked out the front window. They watched his shoulders as he took in a deep breath. They had no way of knowing what Link was thinking or feeling. To them, he was a captor, a kidnapper. But to him, in his mind, he was just as much a prisoner. Trapped in his own circumstances. The truth was that he really did feel remorse and had felt so the entire mission as it pertained to Jude. The Monroes were a family separated by pain and sorrow. He connected with Jude, though he'd never admit it. Link missed his parents and his brother. Everything that he had done and planned to do was for them. He missed when times were simpler. That's why he felt such grief over the mission and what he had to do. Still, he had to continue. Otherwise, what was any of it for?

Link didn't turn around, though he spoke once more to Jude. "Ace, when it's all over and we all go home, I hope you keep that in mind. You can be anything and do anything. I do believe that, and you really do deserve it."

Link sat down in his pilot's chair and still didn't look back at the two behind him. Jude didn't fully understand the meaning of Link's words. He had seen too many movies to know that home was never a part of a villain's plan. Surely that was off the table by now. He looked at his sister, and she looked just as confused as he was.

Link immediately threw the pod in reverse and sent Hazel and Jude onto their backs. He accelerated the pod, and it shook violently as they flew through the air. Jude was unsure as to where they were headed, but after all the things he had learned over the last few days, he knew that he had to prepare himself for anything. As they flew through the Chicago sky, Jude stared at the metal roof of Link's pod. He knew that soon they would have to land. He had faith that Sarah and Grace would find a way to come through for them, but he knew that he had to be prepared to fight this next fight alone with his sister.

He rolled his head over to look at Hazel. As he began to think about what he might say to her next, something caught his eye. When the pod hit a bump of turbulence, the screen from his sister's wristwatch lit up only for a second, but it was all the time that he needed to see what was displayed. He was able to read the lone word that filled the tiny screen: Mom.

He felt butterflies in his stomach as he looked back to the ceiling of the pod. If his mother was back in the 21st century, he and his sister had more than just a fighting chance. He closed his eyes and began to prepare for whatever was to come. Anything could be on the other side of the pod door when they landed, and he knew that. Still, despite any impending dangers, deep within his heart, he felt the tiniest spark of hope.

Twenty Eight

June 21, 2342

Two young boys ran by Peter's legs and to a makeshift house built by random assortments of scrap metal. Peter and Reginald could hear laughter from inside the structure and then the sound of metal scraping the inside walls. The two boys broke out of the metal door once again with objects that were clearly supposed to be swords and shields as they ran around and proceeded to slay pretend monsters. The cheers of victory came shortly after both boys simultaneously imitated monster screams that confirmed their successful carnage. They stuck their swords into the ground and fell onto their backs in the dirt to look at the clouds that floated high above.

Peter took a few steps closer to the boys after removing his part of the Honeymoon Vest. He nodded his head as an invitation to Reginald, but there was no movement in return.

"Come on over. Don't you want to see the house again?" asked Peter, doing the strangest thing Reginald had seen yet, smiling.

"How do they not see us?" asked Reginald, gesturing at the boys who were each pointing at different clouds and identifying what they looked like.

"Olive and I created a different kind of vest with Molly. It's like the Houdini Vests and uses the same technology. You can only create three different portals with them, like the other vests. However, these can do something even more spectacular than the other. We call it the Honeymoon Vest. Essentially, if you wear one, you could escape to any time in the past and walk around it like a 3D movie."

"Like a—"

Peter took a step back toward Reginald. "It's like, if you were to build a museum of the history of time. It could hold any time, happy, sad, historical, insignificant, and you could go back and walk around in it. You won't interrupt anything. You can play in the dirt, walk in the sea, hell, you could grill out, and you would never affect anything. It's like you're living simultaneously with whatever you came back to see, but in some weird parallel dimension. I gotta tell you, it really doesn't get any better than this."

Reginald looked down at the boys as they continued to point at the clouds above. Their mouths were open, filled with laughter, and their eyes were full of hope and potential. There was a tear in his eye as he looked down and saw this beautiful memory from his past. "I remember this," he said. "I remember every day we had like this."

"Times were so much simpler when we were kids, weren't they?" asked Peter, putting his hands in his pockets. "You were always better at the cloud game."

Reginald looked around and then finally worked up the courage to move. He walked up to the boys as they both sat up and continued talking. They weren't talking about anything important, but they were talking as if the topic was the most pressing thing that they could imagine.

He knelt down a foot away from his former self, who was unaffected by his presence. He was simply amazed by where Peter had brought him. He turned his head toward Peter, the old one, and shook his head. "This is where Molly's been?" Peter only nodded his head. "You know, I knew she wasn't really dead."

"We had gone too far fo–"

"Oh, I know, Pete." Reginald's words stabbed like a knife. Peter had known this conversation would go in this direction. He just didn't know how long it would take to get there. Either way, this conversation should have happened a long time ago. Olive and Peter recognized their many mistakes and had come to terms with them. By the time they had to flee, Reginald was far too distant for any reconciliation.

"Reggie," Peter began, but Reginald stood up and cut him off with a look that told him to not even try it. "Look, Reginald, we did what we had to do. We saved the Earth, they wanted everyone to die, even Olive and me… and you and Molly and the girls. We did what we had to do."

"And you did it all without me. I didn't have a say or a par–"

"I kno–"

"Don't you dare. You were gone for more than a decade, but the problems never left. Just because a comet didn't decimate the planet doesn't mean you saved a damn thing."

Peter looked at Reginald as the two boys on the ground stood up, grabbed their swords, and started fighting more imaginary monsters. There wasn't anything he could say to make anything better, he knew that, but he still had to try. Everything was on the line.

"So, what now? You're going to take out your revenge on billions of innocent humans and Volgens?"

"I have my reasons to take revenge out on both... but maybe my hatred of the Volgens is something you'd know all about." Peter let Reginald's words float in the air as the boys ran around the yard, their backs against each other as they were cornered by the new imaginary beasts that had infiltrated their sacred space. The two grown men stood and faced each other as the sun turned to a deeper orange as evening began to settle into dusk. "So, what the hell is this? You bring me back to when we were kids and expect me to remember the good old days?"

Peter walked to the metal house and leaned against it as the boys changed positions and began fighting whatever monster the other one was fighting. "I told you I'd bring you to the comet, and this is where it's at."

Reginald looked to the sky. The intermittent clouds were dissipating as it was quickly getting darker. "Where the hell is it? You heard what would happen to you–" He froze as he heard a voice that he hadn't heard in so very long. He turned around as Peter's mother came into the backyard to bring the boys in for the evening. They immediately hid their swords by tossing them out of sight. Tears crashed the threshold of Reginald's eyes as he watched her walk within a foot of him and to the boys who were only a few feet away. He watched her walk and stop with her hands on her hips as the boys pleaded for five more minutes of playtime. For a second, as he looked just behind the woman, he saw Peter, who was also crying.

Adeline Monroe had taken Reginald in when his parents both died of the plague only a few years prior to this moment. They didn't give vaccines to people living on the south side, and he became an orphan. Peter, his best friend, was all that he had left. Adeline instantly became a second mother, and he loved her with every ounce of his heart. Here she was, standing before him again, and she agreed to let the boys play for five more minutes. She then walked a few steps before stopping once more and turned her head. Reginald would have sworn that she was looking straight at him. "You boys make sure to save the world in that short amount of time, y'hear? I'm counting on you," she said, smiling before she turned again and walked away.

The boys looked at each other and immediately ran to get their swords. "Why the hell would you bring me here?" Reginald, finding it difficult to breathe, asked Peter.

"I told you. This is where the comet is. Give it five minutes."

"Why here? Why the hell would you bring it here?"

"I told you, things that enter into the Honeymoon Dimension cannot affect the time they are paralleling. Just like you and me, here. We can't affect the boys... ourselves. The comet can stay here forever and would never do any damage. It's the perfect solution."

"I get the science, Pete. Why this time? Why this place?"

Peter looked at his old friend as he thought hard about what he should say. "We saved the world so many times back here. It was the only place that could possibly make any sense. Putting the comet here saved the Earth one more time."

The two men looked to the sky, two minutes before curfew, as the two boys found themselves being backed slowly by their foes toward the metal house. "Peter," Reginald finally said. "I'm many things, but I am not a liar. You have your family. You can have them. We'll go our separate ways. I'll take my comet. Just stay out of my way."

"So you can murder all tho–"

"It's time to save the world again, don't you get it? How can you stand here and not get it? Even the Phoenix has to die to grow from the ashes." There were no more tears in his eyes as he glared at Peter, who remained silent.

One of the boys stepped forward and slashed and stabbed, while the other protected the door of the house. The one in the middle of the yard was soon overcome as he took his sword and tucked it under his arm, falling down to the dirt in agony.

"Look at these kids, Reggie. Billions just like them are playing in their backyards, and you want to kill them? What did they do?"

"What world are they growing up in, Pete? We can start over, and we can build a new world where kids can grow up and be in a society that's safe."

The child who was defending the house slew his last villain and ran to his friend lying in the middle of the yard. He slid on his knees to fight the monsters surrounding them. "You're outside your mind if you think that any world built in fire can result in anything but calamity."

"Calamity is here, regardless."

"Think of these kids, Reggie."

"These kids are the exact reason that the comet is needed. It's the only way to better their li–"

"It's not living you're after. It's death."

As the two boys both sat up and began to laugh, the men met in the middle of the yard, only a foot apart. They began to speak as Adeline's voice could be heard from the screened back door. They turned their heads toward her as the two boys ran past them and went inside. When they finally looked at each other again, the sun was completely gone, but the sky was a dark red as the comet sailed high above.

"There's your comet. Now give me my family."

"How does it work?"

"There's a cannon called the Honeymoon Cannon. When we first had our breakthrough with teleportation, we did it with a teleportation cannon. We'd point it at someone, and they'd teleport somewhere else. That technology was then put into the Houdini Vests. So, when we created the Honeymoon technology, we built a cannon first and then the vests. We teleported the comet to Volgeria. However, Molly didn't want us to destroy her home planet. So, we teleported her there, and she used the Honeymoon Cannon to send it to this dimension from there."

"Why didn't you just use the Honeymoon Cannon from Earth?"

"Honestly, we weren't sure it'd work. We knew the teleportation cannon worked, but the Honeymoon Cannon was something completely different. We all agreed that if it failed and hit Volgeria, which only had Shadows, that it'd be better than failing on Earth and killing the innocent."

"I don't understand. In your records, you wrote that you couldn't teleport inanimate objects. Is the comet not an inanimate object?"

"That's actually quite simple. We teleported bugs onto the comet in a fireproof case. They were the live creatures we used to activate the portal. We never wrote that it had to be humans. Technically, they're still up there."

Reginald paused, still deciding if he wanted to believe the fantasy being told to him. If he wasn't already standing in an unbelievable setting, it would have been impossible to accept Peter's words. Each answer he received left him with more questions. "Then how did Molly die? Clearly, she managed to get the comet here."

"Molly was killed by Shadows just after successfully sending the comet to the Honeymoon Dimension. That's when we– That's when we did what we did. Anyway, the cannon is close by and that's all that you need."

"... and it's here whenever we want it."

Peter hesitated before answering. "Yes. It is, and because the bugs are still up there, you can activate a portal. But Reg–"

He was immediately cut off as Reginald pointed the blaster at him. "Get back in the Honeymoon Vest, Pete. It's past curfew, and it's time we end this for good."

Peter shook his head as he put the Honeymoon Vest straps back on and set the coordinates to where his family was in 2019. He thought about finding a way to leave Reginald stranded there, but he couldn't. He'd known since before coming here that he'd have to trade the comet for the rest of his loved ones. Reginald grabbed the Houdini Vests, and the pair of men watched the comet leave the night's sky. When they were alone in the dark backyard that they had grown up in, they triggered the vest and flew through a portal together.

They landed in the front yard of the old Monroe house. The lights were on inside, and the windows were open. Laughter filled the air from a family playing a board game at a table just inside. The two men looked at each other, and then they looked in through the open window. Peter saw the scene of the joyous family as the way the world should continue to be. Reginald saw the same scene, but only as what the world could be. They knew they would never be able to make the other one see things from their point of view. After a few moments, Peter and Reginald stepped out of the grass and onto the sidewalk. Using Reginald's tracking device, they traveled in the direction of where Elise was waiting.

As they progressed into the darkness of the night, laughter and joy were certainly both behind them.

Twenty Nine

July 17, 2019

Olive, Grace, and Sarah tracked Hazel's phone as they cruised through the air in Sarah's pod. Because of the speed at which they were traveling, the entire vehicle shook violently. Grace sat back in her seat next to Sarah, gripped the armrests, and closed her eyes. Olive and Sarah hardly noticed how rough the ride was.

The three women in the pod remained silent as they hurtled forward and gained on the Monroe children. When Olive had stepped onto the pod only minutes before, Sarah and Grace couldn't believe their eyes. It wasn't that they were surprised to see that she was alive. It was that she had come to 2019 early, and both Grace and Sarah were without the only things they were given the task of protecting. When Grace didn't have an answer to where Jude and Hazel were, Olive didn't even attempt to conceal her grief.

Still, it was not Olive-like to sit back. After she saw the pain-filled faces of the women sitting in the cockpit of the pod, she walked over to Sarah, put a hand on her shoulder, and looked at Grace. "They're not lost. Not yet," she said, smiling as she handed the phone to Sarah to plug into the pod to track. "No one messes with the Monroes."

A screen in the front of the pod immediately popped on to indicate where Jude and Hazel were. All three women simultaneously sighed in relief as Sarah lifted the pod off the ground. They had to be careful as they began their chase, of course. Too close and they would pop up on Link's radar; too far and what would they do if they lost the connection to Hazel's phone? When was the last chance that she had to charge her device? The battery life was certainly draining. There was also the chance of Link discovering that she was on the phone and disconnecting it or doing something worse.

They proceeded regardless. All that mattered was getting Jude and Hazel back. Olive moved to sit in a seat at the table, and Grace, always a nervous flier, continued to watch the screen and not outside the window. Sarah pushed the pod to fly as fast as it could. They were in the air and undeterred by any potential danger that could possibly come their way.

Jude and Hazel were roughly thirty miles ahead and moving, but only at half the speed as their pursuers. After taking to the sky, Link didn't say another word to the two Monroes that were tied in the back of his pod. Hazel and Jude were quiet, but still able to communicate. As close and connected as they were, they didn't need to say anything to know each other's thoughts. They knew that when the pod was landed at wherever they were going, tied or not, they were going to have to fight. For their parents, for Sarah, for Grace, for each other, they weren't just going to sit idly by. Hazel would rotate her wrist every so often to make sure that she still had a connection with her mother. It made Jude smirk every time he saw the word 'MOM' on the tiny screen.

Of course, they couldn't be certain that they were being pursued. They only knew that their mother had a cell connection. However, they truly believed that she'd figure something out. Olive always seemed to be the most resilient member of the family. Having someone like that to look up to her whole life was exactly why Hazel was as strong a woman as she was now. If Olive was on the other end of that silent phone call, then there was hope. And if there was hope, then when Link landed the pod, Jude and Hazel would have to do whatever it took to buy enough time for their mother to come through. In their minds, Olive coming to the rescue wasn't so much a matter of if, but of when. They followed each other's eyes as they motioned to different weapons that they might be able to use: a chair, a fork, even a small trash can.

After ten minutes of following Link, Sarah was absolutely perplexed. For whatever reason, he had doubled back to Chicago, which didn't make any sense. Yet, as she watched the screen on her dashboard, and as a small red dot flickered over a digital map of Lake Michigan, there he flew in the opposite direction that he had been heading this entire time. She hesitated before doing an about turn, but did so nonetheless. She held her course steady with a fifteen-mile tail on Link as they zoomed back toward the city.

If only Sarah had known the final destination of the pod that she was following. She knew that there were dangers ahead. Though, she never anticipated that when the pods were on the ground, Elise would be waiting for them. Link had immediately received a notification on his resistance arm band that Elise was in 2019, and the exact coordinates of where she was. Sarah, on the other hand, had no way of knowing the extent of the threat ahead.

Even healthy, the three women were outmatched when it came to Elise. They were far from healthy, though. Grace's chest and Sarah's leg each had blaster wounds, and Olive had been tortured by the resistance only hours ago. Sarah knew she'd have to deal with Elise at some point, but she had no way of knowing that it would be sooner than she had hoped. All three women were tired and in pain, and their entire worlds were crumbling. As they moved ahead believing Link was the only real hurdle in their way, they felt relatively secure. Link was manageable. Though they were injured, they still believed that they could take him down if they worked together. So, they pressed on, unconscious of the magnitude of the consequences.

Link's red dot settled in the south side of Chicago. Had Grace been able to fully comprehend the tracking screen on Sarah's dashboard, she'd have known instantly where they were. One rainy day at this location changed the trajectory of her life forever.

As they began to slow down, Olive made her way to the front of the pod. Instantly, her heart sank as she saw where Link had stopped. Unlike Grace, she knew exactly where they were about to land. She'd been there so many times. Her first thought was that her kids were going to the very park she had taken them to throughout the entirety of their childhoods. Olive couldn't understand, however, why this location? Why would they be going back home? Their home. How would Link even know about this park? Something was clearly awry, but Olive remained silent. She could feel a trap, sure, but her kids were so close. They had to proceed.

Hazel and Jude could feel the pod slowing down as they sat shoulder to shoulder. Link landed the vessel, stood up, and turned around to face the two Monroes. He already had his blaster drawn.

"I know I don't have to say this, but I will anyway. I will kill the other sibling if one of you tries anything." Link's face was solemn as he continued to point the blaster at the pair. He hit the button on the side of the pod with his fist to open the door. On his wristband, he could see that Elise was close, however, she was nowhere in sight. He stepped onto the grass just outside the pod and looked around.

"Jude. What are we going to do?" whispered Hazel, leaning closer to her brother.

"Mom's still on the line. She'll know where we are."

"Do we even know where we are? Besides, how would she get to us even if she did know?"

"Look. I don't know. But what else do we have to be optimistic about?"

Hazel, surprisingly, smiled when he said that. "Only my brother would find a way to be optimistic right now."

Jude smiled back at his sister. "Oh, I'm definitely optimistic... optimistic that I'm going to beat some ass in a second."

Hazel allowed herself to laugh, just a short, quiet chuckle, as her brother was seemingly his old self again. She looked over her shoulder and saw that Link was out of view. "It's good to have you back, y'know."

Jude looked outside, and he only saw the darkness of night. He turned back and looked at his sister. "What do you mean, I was only technically dead for like 20 hours."

Hazel shook her head. "We lost you a lo-" She stopped as she heard blaster shots from outside the pod. They sounded like mini cannons. One shot blasted through the doorway and into the table only feet from Jude's head. He and Hazel fell onto their sides as they ducked for cover. The shots continued outside. They had no clue who was firing or why, but they had a hunch.

A few minutes prior, Sarah had parked the pod a half-mile away from Link's. Her walk, like Grace and Olive's, was slow and deliberate. Olive let out a small laugh as she thought about the condition that the three women were in as they either limped or grunted toward Jude and Hazel.

"You know, Link's not just going to let us walk in and take them," Sarah stated, taking a deep breath with each step.

"No. He's not, but that's exactly what we're going to do nonetheless," said Olive, who, to the surprise of the other two ladies, was grinning. "Sarah, you're a great shot, aren't you?"

"Better than he is."

"Exactly. So, you go in hot, and lay down fire, and I'll get to the pod an—"

"Olive," interrupted Grace, "let me get to the pod. I can get to them quicker."

Olive's smile vanished as she stopped in her tracks and turned around to look at Grace. "Did you just call me old?" She turned to Sarah. "She definitely just called m—"

"No, that's not what I—"

Olive's smile returned as she looked back at her son's former fiancé. "Honey, I *am* old," she said, laughing, then turning back around and continuing to move forward. "Oh honey, some things never change... Grace, you get to my kids. Sarah, you and I will take care of Link."

Slowly, they walked toward the park. They could see Link's pod with the door open, and he was standing roughly forty feet from it. The women got into position behind a small teeter-totter. The three simultaneously took in a deep breath and nodded at each other.

At the same time, Grace went left and began to walk quickly, yet quietly, toward the pod. Olive stood up and moved in a way very similar to Grace, but she went to the right and toward Link. Sarah pulled out her blaster and pointed it directly at him from behind the small yellow and red structure. He was too far for her to be sure that she would hit him with a shot and not just alert him to their presence. In just thirty seconds, however, as Link was looking down at his armband, he was completely oblivious to the fact that Olive was directly behind him.

She stood five feet from Link, knowing that her role was simply to be a distraction for the other members of her trio. "Hiya, Link," she said, "it's your old pal Leo."

Link's face immediately went stark white as he pulled out his blaster and pointed it at Olive. He didn't have any time to do more than that as Sarah hurtled the teeter-totter while firing blaster shots at him. The first two missed, but they were enough to distract Link from firing at Olive. He ran a few feet away to a nearby jungle gym. Sarah kept moving forward and continued a barrage of blasts. Link returned fire as he ducked for cover, though he still couldn't see his target.

After a few more blindly released shots, he crawled to be protected by a metal slide as Sarah kept advancing. The pain in her leg was nearly unbearable, and his shots, even though they were shot without looking, were way too close. As she moved in on him, one shot grazed her hair. She rolled behind a park bench and continued to fire. She planted five shots directly into the slide that he was hiding behind.

The noises from the blasts were bouncing off the inside of the metal walls of the pod as Jude and Hazel agreed that this would be the perfect time to start their escape. They didn't know who was firing, but they knew a good distraction when they heard one. They both stood up and began to creep toward the open door of the pod. As Jude began to stick his head into the opening, Grace jumped into the ship, causing both Jude and Hazel to let out small screams. She immediately grabbed the two and pulled them both in for a hug. The pair of imprisoned Monroes immediately shifted from shock to joy as they were embraced by Grace.

"I was so worried about you guys. I don't know what I would've do–" She was cut off by more blaster shots from Sarah and Link. "Come on, we have to go."

"Who else is here? Don't tell me that's mom firing out there," asked Hazel, trying to connect the dots.

"No dear, it's not," said Olive as she crossed the threshold and into the pod.

Hazel's world immediately stopped turning as she stood only feet away from her mother, who had been gone for so long. Truth be told, she never fully believed Jude. Of all the things that she had been told or had witnessed, the thought of her parents still being alive was the hardest to fathom. Even now, she didn't know how to believe what she was seeing. Tears poured out of her eyes as her mother crossed the pod and held her in her arms.

Jude watched his mother and sister hug, and he looked at Grace, who was already staring back. She smiled as they looked into each other's eyes, only imagining what this moment must have meant to him. This was what she had fought for. This was why she had left. Jude took a step toward Grace and, in an instant, turned his head and looked outside. He knew that if Grace and his mother were here, then someone was missing. He immediately realized who was participating in the blaster fight outside. He didn't hesitate; he immediately ran outside and toward the blaster sounds. He didn't hear a single person in the pod when all three tried to stop him.

Fifty yards away, Elise sat back and watched the entire scene. She was filled with contempt for everyone on Leo's team. Of course, she'd have had no problem stepping forward and joining the fray, but her father told her not to harm anyone for 24 hours, and only a couple had passed. As she watched a shot from Link zoom through Sarah's blonde hair, she continued to sit back. They'd all get theirs, she thought. True, Link was a fellow resistance soldier, and while she had hoped nothing bad would happen to him, she couldn't help but to think that he had put himself in the position that he was in.

She saw Jude for the first time since the prison as he sprinted from the pod and toward the shooting. She only laughed to herself as she thought about the coward she'd met only days before. Jude had clearly changed since they first saw each other. Still, he was Leo's son and automatically an enemy of hers. It didn't matter that he had helped her or that they had shared genuine laughs together. She was prepared to kill him and everyone that he loved. That's how the game was played. She sat back and watched like a panther stalking its prey, tucked away in the nearby brush.

Jude ran forward; the pain in his leg was still ever-present. It didn't matter. Sarah was fighting for his family, and he couldn't stand to the side. He ran as one of Link's rogue shots sliced through the side of his right arm. It tore through a part of his muscle, but he hardly felt it. Sarah pointed the blaster at him when she saw him running. She couldn't believe what she was seeing. What could he possibly be thinking, she wondered.

Jude crouched down next to her at the bench that she had positioned herself behind. "Need a hand?"

"Yeah, from someone who doesn't have a full team trying to protect him. What the hell are you doing here?"

"I came to help. I couldn't leave you alone." Jude immediately put his hand to the new wound in his arm.

"I think that she's thinking the same thing," said Sarah, as she pointed her eyes directly over his shoulder. Grace was running, full speed, directly toward them. "That girl would do absolutely anything for you."

Jude turned and saw Grace sprinting their way. Sarah, on the tail of her previous sentence, thought to herself, 'and so would I.' Why she didn't say it aloud to him, she'd never know. Link stood up and stepped from behind the metal slide. He pointed the gun directly at Grace and began to step forward.

Sarah saw the look in Jude's eyes as Link began to move toward Grace. She hurdled the park bench and began a full assault against their assailant. Both of the shooters were out in the open without any protection. Link, focused on his target and unconscious of Sarah's movement, sent one shot and missed Grace by a few inches. He never saw Sarah coming. Jude dove on Grace to shield her from the last two shots that Link fired. They were the last shots he would ever fire.

Sarah's blasts connected with her quarry as she relentlessly fired shot after shot. Planting five shots in Link's chest, she watched as he staggered and reached out to grab a hold of something to brace himself against. As he stumbled into a post supporting a nearby swing set, he lifted his blaster one more time, this time at Sarah. She released one more shot into his head and finished the fight before he could fire any more at her or at anyone else.

The pain in her leg became overwhelming, and she toppled to the ground. Jude and Grace rushed to her as her eyes remained fixed on Link. He was lying under the swings, completely lifeless. Jude and Grace tried to help her up to get her to the pod, but she was too distracted. She'd never killed anyone before. No matter what he was trying to do to the people that she cared about, it was still the worst thing that she'd ever done.

Sarah knew she couldn't think about it now. Her main objective was to keep the Monroes safe. If Olive was already in 2019 tonight, the situation was definitely still dangerous. Jude and Grace helped her up and walked her toward the pod where Hazel and Olive were waiting. They had watched all of the action from the open door, and while they had wanted to help, they knew that it was safer for them to stay back. When Grace, Sarah, and Jude started back toward the pod, Olive and Hazel ran to meet them to help finish the short journey from the bench.

Elise stayed back as her comrade was killed fifty yards away. Rage poured through her body as yet another child of the resistance perished. She'd avenge him, she knew that. Time would tell. Still, it was growing more difficult for her to be a spectator to all of this. It took everything that she had to remain patient.

When Grace and the Monroes got Sarah to the pod, they set her down at the table. Blood was seeping through her bandages. They opened up the gauze and saw that the charred skin from the wound had all but disappeared, and it was completely open. The other four rushed around the pod to look for medical supplies, which they found under the pilot's seat.

Olive began to treat her; she'd seen wounds like this a few times before when the wars were breaking loose around the globe when she was much younger. Two injections and a new strip of tightly wrapped gauze later, Sarah was feeling slightly better. Olive pulled up a chair and sat next to her while Jude, Grace, and Hazel sat with their backs against the wall of the pod. Link was disposed of and that brought a small sense of security. They had no idea who was watching through the open door from not too far away.

A calm sort of silence crept into the pod. Sarah looked at Grace, who was sitting only feet away from Jude and his sister. She could clearly see a connection between them that still remained. This was a battle, she thought, that was over before it even began. It didn't make it easier for her. Still, she made eye contact with Jude, and she felt no regret about joining the Monroes' cause. Pain or not, she truly felt that her life was better because she had met Jude Monroe.

"Okay." Hazel broke the silence as she looked at her mother. "Where's dad?"

Olive looked at her children, closed her eyes, and took in a deep breath. "He's alive, but he got left behind."

"Tell me where and I'l–" Jude began, but Olive put her hand up to cut him off. Elise moved out of the brush and moved closer to the pod so that she could hear more clearly.

"We had a plan. He had to stay behind to keep you safe. He's got to deal with Reginald first." Elise's blood went ice cold when she heard Olive. It took every ounce of restraint she possessed to not enter the pod. No, she thought, he can take care of himself.

The pod was quiet again as everyone sent their eyes to the ground and tried not to think the worst. "So, what now? What's the plan?" Jude asked the question everyone was thinking.

"Your father will come. He knows how to find us, and he'll be here." The group became quiet yet again, only for a moment.

"Mom," said Hazel, trying to keep her voice light. "If we're going to just sit here and wait, I think it's time that you told us whatever you haven't in the past."

Olive looked at her oldest-born and then looked to Jude, who was watching to see what her next move was. "Everything?"

"I don't see why not," said Hazel, looking at her brother out of the corner of her eye.

Olive leaned back in her chair while everyone, including Elise, sat and listened. "Well, let's see. I guess it all started when two scientists met in a time full of chaos and dreamed of a better world..."

As Jude and Hazel listened to the most fantastic story that their mother had ever told them, everything, absolutely everything, from their lives began to make sense.

Thirty

July 17, 2019

"You know," said Peter, walking only a step in front of Reginald, "there is one thing I don't get."

Reginald didn't respond for a matter of thirty seconds. In his mind, he had told himself not to engage in any conversation. It'd be easier that way. As the tension built, however, he couldn't remain silent. "... and what's that?"

"You could have killed me. You have the vest. You have your daughter. You have a resistance in a building that I'm sure the Shadows have exited by now, meaning the vests I've made are safe to retrieve..."

Reginald took out his blaster. "Well, when you put it that way." Peter stopped and looked back at his old friend. "First, I can't trust that the vests work. Second, I have you right where I want you. You might have noticed from the last time you "died," it's easier to know where you are. Thirdly... Nevermind. It doesn't matter." Reginald began following his daughter's tracker again, and Peter followed. Now he was the one who was a step behind. They were only two and a half miles away from where Link, Jude, and Hazel were about to land.

"Thirdly, what?" asked Peter, trying to keep him talking. Reginald knew what Peter was doing. If they somehow found chemistry again and rekindled even the tiniest of flames from their friendship, maybe everything could be stopped. It was hopeless, though. Nothing could stop his plan. "Thir–" Peter began again, but Reginald cut him off.

"It doesn't mat–"

"If it's keeping me alive the–"

"Thirdly, I wouldn't do that to Adeline's son. She'd deserve better than that. She's the only reason you're alive." He still had the blaster in his hand, and he pointed it at Peter's chest. "She was too good to me, but trust me, if you or your family become any more of an inconvenience to my plans, I will not hesitate to slaughter each one of you." Reginald paused and looked in Peter's eyes. The faded light from a nearby streetlight illuminated his face just enough to show his sincerity.

The two men continued walking. They were silent again for half a mile. The pavement was still hot from a sunny day that had shone oppressively only hours before. Now, something was burning at Reginald's brain, a brand new thought that stemmed from what Peter had just asked. He waited another half mile before breaking the silence.

"Why didn't you kill me or leave me behind in the Honeymoon Portal?"

Peter knew this question would come. In fact, he had thought about it before they even went there in the first place. It was on his mind when he finally decided to give up the comet. "Well, first of all, my family was threatened. Y'know, the whole 'if I'm not there in 24 hours' stuff. That was very evil villain of y–"

"Forget I asked," said Reginald, cutting him off.

"No, no, I'll answer. Second, we're old–"

"Don't even bother with that."

"Honestly? Yeah, I could have killed you and probably made it back to my kids with the Honeymoon Vests. It would have been a long shot, but I probably could have made it."

"So–"

"So, honestly, I couldn't have done that to Adeline's son, either."

Reginald stopped and pointed the blaster back at Peter. "She only had one son. Don't try that senti–"

"She looked at you like a son, Reggie. You kno–"

"Go to Hell, Pete. How da–"

"Reggie, we were... we are brothers. Adeline loved you. Sometimes, I think more than she did me."

Reginald gripped the blaster and immediately looked Peter in the eyes. "You have no right to say any of that. No right. No brother would lea–"

"I know and I'm–"

Reginald lowered the gun slightly as Peter began his apology, but he couldn't stand it. The pain he felt from Peter grew too strong. He pulled the trigger and shot a blast square into Peter's knee. He fell to the ground.

Standing over his childhood friend, he held the blaster at Peter's head. "Not another word." Peter went to speak, but Reginald put the blaster in between his eyebrows. "I never want to hear you speak again." As his finger wrapped around the trigger, he could hear Adeline's voice in his head. This is the last time she saves him, he thought, as he pulled the gun away from Peter and immediately walked into the darkness and out of sight, taking the Houdini Vests and the Honeymoon Vest with him.

Peter, in immense pain, looked up just long enough to watch Reginald disappear. He used a nearby fire hydrant to stand up. He figured Reginald knew he would follow. He also knew that Reginald was heading towards his children. The memory of Adeline had been used up by now, and he knew that he had to get there as soon as he could. He took one slow step followed by another.

Each step felt like being shot all over again. It didn't matter. His vision became blurred as he grunted through the pain. Still, in the back of his head, he could hear a voice. He could hear his mother saying the same thing she said every time he went back to the memory he had just visited with Reginald. "You boys make sure to save the world in that short amount of time, y'hear? I'm counting on you."

He kept hearing that sweet maternal voice saying it over and over again in his mind. "I'm counting on you." His pace became quicker. He had to hurry for his family and for every family alive in the future. No matter what, he thought, no matter how terrible the future may be, there are mothers like Adeline there and children asking for five more minutes to save the world. He couldn't let any of them down. Yes, Reginald had access to the comet, but there was still hope. There still had to be hope.

Step by ever-quickening step, he just had to get there. Confidence grew as one foot was placed in front of the other. His mother's memory hadn't faded or been used up, after all. At this moment, it was stronger than ever. The combination of her voice, her memory, and her love was going to save more than just his family.

It was going to save the world.

Thirty One

July 17, 2019

O live finished her story that was filled with love, different vests, aliens, wars, and everything else. The pod was silent as all of the revelations clicked together. Hazel looked at her mother, who seemed all the more heroic than ever before. Grace and Jude looked deep into each other's eyes.

From his mother's story, Jude understood everything. Grace hadn't left because she didn't love him anymore. She had left and risked everything because she loved him so dearly. As she looked into him, she didn't care about the past, about a kiss, and she didn't care about what had happened since she left. No. She cared that Jude was here, was safe, and had achieved more of his potential than he ever had, even before the alleged death of his parents. He was there, and she was with him, and that's all that mattered.

Jude looked from Grace to Sarah and saw tears in Sarah's eyes. Ironically, the story made everything click for her more than anyone. She looked at the romance in front of her, sure, but she also looked at a family that was reunited. She'd lost hers so long ago. She could see why the Monroes did so much for each other. There was no denying that she'd do absolutely anything to have her family back again as well.

No one spoke after the story. There wasn't a question left to be had. In fact, the silence wasn't broken until Reginald and Elise came into view and were illuminated by the light inside the vessel.

"You really should shut the door. You never know what you might let in," Reginald said, pointing his blaster squarely at Olive. Elise had her blaster pointed at Sarah.

Immediately, everyone's hands in the pod went up as Reginald gestured for everyone to move outside. Olive, standing up last, expected the worst. If he was here and his daughter was here, where could her husband possibly be?

"Where the hell is Peter?" asked Olive, taking a step toward Reginald.

"Whoa, whoa, whoa. The floor has not been opened for questions." Elise stepped between them, her blaster still pointed at Sarah, who was limping to the edge of the pod to step down.

"Go to He–"

Elise punched Olive in the face, cutting her off instantly and prompting staccato screams from everyone in the pod. "Listen," she said, "you've caused enough problems. It's over."

Hazel tried to go after Elise, but Jude and Olive held her back. Blood began to seep from Olive's closed mouth.

Reginald looked around and began to speak again. "Here's the deal. We have our Houdini Vests and our Honeymoon Vest. We've won. It's over. Now, no one here needs to get hurt. You can live out the rest of your lives in peace. We're all going to go our separate ways now. We're going to finish our plans, and you'll never return. If you do, we will kill you all. We will send fighters back here to hunt and kill everything that you love. It's over."

There was only silence as Reginald put on a Houdini Vest. Elise still had the one that she had stolen from Peter only hours before. The pair continued to point the blasters at their rivals. Grace, Jude, Hazel, Olive, and Sarah were all safe, and they believed that Reginald would spare them if they stayed out of his way. However, they still felt like they had failed. How many people would die because they chose to stand there idly? Still, the people who mattered most were present, and they were standing together. Could they really risk losing someone they loved more than anything for an entire generation? It was the most conflicted any of them had ever been. They stayed still and unanimously made their decision in silence.

The only thing moving in the park, other than Elise and Reginald, was Peter. He had heard the thud of Reginald's daughter's fist as he moved into the park only moments ago. Still hearing his mother's words, still refusing to let her down, he moved diligently. He found himself by the swings and nearly tripped over Link's body. Looking down, he saw Link's blaster. He looked to the sky, as if to say thank you. He picked it up and moved ahead.

Reginald and Elise made sure that their vests were secure as they began to set their destinations. It was the last chance that Peter had as he was thirty feet away. He lifted the gun and shot directly at Reginald, hitting him in the wrist of his gun-wielding hand. The two Beckets were completely stunned. Reginald dropped everything: his gun and the extra vests that he was holding.

With all of his strength, Peter moved forward, holding the gun at Reginald and looking squarely at Elise. Olive used the distraction to grab the Honeymoon Vest while Hazel grabbed the two remaining Houdini Vests. Sarah tried to reach her gun, but it was too far away, and she was in too much pain to move quickly enough.

By the time that the two Beckets composed themselves, Peter was standing only feet away with his gun pointed at Elise. "I wouldn't move again," Peter said, unflinching. "Looks like we win." Hazel let out a small scream of excitement after seeing her father for the first time in years. The mood had immediately shifted as hope seemed to be once again rekindled.

Elise didn't move but laughed at Peter. "Oh, no," she said sarcastically. "You'll just send us to where we were planning on going anyway."

"I wouldn't be so sure of that," Peter responded, "those vests don't work yet."

"Is that so?" Elise asked her question while lifting her blaster to point it at Peter. "I'm still wearing the vest that I've taken one trip in. It's the vest that you were going to jump out of the window with. No. It works just fine."

Peter, internally cursing himself for the blunders of his short-term memory, turned his blaster toward Reginald. "You know yours works, but you can't say the same about your father's."

The tension was palpable as the group could hear the leather of Elise's glove tighten around the trigger of her blaster. She was obviously calculating. "You thi–"

"Enough," interrupted Reginald as he reached down and grabbed his blaster, "Pete, I warned you." He turned and pointed his blaster at Olive. Peter didn't hesitate as he pulled the trigger of Link's blaster and sent a shot directly at Reginald. The blast hit the side of the pod as Reginald's vest was triggered, and he instantly disappeared.

The entire group was stunned. Even Elise, who was secure in the safety of her father while he had the vest on, couldn't believe that Peter had the gall to pull the trigger and fire the shot. Nonetheless, it made everything much simpler as he stood there with his gun pointed at nothing but the metal wall of the pod. "Don't move," she said, her smile completely gone. "It's all over, Goliath."

"Please," screamed Olive, "please, you have what you want. Just let us go. Please."

Elise continued to point the blaster at Peter, but she turned her head toward Olive. "Why the hell would I do anything to help you, Leo? You're the reason we have to go and retrieve the comet in the first place. Do you really think Goliath should live while so many martyrs are about to perish?"

"Elise," Jude said, taking a step forward. "Elise, please, that's my father. Please. I'm asking you. Just let my family be together." Elise looked at Jude, and he had tears streaming down his face. He looked back at her, and she was completely emotionless, but he could see her thinking as she continued to point the blaster at his father. "Please Elise, I–"

Elise held up her left hand to cut him off. She slowly dropped her blaster to her side. "Jude Monroe," she said, sighing, "Oh, Jude Monroe, I know you never asked for any of this." The pair continued to look at each other. To the others in the group watching, it felt like an eternity that they waited for either of the two to say anything else. "But none of us asked for any of it. Don't you get it? There are just things that simply have to happen. Whether we ask for it or not, we have responsibilities." She paused as her words hung in the air. After cocking her head to the side to see that Jude had heard every word that she had just spoken, she raised her blaster once more and, without hesitation, sent a single shot through the head of Peter Monroe.

Everyone screamed as they watched his lifeless body plummet to the ground. Sarah jumped in vain to catch his corpse. Grace grabbed Jude as he fell to his knees in immediate agony. Hazel and Olive both jumped after Elise. They weren't quick enough as she hit the trigger on her vest and disappeared instantly.

They all wept as they sat upon the ground only feet from Peter. Even as a warm breeze of summer air softly crashed against them, in their lives, none of them had ever felt so cold. All seemed lost, and all hope seemed to have vanished as they sat there together and felt absolutely alone.

Thirty Two

July 17, 2019

J ude, sitting on his knees and weeping, cradled his father's head. Peter lay motionless in the recently cut grass with the blaster by his side. Jude's tears poured down and disappeared in his father's hair. Grace looked to Sarah as if asking her to use the medical supplies, but both women knew it was too late for that. Hazel was curled into a ball and lying in her mother's arms. Olive, quite simply, remained motionless.

Shock fell upon Olive immediately following Elise's blast. They still had so many plans. The family was soon to be reunited, and they would soon be headed to the Honeymoon Dimension. That was no longer a possibility. Yet, Olive Monroe hadn't connected that yet. She sat frozen as Grace and Sarah eventually moved toward Jude. Sarah put her arm around him as Grace began to take over the cradling. Hazel, making eye contact with Sarah, slowly knelt down next to her brother, helped him to his feet, and led him into the pod. Sarah and Grace moved Peter slowly into the small ship and to the mattress in the back.

Olive stood alone outside, only feet away from the pod. The world turned to slow motion, and she felt her knees buckle beneath her, but she was on the ground before she even knew she was falling. Sarah hurried outside and helped her up and back into the pod. Jude and Hazel sat feet apart on the floor and buried their heads in their hands. Grace stood motionless by the open privacy curtain leading to the bedroom. Olive sat in the chair and stared at the doorway of the pod as it closed slowly. Sarah made her way to the cockpit, and in one quick movement, the group was in the air with no idea where they were headed.

No one knew what to say. Jude and Hazel had lost their father, and Olive, a husband. Grace and Sarah, both on opposite sides of the pod, were both thinking they needed to do something, but they simply couldn't think of a single thing.

Sarah couldn't think of a safe place to go. Elise was volatile. She and her father had won. The resistance had everything they needed, and yet to still kill Goliath in cold blood was pure evil. She knew that evil like that doesn't just rest or take breaks. They couldn't go to any of the Monroe houses or anywhere the group had been since they came back to 2019. They needed a plan, and they needed one as soon as possible. But, who would plan it? Sarah put the pod on autopilot. She figured she would stay in the air until some dust settled and the group could discuss moving forward. Still, she thought, maybe there's a chance that Peter's death wasn't in vain. There had to be something they could do, but at the moment, Sarah couldn't think of anything.

With the pod on autopilot and in its invisibility mode, Sarah left the pilot's seat and sat in a chair only feet away from the Monroes. The shock was beginning to wear off, and life crept back into each of their eyes. Jude stood up and slowly began to pace. Hazel moved a little closer to her mom and rested her head on her mother's knee. Olive looked at Grace, who sympathetically nodded her head.

Jude's slow pace began to quicken as everything moved to light speed in his head. What was once stalled by the shock was now flooding in. He stopped only to stand next to Grace and to look at his father as he lay on the small mattress in the back of the pod. He moved into the back room, crouched on his knees, and took Peter's hand. He could only feel guilty. After all, he had helped Elise, and that had led to where they were right now. Jude cried as he buried his face in the crook of his father's arm. There was no denial left. His father was gone.

The women on the other side of the curtain heard him crying, but they remained still. Silent tears crashed to the ground as they let Jude have his time. The pod rocked back and forth as it hit a few clouds in the sky, causing a small amount of turbulence. No one noticed. Jude's mind was still rapidly going from one thought to the next as he stood up and wiped tears away from his face. The cold pain that rushed through his veins was replaced by a fiery rage.

He came back into view of the other four, and they all noted an obvious change on his face. Only Sarah noticed that his eyes were focused on the blaster that was sitting on the table. Finally, after an hour of silence since the murder of Peter Monroe, Jude was the first to speak. "Why does she get to go on to live her life when dad doesn't?" He looked through the front of the pod and out the windshield. "Someone tell me how that's fair." Everyone remained silent. Sarah kept her eyes on the blaster. "She should be the one lying in the back. Not him."

Grace, standing a foot behind him, moved and put her hand on his shoulder. "Jude. It isn–"

"She deserves to pay for this. She des–"

"Jude, if you talk like that, you're only as good as she is," said Sarah, unable to stop herself.

"Me?" Jude raised his voice. "How could I possibly be anything like her? She kil–"

Sarah cut him off. "She's a murderer, and you're Jude. You're Jude. You could nev–"

"You have no idea of what I am capable of now. That's my father lying back there."

The pod went silent yet again as Jude's words sank in. True, everyone was enraged, and they understood what Jude was feeling. Still, they knew the only thing separating them from Elise now was her actions versus theirs. Jude began to pace again as Grace took a step backward. Finally, he looked at his mother as she sat next to two Houdini Vests.

"Mom. Why don't we just use one of those vests and go back in time and stop Elise from killing him? I have a vest on already. I can just go ba—"

Olive finally spoke. "Jude, it doesn't work like that."

"Are you serious? Hasn't it been done before?"

"Do you know what happened when it's been done before? That's how the Shadows came to Earth. They are locked in the future. You try something now, and they'll be in 2019. They'll kill everything, Jude. That's what they're doing in 2393 right now."

"Is it not worth it? Don't you love him enough to d–"

Olive stood up and looked her son square in the eyes. Though he had overstepped, she could only look at him with compassion. After all, his hero had just died before his eyes. "Honey. I love him enough to not do the exact thing that he would never want me to do."

Jude looked at his mother. They both were crying tears, of which, they were fully unaware. He turned away and accepted what she said until he lifted his head and saw his father still lying there, only feet away. Thinking of the vest he was wearing, he turned swiftly to grab the blaster on the table. He was too late. Sarah had already grabbed it when his back was turned. The two stood locked as they stared at each other. The rest of the pod froze, waiting for whatever would come next.

"Sarah. Give me the blaster."

"No. Your mother is right. There's nothing you could do with it that would make things better."

"You're wrong. I could save dad. I could kill Elise. Both would make this world a better place." Jude took a step toward Sarah. She remained motionless.

"Jude," she said. "Jude. I know you–"

"You have no idea what I'm feeling," said Jude, as he took two more steps toward Sarah. "Give me the blaster."

"Jude," Olive said, her voice shaking. "Jude, we're all heartbroken, but there are other solutions."

Jude paused as he looked at his mother. His rage had slightly subsided as she put her arms around him and brought him in for a tight embrace. He wept in her arms as Hazel remained sitting a foot away, Grace watched from the back of the pod, and Sarah stood on guard with the blaster. The tension decreased slowly as Jude cried into his mother's shoulder.

Slowly, he pulled away and looked at Sarah. "I'm sorry," he said, his eyes bright red, the centers were crystal blue. "I'm just... Sarah, I'm sorry."

She nodded at him and smiled. She could only imagine how painful this was for him and his family. She was there, she thought, for anything they needed. She knew as long as Jude needed her, she would be there for him. It's like she had heard Jude say, as she had eavesdropped from outside the pod earlier, she'd be there whenever he'd fall. Here he was, falling, and she cared for him more than she could ever say.

Jude stepped backward and continued to look at Sarah. He returned her smile as he moved his eyes to his mother. She looked at him with love as he continued to move his gaze to his sister, who was looking up at him. She hadn't said a word since before the death of their father. She had spent so much time being strong after their parents 'died' the first time. How could she possibly replicate that energy again? Jude knew it'd have to be his turn this time. Finally, his glance fell on Grace, who stood staring back. He wanted to cross over to her and take her in his arms. He knew that she, too, was grieving. He was well aware that he had no idea how much of a toll this entire mission had taken on her.

He put his head down as all the women surrounding him watched as he got lost again in his thoughts. He seemed calmer now than ever.

He took in a deep breath and, without looking up, he quickly pressed the button that opened the side door of the pod that was flying high in the air, turned, and jumped.

Olive, miraculously, caught him immediately. She held onto the shoulders of his shirt. Jude looked up at his mother as he dangled below. Grace hurried to help keep Olive from falling out of the pod. Olive held a tight grip on his shirt, but her fingers were slipping. The pod was hurtling forward while flying 7,000 feet in the sky. Olive and Jude looked at each other, and the world felt as though it were in slow motion. There was nothing but sadness in each other's eyes. Jude remained suspended as his mother tightened her grip on the Houdini Vest she had sent back to her son so long ago. Seeing the plea for sanity in her eyes, he reached up to take her hand and to pull himself up. He simply had no strength remaining, and his grip failed the moment his hand touched hers. Before he even realized what had happened, he slipped out of the shirt and plummeted toward the ground below.

Without hesitation, Sarah grabbed the first vest she could reach and jumped out the door to try and catch him before he hit the ground. Jude floundered through the air while Sarah straightened herself for a more aerodynamic fall. As she gained on him, she noticed the vest she grabbed was the lone Honeymoon Vest that Olive had discussed only hours before.

The ground was getting closer as she closed in on Jude. She finally grabbed one of his hands and pulled him into her. Their fall seemed to be quickening, and they could easily make out everything on the ground below them. Her hands worked faster than she thought possible as she managed to put the vest on them. At 500 feet and falling, Jude looked at her with amazement as Sarah tightened the straps around his waist.

She only had to figure out what coordinates to put in. To her, there was only one answer. She typed in the last number of the coordinates at 150 feet. Finally, she wrapped her arms around him as they flew through the air with their cheeks pressed together. A moment before they reached the ground, everything went black. The world around them disappeared as they held each other, flew through a Honeymoon Portal, and landed safe from any harm and not too far away from the time they had just left.

Thirty Three

March 27, 2019

Jude Monroe was nervous as he sat on a stool and couldn't decide if he should cross his legs or just let his feet dangle. He adjusted his posture numerous times while he waited for the camera to be pointed at him. Fortunately, he still had at least two commercial breaks before he went live from the CNN studio that was a lot warmer than he'd anticipated.

He moved his nervous energy from his posture to the buttons of his jacket. Hazel, before Jude hung up to go into the CNN headquarters building in Atlanta, Georgia, reminded him that 'a true gentleman sits with his jacket unbuttoned and only buttons it when he stands up.' He certainly was anxious; he had buttoned and unbuttoned his jacket numerous times without realizing it. The spotlights went out as the anchor sent the broadcast to a commercial break.

"Hey there! Jude, right?" She smiled at him and didn't even flinch when Jude jumped and was brought out of his daydream.

"Hi there, yeah, that's me. I'm really glad to be here."

"It's okay to be nervous." The anchor never broke eye contact; her brown eyes were intense but welcoming. "To tell you the truth, I'm always nervous, even after years of doing this."

Jude dabbed a bit of sweat from his forehead with a handkerchief that he had gotten from his father long ago. "I'm just a teacher. I'm not meant for the spotlights. I don't know how you guys–"

"Hey," she interrupted him with fifteen seconds to go in the break. "You guys are the ones who deserve the spotlight. We're the ones that should be pointing them." She smiled again at Jude as the producer counted in from 5, 4, 3...

Jude looked at her as she seamlessly hopped back into the story that she had teased only a minute ago. He was surprised when he realized that his nerves had slightly diminished. At the very least, he hadn't touched the buttons of his jacket since she started talking to him. He looked down, and his hands weren't shaking or fidgeting. He still had just a few minutes before it was his turn. He knew that he'd be on after the next break. He knew that his students, his friends, and his sister would all be watching. He wondered if Grace would be watching, and that made him more nervous than anything.

He slipped his fingers into the inside of his jacket, and he pulled out a small picture. He looked down and smiled at the small photo of his family. His parents should be home watching him on CNN, he thought. Still, he looked at the picture and for a brief second, he felt joy burst through his veins for the first time in so very long. He still felt like he was making them proud. Truthfully, in this brief moment, he was proud of himself. He smiled and even fought back a slight chuckle as he felt so happy while sitting a few feet off camera in a terribly awkward chair.

Sarah was surprised by the grace with which they landed in the lobby of the CNN Center moments before. The ground had hurtled toward them at such a high speed that the fear had taken their breath from them. The world buzzed by as lunch time began, and no one saw Jude nor Sarah standing in the middle of the large open space. Despite the heroics it took for Sarah to bring Jude to this spot, the most amazing thing was the strange dimension that they were in. Clearly, they were invisible, yet living simultaneously with the world around them. It was only then that Sarah recognized the difference in the vest that they were wearing from the vests that she had known previously. Regardless, they adjusted to their new environment quickly. Sarah grabbed Jude's hand and took him directly to the room where he was about to be interviewed.

They stood about ten feet in front of Jude as he nervously fidgeted, looked at the picture, and awaited his very first television interview. Thanks to the Honeymoon Portal that they had entered through, no one, not the Jude from earlier, the anchor, the producer, nor anyone else was able to see them. Everything felt surreal as Jude stared at himself and looked at the nervous habits he didn't even know that he had. He didn't need to see what his former self was smiling at to know what it was.

He reached into his pants pocket and pulled out the exact picture that he had with him at all times. During the interviews, *The Audacity* takeoff, Chicago, and St. Louis in the future, he always had it. He looked up from his picture and at his former self sitting only feet away. His dad was alive then, and he didn't even know it at the time. He had always looked at the photo as a captured moment of 'what was.' However, during the time of the interview, his parents were very much alive. They weren't truly gone, and he had no idea. He looked down at the photograph in his hands and fell to his knees.

Only now, after a horrible tragedy, the picture truly was a frozen image of the past.

Sarah knelt down and put her arm around Jude as he continued to weep. He let all of his pain overcome him, and he tried to get it out through his tears. The anchor sent the broadcast to the commercial break after teasing her next segment: "The Teacher in Space." Jude slowly quieted down, sat back, leaned into Sarah, and put his head on her shoulder.

"Sarah..." Jude said, his eyes were closed, but tears still broke the barrier. "I'm shattered."

Sarah nodded, her head still touching his. "I know. I know, Jude. I'm so very sorry. I– I'm so very sorry."

She tightened her grip around his shoulder, and the two stayed motionless for a few seconds while Jude collected his bearings for a moment. Finally, he pulled away from her and looked at himself, who was still sitting awkwardly a few feet away. The former Jude's smile had faded to terror as he spoke with the anchor a few moments before the end of the commercial break. He closed his eyes and took a deep breath as the clock hit 30 seconds.

Jude, tears on his cheeks, broke out in laughter. Only now, as he began to come out of the fog that he was walking around in, did he fully remember what he was about to witness. "No. No. No. I'm down. My father just died. And now you're going to make me relive the humiliation of this interview?"

"You must think I really hate you," said Sarah, unable to keep from laughing while looking across the floor and at the former Jude.

"Sarah, of all the places you could have chosen... Why here?" The two looked at each other, and it was the first light-hearted moment that they had shared since she rescued him a day ago. Jude wiped his tears and didn't even realize how wide his smile was until he felt the tension in his cheeks.

"Can't a girl use a Honeymoon Vest to go and watch the moment when her crush began?"

Jude felt his cheeks flush when she said that. He was in an immense amount of pain, his sadness was unbearable, and yet, somehow, Sarah was already helping more than he could ever say. He looked at her, and she continued to stare straight back at him.

The anchor broke their moment as she brought the broadcast back from its break. Jude and Sarah sat and watched as the interview began. Jude ran his fingers quickly through his hair in embarrassment as he watched his former self slowly move his hands to his jacket and button it.

"This is seriously terrible. We should go." Jude's humiliated laugh filled the studio when he spoke, and to his surprise, no one reacted. He still wasn't used to this odd environment that he and Sarah had landed in.

"Oh, shut up. This is vintage Jude," said Sarah, putting her hand on his thigh, as she watched the former Jude field basic questions about his life and teaching. "The only thing I'm upset about right now is that we should have brought snacks. I wonder how that works in this place."

Jude looked around as if to see the borders of their new reality. There was no division, but like anything he had lived through during the last couple of days, he just accepted that he was living in a universe full of more surprises than he could ever dream. He looked back to Sarah, her eyes were glued on the interview, and she was smiling. Her blonde hair was tucked behind her ears, and her eyes were brightly illuminated by the lights surrounding the set.

"Oh, yes... here it comes. The best part." She turned, nudged her elbow into him, and laughed yet again.

Jude looked at the anchor and knew exactly what was about to be asked, and began to stand up, but Sarah kept him on the ground. The two watched as the interview quickly reached a new level of humiliation.

"So, Jude, going to space... are you scared of not being alone out there?" The anchor giggled through the joke. Yet, her eyes still demanded an authentic answer.

"Well, you never know." Jude nervously coughed as he answered.

"Teacher goes to space, abducted by aliens, it's a movie waiting to happen." The anchor still joked, and Jude looked at the camera and then back at her.

"Uhh, yes, I hope I don't get kidnapped by aliens, because I have no training for that!"

When Jude said this, Sarah threw her head back and laughed louder than Jude had ever heard her laugh. "I have no training for that!" she yelled through a cackle.

Jude buried his face in his hands but couldn't keep from joining in the laughter. Neither of them heard another word of the interview for at least a minute as they howled at his response. For the entire minute, Jude was void of the pain that had brought him to the ground where he was sitting in the first place.

Sarah looked at him, and he seemed calmer. "Honestly, I brought you here for two reasons. The first was the certain laugh that I knew would be provided. Secondly—" She paused as she looked at the interview and tried to catch her breath. "Secondly, I thought you needed a reminder." She pointed as the previous Jude was asked the final question of the interview. Jude's former self looked down at his hands that had just nervously unbuttoned his jacket. Finally, he looked at the anchor and said, "I guess I just agreed to do this thing because... aside from the pressure from my sister... because, y'know, after my parents' car wreck, I got so scared of death that I forgot about wanting to live my life... I guess this is me, deciding that I want to live my life."

The anchor was silent for a moment before sending the broadcast to a final commercial break. Jude and Sarah watched as the spotlights faded and the words sank in. Sarah put her arm around Jude yet again and hugged him tightly. "Jude, this universe takes and it takes. I can't fathom what you're feeling. I know that when I lost my mom, I wanted to give up. But that would have been a disservice to her memory. So, I stepped out and tried to make her proud. When I heard you say that..." She broke off as she watched the former Jude stand up and walk away from the uncomfortable stool. "Jude... I know the world is dark right now, but decide, for me, for your family, for you, not only just to live, but to live bravely in the face of all this darkness."

Jude looked into Sarah's eyes, and she tilted her head to the side. She smiled at him and took his hands. "Jude, watching that interview, it's obvious that there's so much light in you. There's no amount of darkness that can compete. Are you going to give up now, or are you going to shine?"

Jude's eyes remained fixed on Sarah's as a million thoughts ran through his head. She continued to hold his hands as he processed every bit of her short speech. Strangely, his mind wrapped around one thought. Sarah's words reflected every bit of what he wanted his students to take away from his classes. They reflected everything that his parents raised him to know. They reflected everything that he wanted to be. Now, at his darkest moment, would he choose to hide or choose to live?

Jude stood up and watched his former self walk past him and to the doors to exit. Before leaving the room, he let out a deep exhale, and then he was gone. The room was silent as Jude was still, and Sarah slowly stood up. He was clearly thinking, and Sarah waited for him to make the next move. He turned toward her, and she could see the smallest of changes. It wasn't much, but it was enough for her to see that she had reached him.

"Thanks," Jude said, still motionless and still clearly in thought. "Sarah. You never fail to amaze."

"One of my quirks," Sarah said, slightly smiling.

Jude took a few steps and looked around the studio. "You know, my parents, they're pretty incredible."

Sarah also looked around the room. "They never fail to amaze, either. Do they?"

"Never," said Jude, looking to his feet. "Absolutely never."

The room was silent again as Sarah continued to wait for Jude to decide what he was going to do next. Jude took a few more steps and paused at the stool that his former self had just sat in. She watched him as he looked at it and shook his head. "Sarah," Jude said, not turning around. "There's one more place that I want to go before we head back to the others."

"Of course," replied Sarah as she took a few more steps toward him and handed him the Honeymoon Vest. "Where to?"

The smallest of smiles crept across Jude's face as he looked at the coordinates panel on the vest. "Somewhere happy. There's only one place I could possibly want to go right now. You're okay with one more trip?"

Sarah slipped into her part of the vest and nodded to Jude. "With you, I'd go anywhere."

"Perfect." Jude typed a few numbers into the coordinate panel. He took Sarah's hand as the pair flew through a Honeymoon Portal and landed gracefully outside of a building that had loud music and bright lights inside.

Sarah looked around, confused, but she followed Jude's lead as he walked directly through the front doors and into the building. They took a set of stairs that was on the immediate right of the entryway and walked upwards toward a large ballroom. LED lights broke through the separation of large ballroom doors, and the music was blaring inside. Jude walked to the doors and paused as Sarah stood directly behind him. He looked, to her, exactly as his former self had the moment before leaving the studio a few minutes prior. Jude turned and looked at Sarah, and she couldn't exactly tell what he was feeling or what he was thinking. After a deep breath, he turned back and opened both doors without hesitation.

The room was filled with people who were dancing, sitting around, or standing while eating as they were engaged in wonderful conversations. The smells from the buffet near the door made the pair realize how hungry they were. It had been far too long since their last meal. Sarah and Jude stood against the wall and took in the party that they had walked in on.

A large streamer was draped over the dance floor in the center of the room that read: "Happy 34th!" There were what seemed like a hundred chairs all around the room, and none of them matched. Screams of jubilation were heard at all times from various parts of the room. Jude looked around the large space and was, for the moment, filled with jovial energy as he stood immersed in his favorite memory. He didn't know what he would feel as he went back to watch his parents' 34th anniversary party, but he welcomed this feeling nonetheless. Sarah, on the other hand, was simply in awe. She had never truly been to a party like this. Actually, the welcome party where she had met Jude was the first party that she had ever attended. She looked around and witnessed more love and joy than she had ever seen before, and she was transfixed. Jude looked at her, and she was smiling widely. He nudged her, and she turned her glance toward him.

Jude and Sarah looked at each other for a moment, and then their eyes went back to surveying the room. They both simultaneously focused on the same thing in the middle of the dance floor. Hazel, with a group of 15 people around her, was stealing the show as she danced to Hall and Oates' "Make My Dreams." They cheered as she grabbed Olive, and they did a perfect duet. The song ended, and the entire room gave a standing ovation. Even Sarah and Jude from an alternate dimension applauded.

"This is incredible," Sarah finally said after a few minutes of watching. "You guys are an incredible family."

"The best," said Jude as he watched his sister not miss a beat as she started dancing to the next song. "Just the best."

Sarah shook her head as she watched Hazel dominate the dance floor. "I see why you wanted to come back here."

Jude slowly nodded as he continued to survey the room. "This memory... This memory might be the happiest that I've ever been. But, I came back here for one specific thing." He stopped moving his eyes as he locked on something in particular across the dance floor. He immediately began moving, and Sarah followed closely behind. She didn't know what he was looking for until she saw it for herself. Fifteen feet away, a former Jude was being led out of the ballroom and onto a balcony by his father, who had his arm draped around his shoulder.

They followed the pair outside, and they were the only four people on the balcony. It was a cool spring evening, and a light wind pressed against them. Jude and Sarah stood back and watched as the two Monroe men walked peacefully to the rail of the balcony that over-looked a small pond behind the venue. Peter reached into his pocket and withdrew two cigars. The two men smiled at one another.

"Oh, Jude. My son," said Peter as he pulled cutters out of his pocket for the cigars. "Tonight has been perfect, hasn't it?"

Jude took the first cigar from his father. "I think it's been the most perfect evening that any of us could dream of."

"I love you and your sister and your mother so very much," said Peter, slicing the end of his own cigar.

Jude nodded and puffed on his cigar as his father held a match. "You know that we love you, too. I think we're all very lucky to have one another."

After starting his own cigar, Peter let out a large puff of smoke. "That Grace is something special, too. I think she's going to make a great Monroe."

"She already is a great Monroe."

There was a quiet moment as the men smoked their cigars and looked to the night's sky. Sarah and Jude stood peacefully behind. Jude watched as his former self interacted with his father. He felt happiness more than anything. He was sad, of course, but seeing the love that was shared between his father and him was beyond cathartic. Sarah fought back tears as she stood next to Jude, who was watching this old yet perfect memory. Jude could have gone anywhere, but he just went back to a simple conversation. To her, he truly was remarkable.

"Do you know why I love cigars, son?" Peter took in a slow puff of smoke. Jude looked at him as if to ask why. "Cigars take patience, and when you enjoy one with someone, the world slows down, and that moment seems to last longer than some others. It always feels like you hit a pause button on life, and everything around you is still."

The former Jude looked at his cigar as he thought about his father's words. "They do take forever, don't they?"

"They sure seem to, and isn't it grand?" Peter put his hand on Jude's shoulder. "I can't tell you how many moments our family has shared together that I wish that we could have hit a pause button and just let it stay paused forever."

Jude continued to smile as he made eye contact with his father. "If only time could work like that. But for now, at least we have cigars."

Peter nodded and smiled. "But for now, at least we have cigars," he repeated and moved his arm all the way around Jude and brought him in for a hug. Jude let out a laugh when his father took his former self in, and tears were rolling down his face. Sarah took Jude's hand as they watched.

Peter knocked on the concrete barrier of the balcony. "Jude, do you want to know something incredible about this building?"

"What's that?"

"During the Chicago fire, the flames rushed toward this building. But a Mr. Milo Henry, armed only with a bucket, defended it. He spent the night running to that pond down there and would run back and splash water on the closest flames. Also, this is not to mention that his wife was also in labor that night. When the fire had been quelled, like the legend that he is, he walked back inside and delivered his only son. Isn't that incredible?"

Jude looked at his father and shook his head. "Dad, what's the secret? How do you make every story seem like it's the most important story in the world?"

Peter turned around and leaned against the balcony rail. He looked long and hard at Jude as he contemplated his answer. "You know, Jude, that is a very good question. I guess I'd have to say that because each story, to someone, *is* the most important story, you see? You and your sister, to your mom and me, are the most important story to us. One day, when people tell our story, they'd better tell it like there was nothing more serious... or more fun."

Peter's words hit home with everyone listening. They had even more of an effect on Jude the second time that he had heard them. After his answer, Peter smiled at his son and took him under his arm once more. They finished their cigars in blissful silence. With one more hug, the two men walked back into the ballroom.

Sarah and Jude stood alone on the balcony, and the air felt as if it were getting warmer. Jude took a few steps and stood right where his former self had stood only a minute prior. He was deep in thought.

"Your father... He's amazing."

Jude looked up at Sarah. "He's my hero."

"He loved you. That is certain."

"I know that he did. Now, he belongs to the storytellers."

"Lucky for us, his son is just as good as his father was at telling stories." Sarah took a few steps and stood only a foot away from Jude.

"I could never do the story of Peter Monroe justice. Not like this," said Jude as he looked around the balcony and reflected on the Honeymoon Dimension.

"I think you do a good enough job keeping his story alive by being the fantastic son that you are."

Jude turned around and looked back at Sarah. The warm glow of the party lights illuminated her as a subtle breeze returned from off the water ahead of them. "Sarah. I'm glad you're here."

"I am too. I really am."

Jude looked back to the doors that his former self and father had just walked through. Life had always been much simpler. He thought about many of the long cigar conversations that he had shared with his father. He thought about many moments that he wished there had been a pause button. Jude deeply missed his father. That wasn't new. He had missed him for years. He reached into his pocket once more and withdrew the picture he so cherished. "You know, his story isn't finished. It can't be finished. He wouldn't want us to stop. He wouldn't want any of us to just give up."

"Tell me what you're thinking." Sarah looked down and saw the picture in his hand. It was obviously from the events taking place just inside the ballroom.

"Sarah, it's not about revenge. Dad wouldn't want that from me or anyone. It's about family. It's about all of the families. It's about our family. We have to stop the comet. That's my dad's legacy. That's your mom's legacy. We need to go back and finish this. We have to do it for our families."

Sarah stared deeply into Jude. As he stood there in front of her, she could see a fire raging within him. "I completely agree. I'm with you all the way."

His confidence radiated from him as he began to type coordinates on the Honeymoon Vest. "Let's go," he said, taking Sarah's hand. "We have a world to save."

Thirty Four

July 17, 2019

O live, Hazel, and Grace had tears pouring from their eyes while they looked for Jude as he plummeted toward the Earth below. After Sarah had leaped out of the open door with only a vest in her hands, they were flabbergasted. They lost sight of the two in the darkness of the night. They were hysterical as they had no way of knowing the fates of either Sarah or Jude. No one on the pod could handle any more heartbreak.

Olive held the shirt that she had designed years ago with Houdini technology built into it for her son. She turned from the door while looking down at the shirt and continued to weep. As she turned, Jude and Sarah, having just reentered the pod through a Honeymoon portal, were standing right in front of her. Olive immediately grabbed her son and pulled him into her for a hug. They tightly embraced as if making up for all the missed hugs since the Monroe parents left so long ago.

Grace, after being completely stunned, joined in and hugged Jude tightly. Hazel followed suit and quickly turned the embrace into a group hug. Sarah stood off to the side and watched the four hold each other until Hazel grabbed her by the front of her shirt and pulled her into the huddle. They all held each other and, one by one, they began to break out in laughter. No one knew why they were laughing, but they were doing so nonetheless. After such pain and terrible grief, they had each other. They remained locked in each other's arms for an entire minute.

The group had been awake for an unbearable amount of hours. They had watched tragedy unfold in front of them several times. They had battled and won. They had battled and lost. Revelations of an unfathomable universe had been placed upon their shoulders at every turn. Here, together, as safe as they could be, they hugged and they laughed. The group embrace dissipated into individual hugs. Olive thanked Sarah for saving her son yet again as the pair embraced.

The group sat down, Grace and Sarah against the wall of the pod and Hazel and Olive at the table. Jude stood in the doorway leading to Peter and paused only for a moment. The others looked at him from behind as he gazed in upon his father. For Sarah and him, it had been two hours since the terrible episode. For Grace, Olive, and Hazel, it had been only a few minutes. One thing was certain to all of the women in the pod, though: Jude was changed. After one more look at his father, he turned around.

"This isn't over," he said, looking straight at Sarah. She smiled and nodded her head. There he is, she thought, he's back. "We're not vengeful people, and that's what separates us from them. They're driven by hate, and that's what separates us from them." He turned and looked at his mother. "You both fought for a world that cast you out, why? Because, hate can never win. There's a comet somewhere out there, and we're going to go find it and destroy it before the resistance can use it. They might have an army and two lunatics, but we have something better."

"A couple of pissed off Monroes plus some extras?" asked Hazel, chiming in while crossing her arms.

Jude looked at his sister and smiled. "Exactly. Plus, as Sarah told me, we have light within us. If we have that, well, no amount of darkness stands a chance."

Sarah stood up and put her hands on her hips. She was beaming at Jude. "What's the plan?"

Grace stood up immediately after Sarah. "Count me in for anything."

Hazel joined the other women on their feet. "We're doing a standing thing? I've always wanted to do the standing thing. There's a crazy bitch in the future whose ass is waiting for me to kick."

The group all looked to Olive, who was sitting back as she watched her son take control of the situation. He looked just like his father, she thought. Looking around the room, she had never been prouder of a group of people. They were ready to take on any adversity that may be ahead. She stood up and put one hand on each of her kids' shoulders. "This is going to be good. Really good."

Hope filled each person in the pod. They had planning to do. They had a long road ahead, and there was much uncertainty. For the moment, however, none of that mattered. What mattered was that they had each other. Each person could feel a fire burning within themselves. Jude looked around at Sarah, Grace, Hazel, and then his mother as they began preparations for the oncoming storm. He looked past the four as they moved and spoke in the main cabin of the pod. He could see his father through a break in the curtains. Everything to come was for the people he loved. That's all that Jude was certain of. He looked away from the curtain and back to the women in front of him. No matter what, everything to come was for family.

Thirty Five

July 17, 2019

After what was a surprisingly good night's sleep for the entire crew, everyone was now awake, relatively refreshed, and ready to move forward with the plan that they had agreed upon hours ago. Using the unique time difference to their advantage, they figured that a little rest would give them the edge that they needed. Sarah parked her pod on the top of Willis Tower as they prepared for the journey ahead. Jude and Grace still had one trip left in their Houdini Vests as they had both traveled to the future and back. Sarah had used various forms of vests built by Olive. The one that she was wearing also only had one more trip left. Olive had two trips left on hers.

The two other vests that they had stolen back from Reginald created somewhat of a dispute amongst the group. They weren't sure if they had been used, so they had no way of knowing how many trips were left on any of them. Olive, Jude, and Sarah were prepared to go on the offensive by themselves, but Grace and Hazel would have none of it. Hazel stood up in the middle of the argument, looked her mother in the eyes, and told her that the family was staying together no matter what. There was no more to be said on the matter.

Of course, as Hazel wore a Houdini Vest for the first time and stood at the edge of Chicago's tallest building, she was second-guessing herself. In truth, all five members of the group were nervous as they stood and felt the building rocking underneath them. Jude stood in the middle and looked down. His thoughts were not of the city below, but of the plan ahead. There was a battle awaiting on the other end of the portal that he and his family were about to enter. Still, he was calm. For the first time in his life, he felt prepared for anything.

Olive put her hand on her son's shoulder. "You sure about this, kiddo?"

"We have no other choice," he said, looking at her with an intense wind blowing through his hair. "We could hide here, or we could do the right thing. Dad would want us to do the right thing."

Olive smiled and didn't say another word. Jude looked to the other women standing on the ledge near him. Hazel looked terrified as she stared back at her brother. Grace, doing her best to stay strong, smiled widely. Jude remembered, for the moment, how much he loved seeing her dimples when joy would overtake her, and he felt his heart flutter. Finally, he looked at Sarah. She nodded and squinted her eyes, clearly ready for battle.

"Everyone knows their moves?" yelled Jude, taking one more look at everyone standing on the ledge with him. They all nodded and simultaneously looked to 1,450 feet below.

"Tell me again why we can't just hit the button and just travel the easy way?" Grace yelled the question as the gusts of wind became more intense. Hazel welcomed the question as it permitted the slightest amount of stalling before the leap to come.

"It's like I said last night," said Olive, leaning forward and looking at the two on Jude's right. "If we hold hands through the portal, we can be 100% sure to land at the same time and place. It's just one more safeguard."

Hazel, acting mockingly confident, crossed her arms and let out a laugh. "Yeah. Nothing safer than jumping off the tallest building in the Midwest."

Everyone shook their heads and chuckled at Hazel before yet again looking to the ground below. They focused and prepared for the journey ahead. As the group interlaced their fingers in each other's hands, Jude looked once more to his mother, nodded, and all five jumped.

The portal opened, and they all flew through it together. To Jude, it almost felt normal. By now, he'd flown twice with his Houdini Vest and once with a Honeymoon Vest. He practically felt like a natural time traveler. He flew and felt no wind in the warm darkness. After a brief moment, he saw the light coming from their destination on the other end of the portal. He knew that when they landed, the fight would truly begin.

* * *

The group landed on the top floor of the St. Louis prison. Hazel was the only one to not land on her feet, and she still had not opened her eyes. Grace put her hand on Hazel's arm and helped her stand. The room was empty, but the desk and cages that had once stood prominently in the middle of the room were now shredded. Cold wind crashed through the openings of the windows, the glass of which was all completely gone. To the left of the group was a pile of Houdini Vests that had been destroyed, but Olive noticed that many were clearly missing. There were two Honeymoon Vests resting near the window which Olive had thrown her son from. There should have been three. Oh Peter, Olive thought, he had clearly given up the comet.

The group felt frozen, but there was something more ominous. They knew that they were flying into a fight when they jumped off the tower, but where was the resistance now? Only Olive, calculating the amount of missing vests, had the answer. Still, she wondered, there had to be hundreds of resistance fighters somewhere without a vest... Where were they? Her thoughts were immediately cut off when Sarah let out a scream.

Everyone jumped at the sound of her shriek as they followed her moving across the room with their eyes. Sarah ran behind the remains of Reginald's large desk. From Jude's perspective, he could only see the feet of a lifeless body. Olive knew what had caused Sarah's reaction, however. She knew that behind that desk was not only Sarah's mother, but the beginning of a conversation that had been a long time coming.

"Mom?" Sarah yelled, crouching out of sight from the group. Jude and Grace immediately ran toward her. Hazel began to move as well, but Olive put her hand on her shoulder and stopped her. "Mom? Wh—"

Sarah broke into tears as the room, with the exception of the loud wind crashing in, was completely silent. She stood up, looking past Jude and Grace and directly at Olive. "What is this? How can she be here?"

Olive took a step forward. "Sarah, this isn't the ti—"

"Don't you dare." Sarah was fuming, and tears rushed down her cheeks. Her mother's corpse was lying at her feet. "How can she be here?"

Olive paused and looked around the room. Hazel was completely confused. Jude and Grace looked from one another and back to Olive. Sarah remained motionless. "Your mom came here to warn us about a breach inside a Honeymoon Portal by the Shadows."

"You said she was dead. How could she—"

"Your mom died, Sarah. That part was true."

Sarah pointed at the lifeless body at her feet and continued to ask the only question that she could think to ask. "Then how could she be–"

"Your mother was our best friend. I told you that. She also died sending the comet through a Honeymoon Portal. That is also true. The way it worked... When we first started with the technology that we invented, we could produce portals using gun-like machines that could generate portals wherever we pointed them. We built a tele-portation cannon to send the comet to Volgeria, your mom's home planet. We teleported the comet to a planet that we knew didn't have any innocent people. Your mother said that it was fully evacuated, with the exception of Shadows running wildly upon it. We sent it to Volgeria with one cannon where Molly would be waiting with an-other that would send it into a Honeymoon Portal. We never knew how overrun the planet was with the Shadow monsters. She managed to send the comet into the portal... but... Anyway, we didn't think it was fair... So then Peter and I did something we should have never done. We went to Volgeria and saved Molly before she was killed by the monsters. Only we did it after she had originally died."

Sarah went silent and looked at her mother. Tear drops rained down onto her tattered shirt near the hole created by the blaster shot from the previous day. Sarah fell to her knees and took her mother's hand. It felt frozen and stiff. Olive and Hazel moved toward Sarah, and all four looked down upon her in sympathy. Sarah wept loudly, and she held her mother's hand tightly to her chest.

Hazel looked at each person standing near her. "I don't get it. What could you ha–"

"She disrupted the natural flow of a person's timeline," Sarah said, still not looking up. All eyes immediately went to her. "There are only a finite number of things that you can change, but the rest are all cemented points in time. A person's death, no matter how much they traverse time, is locked in place. Houdini Vests can manipulate time by using energy, but once a person is truly dead..." Sarah looked up, and she had stopped crying for a moment. "The Shadows break through the cracks of reality when the natural flow of time is disrupted."

The room was silent. Like a pendulum, the eyes of Grace, Hazel, and Jude all went from Sarah to Olive.

"Your mother was furious at what we did. Honestly, we didn't care. Though, we should have."

"Why didn't she come find me? Why did you lie and tell me that she was dead when she was clearly alive all along? I protected your family, and you hid mine from me."

"Sarah, please believe me when I tell you that I wish I–"

"Don't insult me with wishing. Losing her–"

"Sarah. Your mom went into hiding when we brought her back. She knew that if you knew that she was alive, you'd go find her."

"Of course I would have. She's my mom."

"When Shadow monsters break through a portal that disrupts the flow of natural time, they hunt constantly for the person who created the portal. Why do you think they're drawn to people with time residue? It's like a scent they're tracking. They–"

"You mean the Shadows that came after the comet missed..."

"Yes. The Shadows were our fault. Yes. We didn't know the extent of evil that would come from our actions. We brought the Shadows here, and we didn't even know it. We were young fools." Olive broke eye contact to look at the ground. "We never imagined the scale of our actions. We were just trying to save our friend."

Sarah paused, absorbing everything. "Why couldn't I know?"

"Like I said, your mother knew that if you found out that she was still alive that you'd go after her. She knew that the rest of her life would involve her being chased by Shadows. You'd have been in too much danger. Especially if you had opened a portal that connected this dimension with the one that she was living in. She didn't want that for you. I had to promise that I'd never tell you. Peter, too. We brought you into all of this to keep you close." Olive looked back from the ground below and at Sarah. "I know how selfish all of this must seem."

The three absent from the conversation continued to look from one to the other. Both Sarah and Olive had at least one thing in common: there was complete exhaustion in their eyes. After a moment, Sarah put her head down on her mother's stomach and grieved loudly.

Jude crouched down and put his arm around Sarah. She leaned backwards and put her head on his shoulder. The tears were not slowing down, though she welcomed the warmth that he was providing. Only hours ago, he too had lost his hero. She knew that he understood her pain, and it made her feel slightly less alone.

As the group congregated over Molly's body in silence, the reality of the situation slowly crept back in. The fear of the missing resistance fighters made the vacant space all the more eerie. The comet would surely make its appearance soon if they didn't get moving, and they weren't about to let the deaths of Peter or Molly be in vain. Each second that flew by was another wasted for the mission that had already taken so much from each member of the group. Finally, Sarah stood up and looked at Olive. "Who did this?"

"Sarah. You know who did this." Olive's response seemed strange to Grace, Jude, and Hazel. They didn't give it much thought, however. They simply connected it to the murder of Peter. Regardless, Elise clearly had been busy.

Sarah stood up. "We'd better get moving. She's not stopping until she kills a lot more."

"I agree," said Olive, looking from her oldest born to her youngest. "Sarah and I will go and stop Reginald. You guys stay here and stay safe." She moved to where the two remaining Honeymoon Vests were sitting. Picking them up, she moved to Sarah.

"Oh, no. I am coming with you," said Jude, speaking for the first time since landing in 2393. "Together, we have three Honeymoon Vests. I'm coming with you, and we're doing this together."

"It's not safe, Jude," said Olive, taking a step toward her son.

"We all came here to finish this. We're going to finish it together."

Olive looked at her son, who looked more like Peter Monroe now than ever.

"There's one thing I don't understand," said Grace, now taking her turn to speak for the first time. "Okay, so you originally needed a portal cannon to send the comet to the Honeymoon Dimension, right? So, wouldn't they need the same portal cannon to bring it back?"

"Well, yes and no. There are two ways to bring it back. One way, the more dangerous way, is to activate a Honeymoon Vest in the presence of the comet, which has its own Honeymoon tech on it. Because of a safety mechanism that Peter and I built in, if you activate the vest, you'll suck the comet through with you. Using a cannon is the other and much safer approach to returning the comet. I hate to admit it, because looking back, it seems foolish, but we hid everything in the same Honeymoon Dimension. That includes a cannon. If they are there, then they have everything they need."

"You did what?" Everyone in the room said at the same time.

"I know. I know. Stupid now... but listen. We figured that everything from that day was better hidden where we knew where it was, rather than scattered."

The room fell silent, and everyone looked to the floor. "Okay," said Jude, standing next to his mother. He put his hand on her shoulder. "Sarah, you and me, we're going to stop Reginald and Elise. Mom, you and Hazel and Grace will get to the cannon and destroy it. We thought there'd be a fight here, but clearly it's one more portal away. Let's get to the Honeymoon Dimension and put an end to this once and for all."

Grace looked at Jude and blushed. She started to think that she didn't recognize him, but the truth was that this Jude that was standing in front of her was the very Jude that she had originally fallen in love with. Sarah and Hazel nodded, and their postures straightened. Seeing Jude like this made them feel like they could do anything. Finally, Olive put coordinates in each of the Honeymoon Vests, handing one to her son. "Jude," she said as she brought him in for a hug. "I wish I could only find the words to say how proud I am of you."

"Get in line!" yelled Hazel as she moved up closer to the two and put both of her hands on Jude's shoulders. "This guy... I am so pro–"

Hazel's words were cut off abruptly, and no one, not even she, had any idea why. As the group had moved closer together and began to prepare to head toward Reginald, Elise, and the comet, no one had noticed that the golden elevators on the far side of the room had opened; nor had they been aware of the group of men with blasters that had entered the room. Smoke slowly flowed out of the barrel of one of the blasters pointed at the group. The smoking gun was held by a man with deeply sunken eyes. Jude recognized him immediately.

The group of men continued to point their blasters at Jude and his company. In one quick motion, Hazel fell into Olive's arms, who fell backward behind Reginald's broken desk. Grace threw her arms around the two women to shield them from the shots that were starting to be fired by the resistance fighters.

Only Jude stood still as Sarah grabbed the Honeymoon Vest from him and began to pull him toward the open window that was only feet away. To Jude, after watching his sister hit the ground, his world had crashed to a halt. He didn't even notice that he was being dragged backward. Within seconds, Jude and Sarah stood at the edge of the window. The shots from the resistance fighters exploded against the metal frame of the opening. Each shot only slightly missed the pair. The Honeymoon Vest wasn't attached yet, but it didn't matter. Sarah grabbed Jude by his shoulders and pulled him out of the window and, yet again, they were flying. The last thing Jude saw before his freefall was Grace protecting his mother and his sister while Hazel's eyes slowly closed and her body became limp.

Quickly, with the cool wind crashing against their faces, Sarah slipped the Honeymoon Vest around her and Jude. Within seconds, a new portal opened up, and they flew through it ever so quickly and to the fight of their lives.

Thirty Six

November 15, 2393

H azel was still breathing, and that's all Olive needed to see to feel relieved. Still, she was severely worried about her unconscious daughter, who was lying in her arms. Grace and Olive knew that sunken-eyes was only a few feet away and slowly moving toward them. It was eight guards plus the man who had fired at Hazel against only Grace and Olive. They had to act quickly. Still hiding behind the broken desk, Olive gently set Hazel into the opening of the still remaining leg space. She looked at Grace, whose eyes were filled with fear.

"What are we going to do?" asked Grace, her face pale white.

"They're going to come around the corner of that desk any moment. We can either take the Houdini Vests and run or fight."

"If we run, who does Jude come back to?" Grace, thinking of Jude's face as he was pulled out the window, began to fight back tears.

"Fight it is then." Olive's voice, to Grace's surprise, had a tinge of excitement. A few seconds later, they heard a footstep near the desk, and Olive jumped up with a piece of broken wood from one of Reginald's chairs and landed it square in the face of one of the resistance fighters. Grace jumped up too, wielding what was left of the broken chair, and swung it at another fighter.

Suddenly, a blaster shot from the man with the red tie was fired directly at Olive. Because she hadn't taken her vest off, she immediately disappeared through a portal, and Grace was all alone. She held her hands in the air as eight blasters were pointed at her. She could feel her knees shaking when all of a sudden, Olive appeared right behind sunken-eyes with a blaster pointed at his head and a brand new backpack on her shoulders. She had used her third trip of the vest to come back and finish the fight. Fortunately, when she was sent back to 2019, she knew where Sarah might have hidden a blaster. She had brought it back with her.

"Everyone put their guns down or I ruin this man's pretty little red tie," said Olive, complacently looking around the room. Each guard did what she said, and they raised their hands toward the ceiling. "Now, here's what's going to happen. All of you are going to head back down the elevator, and she and I will be having a long conversation with the man who thought it was a good idea to shoot Leo's daughter."

"Do it. Leave us," he said with his sunken eyes fixed on Grace. His gaze sent shivers down her spine. The room emptied, and Olive led him to the only unbroken chair in the room. She tossed the backpack to Grace, who opened it to find Sarah's medical supplies.

"These are getting a lot more use than they need to," said Grace as she rushed to Hazel's side.

"That's what happens when you have to deal with the scum of the resistance," said Olive, still pointing the blaster at the man who was now sitting in front of her.

"We want the world to be a better place. Just like everyone else," he said, adjusting his tie.

"You want the world to be an empty place. That's not better."

"We'll agree to disagree," he smirked at Olive, but she didn't budge.

"I'm actually glad to have this conversation. Tell me, where did you keep the large chest of my husband's and my belongings? It was the biggest one locked away here. Where is it?"

"Why the hell would I tell you anything?" He laughed to himself as he allowed his military-like posture to subside in the chair.

Olive matched his laugh with one of her own. "I'm glad you asked." She immediately pointed the blaster at his right thigh, pulled the trigger, and shot straight through it. Then she pointed at the left thigh and put an identical wound on the other side. She pointed the gun directly between his legs and spoke again. "Look at me." The man with the sunken eyes groaned in pain. "Look at me. Now." He looked up, his eyes were wet, and he was trying to stay conscious. He was in severe pain. "I will put my next shot directly in the middle of the last two if you don't tell me in the next five seconds."

Grace watched the entire encounter with complete shock. Sure, everything that she had witnessed from Olive since her first trip to the future had been surreal, but she never imagined that she had any of this in her. It wasn't that she was repulsed in any way. Rather, she found it heroic. Olive's family was in danger, and here she was being as much of a mom as any mother could be. Of course, she had no idea what Olive could possibly be looking for. Grace directed her attention to Hazel and started treating her with the medical supplies. She cut open her shirt. The wound on her breast was in terrible condition.

"Five… four…" Olive stepped closer, still pointing the blaster.

"Okay. Okay. Just don't shoot me again." He paused. Olive remained as calm as she could. "It's in here. It's hidden under that pile of scrapped Houdini Vests. We brought it up here as a scapegoat if something went wrong with the comet. We know it's your teleportation cannon, and we have your journals on how to use it. None of it will matter, though. Not if Mr. Beckett is successful."

Grace stood up and nodded to Olive in a way that affirmed that Hazel was okay or as okay as she could be. Olive nodded back but still pointed the gun at the man in front of her. "Grace," Olive said, not looking at her. "Show me what's under those vests over there." Grace went to the pile, moved some vests, and underneath was a large black case. She opened it, and Olive immediately showed a sign of relief. "Now, that's some good luck after all."

"Mr. Beckett will be back. You're going to—" Olive cut him off by slamming the butt of the blaster directly against the side of his head. He crumpled to the ground.

"Come on, Grace. We don't have a moment to lose. If Jude and Sarah can't stop that comet, then we'll be this world's last line of defense."

As the two unloaded the black chest, Olive noticed that of the two notebooks that she and her husband had once hidden within it, one was missing. She grabbed the only remaining notebook and refamiliarized herself with the notes that she had written such a very long time ago. As the two women got to work, neither of them heard the portal open behind them. They were completely ignorant to the fact that they weren't alone until they heard a shoe scuff the floor. They turned around quickly, and both of their hearts sank into their stomachs when they saw who was standing before them.

Thirty Seven

June 21, 2342

Jude and Sarah hid behind a large rose bush, only thirty feet from where two boys were playing in a backyard. On top of the boys' clubhouse stood Elise and Reginald with the portal cannon that Olive had described only moments before the group was separated. They had read about the cannon in Leo and Goliath's notes and found it stored away close by. Neither Jude nor Sarah had any idea where they were, nor did they know the boys who were running around in front of them. As always, the Honeymoon Dimension prevented any interaction.

Sarah put her hand on Jude's shoulder as he watched the happenings in the yard with rage. He had cried too much in the last several hours, and no more tears could be found. The images of his father and of his sister being shot were scarred into his brain. Every time that he closed his eyes, they were there. Their deaths weren't a reason to stop for Jude; they had become motivation. He looked at Sarah, and he knew that they were too far past the point of return.

"Jude, are you alright?" Sarah looked at him in complete sympathy. As far as they knew, the room in St. Louis held two dead loved ones. They were carrying similar burdens.

Jude nodded. "It's time we finished this. For dad, for Hazel, for your mom, for everyone; it's time."

Sarah looked at the deeply faded grass below her feet. "Okay. What's the play?"

"I'm no match for Elise," said Jude, looking back into the yard. The two boys began flailing their makeshift swords through the air. "I don't mind being a distraction, though. You sneak around to the clubhouse, and when you get there, I'll jump out, distract them, and you take the cannon."

"Jude, they're going to shoot to kill. It's too dangerous for you–"

"Don't you think we're beyond danger here?"

Sarah looked back to Jude and saw that there was no convincing him otherwise. "Okay. I'll make it over there. Wait for my signal..." She paused. There was more that she wanted to say, but she stopped herself. In the silence of the pause, the two looked back into the yard and prepared to go. At no point in their journey was there a moment so dangerous. They didn't care as it was now or never. Sarah looked at Jude one more time. "Jude, there's something I need to tell yo—"

She was cut off by the sound of the cannon beginning its process. "Two minutes and then we'll have everything we've ever wanted," Elise yelled, looking to the sky above.

Sarah looked at Jude, who, for the first moment in a while, had fear in his eyes. "Jude I—" Jude looked at her, and then she immediately closed her mouth. It wasn't the time. "... I'll see you on the other side. Be careful."

Jude took her hand and smiled. "The good guys are going to win today."

Sarah looked deeply into his eyes once more and then turned around and began to sneak closer to the clubhouse. She used the trees and bushes to get nearer Elise and Reginald. Jude watched from a distance, and the pair on top of the clubhouse never noticed her. When she was only feet away from their adversaries, she turned and looked at Jude. On her hand, she counted down: five... four... three...

"Get your ass up, Jude. Who taught you how to hide?" Elise interrupted Sarah's counting, and her voice sent a cold shiver through Jude. He complied as he stood up with his hands in the air. Sarah remained hiding, hoping that she wasn't seen as well.

Elise watched Jude from the roof of the building as the two boys ran between her and him. She smiled as Reginald continued to read Olive and Peter's journal to see the next steps in the process of the cannon.

"Hello, Jude. How'd I know you'd come?" Elise said, crossing her arms.

"Elise. You're better than this. I know–"

"You don't know a damn thing." There was a pause as the two continued to look at each other. The boys ran around Jude's legs. "You may not believe it, but I am genuinely sorry about your father. You deserved better than that. Still, your father was a criminal and he pai–"

"No. No, he wasn't." Jude couldn't stop himself from yelling. "I trusted you. I helped you and yo–"

"This is so much bigger than you and me, Jude! Don't you get it?" Elise hopped off the roof of the house as the two boys were finding their way to the center of the yard. "None of that matters now, anyway. Our fathers had a deal, and you showing up here breaks it. Thanks for your help, Jude. Believe me when I say that I don't like this, but you can't keep getting in our way." Elise took out her own blaster and pointed it squarely at Jude. He didn't flinch.

Reginald raised his head up from the cannon to look at the son of his old best friend. Behind Jude, Adeline was beginning to come into the yard. Reginald relished in the moment as he finished the preparations on the portal cannon. It was time for victory. He watched as his daughter moved closer to Jude for the kill. No matter, he thought, here or there, Jude's death was inevitable.

Elise stopped walking when she stood only three feet from Jude. She took a deep breath. She'd never admit it, but she truly did sympathize with him. Of course, that didn't matter. She began to squeeze the trigger of her blaster when something unimaginable occurred that stopped her from shooting Jude. It wasn't a bullet or any type of force that stayed Elise's hand. It was just a single word, barely audible from just over her shoulder. "Elsie?"

Elise paused with her gun still pointed at Jude as she turned her head to see where the voice had come from. Standing behind her was a redheaded woman, the exact same height as Elise. At first, Jude didn't recognize her, but after a moment, it was clear to him who it was. Despite the complete change, those were still Sarah's eyes looking from across the yard and straight at Elise.

"Who the hell are you?" Elise said, quickly pulling out a second blaster and pointing it at Sarah who, for some reason, was walking toward the gun that was pointed at her.

"Don't you know?" Sarah asked, doing her best to seem warm and almost loving. "How many people have ever called you that?"

"Only one, and she's dead now. She died in the camps." Elise took a step closer to Sarah, her gun was still pointed at both of her targets. Jude could hear the tightening of Elise's gloves.

"No. That's just what you were to—" She was cut off by Reginald sending a blast into the yard.

"We really need to get going, Elise. Come on. Kill them both and we'll get moving." As Reginald spoke, Elise immediately noticed the change in his demeanor.

Sarah took another step closer to Elise. "He doesn't want you–"

Reginald sent another shot toward Sarah. It grazed her arm. "Kill them, Elise, and let's get going."

"Wait," said Elise, looking deep into Sarah's eyes. "Dad, do you know–"

"What I know, Elise, is that we better get going if we're going to capture this comet at the right time. The journals are very specific about when to launch the cannon. Kill them, and come on."

"Elsie, don't."

"Stop calling me that. You're clearly Volgen trash. It doesn't matter how good you are at changing your appearance, you're not her."

Jude still had his hands in the air. "Elise, wha–"

"Shut up," Elise and Sarah said in unison as they turned their heads toward him.

Reginald pointed his blaster at Jude. "If you won't do it, then I will."

"Elsie. I'm alive. Mom and me, we lived w–" Reginald shot a blast that landed square in Jude's shoulder. He hit the ground quickly, writhing in pain. The shot went straight through him and kicked up dust from the ground.

Elise looked into Sarah's eyes. Somehow, and she couldn't figure out why, she was captivated by the woman standing in front of her. Appearance change or not, she had spent her whole life missing her sister, and the person standing in front of Elise looked just like her. Not only that, but she was looking at Elise in the exact same way that Elise's sister used to look at her. "I can't trust a Volgen. No matter how much you may look like her or seem like her." She tried to pull the trigger, but she just couldn't.

"Then trust your sister. Please." Sarah wanted to run to Jude, but she knew that would only put him in more danger. Not only that, but she could see in Elise's eyes that she had her. Elise was listening. "I never got your name right... Like I never got your braids right when we'd do each other's hair."

"That's enough, Elise. Kill her!" Reginald pointed his gun at his only standing rival and aimed to fire.

Elise didn't move, and she never took her eyes off of Sarah. Appearances could be changed, sure, but no one could possibly know about the one name that she used to be called by her sister; her sister, that she was certain was dead until now. In one quick second, everything in her mind clicked. "If... you're my sister, then... that means..." Elise struggled to breathe as she realized exactly who she had murdered at the top of the St. Louis prison.

Reginald, seeing the reaction of his daughter, knew that she was lost to him. He pulled the trigger and sent a blast at Sarah. Elise, knowing her father's moves better than any, anticipated the shot as she hurriedly ran, dove, and pushed Sarah to the ground. She had saved Sarah from the fatal blow as she rolled back onto her feet and turned around to face the portal cannon. Reginald was already back at work as he pointed it to the sky. With both blasters in hand, she ran at her father and pointed them at him.

She would have pulled the trigger if the comet in the sky hadn't fully distracted her when she made it to the side of the clubhouse. Reginald hit the lever on the cannon, and he and the comet simultaneously disappeared.

Elise looked to the sky where the comet had been. Her arms fell to her side as she turned around and looked. Jude was holding his shoulder, but sitting up and looking. Sarah, still redheaded, sat in the dirt where the two boys had finished their battle with the monsters only a few minutes prior.

Elise began to slowly walk away from the clubhouse. She threw both guns to the ground, moved over to Sarah, and held out her hand. Sarah took it, and the two women stood looking at each other. Elise's balance became uneasy. "Could it really be you?"

Sarah didn't respond; she simply reached into her pocket and pulled out a metal chain. Hooked on it was half of a metallic heart. Elise reached into her pocket and pulled out a necklace that was seemingly identical.

Elise, after looking at the necklaces that the pair had worn as young girls, fell into Sarah's arms. Through heavy tears and deep breaths, Elise was able to conjure only a few words. "Oh, Kate, I've been so wrong."

Thirty Eight

January 30, 2373

E lise Becket immediately loved her younger sister. Blood or no blood, they were family, and nothing else mattered. When Reginald introduced Kate and her mother, Molly, to Elise, excitement filled the house. The two girls were too young to understand the tumultuous situation in the world. Everything that they knew existed only in the small apartment where the four people lived together. From the moment that they met, Kate and Elise were immediately the best of friends.

Honestly, it was a wonderful situation inside the apartment. Molly and Reginald, Reggie she called him, were passionately in love with each other, and they deeply loved both of their daughters. Even though food was hard to come by and the lights were off most of the evenings, nothing took away from the jocund feelings that reverberated off the walls of their small living quarters. They had each other, and that's all that they needed. Late nights of blanketed forts, storytelling from before the banning of information, and board games filled their lives. Happiness was the only thing that was not in short supply.

Outside the apartment was a completely different story. When Reginald and Molly fell in love and brought their daughters together, the world had been at war. No country was safe anywhere in the world from the destruction caused by the wars. A battle for resources threatened the lives of billions of people living on Earth. Diseases also raged across the globe, and medicine only went to those who could afford it. Both Reginald and Molly had lost their previous spouses to the plague. They found each other early one morning at a secret market that only locals knew about. It took just a few months for them to move in together and create a small family in their third-story apartment.

Kate's birthday was only a few months after they began living together. She was taller than Elise as she turned four years of age. On that special day, both girls received a present. Molly gave them both a separate necklace. The necklaces themselves were divided pieces, but if placed together, they formed a perfect heart.

The morning that she gave the pair their present, Molly walked into their bedroom and sat on their shared mattress. They scooted to the edge of the bed to join her. She put her arms tightly around them both. "Now, you both know that I love you very much," she said. "The world can be difficult out there, but not if you stick together." Smiling, she took out the necklaces for the two young girls. "Look, disconnected, the heart is broken, but together, they make the perfect symbol of love. Just like you two. We're a family. We have to stick together. You girls need to stick together."

Elise and Kate giggled as they helped each other put their necklaces on. They were always determined that nothing would separate them. It was an easy idea for two young girls unaware of the dangers of war or of The Imminent Collision.

As a few years came and went, the girls only became closer. The love their family shared became a much deeper bond. Still, it was undeniable that the stress became much more potent. Molly was working much later nights, and Reginald did most of the raising of the children in the months leading to the collision. Even when the packages arrived with Leo and Goliath's Houdini Vests from The North American Government, the stress only grew. There was an uneasiness of what was to come in the new world. Molly's frequent absences only made the situation harder.

Still, Elise and Kate found comfort in each other, playing games around the apartment and in the halls of their building. Elise could often hear Kate yelling 'Elsie' from another room. Despite the fact that she had finally become old enough to know her real name, Elise would always be Elsie to Kate.

Things went from bad to worse in the weeks leading up to The Imminent Collision. Molly was rarely home because of work, and Reginald didn't understand. Why she would spend the last few days before the collision working instead of with her family made no sense to him. She would come home in the evenings and face late nights of fighting. Elise and Kate heard every word, and they would lie in bed and hold each other. They were each other's shields.

The worst day was the morning of the collision. Reginald woke up to a note from Molly. She told him that she loved him and the girls, but she had to go. The girls woke up to the sounds of Reginald destroying the kitchen. They stayed locked in their room until he came to put their vests on them. There they sat in the yard outside of their apartment building and awaited the comet. The disappearance of the comet only made Molly's leaving worse for Reginald and more confusing for the girls.

Of course, things only got worse. Rumors of the North American Government searching for Volgens and limiting children per household began to circulate. No one wanted to believe that level of evil existed within their government. Reginald, like most others, agreed with the capturing of the Volgens. After what they did, he thought, they deserved worse than death camps. But in the mornings, as he fed his daughters crumbs of bread, he looked at them and only felt despair. He couldn't imagine how anyone was feeding their children. As time moved on, the more believable the single-child law seemed.

Late one night in September of 2376, Reginald's door was kicked open. 10 men entered the apartment as Reginald, Elise, and Sarah hid under the girl's bed. They could hear the men slowly walking around the apartment and searching each room.

The men entered the girls' room and stood at the bed as the three held their breath. It was useless. The bed was flung to the side, and the men immediately grabbed Kate and hurried out of the room. Reginald stood to fight, but a punch from a guard sent him backwards and off his feet.

The last thing they heard was, 'Elsie!' Elise buried her face in her hands and sobbed. There was nothing that she could do. She was no match for the firepower that infiltrated the apartment. Reginald went to stand again to chase after his youngest daughter. He made it to the doorway and stopped when he saw the oddest thing illuminated by the faded overhead light. The intense fear that Kate was feeling was causing something extraordinary. Her red hair was rapidly changing from blonde to black to red to brunette, while her skin colors also changed in a spectrum of shades. Suddenly, Molly's strange behavior leading up to the collision made perfect sense. Volgens, he thought. How could he have missed it under his own roof?

That night, there were two vendettas born within Reginald. How dare The North American Government kick down his door and attack his family? They would pay. Reginald was cunning, he was smart, and he had resources. Thus, in the hallway of his third-floor apartment, the resistance was born.

The second vendetta that came, though, overpowered even that of the government. Volgens. They had come to Earth. They had lied about their intentions. They came out of hiding, and they seemed incredible. Why did Molly keep her secret? Perhaps she knew all along about their deception. She, as well as each Volgen, had lied enough. They had caused enough damage. From that moment on, Reginald wouldn't stop until both groups, the Volgens and the governments alike, faced consequences.

* * *

The next several years, through her teens and into her early twenties, Elise only knew one thing: the resistance. She learned everything that she could from her father, such as the hatred of the government and especially the hatred of the Volgens. Mission after mission, she slowly became a machine for her father. She was cold, vicious, and virtually the opposite of everything she was as a young child. Volgens and the government had taken everything from her. There wasn't a day that went by that she didn't think about her sister. Her love for Kate was the only thing that remained from her youth.

They didn't know the full story, but they knew their version of the events, and that was enough to motivate them toward their cause. Upon the discovery of some of Leo and Goliath's materials in St. Louis and the information that they had about their technology in Chicago, the stage was set. They had to go after Leo and Goliath. Fortunately for Reginald, his deepest secret that no one knew, not even Elise, was that he knew exactly who Leo and Goliath were. He also knew where they were. More importantly, it wasn't difficult to find out who their kids were in the 21st century. One was Jude Monroe, the teacher astronaut who was supposed to have died on *The Audacity*. It was all in the hacked information that he had hidden away. He knew of Peter, Olive, Hazel, and Jude long before the mission to bring the comet back was finalized.

He knew everything that he needed. He had everything that he needed to acquire the materials required to end the world's governments and the Volgen race. Link was sent back to the 21st century, and Elise was sent to Chicago to wait for Jude. Reginald and a few resistance fighters knew exactly where to go to find Olive and Peter when they came back. Trap after trap, they slowly came closer to achieving a full victory for the resistance.

Somehow, though Reginald would never tell how, he knew that Kate was still alive. It was just one of the many secrets that he kept. He underestimated her, and he knew it. Reginald told Elise that Kate had died in the camps due to the single-child law. For all Elise knew, that actually was the truth. Yes, he had underestimated her, but he never imagined that Kate would show up in the Honeymoon Portal.

* * *

Kate's journey to Reginald and Peter's childhood backyard was somehow more convoluted than her sister's. She had learned to control her appearance changing long before she met Elise. Still, as she was carried out of the apartment building, her emotions got the best of her. At six years old, it was an unbearable occurrence.

The guards were unfazed as they cuffed the six-year-old child in their control and tossed her in the back of an armored van. Despite her screams, they slowly pulled onto the road and drove toward the Chicago Death Camps. She wasn't alone. There were ten other children in shackles. They were all older, but they were crying just as hard.

The ride was bumpy and completely dark. Kate reached out for something to hold, but she only fell onto the floor of the van. No one helped her up. Instead of attempting to stand, she curled into a ball and cried harder. She had lost everything, and she was simply a scared child who wished her sister were there to hold her.

Suddenly, the van crashed to a standstill, and there were thuds heard in the front of the vehicle. The sound of ten thumps vibrated through the metal interior of the van. Every child went silent. There was no noise or movement for a solid minute. Finally, one more sound against the van, this time against the back, was heard, and the doors immediately opened.

No one recognized the woman standing there alone with a blaster in her hand. "Hurry. Get out and run. There'll be more guards here soon." As soon as the strange woman said this, the children flooded past her as they jumped onto the damp road. Only Kate remained inside as she continued to lie on the ground. She didn't look up as she continued to cry.

The woman jumped into the van and crouched right at Kate's head. "Sweetie. We have to go." Kate didn't move. "Come on, dear. There'll be more bad guys here. We have to move." Still no movement. "Kate. I know your mother." As the woman said her name, Kate immediately looked up. She took the offered hand and ran away with the complete stranger.

The wailings of sirens filled the air as the two ran through back alleys and abandoned buildings. Kate was exhausted and heartbroken. She simply wanted to go home. When her tiredness became too much, she sat down on the wet pavement and leaned against a brick wall. The stranger, out of breath, slumped down next to her when the coast was clear, and she decided it was safe for a breather.

"I just want to go home," said young Kate, looking in the eyes of the woman sitting next to her.

"I know you do, and I'm sorry, but you can't ever go home again."

"Why? Where's my mom? If you know her, where is she?"

The woman rubbed her hands together and looked at the wet concrete of the sidewalk the two were sitting on. She took in a deep breath and let out a long exhale before responding. "Kate, I'm about to tell you a story and it's going to be really hard, but I need you to listen to me and to trust me."

"Why should I tru–"

"You should trust me because your mom sent me here to help you. She told me about the sweetest pair of necklaces that you and your sister wear. I'm guessing that not too many people know about them." The woman moved Kate's hair, which was now black, to the side and revealed a small piece of gold around her neck. "Your mother loves you so much. Don't you know?" Kate shifted her eyes to a puddle that was only feet away. She nodded in a silent agreement to trust the woman.

"Kate." The woman paused as she worked up the strength to continue speaking. "Your mother is dead. The reason that big comet didn't come to Earth was because she stopped it with the help of some scientists a few months ago. She gave her life to save your family. I'm so sorry, sweetie. I am so very sorry."

Silent tears rolled down Kate's cheeks. Truthfully, she had known all along, and she wasn't surprised to hear it be confirmed. Though she was young and scared, she knew the world that she had spent her short life in. She missed her mother dearly, but even in her wildest imagination, she never dreamed of seeing her again. It didn't make it any easier to hear. Her hands immediately went to the necklace around her neck.

"Here. Take this," the woman continued, handing Kate a small envelope. "She wanted me to give you this."

Kate opened the envelope and removed a letter that was inside. After wiping the tears away, she read the last words that her mother would ever say to her.

Kate,

If you're reading this, well, I guess the comet's gone and you're okay. Everything I ever did, I did for you and because I love you very much. I know this is hard, but you've always been braver than you know. I'm so proud of you. So very proud.

There are harder days ahead. No one, not even Reginald or Elise, can ever know that you are alive. That would only put them in more danger. The people that you can trust will be far fewer than the ones you can't.

The person who gave you this letter, she will take you to a home where you will be safe for some time. I trust the people that you are being taken to. I trust the woman taking you there. And, should you ever meet them, I trust a pair of people named Leo and Goliath. You'll hear their names in the coming future and no matter what is said by the governments around the world, it isn't true. Whatever is said about them, only remember this: I trusted them, and they were family.

I wish I could hold you and tell you all of this. Just know, I love you more than anything.

You are the light of my life and so much more.

Yours,

Mom

Kate read every word. She would read the note a thousand more times throughout the years, and every time, new questions would come into her mind. Regardless, the love of her mother always shone through the words. On that September night in a back alley deep in the heart of Chicago, Kate didn't look at the woman sitting next to her until she had read the note three more times.

Kate finally looked up, and the woman had a deep pain in her eyes as she returned the mournful gaze. "Your mother loved you more than anything."

Kate stood up and stared at the graffitied wall across the alley. She changed her hair to blonde, the color that she would keep for the next many years. The woman stood up and looked down at her. "If you could pick any name, what would you pick?"

Kate closed her eyes, and memories of her mother piled in. She began to smile as she thought of a story that her mother used to tell her. Before Reginald, her name wasn't Molly. Only Kate knew her original name. It was a secret that the two shared. Her mother's name was

Sarah, and it was the only name that Kate could think of. To her, it was the most beautiful name that she'd ever known.

"I'd pick Sarah," Kate said, her eyes still closed as she pictured her mother.

The woman knelt down and put both of her hands on Kate's shoulders. "Sarah it is. No one. Absolutely no one can ever know your real name." She took Kate's hand, and they moved onward toward their destination.

Kate and the woman continued their journey for ten more miles until they found themselves on the doorstep of a dark house. They knocked, and the sound echoed throughout the seemingly vacant residence. Only a single candle illuminated the inside. The woman turned to Kate, crouched down yet again, and brushed the blonde hair away from her eyes. "You're going to be amazing. I just know it."

The door opened, and another woman, who was a little shorter than the one who had saved Kate, stood there. The two looked at each other, nodded, and never said a word. The woman who was inside the house put her hand on Kate's shoulder, led her into the dark foyer, and shut the door quickly.

Alone on the doorstep, Molly, with a completely new appearance, had just delivered her daughter to safety. She didn't know what the future held for Kate, but she knew that her daughter would be safer this way. She had seen what came as a consequence of messing with the natural flow of time. She could think of nothing more evil than the Shadows. She reached inside her leather jacket and put her finger on a small button. The coordinates were set on her Honeymoon Vest. With her daughter safe, it was time for her to leave.

Throughout the next few years, Kate was all too aware of the resistance. Everyone was. More specifically, she knew about Elise and Reginald's leadership. Unfortunately, she also knew of their wish to destroy the Volgens. She understood that the resistance blamed the aliens for much of the hell that the world was facing. Still, her sister, her best friend, was clearly going down a dangerous and violent path. Yes, family was more important than her race, but she had no desire to encounter her sister. It was safer that way. Being a part of the lower ranks of the resistance allowed her to watch from a distance.

Some time after leaving her foster family, she was in Chicago attempting to help the resistance. Kate, now Sarah, sat alone on a park bench in the early morning hours. She was exhausted from a hard night's work. She took out the tattered letter that her mother had written to her and began to read. She always did this as a way to find a calm center when things seemed bleak. After what she had seen the night before, things seemed bleaker than ever.

She didn't notice the woman who had approached her until the pair were sitting next to each other. "Hi. Sarah, right?"

"Who the hell are you?"

"I'm someone who knows that your real name is Kate," said the stranger, who folded their hands and looked up toward the sky.

Kate immediately took out her blaster. "How could you possibly know that?"

The woman didn't flinch. Her tone remained calm and cordial. "Because I knew your mother well. I could tell you my real name, but you're probably more familiar with my alias, Leo. I need your help."

Kate continued to point the blaster at Olive Monroe as she let the words sink in. Then, she lowered the gun and nodded. She remembered her mother's words from the letter. "I was wondering when I'd finally meet you. Tell me, what can I do for the family?"

* * *

Sarah knew that one day she would be standing in front of Elise. It was inevitable from the moment that she agreed to help Leo. Much had happened since that fateful night that she was taken away. Everything she had ever done since was for family. Her sister, whom she still loved so dearly, was more of a danger to herself than to anyone. When Olive told her what the plan would be and what part her sister would play in it when Jude came to the future, Sarah was ready to do anything. Yes, she truly wanted to help Olive. However, most importantly, her goal always remained to be as much of a sister as fate would allow her to be.

Here in the Honeymoon Dimension, the two stood face to face after being apart for the majority of their lives. Elise had heard of Sarah, the Volgen, chasing after Link, who was a captain in the resistance. Though, even with all of the appearance manipulation that a Volgen could have, no one could fabricate the necklace or the name that her sister used to call her. This was her, alright. This was Kate. And if this was Kate, then that was Molly in St. Louis. Reginald had watched as she killed the person who was as much of a mother as anyone ever was to her. Then, Reginald was going to watch as she killed her sister. She always knew that he had information that he kept to himself, but these were secrets only a monster would hold. What he made her do and what he let her do were beyond evil. In her mind, it was a betrayal far more malicious than anything that any government or alien had ever done. Everything sank in with incredible speed as her world collapsed. Elise's knees buckled as she fell into her sister's arms and wept.

Kate held Elise tightly as they let out every emotion that they had held in for so many years. So much wrong had been done, and they were far past returning to the innocent children that they once were. In that moment, however, none of the past mattered.

They were together again.

Thirty Nine

June 21, 2342

Jude remained motionless and baffled as he watched the reunion in front of him. For the first time, he saw real joy radiating from Elise. This entire journey was, of course, filled with twists and turns, and he had to accept more unbelievable things than he ever dreamed he'd have to in his life. And yet, here he was, tasked with accepting something outside the realm of possibilities. Sarah and Elise, his friend and foe, were hugging, and he was feet away watching.

The two separated and looked at each other with tears in their eyes. "Kate... Mol— I am so sorry."

"We can't worry about any of that now. We have to stop the comet. Reginald has to be stopped."

Elise breathed deeply as she looked at her sister. In this moment, she had to decide to either turn her back on everything she'd worked toward throughout her life or on her sister. The choice was easy. "I have my sister back," she answered. " That's all that matters, and I'm with you all the way."

Sarah put her hand on Elise's shoulder. "So much has happened, Elsie, and there's a lot to sort out. Let's finish this thing, and we'll work everything out later."

Jude continued to observe Sarah as she had her hand on her sister, and he was filled both with rage and with wonder. Elise had murdered his father in cold blood. She had done the same to Sarah's mother. How could she be so forgiving? Forgiveness was the furthest thing from his mind. It was taking everything for him to stay put where he stood.

Elise turned toward Jude, but it took a moment for her to actually look him in the eyes. "Jude. There's nothing I can s–"

"You're right. There's nothing you can say. You killed my dad," Jude cut her off, and he stared deep into her eyes. His words reverberated throughout the backyard.

Elise paused while Sarah looked squarely at Jude. Neither of the women could blame Jude for his response. To them, he was absolutely right. Everyone in the yard knew there was nothing that could make any of it right. There was nothing to be done to make the situation even.

"All my life, I've fought for one thing," said Elise, looking to the sky. "And my father just took the cannon, ran away, and left me. How stupid could I possibly be? And Jude… How terrible could I possibly be? And here you are, Kate. I feel like my whole life is a lie. Everything has been a lie. Everything that I've done has been wrong and meaningless." She fell to her knees and wept loudly. Shrill cries erupted from behind her hands that covered her face. "All of those people. I– I'm a monster."

Sarah and Jude looked at Elise as she broke down. Even Jude felt the slightest amount of sympathy for her. He knew what it was like to have his entire world blown up or flipped upside down. He felt genuine hatred toward Elise. What she did was beyond reconciliation. How many fathers had she murdered, he wondered. Nothing could repay that debt. While the rage rushed through his mind as he watched her weep, there was another thought that crept into his mind. To what lengths would he have gone for his own father? He closed his eyes, and he could see his father smoking a cigar right next to him. He missed him with everything he had.

After a moment, he looked to Elise, and his anger subsided. She, too, in some way, just lost her father. Jude walked over to Elise as she was on the ground. Sarah stood still as she watched him move. She couldn't stop herself from showing her surprise when he held out his hand and offered assistance to Elise to help her stand up. Both women stared directly into his unblinking eyes.

"You killed my hero. My father. You can't make it right. But, you can help us finish what he started." Jude held out his hand once more to offer a handshake.

Elise looked at him and then at Sarah. She took Jude's hand. "I honestly don't know what to believe anymore, but I will help you. Just tell me what you need."

Sarah took a step forward and placed a hand on both Elise and Jude. "We can do this. We have to work together, but we can do this."

"Elise," Jude said, nodding. "Your father just escaped with a comet and a cannon. What's the plan when he gets back to 2393?"

Elise paused in thought for a brief second. "The cannon we just used will put the comet roughly five minutes away by the time he gets there. That will be enough time for him and some of the resistance fighters to get Houdini Vests on. Then, it's the end of the world."

Sarah and Jude looked at each other, and fear was in their eyes. For all they knew, Olive and Grace were still there waiting to become victims of the end of the world. "Mom said something about a teleportation cannon. If you already had one of their cannons, is there any chance you had the other?"

"Funny you should mention it. We had the other teleportation cannon on the top floor of the prison. What are you suggesting?"

"Let's just do what our parents should have done. Instead of sending it to a Honeymoon realm, let's put it somewhere that destroys it."

"Like where? Wherever you send it brings calamity," said Elise, trying to follow.

Jude turned his head to Sarah. "Reginald wanted to rid a planet of evil monsters. What if we collided with an actual planet filled with evil monsters?"

"Volgeria," Sarah said, as she connected the dots. "Take out the comet and the monsters. Do exactly what I thought mom did originally."

"Exactly. For Molly," said Jude, still looking at Sarah.

"For Peter," Sarah reciprocated.

"Wouldn't that destroy the entire home planet of your people?" asked Elise, bypassing the look the two were sharing.

Sarah turned to Elise. "The planet is already lost. It was lost a long time ago."

The three paused and took in the moment. "Okay," Jude said, walking and picking up one of the two Honeymoon Vests he and Sarah had brought with them into the dimension. "I'll get to Grace and mom. Sarah, you get to Reginald. Elise, you get to the cannon. When we get back, we'll have only a few minutes to save the world."

"How do you guys know you can trust me?" asked Elise, after a moment's pause.

"I don't think you'd still have the necklace if you had it in you to hurt me," said Sarah, taking her sister's hand.

"I don't trust you. But I trust her," said Jude, as he secured his vest. "But, we're all we've got. Let's go finish this. Once and for all."

The three looked at each other as they prepared to head back to 2393. They triggered their vests and quickly made their way to an imminent collision.

Forty

November 15, 2393

"Oh, Olive," said Reginald, pointing a blaster directly at her chest with a sense of victory on his face. "Believe me when I say how sad I am that Pete's not here, too. He was a friend and, despite everything, I really did want a different end for him. The Monroes have always been stubborn."

Olive refused to look at him. Grace, on the other hand, had her eyes locked on him. "You're a monster."

"I believe the monsters are what came after the Monroes did their little magic trick in the sky. Still, it will all be taken care of." Reginald looked over the shoulders of the women and could see the comet lighting up the night sky. "It looks like it's my turn for a magic trick."

"Don't you care? Don't you care how many billions of people you are about to murder?" Olive took a step toward Reginald, but he didn't budge. "This is how you save the world? By murdering everyone in it?"

Reginald remained unfazed. "I save the world that deserves to be saved. There's too much evil. We're going to build it from the ground up to be what it always should have been."

"It's the same plan the governments had to begin with. That's why Molly, Peter, and I did what we di–"

"Save it, Liv. Pete already tried. Same plan? Maybe. Better people living this time? Most certainly. Don't give me any high and mighty nonsense. I know what you did for Molly, and I know you're the reason that the Shadows are here. You pushed my hand on this far more than you'll ever realize."

Olive went to say something, but was immediately cut off by the golden doors opening behind Reginald, revealing 20 people with large cargo boxes. Two men carried the man with the sunken eyes and took him to a chair near their leader. Almost methodically, each person went and grabbed vests and put them on. Following Reginald's eyes, though, Olive and Grace turned around, and their hearts felt like they had stopped beating. The comet was hurtling in the sky directly toward them. It was getting larger by the second.

Of course, Olive had seen it before, but she had an escape plan the last time. Grace, on the other hand, had never seen calamity face to face. They were beyond terrified. The cacophony of preparations around the two women went unnoticed as they were stunned by the certain death heading directly at them.

Reginald took a step forward, put his hands on the shoulders of the two women, and let out a short chuckle. "Stunning, isn't it?"

Olive let her elbow fly, which landed directly in Reginald's stomach and sent him backwards in pain. He lifted his blaster directly at her face and pulled the trigger. Grace, thinking quickly, threw her hip into Olive, sending her to the right, and the shot missed.

Reginald pointed the blaster at Grace, but before shooting, his attention was immediately grabbed by the three people who had just suddenly appeared ten feet away. Jude, Sarah, and Elise seemingly came out of nowhere. They did not hesitate. They removed their Honeymoon Vests quickly so that they could move freely and implement the plan that they had made before leaving the Honeymoon realm. Sarah and Elise each began firing at resistance fighters. Jude ran directly toward his mother, who was lying on the ground at Reginald's feet.

Shots began to ring through the cold air as each individual ducked for cover. The comet was three minutes away from the Earth's atmosphere, and it looked closer to daylight outside than nighttime. Reginald took only a few steps backward as Elise and Sarah sent blaster shots through the air in his direction. Jude slid on his knees to his mother's side.

Looking to his right, he saw the open box containing a portal cannon. "Mom, is that the teleportation cannon? Can you get it working in the next two minutes?"

Olive looked at her son, who looked ten years older than when she had seen him only a short time ago. She nodded at him. "I need two minutes, minimum." She looked at Jude's former fiancée. "Grace, I need your help." Grace nodded and got to her feet, and Olive looked back at Jude. "I need all the time you can give me. That comet is getting awfully big." She handed Jude her blaster, and he had never seen her look as tired as she did in that moment. "You're not a killer, Jude. But if you aim for the people in vests, you'll just send them out of sight for a minute. It's better than nothing." She took his hand and squeezed. "Go. Grace and I have this covered."

Jude turned around and saw a resistance fighter wearing a vest and fired. Absorbing a direct shot, the man disappeared into a portal. With Grace and his mother behind him, Jude gave them cover by sending blasts everywhere else he could see a Houdini Vest.

Shots flew through the air as Elise and Sarah sat next to each other and continued to make resistance fighters disappear. A piece of the desk they were hiding behind splintered as a blast from a resistance fighter collided with it. "Damn it," said Elise, looking at Sarah. "I swear I've shot him already."

"I know. It's the vests. They keep sending themselves back here."

"Three, right?" Elise said, catching her breath. "That's all the trips that they get?"

"Yep," said Sarah, standing up quickly and landing a shot that made another fighter disappear. She crouched back down. "Aren't these your friends? Aren't y—"

Elise looked at Sarah and cut her off. "They're not my sister. They're not my priority now." As she said this, a resistance fighter appeared directly behind Sarah and prepared to fire. Elise put a blaster shot toward his head, sending him backwards as a portal took him, and he vanished. Sarah gave a nod and a grin to her sister as a thank you.

Olive continued to fix the cannon with help from Grace. She was surprised at how quickly everything came back to her. Her hands moved methodically as she attached wires and locked down bolts in the side of the cannon.

Jude continued to give his mother and Grace cover as they worked, but one thing was bothering him more than anything. Where was Reginald? He looked around. He watched as Elise shot someone who had just appeared behind Sarah. Good, he thought, she's living up to her word. Still, he couldn't see the one person that he was looking for.

When Olive was 90 seconds into building the cannon, she was moments from being finished when she and Jude heard Grace scream. Reginald had used his vest to leave, only to come back directly behind Jude, and then grab Grace. Holding her by the throat, he held the blaster to her head.

"Enough!" he yelled loudly enough for everyone in the room to hear over the fray. He stood with Grace in the middle of the room. The shots subsided as two more resistance fighters fell to the ground from the final two shots sent by Elise. They were out of trips in their vests. Only four fighters remained in the room, and they stepped out from where they were hiding. Each of the guards pointed their guns directly at Reginald's two daughters. "Here's how this is going to play out. You are going to leave now, in peace, and I won't blow her head off."

Too distracted by the size of the comet in the sky and the battle that had just paused, Reginald never realized Grace was wearing a Houdini Vest under her jacket. He also didn't see the thumbs up Olive sent towards Sarah to let her know that the cannon was ready. Elise saw the subtle interaction. Noticing the vest that could barely be seen at Grace's collar, she stood up and sent a blast directly at her. Grace immediately disappeared, and Reginald fell to the ground when the blast continued through to his hip. It was not a fatal shot, but the shot brought him to one knee.

The four remaining resistance fighters released more blasts at Sarah and Elise. The two women returned fire as well. Olive and Jude, taking advantage of the new distraction, began to move the cannon toward the window as the comet was only a minute away from the Earth's atmosphere.

Jude immediately felt a hand on his shoulder. "I don't think so," Reginald said, as he pulled the youngest Monroe backward. Sarah's heart sank as she saw Reginald pull Jude to the ground and point a blaster at him. She knew that his vest was out of trips as she jumped over the desk and ran toward the two to save him. She stopped in her tracks when she saw Grace appear through a portal, just as Reginald had done just a few seconds earlier.

There she stood behind him with a wooden chair from Sarah's pod and broke it on Reginald's back. He crashed forward with the debris of the chair and couldn't find anything to catch as he stumbled out the window and fell to the ground below.

After seeing their boss tumble out of the room, the four remaining fighters threw their guns to the ground and sprinted for the elevator. Sarah and Elise pointed their blasters at them, but let them escape. The fighting was over, and the room, with the exception of the cold wind blasting through the window, was quiet. They walked to Jude, Grace, and Olive and stood at the cannon as they prepared to teleport the comet. Sarah typed in the coordinates of Volgeria, and Olive moved to hit the trigger.

It was all over, they thought. However, they didn't realize that Reginald still had one final trip left in his vest. Olive hit the switch as

Reginald landed back at the top of the tower and only feet away from the group. The comet, just as it began to fry the atmosphere, disappeared. They had victory in their grasp. They never saw him until he grabbed Sarah by the collar of her shirt and pulled her backward.

"You horrible, miserable fools," Reginald said, holding a blaster to Sarah's head. "That plan was in the making for years. Don't you understand what's coming? Don't you get it?" He pointed outside the window. "Out there, Shadows are only getting stronger. The governments are planning on exterminating 75% of their citizens by next year, and we could have stopped it. You thought I was evil? You don't know evil."

Jude stepped forward with his hands up. "Let her go. No one else has to get hurt. It's over. Just let her go."

Reginald looked at Jude in disgust. "You're the son of failures. This wasn't a victory. What you've done..." He looked at Olive. "Bring it back or I kill her."

"I can't. It's already gone," said Olive, not moving.

"Dad, you couldn't kill your own daughter. That's Kate. Don't you recognize her?" said Elise, pleading.

Reginald looked at Elise. His eyes were filled with disappointment as he gazed upon her. He turned his attention to the sky. The comet was gone, and he was alone. Everything that he worked for and sacrificed was now a thing of the past. The resistance had been thwarted by this small group of people who seemed completely insignificant. The only question that remained: How?

"Let her go, dad. We have our family back. We can do good without murder. We can do it together." Elise spoke, and everyone in the room noticed the drastic change from the woman who had killed Peter Monroe only hours ago. She took a step further and held out her hand. "Please. She's your daughter."

The entire time, Sarah only kept her eyes locked on one place: Jude. There he stood in front of her, so brave, so strong. He had really grown since she had first met him. She looked at him, and though Reginald's hands were wrapped around her and she could feel the blaster pressed against her temple, she felt no regret about her situation. She had found out the truth about her mother. She had fought for good in such an evil world. She continued to look at Jude. She felt love more than any emotion. The journey was long and often punishing, but it led her to him, and she wouldn't have changed any of it.

Reginald's grip tightened as he looked at Elise. The disappointment had left his face, and he looked completely void of emotion. "This Volgen bitch was never my daughter," he said through gritted teeth. Sarah didn't have time to say anything. Her eyes stayed fixed on Jude as Reginald pulled the trigger, and her body crumpled to the floor.

Everyone shrieked in horror as Jude fell to the ground to catch Sarah's lifeless body. Reginald wasn't finished. He lifted the blaster again and pointed it directly at Olive. Elise jumped and grabbed his arm as he pulled the trigger, and his shot only grazed Olive's shoulder. Reginald and his daughter wrestled for the blaster. Their strength was too even of a match as they fought in a stalemate.

"The cannon!" yelled Elise, holding Reginald's arms as he managed to keep his finger on the trigger and continued firing. Scraps of the ceiling fell to the ground. "The cannon, Leo! Now! Teleport us!"

"If I do that, then you will both die!" yelled Olive, in severe pain as she held her shoulder.

Jude stood up and tried to help Elise as they fought for the gun. Two against one, they still struggled to overpower Reginald. As they were about to release his grip from his blaster, another shot rang through the air. In all of the commotion, all of the battling, and the final struggle to save the planet, no one in the room, including Reginald, remembered the man with sunken eyes sitting in the corner. He sat back and watched the entire episode play out.

Reginald was losing his ground, and his fingers were slipping when a shot flew under his arm and into Jude's side. Jude fell onto his back next to Sarah. He was in agony as he held his stomach and rolled on the ground. Olive was frozen in place as she stood next to the cannon.

Elise, taking advantage of the distraction, gained control of the blaster and sent a shot that directly landed between the man's two sunken eyes. His body went limp, and his chin sagged against his red tie.

Reginald noticed that Elise was off balance after the shot, and he planted his elbow directly into her jaw. She fell to the ground as he grabbed his blaster and pointed it at Jude for the kill shot. In a last-ditch effort, Elise grabbed him at his ankles. She tripped him, and he fell to the ground with his blaster still pointed at Jude. Elise threw her arms around her father.

"Now!" she yelled, holding onto Reginald. "He won't quit, and I'm not strong enough to stop him."

Olive quickly put in coordinates and turned the cannon as Reginald released two more shots that grazed too closely to her son. She hit the trigger and, like the comet a few moments prior, Elise and Reginald vanished automatically.

It was over.

Olive ran away from the cannon and to Hazel, who was still unconscious and lying twenty feet away. Jude grunted through the pain as he sat up, and he took Sarah in his arms. Grace moved to him, crouched down, and put her hand on his shoulder.

"Jude. I'm... I'm so sorry."

Jude's tears poured down his cheeks and fell into Sarah's hair. It was now red as it lay across his arms. They had won their struggle. They had accomplished everything they fought for, but at what cost? It didn't feel like a victory.

The time for mourning was immediately cut short as an all too familiar shriek filled the air. The pounding of large footsteps below the group could be heard, and Olive and Jude quickly looked at one another. Grace had never heard the noise before, and it terrified her. The group exchanged their vests for four new ones that were sitting untouched on the other side of the room. They heard the steps getting louder as they put in the coordinates for 2019 and moved towards the window. Jude paused a few feet away from their exit as he turned and looked back at Sarah.

"Jude. We have to go. We can't help her. I'm sorry," Olive said, putting her hand on her son's shoulder.

"We cou–"

"Jude. We have to go." Olive and Grace were holding Hazel as they stood at the window. "Now."

Jude hesitated. He wanted to take Sarah with them; maybe give her a proper burial somewhere in 2019... but he knew that he couldn't. With the Shadows crashing their way toward them, he knew that they had to go and go fast. He took a final step toward the window, took his mother's hand, and turned around once more to look at Sarah as they fell backward and left 2393 behind them.

Forty One

Volgeria: Year 9737: The Second Age

A sea of black crashed upon the base of the mountain Elise and Reginald found themselves on. Pillars and beautiful statues lined the stone terrace on which they were standing and looking below. The loud screeches of the Shadows were the only thing that they could hear as they looked around the abandoned kingdom to which they had been teleported.

The only light they had, as they stood on a balcony of a beautifully ornate castle, was from the comet that was headed directly toward the two. Neither of them were scared. They had accepted the fate that had come upon them. The Shadows below became more and more violent in their howling as the comet became larger in the sky.

"It's fitting that you die here," said Reginald, watching the comet get brighter. "Choosing a Volgen over family. You're no better than they are."

Elise said nothing. She had no words. Truthfully, she wanted to tell him that she loved him and that she was thankful for every day with him. After all, he was her father, and that was really how she felt. However, she knew that he wouldn't accept anything that she would say. So, she sat quietly and did the only loving thing that she could do for him: sit with him while he died.

"No last words? The comet is getting quite large up there. It's probably thirty seconds away from where we are right now."

Elise maintained her silence. Her heart broke for her father, but he had chosen this path. While she always did his bidding, she never felt as carefree about the genocide as he did. Yes, she aided in it, but when Kate had come back, she snapped out of Reginald's brainwashing. It was her father; she cared deeply for him, but it was all over now.

The comet broke the atmosphere, and the loud noise of an explosion shook their very cores. Elise looked at her father, who had a tear rolling down his cheek. It was the first time that she had seen him vulnerable since that night they hid under the mattress and Kate was taken away.

Seconds from death, Reginald turned to his daughter. He began to say something, and then he noticed the Houdini Vest that she was wearing under her coat. There wasn't much there to see, but it was enough for him to identify it. He smiled at her and began to laugh. "You always were the brains of the operation," he said, looking deep into her eyes. "Take care of yourself, kiddo."

His smile was the last thing that she saw as the comet collided with the planet, and she was sent backward into a portal, never to see her father again.

Forty Two

July 23, 2019

H azel sat at the Starbucks table near a window and fumbled with the small green splash stick that she had removed from her drink a few minutes ago. Though technically, she only left Florida a week prior, it felt so much longer. She had come back despite the fact that, on her plane ride a few days ago, she vowed never to return. The hot Florida summer air outside somehow seemed refreshing after everything she'd been through. That's not to say she didn't appreciate the air conditioning inside the small coffee shop. Hot or cold, either way, she had a new appreciation of things after the events she had witnessed.

The door opened up, and she met the eyes of the person walking through it. She politely grinned and waved him over. He made a small gesture in return, adjusted the collar on his button-up shirt, and slowly walked over to Hazel. Before pulling out the chair to join her, he paused and gave a sympathetic nod to her. He was clearly uncomfortable.

"Thanks for coming. I know this is probably awkward." Hazel looked down at the table while she spoke. Truth be told, she too felt uncomfortable. However, she knew that this had to be done. "I didn't know what you would want, so I got a scone and a black coffee."

Tom Metzlebaum waved his hands in the air as if fanning out Hazel's words. "A scone and coffee are perfect. You really didn't have to do that. Thank you, Ms. Monroe."

Hazel paused and looked up from the table. "Mr. Metzlebaum... I... I'm sorry about your job."

"You've lost far more than I have. I'm the one that's sorry."

"Mr. Metzlebaum, yo–"

"Call me Tom, please. Formalities can be dropped when scones are involved. Don't you think?"

Hazel smiled, a genuine smile. "Tom. You have nothing to be sorry for. You were doing your job. I hold no malice toward you."

Tom nodded as he looked at the steam coming out of the small hole at the top of his coffee cup. "Thank you," he said. There was obvious sadness in voice. "That means a lot."

There was a brief silence that took over the table. Both people looked at their drinks and not at each other. Clearly, there was more to discuss, though the longer the pause in the conversation lasted, the harder the quiet was to break.

"Tom. I really am grateful that you came... I just... I had a few questions that I had to ask."

"I figured you did and, really, I'd like to answer them the best that I can. Though, NASA will release their findings from their investigation later on. I... Look, what I'm trying to say is, I'll answer what I can."

Hazel's head bounced for nearly ten seconds as she nodded in contemplation. She knew her list of questions, but she still wasn't sure the order in which she should ask them. No matter, though, no investigation would truly answer what she came here today to find. "That's fine. I understand completely, Tom. I just appreciate you taking the time to be here."

Tom studied his cup yet again, and lifted it for his first drink. He set it down on the table and awkwardly smiled at Hazel. "I can't tell you the last time I had coffee that I didn't make at home." Hazel let out a small chuckle as she looked at Metzlebaum, and she could clearly see the gears turning in his head. "Go ahead, Hazel. Ask me what's on your mind."

Hazel opened her mouth but said nothing. She paused in disbelief at what she was about to ask. It still didn't seem natural. "Mr. M– Tom. What I'm about to ask... I– Well, the thing is... Tom, are you a Volgen?"

"Am I what?"

"Are you a Volgen? You know, an alien?"

"Ms. Mon– Hazel, what are you talking about?"

Hazel's speech quickened. "I'm just asking because if you are, it's fine. We–"

"Wait, wait, wait. Slow down." Tom waved his hands in the air again. "Hazel. Forgive me, but what are you getting at?"

"I'm trying to figure out if you're an alien or from the future or... I had all of these questions for you, and they're just not coming out the way I want them to." Hazel put her elbows on the table and buried her face in her hands in embarrassment.

"Forgive me, but what does this have to do with your brother?"

Hazel hesitated as she continued to conceal her humiliation. After a moment, she opened her fingers to unveil Tom, with utter confusion on his face, from across the table. "I came here today to see why you put my brother on that rocket. If you're from the future, or past, or an alien... You can tell me. There's nothing that you can tell me that I wouldn't believe."

Tom put his hand on his coffee cup again and spun it completely around as he thought about his answer. "Please believe me when I tell you that I have no idea what you're talking about. But, I get it. Trust me, I get it. We try to find answers in impossible places when the worst things happen. Let me be the first to tell you that I'm not an alien or from any time but now. Vol– Whatever you called them, I don't know what those are. Whatever they are, believe me when I say that I am from this planet just as much as you are."

Hazel nodded, looking into his eyes. There was nothing but truth there. "So. I guess my question is, why Jude?"

Tom smiled widely as she asked him that question. "Well, I'm certain you know the answer to that even better than I do. He was unequivocally the perfect choice for the job. He was charismatic and passionate. He was... Hazel, he was just so very human. He had everything we wanted the person that the mission focused around to have. Just a great guy who, honestly, seemed destined for the job. When I first saw him looking at the *Apollo 11* poster in the hall of our building, I just knew it was him." Hazel was beaming from across the table as she listened to every word. Prideful tears began to fill her eyes. "I'm sorry that there's not more of an explanation. He was our guy. He was so full of life. He may not have seen it in himself, but we all saw it. He was our guy."

Two people from behind their table stood up and headed for the exit. They turned back and looked at them, but never made any expression. Hazel watched them for a moment, and then she reached across the table and put her hand on Tom's wrist. "Any question I could have asked, you just answered. I can't thank you enough."

Tom looked back at her, tilted his head, and furrowed his brow in sympathy. "Anytime," he said, his voice was soft and kind.

Hazel retracted her arm and watched the pair of people who were sitting behind them cross in front of the window. They disappeared from view, and she could see the heat beating off the asphalt pavement of the road. "Tom, I need to be going. Thank you for everything. Not just for this, but for everything you did for my brother. You saved him more than you'll ever know."

Finding it hard to accept the generous sentiment, Tom Metzlebaum's eyes focused on his coffee cup as Hazel stood up, put her hand on his shoulder, and headed for the exit. He shifted his glance outside and smiled at her as she too crossed in front of the window and walked away from the small coffee shop. Looking down at his uneaten scone, his smile faded. He truly had no clue what she meant by Volgens or the future, but he simply shook his head, chalking it up to illusions from grief.

Unemployed, alone, and without a current direction, he looked back up at the chair that had just held Hazel Monroe, and he began to feel the slightest amount of optimism. Something occurred to him; a thought that would take him through the next big steps of his life. It was something that Hazel's brother had said just a few months ago: 'I think I love history because it's filled with everyone's most treasured memories... Good versus evil. Happy versus sad. It's all important to someone.'

He closed his eyes and replayed the words twice more in his mind. When he reopened them, he looked around at the nine people sitting with their drinks in the surrounding space. Some were alone, some were laughing with friends, some were clearly in love. He shook his head and felt a sort of peace that he hadn't felt in quite some time. As he watched the ongoings of the lives around him, he thought of Jude's words one more time.

There really are stories everywhere, he thought, and each one truly does matter.

* * *

Hazel caught up with Jude and Olive a few blocks away as they stood on a street filled with signs, candles, and bouquets. The impromptu memorials for the five astronauts of *The Audacity* stretched as far as the eye could see in both directions. Olive and Jude were standing in front of a large portion of the memorial dedicated to Sarah. A five-foot-tall poster of her official NASA portrait was lined with flowers. To their right, the exact same photo, but of Jude, smiled in their direction. Flowers and cards built a bridge between the two.

"I hope this doesn't give you a complex," joked Hazel when she finally stood next to her brother.

"Kind of weird to go to your own memorial, isn't it?" said Olive, joining in the laughter. "Welcome to the 'I've had a funeral and lived to tell about it' club."

"Mom, don't add to his ego," said Hazel, rolling her eyes.

There was a brief silence until Jude lightly bumped his shoulder into his mother. "I think someone's jealous. I can't help that my memorial is so spectacular. People love me, what can I say?" Olive and Jude cackled loudly while Hazel playfully pushed her brother.

"Yep. I was right," said Hazel, taking a small step away from the two. "Complex."

The three wiped tears from their eyes as the joy of being together was beginning to feel normal again. As a calm came over the group, the reality of where they were standing brought a heaviness to their hearts. Sarah's portrait continued to smile directly at them. Two kids walked up with their parents, and each put freshly picked daisies underneath the portrait. The kids and their parents stood in silence for a moment until they walked to Jude's portrait and left an envelope that the smallest child was carrying. The mother dabbed tears away with a tissue. They never noticed the Monroes.

After the family walked away, Olive collected herself. Even knowing that her son was okay, seeing the memorial was no easy sight. She breathed in deeply and then looked at Jude. "Did Metzlebaum validate what I told you before?"

"He should have," said Hazel, turning and looking at her brother. "I promise. There was no lying in his eyes."

"It's like I told you," said Olive, smiling at her children. "There are things in this world that are destined to happen. Something that could never be changed. Jude, you were always supposed to be on that rocket. You deserved to be."

"You really did, bro."

Jude looked at his shoes to avoid eye contact as he let his mother and sister's words sink in. Deep inside, he knew that they were right. That didn't mean he wanted to accept it. His Imposter Syndrome was a mountain that he'd spend a long time trying to climb. Nonetheless, he felt a warmth inside that he had dreamed of long before the launch of the rocket. Life flowed through his veins, and he relished it. A bright blue summer sky sat above him, and a warm breeze ruffled his hair as he stood in the shade of a nearby palm tree.

Jude put his arm around his mother and the other around his sister. "I love you both so dearly," he said, looking from one to the other. "I finally feel like I've made it back home."

Both Monroe women hugged him tightly, and the three felt the purest joy as they embraced. They had journeyed a long road in the adventure that now lay behind them. With all the losses and victories that they had endured, they couldn't help but feel as though they had saved much more than a planet or its future. They were alive, and they were together. Those two facts were more than enough to be at peace with the world and within themselves.

Olive and Hazel took a step back as Jude remained looking at the portrait in front of him. Sarah had given everything that she had to give to him, his family, and to so many others. He felt a genuine warmth as he thought about what she said that night on the roof of the NASA facility about the enormity of the universe. How lucky, he thought, that in so much space and so much time, he just so happened to have had Sarah Lazerous come into his life.

He knelt down and put a rose underneath her portrait as another breeze crashed through the shade yet again. He stood up and looked once more at the woman who promised to always be there when he fell. Hazel stepped forward and put her hand on his shoulder for comfort. He moved his hand and placed it on top of hers.

He knew he'd never be able to thank Sarah for bringing his family back together or for the sacrifice that she so bravely made. He stood there with his sister and his mother and said a final goodbye. He could still hear her voice in his head, and he knew that she'd want him to face any upcoming adventure with a sense of purpose and a belief in himself.

"Okay," Jude said, radiating confidence and looking at Olive and Hazel. "I'm ready for what's next."

Forty Three

October 1, 2021

Leaving Chicago wasn't easy, but it was for the best. With new identities and new jobs, they made a fresh start in Colorado. Olive was the one who chose where they would relocate. After all, and this was a surprise to Hazel and Jude, they had a cabin just outside of Breckenridge, Colorado.

The surprises didn't end there. In the shadows of the nearby mountains, the cabin was tucked away, and while the inside looked completely normal, it wasn't. Under the fur carpet in the living room resided a titanium door. The door was locked by the same technology Leo and Goliath had used to secure their materials in the Chicago prison.

Dust blew to the ceiling as they unlocked the door and revealed a metal staircase. Underneath the house was a room that was three times the size of the actual cabin. Though it had clearly been years since anyone had been in this room, everything still looked like something from the future.

Jude shook his head in amazement as he looked around his parents' lab. Rows upon rows of notebooks and gadgets took up the majority

415

of the space. The only thing that he could think of as he analyzed everything around him was a feeling of adventure that was calling his name.

* * *

A little more than two years after moving from Illinois, Jude found himself sitting on the tailgate of an old red truck in the parking lot of a locally owned grocery store. Fall was in full swing on this particular weekend, and a cool breeze made him pull his jacket snugly to himself. The cold air was welcome, he thought, watching leaves fly through the air above him. Snow covered the tops of nearby mountains, and he looked forward to another round of a Colorado winter that was only a short time away.

He could wait, of course. After all, each day was a gift, an opportunity for new adventures or stories made with those that he loved. Much like the trees that were shedding their leaves around him, changes come and go, but life moves on. Life finds a way.

The sliding doors of the store opened, and Jude smiled at the woman skipping toward him. Her brown hair bobbed against her shoulders, and she smiled as she held two pints of recently purchased ice cream. The frozen delicacies added to the frostiness of the evening, but tradition was tradition.

"I felt like today was a cookie-dough flavor kind of day," said Grace, as she sat next to Jude, kissed his cheek, and nuzzled closer for warmth. "I went in thinking chocolate, but it was just calling my name, y'know?"

Jude smiled as he rested the side of his head against hers. More leaves flew through the air. Next to her, despite the frigid wind that lightly floated around them, he felt warm. He took off the top of his pint, gave a plastic spoon to Grace, and started to laugh.

"What? What is it?" asked Grace, joining in his laughter.

"This. I always loved this," said Jude, taking a bite that contained more dough than actual ice cream.

"This is the life. Don't you think?" Grace took a bite out of her own pint and leaned backwards. She looked at the mountains as they stood tall behind the small store.

Jude looked at her and then again at the trees around him as some branches still continued to hold onto their leaves. "This really is the life," he replied, more to himself than to her. "This really is living."

The pair sat on the tailgate together and ate their ice cream in silence. There was nothing more that needed to be said. The sun slowly began to dip behind the mountains in front of them, and a gold complexion seemed to grasp hold of everything in sight. Taking in a deep breath of cool air, a sense of calm came over Jude.

He had traveled so far and had done things that he never could have imagined in his wildest dreams. Yet, here with all of that behind him, he sat with Grace as they continued to recapture the past. While the universe seemed larger and the world seemed changed, Jude felt peace as he stared up into the dark yellow sky.

Life is an adventure worth saying yes to, he thought. For so long, he believed that all of his best days were behind him. He took Grace's hand and looked into her eyes that reflected the sunset. In this moment, it was clear to him that all of his best days were only just beginning.

EPILOGUE

November 15, 2393

I t wasn't much, but it was dinner. Elise laughed as she thought about the vile meal that she had fed to Jude a few days ago. No matter their differences, he deserved better than that. Her laugh faded as she thought about all of the things that Jude had deserved to be better. There were a lot of wrongs in her past; she knew that. Carrying out the punishment on her father was the hardest act that she had ever done, however, she also knew that she had only begun her penance.

She spent her entire life fighting on the wrong side of the battle. Although there were many different villains besides her family and the governments of the world, she hated that her life had been filled with evil and hate for so long. She had to be better. That's why she made sure Reginald was the only human victim of the comet. That's why she did what she did next.

Still, as she ate a plate of breakfast while watching the sun set on Lake Michigan, she couldn't help but feel a little satisfied with herself. She had a long road ahead, sure, but Rome wasn't built in a day. She felt like she'd done enough for now.

She could see golden waves on the lake as the sunset cascaded down upon it. For the first time, she saw what Jude loved about it. For so many years, she walked through life only seeing the evil that ran rampant upon the Earth, that she completely forgot about all the beauty it possessed. She thought she was working to save the world without realizing that it had been lost to her long ago. Here she was, though, sitting outside of her pod on top of the building that she had sat with Jude a few days prior, taking it in.

Despite the screeches of the Shadows below, she remained content in the face of the dangers all around. Looking down to the city, it resembled Volgeria with a sea of black overwhelming everything in sight. She knew that the large multiplication of Shadows was her fault. She knew that she caused their presence. The only thing that surprised her was that they made it to Chicago from the broken portal in St. Louis so quickly. She wondered how many there were and how far they had stretched across the planet by now. She'd figure that out eventually. For now, she could wait for the full assessment of the consequences to her most recent decision. There was only one thing that mattered anymore, and it lay only five feet behind her.

After a series of much louder screeches and sirens wailing through the air, she heard a moaning behind her. Elise felt excited as she turned around. Sarah was finally waking up.

After being unconscious for hours, Sarah sat up and looked directly at Elise. Shock and fear set in quickly as she patted herself down and tried to figure out where she was. Her eyes locked on the sunset deep into the horizon. More screeches filled the air, and the two women could hear the stompings from the creatures overtaking the city.

Sarah stood up, with some assistance, and walked over to the edge of the building. She looked down and saw the monsters and the entire world turning black. Watching all of this for just a moment, she found it hard to breathe, and she fell to her knees. Elise crouched down and put an arm around her.

After another pause of collecting her bearings, Sarah fully understood what had happened to bring her, the monsters, and everything else to where they were.

"Elise," she said, looking deep into her sister's eyes. "What have you done?"

Acknowledgements

Far and above, creating this page is the easiest part of the writing process. I am beyond fortunate to have the life that I do. My gratitude to everyone that has supported me cannot be overstated. Let me begin by thanking you, dear reader. By reading this book, you have turned my dreams into a reality. You have welcomed my words and my characters and my creation into your world and I am eternally grateful to you.

Words cannot express the gratitude I have for my mother and her fostering of my dreams. The journey of this novel began with the first books she shared with me, with the first television series and movies she shared with me, and with the love that she showered me with. She edited this book, yes, but her influence runs much deeper than the corrected grammar and ironed plot details. To simply say thank you, does not seem enough. Nonetheless, my life has taken the direction of writing this novel with the guidance of her presence in my life.

I want to say thank you to my father, as well. This is a man that has never doubted my dreams nor my capacity to accomplish them. That support means more than he will ever know. With a tenacity for working hard and a compassionate disposition, I've learned to be bold and caring at the same time. Perhaps so much of this novel came from the first time dad showed me the VHS tapes of *Star Wars*... What a blessing to have had a man like him growing up.

How else could I write parental figures that are so bold and daring and courageous and amazing without folks like mine? Normal figures, but so much larger than life. These are people that care deeply and wear their hearts on their sleeves. I am the man that I am today because I had people like my mom and dad who supported me throughout the highs and the lows of each day that brought me here.

My family is something that matters so much to me. My brother and my sister and their families are so very precious to me. Their influence on my life is also present throughout this novel. Influences from shared shows and movies and music. My older siblings and the lovely people they've surrounded their lives with have influenced my everyday and my every word. So, Alex and Carissa and Holly and Nick and all of my wonderful nieces and nephews, thank you for being you and for being there for me through it all.

At its heart, this is a story of family and love. No matter the twists or turns, family stays constant. I'm so blessed to have a group of people that have always been there.

My friends are also constants. I believe that I have discovered the theme of this thank you letter. Consistency. I think that's why we like the stories that we do, right? You watch someone go through hardships and challenges, but the constants are always the things you rely on to know that everything is going to be okay. My friends and my family are the constants. My inner circle is filled with people that are deeply human and they are indefatigable with their love and their support. My friends are dear to me and they are written into my characters and into my stories.

I am a teacher, afterall, and my life and career has been filled with many wonderful students. Many have known of my writing dreams and I promised them a shoutout in the thank you section if I ever found myself here. Well, guys, we made it. As I've always said, we can never yield in the endeavor of our dreams. In teaching, I have laughed and enjoyed every day in the classroom. That's because of all the joy I have known from such wonderful humans that sat in the desks of my classroom. Thank you to you all. I know you are all out there making the world a better place and making the difference that I always knew you could.

My life is one that is filled with wonderful people and I have known the compassion of family, friends, and strangers. There has been support along the way from many people. Fellow authors, colleagues, and close companions have extended an arm and have been there for me every step of the way during the journey of the writing of this book. I've never felt alone during this process. I never had doubt. When rejections came and time flew by, I never felt alone.

There's kindness in this world. My life has had the good fortune to know it well. No amount of words could ever capture the breadth of love and support that I have known throughout my life. Here, in the final pages of print, allow me to just say one more time:

To you dear reader, to my family, to my friends, to all of the people along the way, thank you from the bottom of my heart. The joy in my life is beyond measure because you have been a part of it.

Always with love,

Noah Coleman

Noah Coleman is a dog dad, a writer, a traveler, a teacher, and a true believer in seizing the day. As a devout optimist, his writing is always filled with hope and the journey toward happiness. To him, these themes are important to be displayed in characters that are not often typical heroes, but ones that are deeply human. *The Audacity* is his first novel. After years of telling his students to chase their dreams, this novel is the fruition of him listening to his own lessons.

Website: www.noahkcolemanbooks.com **Instagram:** @noahkcoleman